A Wide and Pleasant Place

A Wide and Pleasant Place

FARM FRESH MARKET ROMANCE 1

VALERIE COMER

GreenWords Media

His love broke open the way,
and he brought me into a beautiful, broad place.
He rescued me — because his delight is in me.
Psalm 18:19 (The Passion Translation)

I'll stride freely through wide open spaces
as I look for your truth and your wisdom.
Psalm 119:45 (The Message)

CHAPTER ONE

Small towns were boring, stupid, and pointless, and nothing about Galena Landing would ever change Brittany Santoro's mind.

Arrival was inevitable, but why rush it? She pulled off at an overlook above the lake nestled at the edge of the valley and stared down. The blue water rippled and glistened in the late morning sunshine. The town's few streets had been laid out in an even grid, the only curvature being the lakefront drive. Beyond, the broad farming valley swept to the west and north, with pastures and fields like a gloomy patchwork. Spring had yet to lend any color to this drab place.

Happy April Fool's Day, Britt.

She sucked back the bitter laugh. Yup. She was the fool who'd burned bridges at Marketing by Design in Spokane. This gig was her boss's offer of redemption. Six months to prove herself so that Janice Durant and her sister, Galena Landing's mayor, would both write glowing recommendations.

Brittany would be in New York City before harvest. That

was sometime in fall, right? She didn't know. She was no farmer.

So, wasn't it ironic she'd be designing ads to entice local foodies to this Idaho town practically shoved up against the Canadian border? She, who wanted nothing more than to be elsewhere, was tasked with making this blip on the map attractive to new residents, new farmers, and new shoppers for the farmers market.

Go her.

She took a deep breath and scanned the town again, working out roughly where her cousin's house must be according to the digital map program. Then she looked back at the lakefront, where half a dozen white canopies proved the market was in full swing. Might as well see what she was up against.

The road curved down the hill past a newer subdivision then shot straight north for a few blocks. And wasn't it just her luck that the town's one-and-only stoplight turned red just to spite her? Whatever. This was where she turned right.

Was this the heart of downtown? Ugh. That didn't bear thinking about. A tiny log post office. A bakery... she'd definitely check them out. A health food store, which she definitely wouldn't. A few other stores that looked nearly too exhausted to carry on.

Brittany parked near the market, swung her purse over her shoulder, and crunched across the gravel parking lot to the sparsely populated market. So much for it being in full swing. Of course, if it were a bustling place, she wouldn't have been sent here to the middle of nowhere to crank up their marketing.

The thought still rankled. Yeah, she'd been indiscreet.

She got that. But this punishment was excessively severe for the sin she'd committed.

In the recesses of her mind, Jesus shook His head in disappointment. Okay, so He represented the ultimate in undeserved punishment, and there were average human beings who had it worse than she did.

But still.

She stopped cold and stared at the hinged sign announcing the farmers market. It had an apostrophe after farmer. And wasn't the text in Comic Sans? She cringed. Retreating home had never looked so good.

Not an option, Britt.

A guy grinned at her hopefully from behind a table laden with tiny garden seedlings.

She forced a smile and kept walking, tugging her coat closer before she froze to death.

At the next booth, a thirty-something woman arranged jars of honey beside a stack of egg cartons.

That was more like it. Even if her cousin had both in her kitchen, more wouldn't go to waste. Brittany angled closer.

The woman looked up with a smile. "Hi, there!"

"Hello." First rule of farmers markets: if you didn't want to interact with the growers, you should shop at the super-market instead. "I'd like one of those jars of honey and maybe a dozen eggs."

"Sure thing." The woman quoted the total, not that Brittany couldn't do her own math. "Visiting Galena Landing?"

Brittany fished in her purse for her wallet. "I'm here on a short-term contract with the town office."

"Oh, how wonderful! My name is Sierra Rubachuk. I'll be

3

here at the market every week. As summer comes on, I'll have more and more things to sell."

"That's great." Brittany exchanged cash for the two objects. "Do you have a bag to make carrying easier?"

"I'm sorry, no. Most locals bring a cloth bag or two for their purchases."

Brittany should have guessed. "Okay, thanks." She flashed a smile at the woman. It would never do to alienate the vendors before she'd even started with the town office.

"Welcome to Galena Landing. I hope you enjoy your stay."

"Thanks." Brittany backed away, turned to the next vendor, and squelched an involuntary shudder. Hadn't toilet paper holders made of plastic canvas died out long before her birth? This market had no standards.

Not a single booth served hot food, unless she counted that one table with a church-sized coffee urn beside a stack of Styrofoam cups. A carton of half-and-half and an open box of sugar cubes rounded out the display. The honey-and-egg lady should hand out bags and ban disposable cups instead.

Brittany shuddered. Plain bulk brew was not on her radar. The town must have an actual coffee shop. She hadn't seen a Starbucks, but then she hadn't hunted any side streets. *Please, Lord, have mercy. I need real coffee.*

Not that God was answering these days. They weren't really on speaking terms since Brittany had spent a desperate few days praying her beloved father would recover from the horrific accident that ultimately took his life. Still, the ingrained lifelong habit of talking to God inside her head hung on. At least she knew that was all it was, a habit. God didn't much care, or He'd have spared Dad.

4

Brittany turned at the end of the row of canopies and surveyed the small market from the other end. Six booths. The seedling guy. The honey-and-eggs lady. The plastic-canvas lady. The coffee couple... from this angle, she could see a container with film-wrapped cinnamon rolls. One of those was a temptation until she remembered the absolutely amazing delicacies from the bistro back home. This rendition would only taste of disappointment and despair.

Another vendor sold jams, jellies, and pickles, while the final booth contained a smattering of somewhat crafty objects. She would not call the hideous plastic-canvas boxes crafty.

She shuddered, and it wasn't just from the chilly wind.

The middle-aged woman from behind the coffee table poured a cup and came toward her. "You look frozen, dearie. Have a coffee on Bart and me."

"No, thanks."

"Aw, go ahead and take it. You can fix it up over at the table if you don't take it black." The woman smiled. "I don't think I've seen you around before. I'm Jean Stedman."

"Nice to meet you. I'm Brittany." She wasn't giving her surname any minute soon. It would be recognized, since her uncle and aunt had lived here for decades. "Thanks for the coffee." She accepted the cup and eyed it. Had she ever sipped unadorned caffeine before? But she didn't really want to linger at Jean and Bart's table.

"Well, if you're stopping in town for a bit, you're welcome to join us at Galena Gospel Church tomorrow morning. Sunday school starts at nine forty-five — there are classes for adults as well as for kids — with worship at eleven." Jean turned slightly away from Brittany and pointed. "The church is over there on Third. You can just see it between those houses."

"Thanks. I appreciate the invitation."

That was likely where Gina and Chris attended, as well as Uncle Matt and Aunt Connie. The Santoro clan was nothing if not churchy. Of them all, only one cousin had ever walked away from the faith, but he'd returned to the flock and married his first love just a few months ago. That left Brittany as the sole holdout... unless someone else was hiding their status as carefully as she'd been.

A state she needed to keep to herself, so church looked to be in her future. Why couldn't she simply stop with the charade? Six more months, then she'd be safely in New York with a job earned on her own merit, far from family and anyone else who cared about her spiritual condition. Then she'd be free to live her own life.

Cradling the warm cup between both hands, she turned to Jean with a smile. "Where's a good place to get lunch?"

"There's The Sizzling Skillet on the other side of the park." Jean pointed out a log building near a tired-looking hotel labeled "The Landing Pad." The inn's chipped sign bore a cartoon of a frog on a lily pad.

Brittany shuddered. The town had more troubles than attracting residents if this was where people needed to stay while they considered real estate. She hadn't seen a major hotel from the overlook.

Janice and her mayor sister had gotten one thing right.

Galena Landing needed the talents of Brittany Santoro.

BRITTANY EYED the sixties-era house as she slowed at the curb. Her cousin's place seemed well-maintained. The double carport only had one vehicle in it, and Brittany pulled into a paved spot beside it.

They might be cousins, but Gina Zima was nine years older, and they barely knew each other since Uncle Matt and Aunt Connie had raised their kids here in Galena Landing, far from the bosom of the clan. Their son, Tony, had moved to Spokane's Bridgeview neighborhood and opened an Italian restaurant a few years ago, but Gina had stayed put.

Thankfully, the family ties were strong enough for Gina to welcome Brittany to their home with open arms. There was no point in looking for a rental for such a short stint. Not when she needed to save every penny for New York.

Okay. Brittany exited her car, grabbed her purse, and marched to the front door, which swung open at her approach.

"Brittany! It's so good to see you. Did you have a good drive?" Gina hugged her tight.

"Yes, thanks. And thank you, too, for putting me up for a while."

"Oh, no problem. Chris finished up the bedroom in the basement last fall, and we've been praying about what to do with it ever since."

Of course, praying. Brittany smiled at her cousin. "And here I am. That worked out well."

"Come on in. When Chris gets home, I can get him to haul your stuff inside if you like. Everything's in the car?"

No, there was a moving truck arriving in minutes. Brittany stifled the eye roll. "Yep. I didn't need much for just a few months. All my winter stuff is at Mom's, and the furniture in the apartment is mostly Ava's. She'll be living there until the wedding."

"I'm so excited for her and Seth. But I'm also super excited for us, because we get to have you here. You're going to love Galena Landing, I promise."

That was quite the guarantee when the answer was a big, fat, no way. But she didn't need to announce her peevishness at the entire project to her cousin or anyone else. *Zip it up. Smile. Pretend you think this will be the most fun ever.*

"I guess we'll see! I've lived in Spokane all my life, so it will be different, for sure."

Gina chuckled and tugged her inside. "It's not as different as you might think. Bridgeview is just like a small town in the middle of a city."

"Sure. Whatever you say." Brittany looked around the tiny entry. A half-flight of stairs went down to a daylight basement level, and another set rose to the main floor.

Ethan, Gina's eight-year-old, used the railing as a dance partner. "Hi, Brittany!"

"Hey, buddy." It didn't seem that long ago since her youngest brother had been Ethan's age. Michael had been only ten when Dad died. Poor kid had been scarred for life. Or until Mom's new husband came along and won him over.

Brittany liked Charlie. She did. But he wasn't Dad.

"Did you have lunch? I'm sure you're hungry. You've been on the road for three hours. I can fix a quick sandwich."

"I stopped for lunch. Thank you."

"Oh. Well, maybe a cup of coffee and a few cookies?"

"Sure. And this must be Emma. She's sure grown."

A pixie plopped onto the top step wearing a tutu and a plaid shirt buttoned up askew. "That's because I'm almost five."

"Wow, that really is big."

"Yes. I'm going to kindergarten next year, but that's not for a long time."

"I bet you'll be really good at school."

The little girl nodded and leaned closer, pinning her blue gaze on Brittany. "Mama will miss me."

Once, Brittany'd had all that confidence, too. It had vanished somewhere between four and twenty-four. "I'm sure she will."

Gina chuckled. "Come on, Emma. Wash your hands, okay? Then you can help me put some cookies on a plate."

"Okay." The pixie studied Brittany. "They are molasses cookies, and they have sprinkles on them."

"Oh, yum. My favorite."

"Mine, too."

Wow, that little girl was going to be a major bright spot in the next few months. Brittany would take any available positivity. She followed Ethan into the dining area and watched as Emma climbed on a stool, washed her hands, and took her assigned task seriously while her mom poured two coffees and two milks.

"Take anything in it?" Gina asked.

"Sugar. Cream. Everything you've got."

"I won't tell Nonna." Gina winked as she set the mugs down then opened the fridge.

"Thanks... but I don't know anyone from our generation who drinks their coffee like Nonna. My mom does when she's visiting — to be polite, you know — but she'd sure never go to all the trouble of ordering a moka pot from Italy and making pressurized coffee several times a day."

"And that brew is so potent!" Gina laughed.

"I know, right?" Maybe Brittany would get along fine with her cousin, after all, though the interior design aesthetic leaned a little too deep into modern farmhouse. The gray wood-look floors and furniture were brightened with turquoise accessories and splashes of red, like the tulips on the sideboard.

Tasks completed, Gina sat across from Brittany. "I was never so surprised as when you called to say you were moving to Galena Landing! Tell me all the details."

"Six months isn't exactly moving here." And *all* the details? Not on Brittany's life. She needed to reserve some dignity, after all. Save a little face.

"Aw, you'll like it so much you'll stay forever. I just need to hook you up with some cute farmer—"

"Stop it!" Brittany held up her hand and laughed. "Definitely no guys in overalls and straw hats."

"Not even if he looks hot cleaning the muck in his barn with a pitchfork and a wheelbarrow?"

"Eww."

Gina laughed. "That's such a stereotype, cuz. Lots of farmers today have college degrees. A few even have fashion sense. I'm betting your guess whether a guy was a farmer or not would be wrong at least half the time."

Brittany lifted her eyebrows. "That might be a bet I'm willing to accept. How long do I get before I decide?"

"Five seconds. Before he speaks or anyone tells you about him."

"You're on." Brittany reached across the table and slapped Gina's outstretched palm.

"This should be entertaining." Gina giggled. "No prize, by the way. This is just for fun."

"Fair enough." Over the next six months, Brittany was sure to meet dozens if not hundreds of men in one guise or another. The town's population was just over five thousand, and probably at least that many more lived in the outlying area but did their shopping in Galena Landing. All of those would-be farmers for sure.

The kids polished off their milk and cookies and asked to be excused. They dashed down the hallway.

"You sure landed a plum job with the town! It must be nice working for our mayor's sister. I'm so glad your boss could spare you for a few months, because Galena Landing certainly needs some help."

That was an interesting spin on the situation, one Brittany could run with while she kept the real reasons locked in the vault. "It will be an interesting challenge. I popped by the market as I came into town — which reminds me, I should run out to the car and get the honey and eggs I bought you."

"Oh, thanks! They'll be fine out there for a bit longer before they freeze solid. Do tell me more about what you'll be doing."

"Just designing marketing materials and getting word out. What I really need is an insider's view of the town. Do you frequent the market? It seemed pretty small and quiet."

"Today was the first day of the season, and I didn't make it down. As the summer wears on, there will be more vendors. We didn't have a market for years. This is only the second year they're really trying to put something together, and I can't believe they thought April first was a good starting date. I'm not sure why the manager thought it was a good idea."

"I see. So, this is totally the ground floor." That did make Brittany feel better. The town depended on her.

"Last summer it struggled, though the manager — Paula — tried hard. She's super nice; don't get me wrong. But she has no background in running something like this."

"Oh. That doesn't sound good. They need someone with experience and vision."

"You tell me. Paula needs all the help she can get." Gina leaned over the table and lowered her voice. "The biggest problem is that she doesn't know it."

Comic Sans and all.

CHAPTER
TWO

Treyan Ackerman shifted in his seat as the Sunday service drew to a close. Seemed like he couldn't go five hours without someone mentioning contentment. Now Pastor Ron was even preaching it from the pulpit, so Trey'd had to contemplate it for the past half hour.

Why, God?

He wasn't even sure he wanted the answer, but at least church was over for another week. And that was a bad attitude. He knew it, but seriously? Where were the sermons and prompts for some good old-fashioned fire-and-brimstone for those who flouted God? He could get on board with that. If anyone deserved it, his ex did.

But contentment? That was like saying it was okay what she'd done. What she was still doing. What she was dragging their daughter through.

A little judgment, Lord? It could go a long way.

Instead, he got an elbow in the ribs, and it definitely wasn't God's. Trey angled a look at his brother. "What?"

"I'm taking the boys to the diner for lunch. Want to come?"

Trey shook his head. "No, I've only got Scarlett for a few more hours before I have to give her back to Kayla."

"Dude. It's like saying you don't get to see your kid if you're eating lunch out."

Was it fair to remind Mitchell how the boys intimidated Scarlett? No. That was a battle for another day, though maybe they'd simply outgrow it. Best case scenario.

"Nah, we're headed back to the farm. Thanks, anyway."

Mitchell shrugged.

The guy didn't know how good he had it, being widowed instead of divorced. Sure, Mitchell grieved. Trey got that. But at least Mitch didn't have his wounds scratched open time after time, week after week. He didn't run into Lindsey at the Super One or at the farmers market. He didn't have to see her cling to some other man's arm and notice that baby bump growing on her slight frame. Didn't have to hear his kid talk about the upcoming baby as her sister.

And God wanted Treyan to be content. Yeah, that was going to take a bigger miracle than he could begin to contemplate.

He rose to his feet just as his daughter slammed into his legs, nearly sending him back down.

"Daddy!"

"Hey, pumpkin. Junior church is over already?" Trey picked up the five-year-old and gave her a noisy kiss.

"Daddy, can I go play at Emma's house? Please?" She dragged out the begging and batted her eyelashes, looking and sounding way too much like Kayla in that moment.

"Not today."

Scarlett sighed. "You always say that."

She wasn't wrong. She didn't get how short weekends were, how much he missed having her around the other five days of the week. He'd moved in with Mitchell after the divorce just months after Lindsey's death. It just wasn't right that he saw his nephews so much more than his own child.

"Can we go to the lake?"

"It's April, baby. It's too cold."

"I don't want to *swim*. Just play."

"Not today."

She scowled at him and pushed against his chest, so he lowered her. "Five minutes, Scarlett."

If she heard him, she didn't let on as she darted toward a few other small kids.

Trey glanced around as the sanctuary emptied, noting that Steve Nemesek struggled to his feet while his wife chatted with a friend. The older man had contracted Guillain-Barré before Treyan's time, but always seemed to have a pleasant attitude. Trey could learn from the man, for sure... although at least his wife hadn't left him.

He leaned over the pew. "Need a hand, sir?"

"Thanks, son. I'm good." Steve pulled his walker around and grinned at Trey. "And how are things out on the Ackerman home place?"

Trey glanced at Scarlett, but she was occupied. "All right, I guess. Mitchell's got lots of seedlings in the greenhouse, and I'll be tilling the field as soon as it's dried out enough."

Steve brightened. "Rosemary will want to see what you boys have for plant starts."

"Sounds good. Mitchell's the one to talk to about all that, though. He's the mastermind, and I just do the grunt work."

"Oh, I doubt that's all." Steve grinned as he took a wobbly step with his walker. "Talk to you soon, son."

"Thanks." Trey ought to be the one cheering up the other man or, at least, listening to his woes. Pretty sure Steve Nemesek had more to complain about than Treyan did. Trey's ex-wife might be flaunting her affair in his face, but he was young. Healthy. Strong. He had a decent job plus the farm. A place to live.

He sighed and turned to see Scarlett dashing toward him, Emma Zima in tow. And he had an amazing little girl. So, he didn't get to spend as much time with her as he'd like. His whole life hadn't turned out quite like he'd expected when he and Kayla had been just out of college and crazy in love. Or at least *he'd* been. It turned out she'd been playing him from the beginning.

"Ready to go, pumpkin?"

"Mr. Trey, can Scarlett come to my house to play?"

"No. I already told Scarlett not today." He leveled a look at his little daughter. "And it's not cool to get your friends to ask when we already talked about it."

Curly-haired Emma backed away, shrugging as she glanced at Scarlett, clearly apologizing for her failure.

"Coming, Emma?" The girl's mom, Gina, called from the back where she stood beside someone Trey didn't remember seeing before. The newcomer looked a lot like Gina, both with long dark hair and similar features. Maybe a younger relative or something.

Scarlett embraced Emma as though they might never meet again in this lifetime before Emma ran to her mom.

Gina waved at Trey, and he nodded as he took Scarlett's hand. "Time to go home, pumpkin."

"You mean Lincoln and Hudson's house."

Scarlett couldn't know how deeply the words stabbed. The thing was, she wasn't wrong. The house — the entire farm — might belong to Trey and his brother equally since their grandparents' passing, but Mitchell and Lindsey and the boys had already been living in the farmhouse. Trey had thought he and Kayla would build out on the property, but she'd rejected the idea outright. She'd never liked Lindsey. Should have been Trey's first clue, come to think of it.

When Kayla left him months after Lindsey's passing, Mitchell invited Treyan to move into the basement. Mitch had needed help with the boys, and Trey hadn't wanted to go home to an empty house five nights of the week. It seemed to make sense for the brothers to team up and share parenting.

It still did, but Trey hated hearing Kayla's snide comments coming out of their daughter's mouth.

Contentment. Trey wanted to whine at the writer to the Philippians that he didn't know anything until he'd experienced a back-stabbing wife. And yet... no one had tried to kill Treyan lately. He hadn't been stoned or shipwrecked or flogged.

Perspective was everything. Even though he hated to admit it.

"Good morning, Treyan. The mayor would like to see you in her office."

Trey set his coffee cup on the high counter dividing the town hall's front office from the foyer. "First thing on a Monday morning? I'm not sure what I did wrong."

Mrs. O'Neill smiled. "You have nothing to fear."

He always had something to fear from Ms. Kozak. He was intensely grateful for his nine-to-five in the planning office — he didn't make enough from the farm to keep body and soul together — but he only survived the monotony so he could see his daughter on weekends. If he had full custody of Scarlett, things would be different, but he didn't even have half. For some reason, he'd agreed with Kayla's suggestion for a five-and-two split, since it fit better into his work schedule than alternating weeks.

"The clock's ticking," Mrs. O'Neill reminded him.

"Right." Trey offered a grin that no doubt looked as awkward as it felt. He knocked on the counter twice then headed down the corridor to his own space where he parked his coffee on the desk, set his briefcase on his chair, and hung his raincoat. Then he tucked his button-down into his slacks, took a deep breath, and followed the hallway to the corner office, where he tapped on the slightly open door.

"Come in, Mr. Ackerman."

"Good morning, mayor. You wanted to see me?"

The fiftyish woman sat behind her polished walnut desk, semi-casual with her fake-red hair mounded up in her signature casual bun. But the mayor wasn't alone. In the visitor chair sat the young woman he'd seen in church yesterday, dressed in a lavender blazer and skirt. The bun pulling her dark hair to the nape of her neck looked as formal as Ms. Kozak's looked artless.

"Mr. Ackermann, I'd like you to meet Ms. Santoro. She'll be working with us for the next six months, whipping our marketing into shape, both for the market and the town as a whole. I'm sure you'll be relieved to have all that off your plate so you can focus on the challenges of the fire hall."

Trey opened his mouth and closed it again before mustering his courage. "I had completed some preliminary work on the marketing angle."

The mayor held his gaze. "I'm sure Ms. Santoro will be happy to take a look and see if there's anything she can use moving forward."

But... Somehow, Treyan managed to freeze his rebuttal inside his mouth. He needed this job, but the only bright light was pivoting away from him and now shining on a mere girl who looked barely old enough to have graduated college. Wasn't he the one who'd talked the mayor into looking at the town's branding? Who'd pointed out the newly hired market manager might be fine with people but had zero marketing sense?

Yes, that had been him. He wanted this project. Needed this project. He'd been going crazy as he listened to tightwad citizens argue that the 1950s-era building was good enough for today's firefighters because it might cost them an extra hundred dollars a year on their taxes and they were on a fixed income.

Money didn't grow on trees. He knew that. But the ancient clapboard fire hall was likely to be the first building to burn down if a fire blazed through Galena Landing. Didn't their volunteer department deserve to be kept safe? Didn't they deserve to have an up-to-code place to decontaminate their gear and park their trucks? Just wait until the new building was approved. The next hurdle was going to be a new ladder truck.

Treyan was staring at the young woman.

She was staring back, eyebrows raised as she eyed him coolly.

He dipped his head in acquiescence. "That sounds excellent, Ms. Kozak." What else could he say? He needed this job. There wasn't another one in Galena Landing that even remotely touched on his Bachelor of Science in Geography. There wasn't another that paid more or offered better hours or benefits. He managed a smile to the mayor. "Is there anything else?"

"Yes. Since you'll be working closely with Ms. Santoro *and* have one of the larger offices in the building, maintenance will be in shortly to make room for Ms. Santoro's desk. That sounds like the best arrangement to me, since she's only here on a six-month contract."

Treyan took a deep breath and managed not to glare at the newcomer. Did the woman have any idea what she was stealing from him? Not only the bright spot in the midst of a very gray budget fight, but his actual space? How could he make nice with her for six months?

He forced a smile at the mayor. "Certainly. I'm not sure where maintenance will fit another desk, but—"

"They'll remove the visitor seating. You may use the conference room for any meetings for the next while."

Either Ms. Kozak didn't know or she didn't care that Kayla dropped Scarlett off on Fridays an hour before the office closed. Perks of a small town, and one that looked about to be turned into a trial. There was no point in arguing, though. He couldn't deny the mayor simply so Scarlett's space to color for an hour was left intact, and getting Kayla to wait until closing was equally as futile. Apparently, she had things to do on Fridays.

"As you wish." He didn't miss the irony of reciting the line from *The Princess Bride* at his boss.

Ms. Santoro's lips tightened in his periphery. Maybe she was amused. Maybe she was annoyed. He wasn't sneaking a closer look to figure out which.

"Take a few minutes to clear whatever objects you can, Mr. Ackerman. Oh… and the traffic-pattern analysis should be in your inbox. I'll expect to hear your thoughts on that later today."

"Yes, mayor." Gritting his teeth, Treyan backed into the corridor then fled to his office. His own space, his refuge, but no longer. He eyed the area with two chairs and a small table between them. They were going to wedge a workspace in there? Good luck. Oh. But if there truly wasn't enough room, they'd be pushing his desk back.

He ran both hands through his short hair and shook his head. Six months. How on earth was he going to survive? And didn't the intruder just *have* to be a pretty city girl?

"I'm sorry. This wasn't my idea."

Treyan whirled. There she stood, a look of apology on her face. "Why did you apply for the job, then?" He hadn't even seen the posting. Maybe it wouldn't have gone through the normal channels since it was a contract position, but he hated being blindsided.

She lifted a slight shoulder in a shrug. "It's a long story, but I'm here now. My name is Brittany, by the way. No need for the Ms. Santoro bit, since it seems we get to work together closely."

Get to? That was a stretch. "Treyan," he said.

"Pleased to meet you."

He was a decent church-going man who'd been taught not to lie. He couldn't, in good conscience, parrot her polite phrase back to her.

She stepped into the office, scanning the space, and he shifted aside to allow her access. What did a newcomer see? A window overlooking Third Street sat across from the door. The guest seating occupied the shallow space on their right, while his desk, shelves, and file cabinet filled the remaining space.

Brittany crossed to look out the window, her high heels clicking on the ancient hardwood floor.

No one in Galena Landing dressed up in a suit and heels to come to work. Not the mayor. Not the bank manager. No one. But Trey couldn't deny she looked good in it, both the lavender color and the tailored fit. She was slender but curvy. Her dark brown hair in its bun brushed the collar of her jacket. Her sculpted calves—

She pivoted and caught him staring. Those eyebrows came up again as though she knew he'd been assessing her. At least she couldn't know the admittedly appreciative tone of his thoughts.

He could match those eyebrows. "Does this office meet with your expectations?"

Brittany slowly turned and took in the remainder of the space. "I had no expectations. I'm simply grateful not to have taken over the janitor's closet."

"That would have been a nasty fate."

"I'm sure." Her focus lingered on the bulletin board along the window wall by his desk. "Is that your daughter?"

Treyan whipped his gaze to the snapshot of him and Scarlett that Mitchell had taken on a tobogganing day back in January. She was in a bright pink snowsuit with most of her beanie coated with snow. They were both laughing. "Yes. Her name is Scarlett, and she's five."

"She's a cutie."

It was true. He nodded.

"Trey?"

He turned to see Joe from maintenance. "Hey. You're quick."

The older man hitched his sagging tool belt up on his hips as he stepped inside. "So, you want another desk in here."

Want was rather a strong word. The room was crammed with three bodies. Why hadn't Trey retreated behind his desk when he could? At least then no one could bump into his bubble. That whole bubble was pretty much burst for the next six months. He was going to have to deal with it.

"Well, the first thing is to get rid of the extra stuff." Joe stacked the two visitor chairs and moved them to the corridor. Then he snapped out his tape and measured the window wall. "Hmm. If we shove your desk back six inches, we can fit another here under the window."

Six inches? Treyan swallowed his panic. "That's a mighty big desk you're bringing in if you need that much room."

Joe shrugged. "Not a lot of options down in the storage room. There's a smaller one, but it needs repairs, and the mayor specifically said the new hire needs a lot of surface area."

Of course, she did. "Do whatever it takes." Treyan grabbed his briefcase. "I'll be down in the conference room if anyone needs me for anything."

Maintenance might be out in an hour, but Ms. Santoro — Brittany — was going to be sitting directly in his line of vision for six months. Working on his laptop in the conference room might be his new normal.

CHAPTER

THREE

How are things at the office?" Gina asked.

A definite perk of this job was the proximity of town hall to Gina and Chris's house. Brittany could walk to work in five minutes... which meant she could walk home for her lunch hour. Total bonus since the cafés downtown didn't look all that great, and every day Britt avoided them saved a few dollars more for her New York fund. All that walking saved money, too, though it did mean Brittany carried her heels in her messenger bag and wore her ballet flats for the walk.

She shrugged. "It's okay. I'm finally meeting Paula this afternoon."

"Great! You'll like her."

"I hope so. If she's hard to work with, this whole contract is going to be a total pain." But she'd keep her goals in mind. Brittany was nothing if not focused.

Gina set two plates with paninis on them on the table. "Aw, don't worry about it. Really. Her heart is in the right place."

"I only hope she can accept criticism."

"As well as the next person, I imagine." A bowl with fresh-cut veggies landed on the table along with a queso dip, then Gina took her seat. "Let me pray over lunch. Lord, thank You so much for today. I ask You to bless Britt's afternoon with Paula. Please bless this food and our time together. In Jesus's name, amen."

Britt pulled her plate closer and lifted the panini. "Where's Emma today? Also, yum. This smells amazing."

"I'm going to work at two, so my mom picked her up already." Gina worked as a nurse at the Galena Hills Care Facility. "Which reminds me, Mom figures she needs more time with you, so she invited you and Chris for dinner tonight since she'll already have both kids."

"Oh, that's nice." Not only were Uncle Matt and Aunt Connie the relatives Brittany knew the least but, of all five brothers, Uncle Matt sounded the most like Dad. Just hearing his booming laugh reminded Britt of how much Dad loved life and his family. Of how much she missed him. All that made Uncle Matt a bittersweet person to be around. It was worth it, even though it hurt. She'd never dreamed her own pain would linger longer than Mom's. She munched on the panini.

Gina dipped a carrot stick into the queso. "So, have you met any cute unattached guys yet?"

"No, not really."

Treyan Ackerman might be sort of cute, but he was married, so he didn't count. At least, he had a child, so Brittany assumed there was a wife, though he hadn't said anything and didn't wear a ring. Lots of men didn't wear rings. Dad never had. He'd been a tree trimmer and said wearing a ring was dangerous in his line of work. Not, apparently, as dangerous as driving down a residential street midafternoon and being T-boned by a drunk driver.

Brittany shoved the memory of the crumpled truck aside and took a deep, cleansing breath. "Besides, you're conveniently forgetting I'm leaving in just a few months."

Gina grinned. "You can't blame me for hoping you'll fall in love and stay right here. Trust me, I'm aware of how much family time I missed growing up here instead of in the middle of Bridgeview."

"It's not too late to move. Ethan and Emma would love being around all their second cousins."

"Well, they have second cousins here, too, on Chris's side. Just not as many of them. And I honestly can't imagine living anywhere else. Haven't you noticed how absolutely gorgeous this valley is? How pleasant the slower pace is? How everyone knows everyone?"

Brittany raised her eyebrows at her cousin. "You say all that as though it's a recommendation."

"But, of course!"

"As if."

"Oh, Galena Landing will grow on you yet. I'm sure of it."

"Dream on." Brittany glanced at the clock as she took another bite. "Whoops, I'd better get going. I'm meeting Paula down at the park at one, and that's a few blocks further than the office. Are you sure she'll be okay with me meddling?"

"You're not meddling, cuz. The town oversees the market, and they've hired you to put it on the map. It's nothing personal."

"Easy for you to say. You didn't see the sign down by the market on Saturday."

"I've seen it." Gina chuckled. "You're right. It's bad. But surely Paula knows. I'm certain it was just a stop-gap measure, and she'll be thrilled to have a beautiful new sign."

"As you say, Pollyanna."

"Hey, I've been called worse."

"I'm sure." Brittany took one last, rather large bite as she rose. Then she grabbed her messenger bag, snagged a few sugar snap peas and the remaining sandwich, and waved at Gina. "See you later."

She hated to admit it, but the town *was* pretty. Some of the homeowners between the Zimas' and downtown had lovely crocus and daffodil displays. Most of the snow was gone, and a few bushes showed signs of leafing out. An older woman, out raking her yard, waved at her.

Brittany waved back but didn't slow. This was a day she should probably have taken a sack lunch or stopped by the bakery, but the novelty of a fresh-cooked meal with her cousin hadn't worn off yet. Honestly, it might take all six months. Britt was okay with that. Starting completely on her own in New York would be challenging as well as freeing.

Walking everywhere in Bridgeview had prepared her for Galena Landing. The biggest difference was that in Spokane, transit was available anywhere outside of the neighborhood. Here, she actually could get anywhere she needed to go by foot. But she stepped up her pace as she approached the park.

A woman with shoulder-length black hair sat at a picnic table by herself.

Brittany approached. "Paula?"

The other woman surged to her feet and gave Brittany a guarded once-over. "Yes, I'm Paula Dye."

"Brittany Santoro." She stretched her hand and shook Paula's. "I'm so pleased to meet you."

"Same. Santoro, huh? Any relation to Matt and Connie?"

"Guilty. My uncle and aunt."

"They're good people. I'm Italian, too, though you can't tell by my married name."

That explained why Paula looked somewhat familiar, though Brittany didn't think she'd seen the other woman around town in the few days she'd been here. Brittany set her bag on the picnic table. "Why don't you tell me your plans for the market?"

Paula's eyebrows rose. "Why don't you tell me about yours?"

"Excuse me?"

"Well, I've been doing just fine here. There weren't many complaints about our season last year, but the next thing I know, the town has hired someone to check up on me and tell me what to do."

So much for the manager being chill about accepting help. Diplomacy. Surely, Britt could find some somewhere. "That's not quite how I view it. The mayor sees that you've got a great start and the market has potential. My job is to support and amplify that."

"What do you know about running a market?"

"Not as much as you do, I'm sure. My expertise is in marketing and design. Together, we can make the market a smashing success."

"No offense, but you seem too young to have experience in anything at all."

Claiming she was twenty-four wasn't going to win her any points, that was clear. "And yet, I have a degree in graphic design, and the mayor hired me for this purpose. Paula, we're both on the same side. We both want the market to succeed."

Paula sighed. "What do you want to change?"

Besides the sign? Besides the fact that no one had shopping bags and there were no food trucks or entertainment or...? Brittany could go on and on, but today wasn't the day.

She eyed the picnic table bench then brushed a few twigs off of it before taking a seat. Thankfully, today she'd worn a flared multicolored skirt that stood a chance of camouflaging any specks of dirt that clung.

Brittany gestured to the other woman. "Please, have a seat, and tell me your dreams for the farmers market."

COME GET HER.

Treyan winced at Kayla's terse text. He'd phoned her last night and explained why she couldn't drop Scarlett off at town hall so early on Fridays. He should have known her response would be that she and her boyfriend, Tyrell, would have to take Scarlett with them to Kalispell for the weekend in that case.

He rolled back his chair, thankful that Brittany was out of the office. He didn't know where she was, and he didn't much care, so long as she wasn't in his space. He tucked in his shirt and made his way down to the foyer where Kayla stood, holding Scarlett's hand.

"Daddy!" His little girl broke away and darted over.

He scooped her up. "Hey, pumpkin."

"Be good for Daddy. See you Sunday afternoon." Kayla blew a kiss and scurried out of the building.

Had Kayla ever been sweet and motherly? Every time Trey saw her, she seemed less attractive, but he'd once loved her. Without her, he wouldn't have the love of his life, his precious daughter.

"What's her big hurry?" Mrs. O'Neill asked from behind the counter.

Treyan shook his head. "Who knows?"

"Mommy and Tyrell have a date."

Is that what you called it when you lived together and had every weekend free? Treyan wouldn't know. He might only have Scarlett two-sevenths of the time, but he was committed to making those days as wholesome as he could, which included taking her to junior church even when he'd rather have her all to himself.

Mrs. O'Neill mumbled something, but Treyan could ignore that. He took the stairs back up to the second floor and set Scarlett down at the door to his office. "There's been a little change—"

Brittany pivoted from standing beside her desk. Her eyebrows shot up at the sight of Scarlett. She looked at Trey then back to Scarlett.

And here he'd thought — hoped — she was gone for the day. No such luck. He put a smile in place. "Ms. Santoro—"

This time her eyebrows nearly met her hair. Okay, so he'd

called her Brittany on the few occasions this week he'd had to call her anything at all.

"Ms. Santoro, this is my daughter, Scarlett. Pumpkin, this is Ms. Santoro."

How Brittany managed to squat to Scarlett's level without toppling in those heels or flashing him — not that he was checking — was a mystery for the ages.

"Hey, Scarlett. It's nice to meet you. I saw your drawing of a princess on your dad's bulletin board. You're a really great artist."

"She has a crown with jewels on it." Scarlett fired a glance toward the drawing and took a step toward Brittany.

"I saw that. Jewels are very pretty."

Treyan dared breathe. Brittany was being a thousand times nicer about Scarlett being there than he'd expected. Yes, he should have warned her, but he'd clung to the hope that she'd take off early on a Friday afternoon. Surely she didn't have as many deadlines and projects looming over her weekend as he did.

The anti-fire-hall group was spamming social media with their budgetary fear-mongering and deluging all the town's posts with negative comments. The people who should most want a second stoplight installed at the corner by Super One were equally appalled by the town's proposed expenditure. You'd think they were robbing the population instead of adding safety to a location with more fender-benders than any other intersection in Galena Landing.

Scarlett dropped her hands to her hips in a credible imitation of her mother. "Where's my table? I want to make a picture of a castle."

Brittany stood and smoothed her pleated skirt as she looked at Treyan.

"Sorry, pumpkin. My boss decided Ms. Santoro needed a desk more than you needed a coloring spot."

"But it's *your* office, Daddy."

"Not anymore," he muttered.

Brittany's eyes flared. How had he not noticed how blue they were before? Blue like sapphires or Galena Lake just before a storm. "Look, I'm sorry..."

Treyan shook his head, cutting off her words. "It's not your fault my ex refuses to believe I can't walk out of the office at four o'clock on Fridays to suit her whims."

"Your... ex?"

Right, he hadn't told Brittany about Kayla. Why would he have? He'd spent the past five days trying to pretend Brittany didn't exist and wasn't breathing his air, the air her perfume sweetened. The conference room was booked far oftener than he'd ever guessed, but Brittany spent a fair bit of time in meetings elsewhere. Somehow, he'd skated through until today, talking to her as little as possible.

He took a deep breath. "My ex. Scarlett's mother. We've been divorced for three years." Three long years in which Treyan wished he could take his daughter and move far, far away. Unfortunately, that was called abduction and legally frowned upon. Didn't stop the temptation, though. "Her name is Kayla," he added as an afterthought.

"I see."

She probably didn't. Also, she didn't need to. Brittany was nothing to him other than an annoyance for the next six months. But hey, he'd survived the first week. Only twenty-five more to go, and he'd get his space back. His and Scarlett's.

"You can't head out early, huh?"

Treyan glanced at the clock and shook his head. "I still have a traffic report to file. That's what they pay me the big bucks for."

Brittany wrinkled her nose. "Sounds exciting."

"You have no idea."

"Well, listen. I've got my projects wrapped up for the week."

Of course, she did. "Congratulations?"

She tossed him a smile. "So why don't Miss Scarlett and I go down to the bench by the sidewalk, and she can play a game on my phone until you're done."

"You'd do that?"

Scarlett stomped her foot. "But I want to color."

"Or I have a notebook and some pens in my bag. Do you like glitter gel pens, Scarlett? I have lots of colors."

His daughter sidled closer to Brittany, clearly intrigued. "I like glitter."

Wasn't that just like females, bonding over sparkles?

"If it's okay with your dad."

"I can't believe you're offering." He couldn't believe Scarlett looked okay with it.

Brittany shrugged. "It's not like I have anything exciting to do for the next hour, and I happen to like hanging out with kids. They're a lot more fun than many adults."

"You're not wrong."

"I know." She grinned and slung her messenger bag over her shoulder. "What do you say?"

"Um, sure. But I owe you one." A big one.

"I'll collect sometime." She held out her hand. "Want to come? I have almost one hundred gel pens in my bag."

Holy Toledo. She could be the Pied Piper of all the kids in Galena Landing with that stash.

"Okay." Scarlett tucked her hand in Brittany's and gave a little skip. "See you later, Daddy."

"Text me if you need me. You've got my number, right?" Man, it sounded like he was trying to pick his coworker up. So not the case.

Brittany nodded. "I entered everyone's number into my phone from the inter-office memo. A person never knows when she might need to get in touch with someone."

"Right. Exactly." Treyan stepped aside and watched as Scarlett and Brittany walked down the corridor, swinging their joined hands. He scratched the side of his head. What had just happened?

The woman who'd pushed her way into his office maybe wasn't so horrible after all. She sure hadn't needed to take on Scarlett for an hour.

And he was standing in the middle of the room thinking about her instead of finalizing his workweek. That traffic report wasn't going to wrap itself into a nice, neat bow without his attention.

Treyan settled behind his desk and jiggled the mouse, but the screen didn't quite come into focus. Or maybe it was him.

He'd said he owed her one. What would be a suitable thank-you for such a big favor from a near-stranger? Dinner out? No. That would be too much like a date, and word would get back to Kayla in eighteen seconds flat. This was way too early for that.

Too early? What on earth was going on inside his head? He wasn't interested in dating. Which meant he wasn't interested in taking someone like Brittany out for dinner. Besides, her favor to him was more work related than personal. Well, it was personal, but...

Treyan James Ackerman. You've wasted five minutes thinking about whether or not to invite a woman out for dinner when you absolutely know you don't want to. Remember that report that won't compile itself? Do it, already.

CHAPTER
FOUR

T hanks." Brittany noted the comfy-looking camp chair behind the low table. A chair she wouldn't be sitting in for the next few hours, at least not much. If she wanted to engage the market shoppers and chat with them all, she needed to look eager to do so.

"You're welcome." Paula hesitated. "It's not much. Sorry."

"It's fine. Thanks for scrounging up a canopy in case it rains." It very well might, by the gusty wind and gloomy clouds. Hopefully, the tattered canvas would keep any raindrops at bay, but Brittany wasn't counting on it.

"Okay. Well, I should make sure no one needs any help." Paula glanced around the space, where several vendors struggled with their pop-up shelters. "We might not get many visitors today."

Shoppers. Not visitors. Brittany bit her tongue. And those shoppers were the lifeblood of the market. Without people arriving to purchase fresh produce — or whatever was available in early April — there was no point in the dozen vendors setting up stalls at all.

She spread a bright turquoise tablecloth on the plastic folding table and set a bouquet of pink tulips in place. A vintage bowl with wrapped candies to lure people over would not go amiss. Okay, fine, she'd happily bribe them to take her survey.

Brittany pulled the file up on her tablet. She'd had Gina go through the questions last night to make sure everything was working correctly. Then she set a stack of print-outs beside the tablet, with several sharpened pencils in a short cut-glass vase. She was ready to discover what the locals expected from their market. What they envisioned in their wildest dreams. What they'd seen in other towns and wished Galena Landing could emulate.

If she was going to make this market a smashing success — with Paula's help, of course — she needed to know what she was up against.

Across the way, the honey-and-egg lady set up her canopy with the help of a tall blond man. After he unfolded the table and righted it, he gave her a kiss and strode away.

The breeze fluttered the stack of surveys, and Brittany anchored them with the candy dish. Outdoor markets had their challenges, but it looked like the papers were staying put for now. She crossed the grassy aisle. "Hi. Do you need a hand with anything? It's Sierra, if I remember correctly?"

The woman straightened and turned. "Thanks. Brittany, right?"

"Yes. Happy to help."

Sierra swept a loose strand of hair behind her ear. "I've

got everything covered, but I appreciate the offer. Didn't I see you Sunday in church with Gina and Chris?"

"That would have been me." Not that she remembered seeing Sierra. There'd been at least a hundred strangers present, but she'd soon find her way around. She couldn't very well skip church.

"You mentioned something about a short-term contract with the town." Sierra glanced at the unmanned tent across the way. "What kind of contract?"

Here went nothing. "I'm a graphic designer with several years' experience in Spokane. I've been hired to reimagine the town's image as well as help position the farmers market for success. I've got surveys for the vendors and visitors to fill out — paper or digital, your preference. Would you mind completing one?"

"I'd love to, but I don't have time before the market begins. Is there an online option for later? Trust me, I have ideas."

"Great!" Hopefully they were in line with Brittany's own vision. A ray of hope shone in the clean, simple table display. Sierra had a decent design aesthetic. "As for an online survey, yes. I can give you the link, but it might be easier to take a paper copy, fill it out at home, and drop it by town hall. Or return it next Saturday."

Sierra held up both hands. "I'd prefer not to waste a tree." She pulled a tablet from her cooler of egg cartons. "If you know the survey URL offhand, just tap it in here. Promise I'll get to it within the next couple of days."

Thankfully the mayor had approved the simple link Brittany had set up, so she entered it.

"Perfect. Nice, neat, and easy to read. I appreciate it.

Some of my neighbors might like to take the survey, too. Is it okay if I pass the link around?"

"The more input, the better. I appreciate it."

Two men in jeans and hoodies began setting up a canopy next to Sierra's. Brittany shifted to get out of their way. She should probably have gone for jeans as well. Everyone around here seemed to wear them, but she was representing the town, so she'd stuck to slacks, flats, and a blazer. If the wind picked up much more, she'd live to regret her clothing choice. Maybe she already did.

One of the men turned as he extended the pop-up's leg. Wait. Treyan?

Brittany blinked as the guy moved to the next leg. She couldn't be sure, of course. He looked very different from the man in her office. But when he faced her again as he tapped a stake through the foot of the support, she knew.

She looked at the second guy, but his back was to her as he set up the other side. She shifted a step closer. "Treyan?"

His head snapped up then and his dark eyes lasered onto hers. "Brittany?"

"What are you doing here?" She indicated the canopy.

"Setting up for the market?"

Duh, that was obvious. "I didn't know you were a vendor."

"Technically, my brother is. I give a hand at times."

She glanced at the other man, who'd turned to her with a curious expression. "Hi. I'm Brittany. I work with Treyan."

The guy glanced at his brother and smirked. "I've heard your name a time or two. I'm Mitchell. Mitchell Ackerman." He extended his hand.

Brittany shook it. Man, his was a ton warmer than hers.

She'd be a solid ice cube by the end of the morning. "Pleased to meet you."

"Likewise."

The wind picked up, and a corner of the canopy lifted. Treyan grabbed the long leg. "Pass me a stake, please."

His brother obliged, and Brittany backed away. The research she'd been doing divulged that a lot of other markets required weights for each corner of every canopy. With this market set up beside the lakefront, it seemed that ought to be a rule here.

She glanced over at her own booth just as the candy dish tipped over, freeing the papers beneath it. Half a dozen of them fluttered away. She dashed across and parked her messenger bag on the remaining stack then began rounding up the escapees.

"Here. Got them." Treyan handed her a few pages.

"Thanks." She met his gaze. "I was unprepared for the wind gusts."

He gave her a nearly imperceptible once-over.

Okay, fine. She was unprepared for the weather as well, but she'd survive. She always had, so far.

"Doing a survey?" He glanced at her display, where the turquoise tablecloth had billowed off the end nearest the lake and now covered the messenger bag.

Brittany took a deep breath. "That's the plan. Would you and your brother like to take it?" She looked over at Mitchell, who was setting flats of seedlings on an unadorned plastic table. It might be utilitarian and ugly, but at least he wasn't fighting with a tablecloth ready to lift off.

"Sure. I heard you tell Sierra there was an online option. Mitch and I would prefer that, too."

"Okay... but the trees have already been cut down." She grasped at a straw. "And paper is recyclable."

Could that possibly be humor glinting in his eyes? But it faded quickly. "You've got a few things to learn about Galena Landing, Ms. Santoro. One of them is we take the environment seriously around here. Recycling is great. We do that. But we try to minimize the need for it in the first place."

"I get it." After all, her family was big on homegrown food and minimizing their global footprints. She hadn't thought about it a ton — leave that for the bleeding hearts like her cousin Jasmine — but she was certainly aware.

Treyan's eyebrows spiked. "Do you?" Then he pivoted and strode back to his brother.

What was with him? He'd been the most unwelcoming person she'd met so far in this hick town. He'd loosened slightly yesterday when she'd offered to watch Scarlett for an hour, but it seemed that interlude had been an anomaly.

Hostile Treyan was back.

Yay.

TREYAN HAD NO SOONER PUT the truck into park when two seatbelts in the backseat unclicked. Hudson's plaintive voice from the middle begged to be released. Just a few more months and Mitchell's youngest would be in a booster, same as Scarlett and seven-year-old Lincoln. That would make things easier in some ways.

"Stick close," he warned Lincoln as the older boy shoved

the truck door open. At least Scarlett couldn't quite manage that yet, but it wouldn't be long.

Treyan leaned in to liberate Hudson as Scarlett clambered over her cousin, under Trey's arm, and out the open door. Sheesh. You'd think these kids had been locked in the truck for seven hours instead of the seven minutes coming in from the farm on Thompson Road.

When he straightened out of the truck and set his nephew down, the older two were already in the market pestering Mitchell. Hudson darted off to join them.

Looked like Mitchell had sold some of the bedding plants. It was hard to know how much of anything to plant and nurture in the greenhouse. Treyan had a black thumb — after accidentally killing half the hydroponic lettuce a few weeks ago by forgetting to stoke the greenhouse's wood heater when he'd been sidetracked by one of the calves, his brother had banned him from the production.

That was fine. Unlike Mitch, Treyan had a full-time job. Growing hay on the hundred acres not taken up by the home-place and managing their few livestock filled his remaining time nicely. They had a few animals, but that was mainly Mitchell's department again.

It didn't feel like he contributed much. Which, maybe, wasn't technically true, but some days it seemed like it.

Now, he approached the market where a dozen shoppers still lingered at several of the stalls. The couple who owned the health food store stood beside Brittany, deep in conversation. She looked cold, the way she rubbed her hands together.

He shook his head. Being all dressed up city-style was more important to her than keeping her fingers from getting frostbite. Okay, it wasn't quite *that* cold, but it wasn't all that warm, either. Surely even in Spokane they didn't have toasty sunshine every single day in early April. She should know better. Be prepared.

Yeah, well, it wasn't his place to judge. He turned to Mitchell. "How was the market?"

"Not bad."

Which meant not that great. Paula shouldn't have started up the market until the beginning of May. There just wasn't that much call for fresh stuff in April. Probably because there wasn't much fresh stuff to be had. He'd definitely fill out a survey and point out the ridiculousness of an April market.

"Sold out of the romaine."

"Excellent." Mind you, that had only been a couple of dozen heads, thanks to Treyan's snafu a while back. Nice of his brother not to keep rubbing his nose in it, though.

Mitchell slid his phone into the back pocket of his jeans. "Of course, people are asking for vegetables I haven't started."

"Of course. Is it too late?"

"For some of them. I'll look into the others." Mitchell sighed. "Short of getting people's lists in January, it's impossible to know what to plant."

Treyan stacked seedling trays. "So do that, next year. Or in one of the fall markets."

"I hate to say you're a genius."

"I can't help being smarter than you."

Mitchell rolled his eyes. "Dream on."

Lincoln shoved his little brother against one of the supports, and the whole canopy shuddered.

"Stop it, you two." Mitchell's reproof sounded automatic.

But where was Scarlett? Treyan pivoted and scanned the area to see her across the way, where Brittany squatted at his daughter's eye level to talk to her. Hardly anyone gave Scarlett the time of day. Sometimes that included Treyan, for all he craved time spent with her. Once he had it, he didn't always know what to do with it. Besides, life was busy on weekends. All three kids went with whichever father could keep an eye on them. When Trey was out seeding or harvesting, that was Mitch, not him.

His life sucked. Plain and simple.

And Scarlett craved female attention. She'd talked of Miss Brittany this and Miss Brittany that all yesterday evening. She'd showed Treyan the three pictures she'd drawn. Without actually counting all the colors, he was willing to bet Brittany hadn't exaggerated when she said she had one hundred gel pens in her bag.

"Scarlett!" he called. Not that he needed her right this second, but it wasn't fair to make someone else watch his kid all the time. It made him look like a lousy father. Which maybe wasn't so far from the truth. Kayla was fond of mentioning he'd been a worthless husband. Hard to imagine his parenting was any better.

"Coming, Daddy!" But then she wrapped her arms around Brittany's neck and gave a big squeeze before disengaging.

Oh, man. He'd have to remind his little girl that Miss Brittany was moving away in a few months. It couldn't be soon enough, of course. One week in, and he desperately missed his quiet, peaceful office. Not that Brittany was noisy.

It was just that she came and went at irregular intervals. It was mostly that she existed in his space.

Scarlett darted toward him, her tangled curls flying behind her. Her pink parka was shabby and dirty from playing in the muddy yard with her cousins, and her gumboots only proved the point.

He should have cleaned her up a little before bringing her to town so she didn't look so much like a motherless urchin. But... he'd never had that thought before. Why start now?

Brittany smiled at him as she rose to her feet, one hand on the table for balance. The turquoise tablecloth had been folded with her survey on top. Much less prone to fluttering away, plus it seemed the wind had died down some.

Treyan was staring. He lifted his hand in acknowledgment and grasped Scarlett's hand. "Time to help Uncle Mitchell carry stuff to the truck."

"Then are we going back to the farm?"

"Yep." He'd noticed she never referred to it as home. The term, apparently, was reserved for Tyrell Burke's large timber-frame house a few miles south of town.

Trey didn't much like the guy. Never had, even before the cracks in his and Kayla's marriage had turned into chasms. Even before Tyrell's wife had left him. Tyrell had such a big head, so full of himself. What did Kayla see in him, anyway? What did Tyrell have that Treyan didn't?

Money. But was that all?

Not that Trey wanted Kayla back. Those last couple of years after Scarlett's birth had been a living hell. Sure, his sister-in-law had cautioned him that new mothers' hormones were a mess. Kayla was no exception, but it didn't seem she'd even tried. Hadn't sought help or medication or whatever might have made a difference. No, she'd used that as an excuse to deepen the wedge in their already brittle marriage.

Okay, so he couldn't blame everything on Kayla. He'd been busy trying to establish himself in the town office as well as reclaiming the farm. Kayla had hated the farm. Why was Tyrell's so much better than his? It came back to money. It always did.

Right. He was going to stop thinking that way. He and Kayla were irrevocably over, the only remaining link between them, their daughter. And that meant he needed to play nice for years to come.

He glanced across the grass to see Paula coaching Brittany as the pair lowered the canopy. They were making it so much harder than it needed to be.

Before he could stop himself, he set the stack of seedling flats on the handcart and strode across. "Here. Let me help."

The wind gusted, tearing the tattered canvas a little more. The thing ought to be dropped in a dumpster... unless it were possible to sew and attach a new canvas. Not in his skill set, that was for sure.

He looked at Paula. "This thing's trashed."

She pursed her lips. "I can't argue with that, but we need a spare or two for occasions just like this."

"Isn't there any budget to replace it?" He collapsed one support partway then moved to the next.

"I... I'm not sure. I hate to ask."

"That's what I'm here for." Brittany seemed to have caught what he was doing, as she moved to the third leg. "To ask those questions and make budget recommendations."

"But the mayor said..."

Brittany glanced over at Paula. "Seriously. The town is willing to invest. That is actually why I've been hired. Remember?"

Paula looked away then nodded. "Fine."

The newcomer rolled her eyes where Paula couldn't see her.

No surprise. It sounded like the two of them weren't exactly on the same page, but Treyan had to hand it to Brittany. Seemed she could handle herself professionally, and it had little or nothing to do with her fashion sense.

But she must be freezing. "I'll finish this. You go warm up. Did you get lots of surveys filled in?"

Brittany looked up at him, eyes narrowing. "This is my job. I'll get it."

He stared her down. "Go. Your hands are red."

"It *is* cold."

Well, duh, with that wind gusting off the lake. But he managed to bite off getting after her like he would Scarlett. He pointed at the parking lot. "Seriously. Go."

She gave an apologetic look at Paula then off she went.

Paula stuffed the folded canopy into its equally ragged bag with his help. "I don't know why the town hired her. I could manage this myself."

While being afraid to ask for what she needed? It wasn't until he walked back to help his brother that Treyan realized he hadn't once wished he were the one doing the survey and trying to get Paula's cooperation and vision.

Brittany Santoro could have it.

If only she had her own office and stayed out of his.

FIVE

"This is so much better than Gina's basement." Brittany sighed as the comfort of the apartment she'd shared with her cousin Ava for three years enfolded her.

Ava plopped a bowl of popcorn on the sofa and sat cross-legged on the other end. "But of course. Now tell me everything."

"There's not much to tell. I've only been gone for two weeks." Britt grabbed a handful of buttery popcorn.

"Any cute guys?"

"You told me you'd kill me if I met anyone away from Bridgeview." Was it time to tell her cousin she never intended to live here again? Ava suspected.

"Yeah, well, you can break up with him in six months."

"Oh, doesn't *that* sound like fun." She couldn't quite keep the sarcasm out of her voice.

"Sorry. I just know you haven't been single for six months since middle school."

"It's true. But there's no way I'd put myself through that on purpose at my age."

"Because you're ancient now." Ava tossed a kernel of popcorn in the air and caught it in her mouth.

"Does Seth know you're this talented?"

"We had a contest the other evening. Peyton is surprisingly good at catching popcorn. Beatrice less so. Seth? Not at all. But he's excellent at vacuuming up the evidence."

Brittany shook her head, grinning. "You guys are adorable. Sounds like you're doing okay with the girls?" She still couldn't believe Ava would soon be an insta-mom to Seth's two half-sisters and his toddler son. Personally, she wanted no part of another woman's kids.

"Honestly? There are moments. But having Eliza next door makes all the difference. She seems to have a sixth sense about when Seth and I need some time away from the girls. Plus, they really love her."

Eliza had moved to Spokane after her divorce to help out with her deceased sister's daughters. She wasn't related to Seth... they had a complicated family.

"That's great. I'm happy for you." Brittany really was, while at the same time totally thankful she hadn't been the one to fall in love with Seth Donahue. For more than one reason.

"Come on, tell me everything. How are things with Gina and Chris? Have you seen much of Uncle Matt and Aunt Connie? Tell me about your office. About the market. And *go*!"

"And go? What are we, fourteen?"

Ava pulled the popcorn bowl into her arms and cradled it. "No more popcorn for you until you start talking."

"Okay, fine. Gina's good. She goes maybe a little overboard making me welcome in their home. It's almost smothering, but in a good way." The mothering role would play a bigger part if Brittany were dating anyone, since there would be secrets. As it was, it wasn't a problem.

"I've always liked Gina." Ava extended the bowl. "And their kids are cute. I wish I knew them better."

"The kids are adorable, yes. Ethan is eight, so grown up." Britt remembered when her little brother was that age. Before he became emotionally crippled by the death of their father. Mom's new husband had played a big role in helping Michael adjust, but Britt would keep Charlie at a comfortable distance, thanks. She wasn't going to find healing in a stepfather.

"How's the church they attend?"

Britt wasn't going to find healing there, either. "I've only been a couple of times, but it seemed okay."

"And the office? Do you have a view or a wall?"

The office. Talking about that meant she'd be talking about Treyan Ackerman, and she didn't want Ava's questions there. "My desk is right under a window." Which meant Trey didn't have access to it.

"Oh, nice! What's outside? No skyscrapers in Galena Landing!"

"A magnolia tree. The view is great right now with all the blossoms, and there will likely be a lot of shade all summer." And by the time the leaves fell, she'd be far away.

Ava sighed. "I love magnolia flowers. Like big white tulips, tinged with pink. If we were having a spring wedding, I'd want magnolias."

"June is nice, too. Tell me what you need me to do for the wedding while I'm in town this weekend."

"Well, we have the fittings tomorrow afternoon."

Brittany nodded and leaned forward with her elbows on her crossed knees. "Do I get to plan a bachelorette party?"

"Do we have to?" Ava wrinkled her nose.

"It's tradition."

"If I promise not to embarrass you and your future fiancé, will you promise not to humiliate me?"

"Since I'm never getting married..." Britt waggled her eyebrows.

"Are we still talking about the girl who's never been single for more than a week or two?"

"It's been a month right now, with many more to come." And if she met anyone for a fling in Galena Landing, she definitely wouldn't be telling her cousin about him. Just as she hadn't told Ava anything about Jeff other than his first name.

Argh. Jeff. Now that had been a major indiscretion. How was she supposed to know he was married and baiting her on purpose? He'd seemed so genuinely fun, right up until Janice found out and exiled Brittany. He hadn't even shown remorse.

She'd had plenty of practice lately at shoving him out of her mind. And out he went again.

"So. Your job. You have a nice view out the window, but what's the office like? The coworkers?"

"It's an older building with creaky wood floors and stucco walls. Those little glass doorknobs."

"Ooh!" Ava's eyes lit up as she leaned forward.

"The office building isn't very large, which means they

had to wedge a desk for me into a corner of the town planner's office. He wasn't much impressed."

"Oh, man. Not even your own space. That's a bummer."

"Yeah."

"And he's probably some old guy, ready to retire and resenting you breathing his air."

In Brittany's mind's eye, Treyan Ackerman narrowed his gaze at the side of her face. She hadn't missed that he'd moved his monitor a few inches partway through the first day to block his view of her. "Not that old, but yes on the resentment."

"You can win him over. You earned your position there fair and square."

What Ava didn't know wouldn't hurt her. "I doubt he's winnable, but it doesn't matter. Six months isn't that long." Only half of forever. "Then he can have his space back."

"Right. And if he's still got his desk and computer and stuff, what does he need extra air for?"

"His kid." Drat. Brittany hadn't meant to say that.

Ava's brow furrowed. "His kid? So he's not only not that old, he's pretty young?"

Busted. "Thirty, tops. I haven't asked. His daughter is about the same age as Gina's daughter. They're friends."

"Ah, so he and his wife are friends of Gina and Chris?"

Brittany jumped to her feet and brushed a few stray kernels off her red-and-black plaid pajamas. "Do you have some iced tea made?"

"Does Nonna have a thousand knickknacks?"

"Great. You want a glass? All that salt is making me thirsty."

"Sure. Have you met your coworker's wife?"

Standing at the fridge with her back to her cousin, Britt rolled her eyes. "He's divorced."

Ava squealed.

Brittany poured two glasses of tea. There was no avoiding her cousin when she got this way. She was like a hound with a scent.

"So, let me get this straight. You're sharing an office with a divorced man, younger than thirty, who doesn't like you, and his daughter is friends with Emma? What else do I need to know?"

"Nothing. It is entirely possible to share an office with a person like that for six months and then go our separate ways. Which is exactly what will happen, because Treyan isn't my type at all." Right, because Brittany's kind was only out for a temporary good time.

"You need a new type. Keep meeting the same kind of guy, and you'll keep getting the same results. Losers."

It was like Ava was reading her mind. But Britt couldn't let her cousin have the last word. "You're still bitter about Duncan." She set the two glasses on the coffee table.

"Are you kidding me? Seth is a hundred times better than Duncan. A million times. Even you should know that."

"Even me?" Britt settled back to her spot on the sofa and pressed her hand over her heart. "What's that supposed to mean? Because it sounded like an insult."

"Oh, good grief. Duncan was a jerk, and you know it. He went from me to you to Patsy at the accounting office to... I don't even know who after that."

Seth had been no virgin when Ava found him, either, as evidenced by his toddler son. But, yeah, he'd been reformed. Redeemed. Something.

Something Brittany was still avoiding. Birth control was made for women like her, something she hadn't quite realized until Duncan and the fear she might've conceived. She and Ava'd had a weekend-long party when Britt's period arrived that time around. She was never going to worry about pregnancy again. Right along with not confiding everything in Ava. Some things were meant to stay private.

"So, back to the guy in your office. Why does his daughter need room there?"

Brittany sighed.

TREYAN FIRED up his computer and took a sip of coffee while he waited for it to run through its start-up sequence. He'd brought a thermal mug from home, as usual. The budget didn't really run to stopping by Bella's Bakery for a fresh cup every morning, and whoever made the coffee in the break room downstairs must have been told to make the grounds stretch. The stuff was pale with a vague hint of caffeine.

Where was Brittany?

It was a cloudy Tuesday morning, and he hadn't seen her since he'd retrieved Scarlett from her care Friday at five o'clock. She hadn't been at the market. She hadn't been at church. And she hadn't been in the office all day yesterday.

It had been quietly peaceful. Who knew silence could be just as distracting as someone constantly in his space?

A couple of dozen unread emails streamed into his inbox, all of them from the anti-fire-hall group. Who did they think was going to extinguish their houses if they caught fire? Volunteers with no place to stay on-site, no decontamination area, no ladder truck with extensions? If they didn't build it soon, it would only become more and more necessary, and more and more expensive. Look how the price of everything seemed be going up. It wasn't just commercial construction.

He needed to reply to each and every one of those emails separately, because some of those people would be comparing replies, and they'd smell a condescending rote answer in no time flat.

Treyan took a deep breath and let it out slowly.

"Hey! Have a good weekend?"

And just like that, sunshine invaded his office. He glanced up to see Brittany in her lavender suit with a soft pink top ruffling out the front of the blazer. Her dark hair was pulled into the same low bun she wore most weekdays. All business, that woman, except for the sunny smile.

He couldn't help smiling back. "Good enough. You?"

"Great! I went home for the weekend, hung out with my mom and stepdad, my siblings, my cousin." She waved a hand as though summing up a hundred important people. "And then yesterday I interviewed a couple of market managers from other small towns in the region. Between that and the surveys, I think I've got a much clearer handle on what Galena Landing needs."

Treyan tipped his chair back. She was vibrating excitement. Exclamation points practically popped around her head like an effervescent halo. When had he last been that thrilled about anything? Scarlett's birth, maybe. Possibly not even then.

"Ah, I wondered where you were yesterday. Thought you were skipping out of work."

She grinned. "Ah, so you noticed. And here I thought you were immune."

Oh, he was immune all right. "I got two days' worth of work done yesterday because it was so quiet."

"Sure you did." She set her laptop on her desk, plugged it in, and popped it open. "We need some rebranding. We need a food truck or two, we need live music, we need kids' activities, we need—"

"Whoa. Kids' activities?"

"Yeah, I was thinking of asking if the library would like to do a story hour at the market every week. Wouldn't that be great for parents? They could shop and chat with their friends, knowing their kids were happy and busy."

Trey stared at her, thinking it through. Scarlett would love that. Lincoln and Hudson might, as well.

"Yes? No?"

He blinked. "You're envisioning a community hub."

"Exactly!" She reached out, and Treyan completed the high-five across his desk. "Know anyone in town with a food truck?"

His eyebrows shot up. "In Galena Landing?"

"So, that's a no, huh?"

"Totally a no. We hardly have any restaurants, in case you haven't noticed."

"Oh, I noticed. Thankfully, my cousin likes to cook, so I haven't panicked too much. Besides, I'm only here for a few months."

Right. She was leaving in the fall. He'd get his office back. It would all be good. "You could try some of the community groups. Maybe they could do fundraising with hot meals at the market?"

Brittany pointed a finger at him as she nodded. "Now *there's* an idea, Mr. Ackerman. But a food truck or two would be so much better."

Hadn't she heard anything he said? "But we don't have one."

"There are a couple in Wynnton. And..." She drew out the word, looking at him with eyebrows raised.

Fine. He'd bite. "And?"

"And my stepdad has a couple of coffee trucks in Spokane. He hasn't found a regular spot for one of them yet, and he's willing to come up here once a month or so. Oh! That reminds me." She set her messenger bag on her rolling chair, dug into its depths, and came out with a paper bag. "Here. You like coffee. Try this blend from Redband Roasters. That's Charlie's company in Spokane."

"You're giving me a gift?"

"Sure, why not? Call it a sampler. I have a few to pass around. I'll give one to the mayor." Brittany wrinkled her nose. "Do you think they'd be willing to change up the coffee they serve in the break room?"

Trey accepted the bag and held up his thermal mug with his other hand. "Why do you think I bring coffee from home?"

"Right. That stuff needs to be about four times stronger. It's..." She waved her hands. "It's disgusting. It doesn't deserve to be called coffee."

He laughed. He couldn't help it. "My sentiments exactly."

"I'll see what I can do." Brittany shifted her messenger

bag to the floor by the wall and settled onto her chair. Her lips pursed as she read something on her screen.

Treyan couldn't help the grin that poked at the corners of his mouth. She was the consummate professional, but with a genuine, personal touch. She'd go a long way in this business with that combination. A long way from Galena Landing.

It couldn't come soon enough for him, remember? But maybe the next five and a half months wouldn't be completely horrible.

Brittany glanced over and touched her cheek. "Do I have something on my face?"

Awkward. She'd caught him staring. "No. Not at all." He searched for a quick save. "Do you think a table at the market for info on the proposed fire hall would help our cause?"

"Maybe. I can't believe people don't see the need for a new building. I bet the current one doesn't even meet basic fire codes, let alone protect the equipment for when it's needed elsewhere."

Treyan cringed at the thought of what would happen if the fire hall itself caught fire. "You're right. It doesn't. It's even got asbestos in it."

"Asbestos?"

"Popular insulation material from bygone eras. It was a cheap fire-retardant."

"And?"

"And it can get in people's lungs and cause cancer. It's been illegal to use since the eighties. Unfortunately, there's still a lot of it out there. It's considered safe enough if left alone, but the minute you start a renovation project and uncover it, the whole site needs to be sealed off, and a certified decontamination team is required to remove it."

"Yikes."

"Yup."

"Why are people against a new fire hall?"

"Increased taxes, mostly. We're not that wealthy in this county. Lots of older folks are on a fixed income."

"So, it's a mind game."

"A money game."

Brittany shook her head. "No, a mind game. They're rich enough to own property. Now they need to see why protection is worth a little extra."

"I like the way you think." Treyan pointed a pen at her.

"Why, thank you. And, yes, I think a public campaign will be in order. The town manages the market, after all. Why not use their own venue?"

Why not indeed?

CHAPTER

SIX

Brittany scrolled down the list of survey takers and frowned. What was this greenacresfarm thing? The last six email addresses were hosted there.

"Where is Green Acres Farm?" She glanced over at Treyan. "It's coming up a lot."

His eyebrows rose as he looked at her past his monitor. "You don't know about Green Acres."

"You make it sound like I'm a preschooler."

"You are, in Galena Landing lingo, if you don't know about them."

Britt swiveled her chair to face him, leaned back, and crossed her arms. "Fine. Educate me."

"About ten or fifteen years ago—"

"Educators should know which."

He raised his eyebrows. Raised his voice to talk over her. "About ten or fifteen years ago, three women bought an old rundown farm north of town at the end of Thompson Road. Their goal was to live sustainably and teach others to do the same."

"Sounds noble."

"They apparently thought so. Over time, they each got married, and a few other couples joined them. They started a school... I can't believe you haven't heard of this place. Spokane isn't that far from here."

"A farm school?" It was starting to twig a memory or two. "Do they have weekend workshops on xeriscaping and herbs and stuff?"

Trey pointed his pen at her. "Bingo. You *have* heard of them."

"I think a cousin or two might have come."

"One or two of many dozens?"

"Hey, don't knock my family. My dad had four brothers. I've got a lot of cousins."

"One of whom is Gina Zima."

She nodded.

Treyan looked at her thoughtfully. "You mentioned brothers in the past tense."

Brittany pivoted her chair back to her desk. "I mentioned my *dad* in the past tense. Nothing wrong with any of his brothers." She jabbed the trackpad to awaken her computer. Not that she could see past the moisture pooling in her eyes.

"I'm sorry."

"Yeah. Me, too." Somehow, she kept her voice steady, but the screen still blurred.

"My mom, too."

What? She pulled a tissue from the box on her desk and looked at Treyan. "I'm sorry. That's rough." She should know.

"Car accident. I was eighteen."

"I was twenty-one," she whispered. "Dad was driving

home from work. A drunk driver ran a stop sign by the elementary school and T-boned his truck. He hung in there for a few days, but he didn't make it." She dabbed her eyes again. "Worst thing was my youngest brother exited the school just minutes later. Recognized Dad's truck. He was super traumatized."

"Oh, no. I can only imagine. How old was he?"

"Ten."

Treyan shook his head. "How's he doing now?"

"Oh, just fine. My mom's new husband won him over and helped him heal."

He studied her for a few seconds while she tried to compose herself. "Who helped *you* heal?"

"Nobody." She choked on the word and grabbed another tissue, because this called for a long, hard blow. Too bad what Treyan might think of that kind of honk. She didn't care about him, anyway.

"I'm not sure what I'd have done without my brother. Without God."

Brittany snorted, a second very unladylike sound. "My mom kept saying that. It was a copout."

"It wasn't for me."

"My mom was dating again in two years. Married six months after that. It wasn't God who got her through. It was Charlie."

"Is Charlie a decent guy?"

She rolled her eyes. "Just like Mary Poppins: practically perfect in every way."

"Well, that's good, right?"

"Sure." Brittany took a deep, shaky breath, and willed her tears to dry up. "What about your mom?" And what would she have done if she'd lost Mom that day, too? The situation definitely could have been worse.

"Blizzard conditions. There was a fifteen-car pileup. Five people died."

And... she'd asked Treyan a question then tuned him out. *Nice going, Britt.* "Oh, no. It must have been such a shock to get that news."

Treyan stared at the thermal mug in his hands as he twisted it on the desk. He looked up, his face tortured. "No one had to tell me. I knew."

She stared at him, running his words through her mind half a dozen different ways, trying to get them to add up. "You were there," she whispered.

"I was driving."

Brittany strained to hear his quiet words. Had he caused the accident? Surely not in a pileup in a blizzard. It didn't take much in conditions like that. One person tapping their brakes a little too hard, sliding, taking out others. But she didn't want to ask. "I'm sorry."

"Me, too."

"How did your dad take it?"

"My dad? He'd exited our lives after his brother died in Iraq. Haven't seen him in years."

"I'm so sorry." Here she'd assumed she had the worst history in the world. Turned out he'd had worse.

Treyan blinked and rotated his shoulders as though bringing himself back to the moment. "If you haven't been out to Green Acres, you really should. It's quite the operation."

"Right." She laughed. Maybe it would ease the strain of

the past few minutes. "I'll just drive out and knock on the door."

"Plenty of people do."

"You're kidding, aren't you?"

"Not at all." Trey hesitated. "They're down at the end of our road, so I see the traffic."

Brittany angled her head. "You live out of town?" She'd pegged him for a town guy, since she'd mostly seen him in slacks and button-down shirts. Except for that day at the market.

"Yeah." He looked at the clock and nudged his mouse.

She wasn't letting him change the subject this abruptly. "Don't tell me you're a farmer." She'd have to eat her words to Gina if he was... but didn't some people live on acreages?

"Okay." He made a show of looking at his monitor.

That answer didn't make sense. "Okay, what?"

"Okay, I won't tell you."

What? She studied him, looking for clues. "You're a farmer."

He flicked a glance at her, but a tic in his jaw distracted her. "It's a noble calling."

"Well, I'm sure, but you work full time."

"You noticed."

What was his problem? "So, you have two careers."

"Ms. Santoro, I have quite a lot of work to do today, and I assume you do, too. I have the fire-hall opponents flooding my inbox, and then there's the committee against a second stoplight. And citizens have noticed all kinds of potholes now that the snow has melted."

Ms. Santoro. Hadn't they gotten past that? But apparently, he was all done confiding in her for now. She huffed out a breath. "Okay, fine. I can take a hint."

There was no glimmer on his face that he'd heard her. Whatever.

Brittany opened the first survey from Green Acres. Sierra Rubachuk. Wasn't that the egg-and-honey woman from the market? She'd said she would pass the survey link around, and it looked like she'd followed through, since there were six replies.

What were they all about? Britt looked up the farm website and found all the information. Weekend workshops. Months-long courses. Event hosting. The "who we are" tab did, indeed, reveal six couples, and the mission statement, albeit brief, was loaded. Someone knew what they wanted to accomplish in life.

She sat back in her chair. Huh. Why was the town in charge of the farmers market when, clearly, the group at the farm would have been the perfect admins?

A glance at Treyan revealed a stoic face, his eyes tracking back and forth across the screen as he tapped on his keyboard. The man was a quick typist, and he must be accurate, or she'd see his finger move to the backspace.

He was absolutely ignoring her.

She'd need to get her information elsewhere. Maybe from the mayor or Paula. Or she could drive out to Green Acres and talk to them herself. Maybe she'd do just that this evening. It wasn't like she had anything better to do after work. Gina and Chris and the kids were great, but they had their own life and busy schedule. And wasn't Gina working two to ten today, anyway?

Decision made. For now, she'd compile survey info and

keep a very close eye on what the Green Acres Farm people had to say. Maybe they'd solve their own mystery.

BRITTANY HADN'T DRIVEN across the bridge since she'd arrived in Galena Landing two and a half weeks ago. A pair of tired greenhouses sat beside the river, then the road angled upward, leveling out on a gently rolling plain above the lake. Signage announced the Canadian border just a few miles north, but she wasn't driving that far today. Thompson Road was the second one on her right, with a farm on the north side of the intersection. She passed a couple more as the road curved north then east again.

On the right stood a sixties-style bungalow, mature trees just leafing out, and a barn that had seen better days. Several cows grazed on short green pastures, and a cat crouched beside the driveway, intent on something in the taller grass. Behind the house stood another pair of greenhouses — these in better shape — with a large sign on them: Ackerman Farms.

She hit the brakes and stared for a second before remembering that Treyan would see her if he crossed the yard. He hadn't been kidding. This was a real farm.

A light bulb shone. Greenhouses. The brother he'd been with at the market had been setting up flats of bedding plants. So... they farmed this together?

Brittany eased the car into motion, still staring at the operation. Thoughts tumbled over one another as she contemplated what this meant. What this told her about her coworker. About the fact she owed her cousin one point for not guessing Treyan was a farmer at first glance. Of course, they'd met in the mayor's office, so she'd really had no clues. It wasn't fair.

"Your destination is on your left."

The tree-covered mountain loomed in front of her, but a large timber-frame building with a ginormous sign announcing Green Acres Farm School stood on the left. A garden to put any Bridgeview garden to shame took up a vast area across the driveway, and several other buildings came into view beyond rows of brambles and fruit trees.

That house ahead must be the one made of straw bales. There were apparently additional buildings made of logs, timber-frame, and even grain silos. None of this was as typical as the Ackerman place, but then, the website had given fair warning of that.

She parked by the farm school in front of a door marked "Admin." There might not be anyone at the office in the evening, but it still seemed the best place to start.

Britt swung out of the car and shouldered her purse as she looked around. A tap on the admin door went unanswered. She should probably have called first. This was a place where people lived as well as worked.

A tween girl came running out of the straw-bale house toward her. Clearly this kid had never lived in the city. But even here, shouldn't there be rules about not approaching strangers? Britt might know she was harmless, but she also knew that looks could be deceiving. How did this girl or her parents know Brittany wouldn't kidnap her and split for the border? Maybe the border wasn't that easy to cross, but still. Britt wouldn't know.

"Hi, are you looking for my mom and dad?" The girl's dark curls bounced around her head as she skidded to a stop not far away.

"Sure." Whoever the kid was, if her parents lived here, they'd be a good place to start.

"Everyone's at the big house." The girl beckoned, and Brittany followed her past a duplex and a playground nearly as well appointed as the one by the community center back home. No basketball court, though. Obviously, this place wasn't inhabited by any Santoros, or that lack would have been remedied by now.

The girl bounded across the covered deck and whipped open the door to the house. "Hey, we have a visitor!"

Wow. Brittany shook her head. No way was she going inside without someone other than the child inviting her. This deck looked welcoming enough with a porch swing and a grouping of Adirondack chairs.

A woman with short dark hair came out of the house, wiping her hands on a tea towel. "Hi there! I'm Claire Kenzie. How can I help you?" Her smile seemed genuinely welcoming.

"I'm Brittany Santoro, and I'm here in Galena Landing on a contract with the town." She racked her brain. "Is this where Sierra lives?"

"Sure is. She's inside."

Britt smiled. "I didn't want to assume, though your daughter invited me—"

Claire chuckled. "That firecracker isn't mine, but she

does belong to the farm." She held the door open. "Come on in."

Britt followed her inside. Plenty of light came through large windows facing the road, but her attention was captured by the crew sitting around a long plank table directly in front of her.

"I'd introduce you to everyone but, if you're like most people, you'll forget our names immediately. We're a lot to take in."

No kidding. Britt's gaze skipped over the women, men, and kids of all ages surrounding the table. Looked like dessert had just been served... and it looked good. Smelled good.

"Would you like a bowl of plum-upside-down cake? We've got plenty. Guys, this is Brittany Santoro."

Britt gave a little wave, finally settling on Sierra from the market. "Hi."

Sierra nudged the blond guy beside her, and he grabbed a chair from along the wall and pulled it in between them. "Come on over, Brittany. Everyone, Brittany is the person hired by the town to rejuvenate the farmers market. I've met her there a couple of times."

"Oh, that's terrific!"

"We're so glad you're here."

"We filled in your survey."

"Anything we can do to help?"

The replies tumbled over each other so quickly Brittany couldn't hope to note who'd said what. She took the proffered seat, and the tween set a bowl of fragrant, fruity cake on the table in front of her. She smiled up. "Thanks."

"I'm Maddie Nemesek," the girl said. "And I'm kind of hard to forget."

A few people chuckled, and Brittany joined them. She had a feeling it was true, but that dessert smelled too amazing to let get cold, and many others were eating. She took a small bite, and her eyes widened. "This is really, really good."

A woman toward the end with curly blond hair blushed a little. "Thanks. I've been tweaking the recipe lately. This time I made it with a sourdough topping."

"I can't leave a recipe well enough alone, either." Britt smiled at her. "I'm sure your previous version was good, too, but this? This is amazing."

Sierra leaned closer. "That's my sister, Chelsea. I'm not sure how much you know about Green Acres Farm?"

"I work with Treyan Ackerman, and he told me a little after I observed you-all's email addresses earlier today. Then I looked up your website. So, what's on there, I know."

"Cool. Well, we're all about local foods and sustainability around here. It's been just over fourteen years since Jo, Claire, and I bought this forty-acre farm and started building this house."

The woman who'd answered the door patted her chest. "I'm Claire. The three of us lived in a dumpy old mobile home the first year while we built."

"It was infested with mice." Another woman cringed. "I'm Jo. Maddie's mom."

"So, I'm curious. You guys seem to be the natural answer to the Galena Landing farmers market."

"You'd think," Chelsea muttered.

Sierra gave her sister a sharp look then nodded. "We tend to intimidate people."

"We're really not that scary," Claire said.

"Speak for yourself," put in Jo.

Sierra turned to Brittany. "We did have a farm stand at the end of the driveway for a couple of summers, but it was basically a full-time job for one of us to keep an eye on it, and we didn't have anyone to spare."

"Except it wasn't a full-time job, because not that many people want to drive way out here for their produce." Chelsea shrugged.

"It's not that far," Brittany protested. "It took me all of what, eight minutes?" She only knew because that was what the GPS had predicted.

"You'd think it wasn't far." Sierra laughed. "But you'd be wrong. People in small towns aren't like city people. Chelsea and I grew up in Portland. We never thought anything of driving forty minutes to get to a friend's house. I can't believe how many hours we spent in cars, but... still, that's not how it is here. People really do seem to think this is practically in Canada, it's so far."

Brittany bit back the reply that the sign said Canada was only ten miles away, but these people knew that. She shook her head as she contemplated this revelation. "Okay, so a market in town makes sense to you? But you don't want to operate it? Because Paula——" She bit off her words.

"Paula's great," Claire said. "She's a real believer in the market and has taken quite a few courses from our farm school in years gone by. It's just——"

"She doesn't know anything about running a business," Chelsea interjected. "She means well, though."

"Sounds like you should teach business classes, too." Brittany meant it as a joke, but nods around the table told her they took her suggestion seriously.

"It's on the agenda," one of the men said.

"Okay, so what do I need to know about the town and the market?"

Laughter rang around the table. "How long do you have?"

CHAPTER
SEVEN

"Did you just ask me what the town is doing for Earth Day?" Treyan's hands hovered over the keyboard as he looked up at Brittany. Man, he needed this distracting woman out of his office space. As near as he could tell, the mayor hadn't appointed him as the newcomer's walking, talking, on-demand encyclopedia, but here he was. Problem was, he wouldn't mind the added role if his own workload didn't seem to be more crushing every single day.

"It's this Saturday." Brittany beamed at him. Today she wore a royal blue suit, but her hair was in a full updo. To make up for the fact that this suit had slacks instead of a skirt? He liked her better with her hair loose.

He shouldn't even notice. He shouldn't like her at all, and mostly didn't. He focused back on her face. "I know when it is. April twenty-second is precisely two days from today—"

She clapped twice, interrupting him. "Gold star for Mr. Ackerman."

Did she have to be so juvenile and annoying? He steeled

himself. "Which means anything the town might have planned should have been thought of months ago."

"Too bad I wasn't here then."

Not too bad. He wished she wasn't here now, either. Or, at least, that was what he kept telling himself. It bore repeating because he forgot it often.

She dropped into her chair and whirled it to face him. "Put it in your planner for next year. If the town wants to be taken seriously with the market, this is the sort of day they need to observe." She gave an adorable little growl of frustration. "Of course, next year, it won't be a Saturday. We have to do something *this week*."

"This week?"

"That's what I said."

Yeah, he'd heard her. He just hadn't believed her. "Like, in two days." At her exasperated sigh, he held up both hands. "I know. Gold star."

"You're a quick learner," she muttered, flipping her laptop open. "Just not quick enough."

"Hey, now. I resent that remark. You've been here almost three weeks. Why didn't *you* think of it sooner?"

"I'm not an environmentalist." She tapped her keyboard.

Treyan couldn't help the laugh that bubbled up. "Don't say that out loud at the market."

"I know, right? But it's true. I mean, I'm as aware as most people our age, but it's not like I eat, sleep, and dream about this sort of thing."

Our age? He probably had at least five years on her. Well, that might still qualify as peers in this context.

"Gah." She slammed the laptop shut. "There's nothing we can do in two days."

"Quick learner."

Brittany glowered at him then licked her finger and made a mark in the air.

Treyan leaned back in his chair. He was enjoying this far too much. "Ooh, I'm getting points now? How many do I have?"

"Three."

Interesting. His eyebrows shot up. "Three, huh? How'd I get those?"

Her cheeks flushed. "Not telling, or it will go to your head. Just so you know, you're still way behind expectations."

He hated having her in his office, but man, he was going to miss her when her contract was up. "How did Galena Landing get so lucky as to have you here?"

A stony mask dropped over her face as she surged to her feet. "I need to see if the mayor has any suggestions."

Trey stared at the doorway for a full minute after she stormed out of the office, clutching her laptop. What on earth had he said to cause that? He scratched the side of his head then smoothed his short hair back into place. Women. Just another reminder that he had no clue what made them tick. Or ticked off.

Whatever. It wasn't like his inbox wasn't filling with contractor bids for the fire hall. If they were going to break ground before next winter, they definitely needed to get past the "no" committee. Why couldn't that gang go find something else to be against and leave the fire hall alone? Go protest Earth Day or focus all their attention on the second stoplight. Move to Wynnton and whine to the town employees there.

He studied the incoming proposals then filed them appropriately. There were a few that didn't appear to understand the vision, but there were others that looked promising, like the one from Sutherland Commercial Construction out of Spokane. The town needed to secure a site, and that was hampered by the fact that there was only one highway through town. If the bridge happened to be out — as had apparently happened about a decade back, before his time here — then the whole county north of town was cut off from emergency help.

Maybe he could distract the naysayers by proposing a second bridge. That would give them something else to gripe about, and maybe they'd leave the fire hall alone long enough to get it built.

Maybe what he really needed was another cup of coffee. With any luck, Mrs. O'Neill had switched to the Redband Roasters coffee beans. Treyan was going to have to ask Brittany where he could buy a lifetime supply. They beat the brand he'd been buying at the Super One.

He pulled to his feet and walked down to the staff room, passing the conference room. Wait. He backed up and looked in to see Brittany, Ms. Kozak, and the PR guy, Mark Kestrel.

The mayor looked up. "Treyan! Just who we need. Do you have a few minutes?"

"I guess that's your call."

She laughed. "Come on in and give us your opinion."

Treyan held up his thermal mug. "May I grab a coffee first?"

"We brought the pot in here."

All right then. He poured a refill then took the seat across from Brittany. "What's up?"

77

The mayor glanced toward Brittany. "We're putting together an Earth Day celebration down by the market on Saturday."

"You don't think it's too late to do something?"

Brittany skewered him with a glare before lowering her gaze back to her screen.

Duh. Obviously she did *not* think it was too late, but why had Mark been called in? Because the way the man was leaning closer to her, pointing something out on the laptop, was a little cloying. Like he had designs on her.

Mark glanced at Brittany with a little smile. The jerk.

"So tell me what you need me for."

"Nothing," muttered Brittany.

"Hey, now. Just because I don't have an idea off the top doesn't mean I won't think of something brilliant yet."

"We'll ask Bella's Bakery to make a big cake." The mayor made a note. "I'll give a speech. Paula can talk about why the market is so important. What else?"

"Activities." Brittany looked over. "A scavenger hunt for the kids."

"What kinds of things will they look for?"

"Something that can be recycled, maybe?" Mark asked.

"Good idea." Brittany tapped on her keyboard. "More?"

"You'd talked about seeing if the library would do a story time at the market. I wonder if they could start this week with a suitable book?"

Britt pointed at Treyan. "Phone them, please."

Trey glanced at the mayor, but she only nodded. He pulled out his cell, did a quick search for the number, and gave them a call. While he outlined the idea to the head librarian — how had he been roped into this, anyway? — he watched Brittany field Mark's and the mayor's suggestions and come up with a complete plan before his eyes.

BRITTANY LOOKED around Lakeside Park and gave a nod. She'd done it. And, aside from the fact that there'd been no advance notice in the *Landing Herald*, this celebration looked robust enough to be well planned, not thrown together at the last minute.

Her mom and stepdad had driven up from Spokane Friday morning in one of their two coffee trucks. They'd both pitched in with Brittany and Aunt Connie baking dozens of cupcakes, since the bakery had a wedding to cater today and hadn't been able to supply the large cake the mayor had envisioned.

It'd been good hanging out with Mom... and Charlie wasn't so bad, either. Britt still wasn't used to seeing Mom with another man. Didn't Mom miss Dad at all?

She shoved the thought aside.

Deni, the children's librarian, sat surrounded by a couple of dozen restless kids while she read them a story about a set of twins who saved a beached whale by alerting their community, then pitching in.

Chelsea, one of the Green Acres Farm residents, was ready with the scavenger hunt as soon as Deni would be finished. Thankfully, the farm group had offered to run that event for Brittany, and they'd come through. She didn't need to think about the kids' programming anymore.

Over toward the farmers market, a guy in a cowboy hat set up a microphone and a couple of speakers. Zadok Shirkowski. Wasn't that a handle and a half? Gina and Chris had recommended the guy, saying he had a great voice, his own equipment, and an extensive repertoire. Bingo. Hired on the spot.

The market itself had drawn probably double the number of visitors it had the last couple of weeks. Having more going on at the park seemed to be helpful. Maybe she should see if that Zadok guy was willing to come other Saturday mornings, too. Or there were probably other musicians in town.

"Wow, I can't believe this."

Brittany turned to see that Paula had come up beside her. "Me, either."

The woman's eyebrows rose. "But you did it all."

"I only got the ball rolling." And decorated a zillion cupcakes after they came out of Aunt Connie's oven. "Lots of people were ready and willing to jump in at the last minute, from the mayor to the Green Acres people."

"I see that." Paula looked over at Chelsea preparing for the scavenger hunt. "They're a good bunch."

"You know them?" Wait. One of them had mentioned Paula taking some classes.

"They're the reason I moved to Galena Landing, but then I couldn't afford land, and I didn't really do anything with what I learned."

Wasn't that just like life? "I'm sure it was a good experience, anyway. They say learning is never wasted."

"You're not what I expected."

Brittany managed a laugh. "I'm not sure what to do with that information."

"I thought it was stupid of the town to hire you. A waste of taxpayers' money. But I can see that a fresh perspective might be a good thing."

Wow. High praise. "Thanks. I'm only temporary, remember. And I'd really love to work closely with you to create a market people will drive for miles to visit. From Wynnton or even Coeur d'Alene."

Paula's lips pursed. "I want to say that's a ridiculous vision."

"But you won't say it, right?" Brittany nudged Paula with her elbow. "Because we have to think big, and this has so much potential."

"I'm beginning to believe in that. And I'm open to your ideas. I'd like to hear more."

"It's not just me with ideas. It's you, the town, the vendors, everyone."

"You're talking about the surveys."

Britt nodded. "Lots of interesting info in those."

"I don't know where to even start."

"How about with a new sign? We can freshen that up quite a lot so it's more attractive. And maybe buy a few canopies vendors can rent from the market if they don't have their own."

"You don't like that sign?" Paula extended a quizzical look.

Uh. How to be tactful? "Not really. It's an outdated font, and that apostrophe has to disappear."

Paula laughed. "I found that sign from the market's previous iteration, so I'm not taking this personally, but I didn't think it was that bad. It was in a basement storage room at town hall."

Whew. "Along with a couple of ratty canopies?"

"Yep. But what's wrong with the apostrophe? Isn't that what this is, a farmer's market?"

"There are three ways that could potentially be written. The way it is, with apostrophe s, means that the market belongs to the farmer. One farmer. Does that make sense?"

Paula studied the sign. "Maybe?"

"Then, if the apostrophe was after the word farmers, then it becomes a market that belongs to multiple farmers. An apostrophe denotes ownership."

"Ah, so it belongs after the s. I get it."

"That's closer... but not actually correct, either."

Blank look.

"No apostrophe at all — just the words *farmers market* together — shows that the word *farmers* describes what kind of market it is. If anyone owns the market, it's the town, right? But we don't say town's market. We want a clear description so people will know what kind of market it is. People have certain expectations of a farmers market."

"My head hurts."

"Sorry." But not, because grammar and punctuation were important. Still, she might have hammered the topic enough. Brittany pointed at the Redband Roasters setup. "Hey, did you get a cup of coffee yet?"

"Not yet. And that's another thing. Who just happens to randomly know someone who owns a coffee truck and is willing to come all this way with practically no notice?"

"Me." She linked arms with Paula and pulled her toward

the vehicle. "Mom, Charlie, I'd like you to meet the market manager, Paula."

Mom offered a warm smile through the catering window. "I'm so pleased to meet you, Paula. Please have a complimentary coffee and one of the cupcakes on the table there."

"Thank you."

"Hey, this all looks great." Treyan's low voice came from just over Brittany's shoulder.

She turned slowly and took a step away. He was too close. "Hi. Thanks."

But he'd already approached the truck. "So this is where the improved java in town hall has been coming from. I'm Treyan Ackerman." He thumbed toward Brittany. "Brittany shares my office space."

Charlie shook Treyan's hand then poured him a coffee, but Mom looked between Brittany and Treyan and raised her eyebrows. Trust Mom to think she saw something. Or, maybe, trust Mom to think there should be something to see.

Brittany stepped closer, keeping a solid distance from Trey. "I told them they'd be appalled at the swamp water being brewed around the building."

Trey offered a dramatic shudder. "You've got that right. Thanks to you, I no longer need to bring a thermos from home."

Charlie chuckled. "Sounds tragic, indeed. Good coffee is vitally important in the workplace." He slid an arm around Mom's waist, tugged her close, and kissed her hair.

Somehow, Brittany managed to keep the smile pinned on her face. How could he do that so casually? How could Mom let him, let alone act like it were natural? Had she forgotten Dad completely?

"Mr. Jalonen. It's so good to meet you at last. I'm Laura Kozak, the mayor of Galena Landing."

Brittany backed away as the mayor struck up a conversation with Mom and Charlie. She'd catch up with them again later, when she'd schooled her expression for the hundredth time.

"Your folks seem like nice people."

Treyan again. "They're not my folks. I mean, that's my mom and her new husband."

"They look happy."

She gritted her teeth. They did look happy, but this wasn't something she wanted to discuss with Treyan. "Is Scarlett here this morning?"

He pointed toward the group of kids who now gathered around Chelsea. Scarlett and Emma clung to each other's hands on the edge of the group.

"Is she okay?" As one of the younger girl cousins, Brittany had hated being the little kid left out of things. "Maybe I should—"

"She's fine. She was super excited about coming this morning. She's such a social butterfly, but she usually just hangs around with Mitchell's boys on the weekends."

"Going back and forth must be hard for her." She angled a glance at his face.

He looked pensive. "I'm sure. But there isn't much I can do about it unless I want to let Kayla have sole custody. I don't think I could live with myself if I did that. Scarlett needs me, and I need her."

"That's not what I meant." But what had she meant? That it was cute to see him with a little girl who clearly adored him? Except Treyan wasn't cute. Not in a fluffy way. Handsome, sort of. Strong, for sure.

"Do I have something on my face?"

Brittany's cheeks burned. "Nope." But she also wasn't about to try to explain why she'd been staring at him and cataloging his features.

"So you and your mom just whipped up how many dozen cupcakes yesterday?"

"Ten dozen. She had some in the freezer at home, too, that she donated. We just had to decorate them."

"Oh, that's all?" He angled his eyebrows at her.

"There were four of us working. It didn't take too long."

"You're amazing, you know that?"

"Um." Somehow it sounded different coming from Treyan than it had from Paula. Paula had been impressed with the event going on around them. Treyan... it was probably the same thing. She shouldn't read too much into it. Besides, she wasn't staying in Galena Landing. Nor would she ever get involved with a guy with kids. It had worked out for Ava, sure, but it wasn't the route Brittany wanted to go.

New York City. Times Square. Central Park. The Statue of Liberty.

Brittany needed to keep focused on her exit strategy. In a few months, she'd be far from Galena Landing and Treyan Ackerman. She'd also be far from Spokane and her mom and Charlie.

New York sounded mighty good.

CHAPTER
EIGHT

Treyan hated Sunday afternoons. He hated hanging out at Lakeside Park waiting for Kayla to show up. He hated when Kayla was there first, because then his time with Scarlett ended so abruptly. The thing he hated most was when Kayla sent Tyrell Burke, the guy she was living with. Watching Scarlett climb into that man's brand-new, shiny truck was sheer torture.

He never knew which scenario was going to play out, but he did his part by arriving at the park by four o'clock, Scarlett's backpack in tow.

Today, he pushed Scarlett on the swing for half an hour while she chattered about yesterday's Earth Day activities. Emma this, and Emma that. The two of them'd had so much fun racing around behind the bigger kids.

"Where's Mommy?"

Trey gave the swing a push then peeked at his phone. No messages. "I'm not sure, pumpkin. She'll be here soon." Probably.

"Look! There's Miss Brittany."

It took two pushes for his brain to catch up with Scarlett's words. He glanced off toward town. His girl was right, not that she was given to imaginary conjurations.

"Stop the swing, Daddy!" Scarlett jerked on the ropes.

So much for staying under the radar. He caught the swing to halt its momentum. Scarlett slid off and ran toward Brittany.

This might be the first time he'd seen his coworker in jeans. Of course, they were artfully torn, like Kayla's. It was the dumbest fashion statement he'd ever seen. Why did women think it was cute?

Still, Brittany *was* cute, even in those air-conditioned jeans. She wore a lightweight fitted hoodie, and her dark hair flowed over her shoulders. She always wore it up, so he hadn't realized how long it was.

Not that he cared.

"Miss Brittany!" yelled Scarlett then catapulted into Brittany's arms. Thankfully, Britt caught her. Picked her up. Swung her around.

Scarlett shrieked with glee.

Why couldn't Treyan have met someone like Brittany eight years ago instead of Kayla? His gut froze when he realized what he was thinking. He wasn't attracted to Brittany, so it didn't matter. He couldn't be attracted to her. He forced his mind to think through the logistics. Eight years ago she would have still been in high school. He'd been out of college. He wouldn't have looked twice at a girl her age back then.

He was looking twice now.

Only because she was here in the park. No other reason.

She crouched beside Scarlett, whose little-girl giggle rang out along with Brittany's chuckle.

Treyan's insides warmed. Their age difference didn't matter. He hadn't known her back then.

It also didn't matter because he wasn't going to act on this annoying attraction growing between them... or, at least, on his side. He had no idea whether she felt it or not.

She glanced over at him then she stood and grasped Scarlett's hand. They walked over.

He realized he still held the seat of the swing, so he released it. It bumped gently on his knee, but he ignored it as he watched them approach. It seemed like slow motion, but maybe that was just his head drowning in molasses instead of igniting with coherent thoughts.

Which was it going to be? That he'd keep on ignoring the spark he felt in Brittany's presence, or that he'd see where it led?

The second option was just plain dumb. She was leaving in five months. He knew that. But that rebellious, fixated part of his brain grabbed onto the power of love to change the course of history.

Not that he was in love. He'd only known her three weeks.

They'd spent a lot of time together, though. Seven hours a day, five days a week. Enough time that ignoring the attraction seemed as stupid as cutting off his nose.

Because Brittany's inevitable rejection would hurt so much less.

He was an official nutcase.

"Hey, fancy meeting you here." Brittany stood only a few feet away.

She had a cute nose. Gorgeous blue eyes. Pretty pink lips.

Treyan should definitely not be noticing anything like that. He pulled his gaze back to her eyes. "Hey."

Officially tongue-tied in her presence. Great.

"Miss Brittany, can you catch me on the slide?"

"Of course."

Scarlett dragged Brittany toward the tallest slide in the playground, then pointed at the base. "You stand here." His little girl scurried up the ladder.

It wasn't so long since Scarlett had been terrified of that slide. Look at her now. Treyan swelled with pride.

She settled on the top of the slope.

Treyan's gaze latched onto the woman who stood at the bottom, hands stretched toward his little girl. "Come on, Scarlett! You can do it, and I'll catch you."

Scarlett pointed. "Mommy! Look at me slide!"

That freezing sensation took over in Trey's gut again. What he really didn't need was Kayla noticing Brittany interact with Scarlett. Too late to avoid that now, though how could he have, anyway?

Kayla flicked a dismissive glance at Treyan and focused on Brittany. "I'll catch her. She's my kid."

Brittany straightened and took a step back. "No problem."

"No, I want Miss Brittany!"

Oh, Scarlett. Learn to pick your battles.

She wasn't going to figure that out today, apparently.

Kayla scowled and wrapped her arms around her middle, outlining her baby bump.

The sight of it jolted Treyan back a few years, when it had been Scarlett growing inside her mama. He waited for a flare of jealousy that Kayla carried another man's child, but it didn't come. All he felt was sadness that he hadn't been able to figure out how to make Kayla happy.

And grief over being separated from Scarlett for most of the week, even though she would likely spend her days in daycare since he worked full time. He shook his head. She'd be off to kindergarten in August.

Scarlett squealed the whole way down the slide and catapulted into Brittany's arms.

Britt swung her around then set her down beside Kayla. "Good job, kiddo."

"Who're you?" Kayla narrowed her eyes at Britt, shot Treyan a look, then turned back to Britt.

"My name's Brittany, and I work with Treyan at the town."

Trey held his breath, silently begging her not to mention the shared office.

"I'm Kayla. Treyan's ex and Scarlett's mom."

"Pleased to meet you." Brittany held out her hand.

That woman was something else. Consummate professional.

Kayla looked at Brittany's hand. Surely she noticed the fancy city-girl fingernails. Then she shook it with the least enthusiasm possible.

Three cheers for Brittany, still with a pleasant smile in place.

"Can I play at the park some more, Mommy?"

"No, it's time to go." Kayla glanced between Trey and Brittany as she grasped Scarlett's hand. "Is her bag in your truck?"

"Yes. It's unlocked."

Chattering a mile a minute, his daughter skipped beside her mother as they headed to the truck.

Treyan shoved both hands into his jeans pockets and held his breath until Kayla's car pulled out of the parking lot. Then he glanced at Brittany, who stood a few feet away, studying him. He couldn't come up with a quick diversion.

"It must be hard." Her voice was quiet.

"Watching Scarlett leave for another week? Yeah."

"Is it painful seeing your ex?"

He focused on Brittany's clear blue eyes. "Only because she's taking Scarlett. Whatever we had between us has been over for years. Except our daughter."

"When did you guys split up?"

"It'll be three years at Christmas. Scarlett was only two."

"I can't imagine."

"Be glad you don't have to." Treyan took a deep breath. He should really get back to the farm, but it always seemed so empty without Scarlett. And it wasn't, not really. Mitchell's boys made five times the mess and noise Scarlett did, but it wasn't her.

"Yeah." Brittany rocked on her heels, hands in her hoodie's kangaroo pocket. "I guess I should get going. My cousin is probably wondering where I got to."

"Your mom and stepdad left?"

"A couple of hours ago. My little brother was on a youth retreat this weekend, and they wanted to be there when he got home."

Treyan glanced at the long, low log building across the parking area and had a thought. It was a terrible thought. But... maybe not? "Would you like to have dinner with me over at The Sizzling Skillet? I mean, it's a little early, and Gina is probably expecting you, but..."

"Sure, why not?"

He blinked. Why... not? "That'd be great."

"I'll just text Gina and let her know I'll be home later." She pulled out her phone, and her thumbs flew over the screen.

Treyan should do the same with Mitchell. His brother was going to have a million questions. Maybe Trey shouldn't do this. Who was he kidding? A relationship with Brittany couldn't possibly last, anyway.

Britt shoved her phone back into her hip pocket. "There. She's fine with it."

Too late to back out. And he didn't really want to.

THIS WAS A DUMB IDEA. She shouldn't have accepted Treyan's invitation. It was innocent, though. Just two coworkers who happened to run into each other and decided to grab a bite to eat.

He hadn't meant it as a date. He wouldn't argue when she insisted on paying for her own meal later.

Brittany's eyes adjusted to the dimness inside the rustic building. Antique wagon wheels had been harnessed for light fixtures, and only a couple of the slab tables were surrounded by diners. That made sense, since it wasn't quite five o'clock.

A server gathered a couple of menus. "A table for two? Right this way."

Treyan's hand found the small of Brittany's back as he guided her between the tables. She didn't need the assistance, of course, but she barely caught herself before leaning back just a tad to increase the pressure.

How to give the wrong signals! Just because she kind of felt sorry for him didn't mean she needed to get involved in his life outside the office.

Still, more than five months of working together stretched before them, more than enough time to see if this was something real. Back home, she'd have acted on her attraction already, making sure the guy knew she was interested and available.

Treyan Ackerman was different, though. For one thing, they shared a workspace, and if things went badly, she'd lose the recommendation both her former and current bosses had promised. But it wasn't just that. Treyan had been through enough, as had Scarlett. She couldn't just rip through their lives and not worry about the consequences.

And maybe she was starting to regret her former lifestyle just a little. Sitting in church this morning with Mom and Charlie, she'd been reminded that Christians were the same in small towns as back home. There were a lot of genuinely nice people who seemed to have made this a lifestyle, probably without sleeping around.

Treyan seated her then took the chair across from her.

She managed to pull her thoughts together and study him. The guy was good-looking in a country sort of way. That sounded insulting, even in her own mind. He kept his hair really short, barely longer than the scruff on his chin. His jaw was strong and his nose a little long.

He angled his head to one side, his eyebrows raised.

Brittany flushed. She'd been staring again, and those dark eyes were likely a better place to focus. A girl could drown there, though. She picked up her cloth napkin and unfolded it on her lap. "I saw you in church. What did you think of the sermon?"

Dagnabbit, she really didn't want to talk about the Bible. Why had that come out of her mouth?

Treyan shook his head a little and looked out the window.

A couple of boats cruised by on the placid lake. On the other side, the hills were covered with evergreen trees, reminding Britt that she was in a tiny burg on the far edge of nowhere. It didn't seem so terrible today. It was actually kind of peaceful.

Since when had she ever craved peaceful? Since never.

"I don't know whether it's something Pastor Ron is purposefully focusing on or whether it's coincidental, but I keep being reminded about contentment."

Brittany studied Treyan's face as he looked down and fiddled with his bundle of silverware. Then he looked back at her.

"I feel like I deserve to be dissatisfied with life, you know? I mean, what person gets married and starts a family planning for everything to turn sour? I sure didn't."

Made sense. She nodded.

"I want God to tell me it's okay to hold a grudge against Kayla, that anyone would in these circumstances." He let out a long breath. "But, apparently, that's not what God wants of me."

She hadn't spent a lot of time worrying about God's expectations. Not since Dad's accident, anyway. She'd prayed and prayed along with Mom, her siblings, all her relatives, and the entire neighborhood. If what God wanted was for Dad to die, then who cared what He thought about other things? He was mean. A big bully who picked favorites and pounded everyone else.

Treyan's voice was so low she strained to hear him. "It's hard sometimes, you know?"

"Oh, I know."

"How did you find acceptance? Contentment?"

"I haven't." Brittany looked around the restaurant. The server stood chatting with other patrons. "And I don't understand how my mother has."

"Charlie seems like a nice guy."

"I'm sure he is." That wasn't fair. He hadn't done anything to prove otherwise that Brittany knew of. But she couldn't seem to make her brain accept that it was okay he wasn't Dad.

She didn't want to be here with Treyan anymore. She didn't want him to be all mature and dealing with his divorce when she was mired in self-pity and *liked* it that way. It was disloyal to Dad to get over his death.

Brittany pushed away from the table. "Excuse me. I need to visit the ladies' room." And then she'd what, run away? She couldn't do that. Not if she had to face Treyan in the office tomorrow morning, to say nothing of every weekday morning for another five months.

She took her time in the restroom, though. Man, she

hated acting more mature than she felt. She really, really wanted to be somewhere else. Anywhere else.

Maybe in Treyan's arms, being kissed.

Yeah. Not that. He wasn't her type, and she was here temporarily. Blah, blah. She'd been over it a hundred times and had an equal number of good reasons. She simply needed to keep an image of Scarlett at the forefront of her mind and she'd be fine. That, and not ever see Treyan away from the office again.

She could do that, right? But first she had to get through dinner.

Brittany made her way back toward the table where he waited, a worried frown on his face.

"Excuse me," A middle-aged woman held her hand toward Brittany from a nearby table. "My friend said you made those cupcakes at the Earth Day event yesterday?"

Britt stopped and looked down at the smiling woman. "Um, yes. My mom, my aunt, and I."

"Those were amazing. What kind of mix did you use, if you don't mind me asking?"

"They were from scratch."

The woman's face fell. "Oh, I've never managed to make anything half that good from a recipe."

It wasn't like it was rocket science, but Britt kept her smile in place. "I'm glad you enjoyed them."

"Have you ever thought of having a table at the market? I bet you'd sell lots of cupcakes." The woman laughed self-consciously. "I know I'd pick some up every week."

Was she serious? She seemed to be. "I'll take that into consideration. Thanks for the suggestion."

"Oh, please do."

Brittany offered another smile and slid into her seat across from Treyan. "Did you overhear that?"

He nodded. "I did, and I think it's a great idea."

"Really?"

"Sure. Why not? There's not much for baking. Jean Stedman sometimes has cookies, but she's not consistent."

"Huh." Brittany stared at Treyan, her mind racing. "I need to be at the market most Saturdays anyway."

He nodded, his eyes warming as the corners of his mouth tipped up just a little.

"I love to bake."

At that, his eyebrows rose. "And yet you chose a career in graphic design."

"It pays better. Has better hours… and it's less messy."

Treyan nodded. "Makes sense. But you could dabble a little on the dark side. The market certainly needs a wider variety of vendors."

Brittany could feel herself weakening and tilting over into a sugary abyss. "It really does."

"I'd buy something from you every week." His eyes latched onto hers like a magnetic beam. "I mean, for Scarlett."

Of course, for Scarlett. She matched his raised eyebrows and even stare. "What, you don't like cupcakes yourself?"

"I love cupcakes. Especially ones as amazing as the ones you made."

She ought to rip her eyes away, but it seemed too much trouble. "Cupcakes, huh? Or anything sweet?"

Had his gaze just flicked to her lips?

CHAPTER
NINE

Treyan paused just inside town hall, looking out through the door's glass window. Scarlett and Brittany sat cross-legged on a colorful quilt under the fading magnolia tree, playing some kind of clapping game. Their hands flew faster and faster until Scarlett dissolved into a giggly heap. Then Brittany leaned over and tickled her, and the two of them tumbled sideways, laughing.

"You've got a good one there," Mrs. O'Neill observed through her own window further down the wall.

He wiped the grin off his face as he turned toward her. "It's nice to see Scarlett happy."

The town's receptionist huffed a laugh. "That's not who I meant."

"Ms. Santoro is just doing me a favor. She gets off earlier than I do because she works Saturday mornings as well. I appreciate her help with Scarlett."

"Ms. Santoro?" Mrs. O'Neill's eyebrows disappeared into her frizzy 'do. "I heard you had dinner with her last weekend.

Did you sit there and call her Ms. Santoro all the way through?"

Oh, boy. The town grapevine never failed. He could be thankful the mayor hadn't called him on the carpet over that... but why would she? There weren't any rules in the handbook about dating other employees.

Treyan shook his head. "No, but it also wasn't a date. We happened to run into each other at the park and got talking about Pastor Ron's sermon. Ms. Santoro and I are only coworkers. Barely more than acquaintances."

"Tell yourself what you need to hear," she muttered. "And also, if you're heading out, I need to lock the door before another disgruntled resident decides to air a new complaint."

"It never ends, does it?" The question was rhetorical. "Have a good weekend, Mrs. O'Neill."

"You, too, Mr. Ackerman."

He heard the saucy lilt to her rejoinder, but he'd let it pass. He lifted his hand in farewell as he pushed the bar to open the door.

Scarlett bounced to her feet when she saw him on the steps. "Daddy!"

"Hey, pumpkin." He hoisted her into his arms. "What have you been eating? You're getting so big!"

"Lots of honey," she said with a giggle.

Of course, honey. Kayla's live-in was a beekeeper, after all. "Well, it's making you sweet. Mmm, good." He nibbled her ear until she squealed to get down.

Brittany folded the quilt but didn't glance over.

Things had been rather quiet in the office this week. She'd seemed to have a lot of appointments elsewhere and wasn't chatty when she was in the office. He'd known he shouldn't invite her to dinner, but he'd done it anyway. Now he was paying for it, which was awkwardly funny since he hadn't paid for her dinner. She'd insisted on going Dutch.

Probably a good idea, though it hadn't changed the feel of the entire dinner, at least to him. It had felt like a date. And that had left him with all kinds of thoughts that night and all week long.

She tucked the bundle of fabric into her bag before sending a glance his direction. A glance that didn't include meeting his eyes. "Have a great weekend, Scarlett! See you guys around."

He was pretty sure she didn't intend to accidentally run into them at the park Sunday afternoon, either.

Scarlett dashed over and wrapped her arms around Brittany's hips. "Bye, Miss Brittany. Thanks for the fun."

"No problem, sweetie. Be good for Daddy."

"I'm always good."

The scamp. "Thanks, Brittany. Maybe I'll see you at the market?" He didn't even know for sure if she'd follow through on the idea of having a booth to sell baking. They'd talked about it a bit more last Sunday night, but what had gone on in her head since then, he had no clue.

It had been a rather quiet few days. Quiet enough that he'd wondered if she was still okay with spending time with Scarlett today, but she'd come through. So quiet he'd kind of missed her energizing chatter. Who knew?

"Maybe." She sent another vague smile and headed up the sidewalk.

How did women walk so effortlessly in heels like hers, anyway? She wore another one of her skirt suits — crazy attire for playing with a kid on a blanket, but that was Brittany. She rarely let her hair down, literally or figuratively.

"I like Miss Brittany." Scarlett swung his hand as they walked around the back to the staff parking area.

"She's nice. Ready to go?"

"Mommy put my pack in your truck."

"Okay, good."

"Are we going to the diner?"

"Nope, not tonight. Uncle Mitchell is making dinner."

Her lower lip protruded as she climbed into her seat.

"Hey, none of that. You get to see your cousins sooner this way."

"I want a girl cousin or a sister. Mommy says the baby might be a girl."

Treyan's gut soured. "Maybe, but the baby will be too little to play with for a long time. It won't be close to your age like Lincoln and Hudson."

"They never want to play house."

Hazards of boy cousins who had no sisters. Growing up, he and his brother would certainly have avoided that sort of play, as well. Like Mitchell's boys, they'd been too busy running wild, playing sports, and climbing trees.

They pulled into the farmyard a few minutes later. Thankfully, the mud of early spring had dried up. Mitchell had ordered a load of gravel and spread it on the drive and parking area with the Bobcat. One of these years they might add enough gravel to forestall the mud.

Treyan carried Scarlett's backpack into the house and down the stairs to the basement level. No wonder Scarlett didn't like it here. It wasn't just her roughhousing boy cousins, but sharing this sixties-era space with its gloomy old paneling and small windows, too high for her to see out of.

He was half owner of this farm. He and Mitch had talked about him building a cabin on the property, but it was always so easy to put off. Having a place of their own would mean all the world to Scarlett, though.

Building had its pros and cons. Most of him resented staying in Galena Landing at all. He was so very over this small town. The mayor had overlooked him for the market and town re-visioning, hiring Brittany instead.

He just wasn't appreciated around here, but he was stuck. Stuck because, if he moved elsewhere, he'd lose weekly access to his little girl, and that could never happen. He was mired in Galena Landing for at least the next twelve years.

That was long enough to justify his own home, but it would make it that much harder for Mitchell to buy out Treyan's half of the farm when that time came.

It wasn't just indecision that gnawed at him. Mostly, it was too big a thing to think about. It wasn't like he would ever remarry and really need his own space.

Though Mitchell might.

Treyan tossed Scarlett's pack on her bed in the tiny room that was all hers while at the farm. Then he took her hand and they went back up to the kitchen.

"Scarlett!" yelled seven-year-old Lincoln. "Come play. You can be a bank robber, and I'm going to catch you."

Her shoulders drooped so slightly that Treyan wasn't certain it had happened. "I don't want to."

"Bang, bang. Got you! The jail's under Hudson's bed."

This time she shuddered. "No. I'm not playing with you."

"But…" Lincoln's gaze shifted from his cousin to his uncle and back again.

"She doesn't have to, buddy." Treyan squeezed Scarlett's hand. "She's going to help me set the table. Dinner smells good."

It smelled okay, actually. Mitchell was a very basic chef. A slab of meat, some potatoes, and a veggie or two. Since Mitchell tended a market garden, Treyan guessed the vegetables were a step up from other bachelor pads.

Treyan couldn't complain. Whatever his brother fixed was an improvement over anything he wanted to make himself after seven hours in the town office. He cooked some on weekends, but mostly it fell to his brother.

Scarlett pulled open the cutlery drawer and began carrying forks and knives to the table.

"Hey, bro." His brother looked up from the stove. "How was work?"

"Okay." Treyan lifted five plates out of the cupboard. "How're things in the greenhouse?"

Mitchell's face lit up. He dished up the servings as he talked about which transplants were ready to go out into the gardens in the next week.

Sometimes Treyan envied his brother. They'd both lost wives, sure, but at least Mitchell hadn't been such a terrible husband that he'd driven his away. Cancer did what it wanted, though Mitch and Lindsey had fought hard together. United.

Trey couldn't remember the last time he and Kayla had been united on anything. Trying to figure out his marriage was useless, though. Kayla was gone. She wasn't coming back, and he didn't want her to.

It might be worth figuring out if he ever got the idea to marry someone else. Not like that would ever happen. No one had caught his eye in the nearly three years since she'd walked out, and a woman like Brittany would...

He paused, halfway to the table with a loaded plate in his hand. Why was he thinking of Brittany Santoro? She'd never stay put in a dinky little town like this, let alone on a farm.

Treyan didn't want to, either, but he was stuck. She wasn't.

Besides, just because she was pleasant on the eyes, quick in her wit, and good with his daughter didn't mean there was anything of lasting power in their relationship.

Not at all. They were temporary coworkers.

He'd be wise to keep that in mind.

BRITTANY HAD AN ALL-NEW appreciation for the women, especially the older ones, who set up booths at the market by themselves. Raising a ten-by-ten canopy singlehandedly, anchoring all four corners, setting up an eight-foot folding table... whew. She was exhausted, and she hadn't even begun to unpack her wares.

Around her, she heard the bustle as other vendors set up their booths. The market had doubled since April first, not exactly surprising as the weather had improved immensely. It was still low on actual farm produce, but it was early in the season.

"Looking good, Brittany." Paula paused in her rounds, clipboard in hand. "Need help with anything?"

Where had the manager been when Brittany had been struggling to raise the canvas? "I'm good. Thanks."

Gina's husband, Chris, had taught her the tricks of the canopy they often took camping on summer weekends. They'd worked together until Brittany could raise it by herself, though it would never be an easy task. It was just too heavy and awkward.

Would the town council agree to a market area with permanent stalls? Think how much simpler it would be for everyone to set up. The paths should be paved to make it easier for folks in wheelchairs or pushing baby strollers. There'd been that one older man the other week with a walker. He'd struggled on the uneven ground and finally taken a seat at Jean Stedman's coffee stall while his wife made the remainder of the rounds.

Hmm. Some markets did have that type of setup. It was worth thinking big.

Brittany flipped out the red-checked tablecloth Aunt Connie insisted was necessary for her booth. Her aunt had also insisted on loaning her several antique cake stands to add height to the display. Then Brittany headed back for her car to start carrying the results of two evenings of baking.

There was no way people would buy this much sweet stuff. The town's entire population needed to visit with their wallets out.

Could happen.

She carried a big box toward her booth.

"Hey, do you have more?"

She nearly tripped over nothing. "Treyan! You scared me."

He chuckled. "You must have been lost in thought."

"I guess. Full of ideas for a permanent market."

Treyan's smile faded slightly. "Do you need a hand carrying things?"

"Um, sure. There are a couple more boxes. Nothing is heavy, but they do need to be kept relatively level."

"You've got it." He saluted and turned for her car.

Brittany would linger to watch him, but the box was awkward enough to propel her toward her table. Besides, there were too many people around, and some of them would notice if she stared. It was hard not to, though. He was a fine sight.

She hadn't been single for this long in years. That was all. She craved male companionship, but it was an addiction she needed to break, according to Janice. And, since Janice was the mayor's sister, Brittany needed to keep on her best behavior until she'd gotten the recommendations she needed for her dream job.

Her dream job definitely wasn't in Galena Landing.

It didn't matter that the sun shone, and tulips and hyacinths bloomed in colorful riot where the sunny daffodils had recently held court. Grass around town had greened as though overnight, and Chris figured he'd mow this afternoon. Fruit trees seemed ready to burst into bloom any minute.

It was a good time to be alive. A good place to be.

For now, anyway.

Brittany lifted a cake onto a pedestal platter. She'd cut

that one into twelfths and sell the slices individually. Then she loaded the multi-tiered stand with cupcakes.

Treyan set another box down behind the table and eyed the developing display. "That looks really good."

Were his eyes lingering on the cupcakes?

She lifted one onto a napkin and held it toward him. "Here. Try one and let me know what you think."

He reached for his hip pocket.

Brittany put her hand on his arm. "It's on me. Thanks for hauling stuff over."

Treyan's dark eyes searched hers for a second before he nodded. "Okay. Thank you. But can I buy a couple for Scarlett and Mitchell?"

"You know I can't sell anything until the market opens at nine."

He chuckled. "Right. I'll send Scarlett over later with her change purse." Then he took a large bite of the cupcake, and his eyes widened. "What is this?"

Brittany's heart stopped. "That good? That bad?"

"It's amazing! Salted caramel? I didn't expect that."

She laughed. "Nailed it in one. But why not expect that?"

"I guess I'm just used to everything being vanilla or chocolate."

"There are more flavors in this world."

He met her gaze and held. "So I see." Then he popped the remainder into his mouth, chewed, and swallowed. "Thanks."

Brittany tore her gaze from his before she drowned. She needed to hold strong for five more months. Getting involved with someone here, especially a guy she worked with, especially a single father, was absolutely not in the playbook.

The five-minute horn sounded. In the parking area, people mingled and chatted while waiting for the official opening.

She still had the rest of her display to arrange. Maybe other customers would be as impressed with her baking skills as Treyan was.

Not that anyone else's opinion mattered. Not really.

Her hands trembled as she laid out the last few sweets. Cakes by the slice. Cupcakes. Six-by-eight foil pans of oatmeal cakes with broiled coconut toppings. Two kinds of squares she'd sell by the piece. Napkins and plastic forks. Prices on a small easel chalkboard. Her cash float. A trash can.

Brittany took a deep breath and let it out slowly. She was as ready as she was going to be. She'd binge-baked for years when life got overwhelming. Back then she'd passed the results out among the neighbors or donated them to Spokane's homeless ministry, Blessings Under the Bridge.

This was the first time she'd put it all out there to be judged by people's wallets.

From across the way, Jean Stedman smiled and waved. She brought a few dozen chocolate chip cookies most weeks and sold them for cheap with a cup of coffee.

Brittany wasn't looking for Jean's customers. Not exactly. But were there enough highbrow residents in Galena Landing who'd appreciate her fancier baking?

The timer chimed, and several dozen townsfolk streamed into the market area.

The moment of truth had arrived.

TEN

T f you're hanging around the market today, the least you could do is keep filling up the racks," Mitchell grumbled.

Treyan pulled his gaze back to his brother. "Uh, sure." He took a quick scan of the table and replenished the six-packs of pansies and marigolds. Then he squatted beside Scarlett, who played on his tablet at the back of the booth, and pressed a five-dollar bill into her hand. "Here. Run across to Miss Brittany and buy yourself a cupcake. Or something else if you'd rather."

She sat bolt upright, eyes wide. "Really, Daddy?"

"Sure. You've been so good this morning. You deserve a little treat."

"Okay!" Scarlett wrapped her arms around his neck and gave him a squeeze that threatened to pop his head right off. She set the tablet on the chair and threaded through the thinning crowd of shoppers toward Brittany's booth.

The market had been running for nearly three hours now, and it looked like she'd done a brisk business. He'd sent a few folks over there, to Mitchell's raised eyebrows, but hey, she wasn't competition for Ackerman Farms selling seedlings and hydroponic lettuce. They'd moved a lot of bedding plants this morning, many of them preordered.

"Ask her out already."

Treyan shot a glare at his brother. "No."

"Why not?"

"You want reasons one through ten?"

Mitchell crossed his arms and leaned against one of the posts. "One through five ought to do it."

"One, she's leaving town in fall."

Mitch nodded.

"Two, she's not my type. Three, she's annoying. Four, she's a city girl. Five, I don't even like her."

"Now I'm really curious about six through ten." Mitchell straightened as a woman approached the booth. "But I guess it will have to wait. Good morning, Rosemary."

The sixty-something woman smiled at them. "Good morning, Mitchell, Treyan. Isn't it a lovely day today?"

"Sure is." Mitchell glanced at Trey. "Right, bro?"

"Definitely." And he'd kill his brother later.

"Do you have my bedding plants ready today?"

"Sure do. Trey, they're—"

"In the back of the truck. I know." He turned, pulled out the box labeled "Nemesek," and set it on the table.

"Thanks for your business." Mitchell plucked the invoice out of the box and handed it across. "I know your kids grow seedlings at Green Acres, too."

Rosemary laughed as she wrote him a check. "They do, but they don't grow any extras. Somehow, they wedge every plant that sprouts into one part of their garden or another."

"It gets pretty lush over there," Mitchell agreed. "Need a hand with this to your car? Treyan isn't doing anything useful right now, so he'd be happy to help."

"In a few minutes. I have a bit more shopping to do." She sighed. "I left Steve home this morning. It's a real trial for him getting over this uneven ground with his walker. I wish the market were on smoother ground."

Treyan pointed at Brittany's booth. Scarlett sat on a tall stool behind the table, licking frosting off her fingers while her little legs swung back and forth. "That's the woman you want to talk to about future plans. Did you get a copy of the survey a few weeks ago?"

"Survey? No, I didn't. That must have been while we were away visiting our daughter in Denver."

"Well, let me introduce you to her. It's not so busy Mitch can't mind his own table." To say nothing of his own business.

His brother gave a strangled laugh.

"Besides, you need to try one of her salted caramel cupcakes if she has any left." If Scarlett hadn't demolished the last of them. "They're pretty amazing."

"What's number six, bro?" Mitchell taunted as Treyan rounded the table and took Rosemary's arm.

"Number six?" She looked up at him as they crossed the walkway

"Sibling joke." They arrived in front of Brittany's booth. "Rosemary, I'd like you to meet Brittany Santoro, here on a short-term contract to boost town marketing, especially the farmers market. Brittany, this is Rosemary Nemesek, mother of some of the Green Acres folks."

Brittany extended her hand. "I'm so pleased to meet you."

"Likewise." Rosemary smiled warmly. "If you've met Zachary out there, he's our son and the town veterinarian. Our daughter Liz is married to Mason Waterman and they live at the farm, as well."

"Oh, nice. I've met them both."

"Rosemary's here to try your cupcakes and to tell you what changes she'd like to see at the market." Trey scooped his daughter into his arms. "I should leave the two of you to it." He didn't much want to.

Several fortyish women descended on the booth like a flock of magpies. "Oh, look! I need some of these. And these."

Brittany glanced between the group and Rosemary. "Maybe later?"

"I can help." Treyan rounded the table, noting the price chart, cash box, and take-home boxes. Also, it wasn't like he hadn't been watching from across the thoroughfare for the past three hours when he possibly should have been at home taking the training wheels off Scarlett's bike and spending quality time with her.

Brittany's eyes widened. "Are you sure?"

"Absolutely." He directed his smile across at the women as Scarlett slid to the ground. "What can I get for you? They're all amazing, and all baked by this lovely lady here, Galena Landing's newest resident."

Rosemary chuckled as Brittany drew her aside.

Scarlett set a napkin in each little box as he loaded them with the women's choices. Then he tallied up each and took their cash payment.

One ran her finger through the salted caramel icing and

tasted it. "Oh, this is to die for. I hope she'll be back next week."

"I hope *not*," murmured another, halfway through her own cupcake.

Trey frowned as he tried to dissect that remark.

"I know, right?" asked the third. "I feel like I've gained five pounds just looking at them."

"But what a way to go," the first groaned as they moved off.

Treyan shook his head. He'd never understand women's fixation with weight. Eat a little extra? Balance it with a run or a bike ride. Simple, right?

Scarlett tugged on his pantleg. "We did a good job, Daddy. Do you think Lincoln and Hudson would play store with me?"

"Hey, good idea, baby. You can ask them." He didn't hold out much hope, but... maybe?

On the other hand, Green Acres was less than a quarter mile away. Wasn't the Rubachuks' youngest the same age? And the Watermans had a little girl about that age, too. Why wasn't he more proactive in getting her playdates in the neighborhood on the weekends?

And then there was Emma Zima. His mind raced in that direction. Maybe Brittany wouldn't mind hanging out sometime and bringing her cousin's daughter along to play with Scarlett.

On the other hand, when Brittany was around, Scarlett was already entertained. The fact of the matter was that Treyan wanted Brittany to himself. The two of them sharing an office didn't count. There was that pesky thing called work that filled up every minute.

They had lunch breaks, though. Would she go for that?

Wait. He'd been thinking about a friend for Scarlett.

"A quarter for your thoughts?" Brittany flipped a coin at him and he caught it by reflex. She raised her eyebrows and crossed her arms with an amused expression on her face. "You were miles away."

Treyan stared at her for a few seconds before the end-of-market horn sounded. "I wasn't thinking of anything that would interest you."

On the contrary, she'd laugh in his face. How many times had she commented on how many weeks remained before she moved to New York? He wasn't looking for a short-term fling. Not for himself, and certainly not with his daughter involved. No, there was no point in even pretending to start something with Brittany.

He hoisted Scarlett to his shoulders. "If you need a hand hauling boxes or taking down the canopy, just holler. I'll be over there helping Mitch." And he turned his back on her and strode away.

BRITTANY WAS ACCUSTOMED to sitting in church and blocking everything out. She could sing all those worship songs, keep her eyes on the preacher, and still lay out marketing material in her mind.

She'd never been distracted before by a guy sitting a few rows in front of her. Which probably said something about the quality of the men she'd dated in Spokane, but whatever.

Pastor Ron went on and on — again — about contentment.

Brittany managed to keep her eye roll from manifesting outwardly. Wasn't contentment the antithesis of progress, of change? It was great for older people like Rosemary Nemesek, who'd confided her dreams of a more accessible market. She'd been thrilled to enhance Brittany's existing ideas.

Someone like her had nothing left in life to strive for, right? She had some kids and grandkids and a disabled spouse. Apparently, they'd moved off the farm after her husband's illness and now lived in a cozy little house in town, all on one level.

Rosemary Nemesek could afford to be content.

Brittany Santoro was only twenty-four and had her entire life in front of her to have a good time, to make things happen, and to make her mark on the graphic design world. If she got all contented and boring now, she might as well marry some Idaho farmer and forget all her dreams.

Although one particular Idaho farmer-slash-office-worker did wander through her dreams annoyingly often. No matter how many times she reminded herself Treyan Ackerman wasn't her type.

He turned and looked down at Scarlett, who apparently had refused to run out to junior church this morning. Which conveniently gave Britt the perfect view of his profile.

Strong jaw. Longish nose. Short hair. Broad shoulders. Really, not that good-looking. Not like Jeff or Duncan or... no, she couldn't compare him to anyone from her past.

Was he content?

She didn't think so. Not with that shrew of an ex who did exactly what she wanted with no regard to the fact that Trey worked until five on Fridays. So Kayla attended a yoga class — was it the only one scheduled in the entire week? Britt doubted it. Kayla was abrasive and nasty because she wanted to be. Pity the guy she was living with now, but he had options. He could kick her out.

Brittany blinked as the congregation around her rose for another song. See? She'd done it again: survived church without paying attention. Mental high-five. Britt for the win.

"Our closing song today is not likely one you've heard before, but the tune will be familiar. "O Lord, How full of Sweet Content" was written by Jeanne Guyon, a widow who lived in the seventeen hundreds. Madam Guyon was not always applauded for her views. But the words are so poignant and so perfectly representative of what I have been trying to say for the past few Sundays that I'd like you to sing along and contemplate the sentiments." Pastor Ron turned to the pianist and gave a nod.

The haunting tune to "When I Survey the Wondrous Cross" poured out into the sanctuary, and the reverend began to sing along to the words on the screen.

O Lord, how full of sweet content
Our years of pilgrimage are spent!
Where'er we dwell, we dwell with Thee,
In heaven, in earth, or on the sea.
To us remains nor place nor time;
Our country is in every clime!
We can be calm and free from care
On any shore, since God is there.
While place we seek, or place we shun,
The soul finds happiness in none;

But with our God to guide our way,
'Tis equal joy to go or stay.
Could we be cast where Thou art not,
That were indeed a dreadful lot;
But regions none remote we call,
Secure of finding God in all.

Brittany didn't want to hear them. Didn't want to put herself in the writer's mind. *We can be calm and free from care on any shore, since God is there?* Puh-leeze.

As the third verse rolled around, the no-way in her mind solidified. *While place we seek, or place we shun, the soul finds happiness in none; but with our God to guide our way, 'tis equal joy to go or stay.*

So much no. She did seek a place, and that meant shunning other places. Her soul would find happiness in New York. It would. There couldn't possibly be equal joy in staying in Galena Landing, or going back to Spokane as there would be in New York. It wasn't remotely possible.

The final notes of the song drifted away, and Pastor Ron pronounced the benediction.

Beside her, Gina gathered her purse and Bible while Chris slid out to retrieve the kids from junior church. "Those are amazing lyrics, aren't they? I need to look them up online."

"Sure." But Brittany couldn't summon any passion for the word. Contentment — especially to the level the song-writer proclaimed — was dumb.

"I'm just so blessed." Gina gave her a tight, mercifully short hug. "With my parents nearby, and an amazing husband, and this wonderful place to live, and now with you here... I just don't see how my life could be any better. It's all because God is here."

Brittany managed a smile. "You have an amazing life."

"You do, too!"

Right. There were definitely parts that were more than okay, even here in Galena Landing. She'd taken baking to the homeless in Spokane a few times with her cousins, some of whom volunteered regularly at Blessings Under the Bridge. She'd been thankful then — and was thankful now — not to be among the destitute. Most of them had little spark in their eyes. They had little to live for, and the winters were especially brutal without heated shelters.

She'd never had to endure anything like that. She'd grown up in a comfortably middle-class home with her siblings and parents who loved each other and all their offspring. They weren't rich. Well, unless they were compared to the homeless. Then they seemed extremely wealthy.

And then Dad died.

Brittany forced the memories of sitting by his bed in the ICU aside and re-anchored herself in the here and now.

Which happened to be inside the nearly empty sanctuary of Galena Gospel Church. Treyan and Scarlet were nowhere to be seen. Just as well.

Gina rested her hand on Britt's arm. "You okay? You seemed to be elsewhere for a minute or two."

"Just thinking about my father. How can I be content when he's gone? We had a special bond — I was always a daddy's girl. I just don't know what to do without him."

"It hit everyone hard. I think your dad was the favorite uncle of all the cousins. He was always ready with a story and a corny joke. He loved Jesus so passionately and shared his faith with everyone he met." Gina squeezed Britt's arm and looked into her face. "I know it was a big comfort to your mom seeing how many people came to his funeral. How many people became Christians that day."

Yeah, Brittany knew. That funeral had been instrumental in the salvation of at least two neighborhood men she'd known personally. That was great. Hunky dory. "I wish God had chosen a different way to reach those people than killing my father."

"Oh, honey. God didn't kill him."

Brittany surged to her feet, which effectively and thankfully removed her cousin's touch. "Semantics. He didn't prevent it, so it amounts to the same thing."

The sympathy in Gina's eyes threatened to undo her. Brittany had shoved all those thoughts into a corner and tossed a cover over them. Sure, she'd snuck in and wallowed in them at times, but she'd made sure not to invite anyone else in. Until now.

She plastered a smile on her face, though it probably looked as brittle and fragile as she felt. "Anyway, it doesn't matter. It happened. Dad's gone, and wishing doesn't change anything. So, I think I'm going to go for a walk along the lakeshore. Don't wait lunch for me. I might be gone half the afternoon."

All she knew was she wouldn't be anywhere near the playground at four o'clock when Treyan and his ex traded off their daughter.

ELEVEN

As much as Treyan had resented allowing Brittany into his space a couple of months ago, the past several weeks had been worse than the first few.

She spent as little time as possible in the office. Instead of being grateful to be without her distraction, he wondered where she was and what she was doing. Sometimes she was in the conference room. Sometimes in the mayor's office. Ofttimes she didn't seem to be in the building at all.

When she graced their shared office or had questions for him, she was all business. Her smile was fleeting and lacked genuineness.

The weirdest thing was that Kayla stopped dropping Scarlett off at four on Fridays. She'd called him a couple of weeks back and told him her schedule had changed now that it was May, and she'd be by at five as they'd originally agreed.

That was great. Really.

But it also meant he saw even less of Brittany.

He should be glad. He'd given Mitchell all those reasons

why Brittany was the wrong woman for him back in April. He had plenty more where those came from.

There were indications of her work everywhere. The market sported an all-new sandwich-board sign in a modern font declaring the Farm Fresh Market with a new logo, a barn-and-field line drawing. The market also exhibited a facelifted website: clean, modern, and laid out intuitively.

All Brittany's work.

She'd been busy.

He missed her. He tried not to think about that. The sooner she moved on to New York, the better. He'd be able to put her out of his mind instead of wondering when she'd breeze through the office. Or when he'd spot her in Super One or at the market.

Brittany'd had a booth about half the weekends. It looked like she moved a lot of baking whenever she was there. Every week, he sent Scarlett with money for a treat. The two of them shared a few moments then Brittany sent her back without meeting Treyan's gaze.

Also, he was chicken. He didn't make the trek across himself. It was better this way. Really, truly, better. He probably shouldn't encourage Scarlett to continue seeing Brittany, but what harm could possibly come from ten minutes a week? None.

She'd been at the market last week, the day before Mother's Day. Her mom and stepdad had come with the coffee truck, which had also been a big hit. They really should get a mobile kitchen to come regularly, but that was none of Treyan's business. It was all on Brittany, and she was likely on it, since she was mastering everything else.

It had taken two months, but Treyan was finally relieved

Ms. Kozak hadn't asked him to take on the project of sprucing up the farmers market. He'd never have found the time to do even a minimal job, whereas Brittany would leave Galena Landing on the best foundation to continue the market into the future.

The stupid fire-hall project was back on hold. Nolan Leask, a feedlot owner who lived near the border, kept stirring the pot with the townspeople. Why did the jerk do that? It wasn't like *his* taxes would go up. Tyrell Burke, south of town, did the same thing, but less obviously. Kayla's live-in was probably planting negative ideas in people's ears just to spite Treyan.

Why should Tyrell care what Treyan and the town did? The guy had won Treyan's wife and the paternity of Kayla's second child. He was welcome to both. Kayla had burned all the bridges in the county when she'd left Treyan for the other guy.

Treyan had loved her once. He'd done his best to keep their marriage together. Really, he had. But that was ancient history, since she'd left him when Scarlett was barely walking. He was over her.

Really.

But, because of their daughter, she still had the power to get to him. Burke apparently couldn't resist poking, either.

Treyan sighed and powered down his computer. Friday afternoon, and Kayla would be waiting outside with Scarlett. He'd overheard Brittany tell Mrs. O'Neill that she was headed to Spokane for the weekend. That meant he wouldn't accidentally run into her at the town picnic on Monday.

Good. Memorial Day wasn't for picnics, anyway. He and Mitchell would head over to the cemetery with a few dozen others and decorate their uncle's grave with a bucket of flowers, a small flag tucked inside.

THE APARTMENT BRITTANY had shared with Ava for three years looked bare. It was hard to think she'd never live here again, but they'd given their notice for the end of June. It was still a month until the wedding, but Ava had already moved at least half her stuff over to Seth's place.

Of course, half Britt's belongings were in Gina's basement in Galena Landing, with more at Mom's place. She had no intention of packing up the little that remained until she came back for the week before Ava and Seth's wedding. There'd be plenty of time then.

Maybe she'd just have the thrift store pick up what remained. It was silly to pay for shipping clear across the country when little she owned was worth those fees.

Ava plopped the popcorn bowl between them on the sofa they'd both agreed to donate when they were done with it. "Wow, girl, two months down in Galena Landing, and only four to go! How's it been?"

It wasn't like the cousins hadn't kept in touch. They texted often and FaceTimed several times a week, but it had been over a month since Brittany had been home for the weekend.

"I've accomplished a lot, I think." Brittany grabbed a handful of popcorn. "I might need to pace myself, or I'll have shot through my to-do list before the end of September."

"Then they'll have to let you go early!"

Brittany shook her head. "The contract is pretty firm through September twenty-ninth. Of course, I've barely started on the town's profile. That website has been Treyan's domain, but he's been tied up with the fire-hall problems lately."

"The Treyan you share an office with? Tall, dark, handsome, and *available* Treyan?"

"Not that handsome, frankly."

Ava laughed. "Come on. Your mom says he's really cute, but I do notice you've never sent me a photo. Surely you've got some on that phone of yours." She held out her palm in expectation.

"My mother says he's cute?" Brittany stared at her cousin. No way was she handing over her phone. There just might be a few shots of Treyan and Scarlett. Not many, of course. She wasn't stupid. Or obsessed. Much.

"She said he's all the things. Not only cute, but pleasant. Respectful."

Britt rolled her eyes. "Treyan knows the improved coffee at the office comes from Redband Roasters, that's all. You'd be pleasant and respectful, too, if you had the occasional privilege of rubbing shoulders with the people responsible for supplying your daily addiction in a higher quality than you're accustomed to."

"Probably true. But are you really trying to tell me there's no spark there? You talk about him often."

Did she really? "I work with him all day, every day. That's it." She tossed a handful of popcorn back. Obviously, she needed to excise Treyan's name from her vocabulary.

"Too bad. I kind of fancy you living in Galena Landing for

the rest of your life instead of the Big Apple. I'll never get to see you when you're so far away. I mean, I'd prefer Bridgeview, obviously, but I'll take what I can get."

"New York." Brittany clutched a throw pillow to her heart and managed a dreamy smile. "Just think of all the glamor."

"I hear the cost of living is exorbitant. That people share rent with several others for apartments half this size."

Britt threw the cushion at Ava. "Thanks for the dash of cold water. It will all work out." It would, wouldn't it? Some days it was hard to remember why she wanted such a decisive fresh start.

Oh, yeah. Jeff. And the whole God thing.

"But you don't know anyone there." Ava tossed the pillow back.

Brittany clasped it tightly. "I've been watching some message boards. Vacancies come up all the time. I'll find something. And it will be amazing."

"Why?"

Brittany blinked. "Why what?"

"Why are you so dead set on leaving everything you've ever known? Even you taking that contract in Galena Landing was a huge shock, but New York?"

"Oh, come on. I've talked about New York since we were kids." She was going to leave her reasons for northern Idaho out of the conversation. What Ava didn't know wouldn't hurt her.

And Ava *would* be hurt.

They'd been so close since they were kids, despite Ava being several years older. Brittany was actually closer in age to Ava's kid sister, Dafne, but that wasn't how the personalities had clicked. It might have had something to do with the fact that Brittany and Ava had both been the oldest girls in their families following an older brother.

Brittany eyed her cousin and tried to infuse her voice with certainty. "I need to spread my wings. I just do."

"Isn't that why you moved to Galena Landing?"

"Stage one." She managed a chuckle. "Besides, is it ever really spreading one's wings if they're still living with family?"

"You've got a point. But I didn't know living with me stifled you so much."

Brittany pitched the pillow at her cousin again. "You're getting married, silly. I can't believe you've forgotten."

Ava's expression softened immediately. "Not likely. I just want you to be as happy as I am. Seth's so amazing. I can't believe how lucky I am."

There'd been times last spring and summer Ava hadn't been quite so convinced, but Britt wasn't going to remind her. That would only bring the conversation right back to what was wrong with her own life choices. The ones she'd just as soon her favorite cousin never discovered.

"You asked about planning a bachelorette party. Would it offend you if I don't want one?"

"But..."

Ava leaned over the popcorn bowl. "You know what would be fun?"

"What?"

"Why don't we have a girls' weekend near Arcadia Valley? There are some really neat hot springs in that part of Idaho. Or we could go to a dude ranch in Montana. Or a B and B on the Oregon coast. We could just hang out for a couple of days and talk and watch movies."

"Anything but a dude ranch. Horseback riding doesn't sound like fun." Brittany shuddered.

"Huh. I've always wanted to try it but never had the chance."

"Do it on your own time. Don't drag me along."

"Okay, okay." Ava giggled. "How about the other ideas?"

"I guess we could look at them. I know you don't like the party scene." She shouldn't have left Ava an opening like that.

Her cousin didn't take it. "I don't, really. I thought of a wine-tasting weekend in the Yakima Valley, but... no."

Ooh, sounded fun. Brittany would have to find different friends to do that with before she left for the East. Though there were likely vineyards somewhere over there, too.

She pulled her thoughts back. This getaway was all about Ava, not her. "So, the weekend before the wedding? Is that what you're thinking?"

"Well, not the weekend *after*." And Ava's face reddened five shades in two seconds.

"Ha, ha. The weekend before sounds good. I booked that week off, remember? I made sure of it before even agreeing to the contract in Galena Landing."

"You're the best."

Britt shook her head. "If I were the best, I wouldn't have skipped town right before your wedding."

"But opportunity came knocking. I get it."

No, she didn't, because Brittany hadn't told her. She snapped her fingers as though she'd just thought of something. "Oh, that's Father's Day weekend. Will your dad be okay?"

"Oh, right. Well, we'll be back that evening. Dafne and I can make it up to him then." Ava studied her uncertainly. "What about Uncle Charlie?"

"My *stepfather* will be fine. You don't have to call him uncle, you know."

"Sure, I do. He's married to my aunt."

"By that logic, I should call him Dad, and there's no solar system in the galaxy where that's happening."

"Aw, cuz. Don't punish him."

"I'm not. He's just not my dad."

"You'd rather punish your mom."

"Look, can we not talk about Charlie? He's fine. He's nice and all that. I just... I'd rather talk about the girls' getaway. Which is your first choice? Arcadia Valley or Lincoln City?"

"It's probably kind of late to book anything on the coast since it's only three weeks away. I should have thought of this earlier."

"No, I should have. I would've, if I'd stayed here." Way to heap the guilt on. Brittany surged to her feet and grabbed her laptop out of her messenger bag. "We can poke at options on the Oregon coast and see if anything turns up. How many of us are going?"

"You, me, Dafne, Gabriella..."

"Oh, good. I don't spend much time with my sister, so that will be fun. Anyone else?"

"Maybe one or two friends from work, though that might not be a good mix if everyone doesn't know each other. Should I just keep it to us Santoro girls?"

Um, yes? "Up to you. It's your party." Britt's fingers flew

over the keyboard. "There's a cute one right on the ocean. Oh. Never mind. Not available that weekend. I'll keep looking."

"Or maybe along the Washington coast?"

"My mom was raised near Grayland in cranberry country. The coast there isn't as pretty as Oregon, in my opinion, but we'll be too busy talking to care." Brittany looked up, hands poised on her keyboard. "We could try one of the San Juan islands? Dominic went to med school in Seattle, and Katri grew up there. They might have some suggestions or know someone."

Ava brightened. "You could ask Charlie!"

Brittany stared back for a few heartbeats. "Oh, you know how Charlie is. He's so loaded, he'd probably offer to pay for everything."

"For you, maybe, since you're his stepdaughter. He wouldn't do that for me. I mean, I wouldn't even want him to."

"Don't count on it. He loves spending money. Mom had a hard time reeling him in over Dominic and Katri's wedding." It had been awkward enough that Mom had begun dating Charlie barely two years after Dad's death, but that she'd fallen for the father of her own son's fiancée had been even weirder. They'd met over their kids' wedding planning and then beat them to the altar. Charlie had paid for the whole crew to fly down to Florida at spring break last year for their wedding near Grandma and Grandpa's retirement village.

With five kids in the family, Brittany and her siblings hadn't been raised to jaunt off to Florida just any old time, even after Mom's parents retired there. There hadn't been money for that sort of thing. Nor had they really wanted to go, not as often as Mom and Charlie traveled now.

Maybe Brittany was just jealous.

Maybe manatees flew.

"You could ask Charlie if he has any suggestions, but I'm not looking for a handout."

"Maybe." Britt refined her search terms to the Washington coast.

"He's a good man," Ava said softly. "Your mom seems so happy."

"Uh-huh." Britt opened the next result. "Here's one in Queets." She angled the laptop. Would Ava take the bait?

Her cousin scowled at the screen. "Oceanview probably means you can get a glimpse from the attic window. Is that the best there is?"

Whew. "I'll keep looking." And she'd also do her best to keep the conversation veered away from Mom's husband. "Does Seth have any relatives or friends on the coast?"

"I don't think so. If he has, he hasn't mentioned anyone. He grew up in Spokane."

"Right, I knew that."

Ava hugged the pillow tight. "Brittany, he's so amazing."

"Is he really?" Britt teased. The breath she'd been holding released slowly. Get Ava started on Seth, and it shouldn't be hard to keep the conversation right there for the next half hour.

"I always wondered how a person could just know someone else was the perfect match for them, especially when they knew full well that person actually had flaws, you know?"

"Umhmm."

"It must be a God thing. Because it's completely possible to see someone's flaws and still know they'll be by your side forever."

Unless they died young, like Dad.

"My big brother talked about that when he was dating Sadie. She had so many hang-ups, remember?"

Britt remembered, but she had little desire to divert Ava's musings.

"Even a hotshot family lawyer can be super insecure. Seeing Sadie transform... seeing Peter fall in love and adore her through all of it... well, that gave me hope for myself, too."

"That's sweet." No, not that B&B, either. Too far from the water. Too far from anywhere.

"You'll find someone, too. I know you will."

Brittany stared at her cousin. "Who said I was looking?"

"I know you, remember? You might deny it right now, but with your dating history and all, I know it's true."

"Not anymore. I haven't been on one date in Galena Landing. Which means I haven't gone out for several months. I decided to focus on my career for a while."

"And then find the right guy." Ava still looked all soft and dreamy. "Or you might find him there. Sometimes God surprises us when we're not really looking. Or *because* we're not looking."

A forever love would be nice. Every time Brittany thought she might be coming close to discovering that, she discovered the guy was a jerk instead.

Maybe she'd been looking for guys in all the wrong places.

Maybe Treyan Ackerman was one of the good ones.

Not to hear Kayla talk about him, of course. But he might've learned something. Might have changed. Seth had. Charlie had.

But staying in Galena Landing? That really wasn't for her. Was it?

TWELVE

Brittany gave Treyan a little wave without meeting his eyes as she grabbed a file folder off her desk and pivoted back toward the office door.

He'd had enough of her cold shoulder. Maybe he didn't want an actual relationship with her — okay, he kind of did, but she obviously felt differently — but he could do without the indifference she'd shown him over the past few weeks. "Hey, how was your weekend? Did you head back to Spokane?"

"I, um…" Her gaze bounced off his. "Yes. I hope you had a good weekend, too."

"Brittany, what did I do to deserve being completely shut out?" Now he sounded desperate, but she was almost to the door. If the past few weeks were any indication, he might or might not spot her anywhere in the building again before office hours ended.

"Nothing."

Treyan wasn't buying that for a second. "Can you look me in the eye and say that?"

She huffed a breath as she stared past his head. "I have a lot to do."

"I know. And I think you got a lot done in April when we were actually on speaking terms."

Brittany shifted from one foot to the other.

"Is it because of dinner that night at The Skillet? We went Dutch, remember? It wasn't a date." It still shocked him how much he'd wanted it to be, but she'd made herself clear. She'd been making herself clear ever since.

"Of course not."

"But we could try an actual date."

The words hung in the air. Had they come out of his mouth? He'd told himself all the reasons not to pursue her, and they all still stood. She was a third into a short-term contract. He didn't want Scarlett hurt. Didn't want himself hurt. Blah, blah, blah.

His heart and his brain apparently weren't on the same page, which was all kinds of dumb. Especially when his mouth acted as a third party, having consulted neither.

Brittany sucked in her lower lip for just a second, but that did strange things to his insides. "Bad idea, Mr. Ackerman."

"Why, Ms. Santoro? We're colleagues. We, uh, don't have to become romantically involved. We could just hang out, be friends."

"That's not dating, Mr. Ackerman. The very definition of dating screams romantic involvement."

"And you can't see that ever happening?" Whoa, man. But what did he have to lose? She seemed perfectly capable of freezing him out for the next four months and then disappearing forever, so it wasn't like things could get much worse. She could talk the mayor into a work-from-home option or taking over the janitor's closet.

Her eyebrows peaked. "No, I can't. Can you?"

Treyan had her full attention now. He took a deep breath. "I could see us dating with that intention, yes. Or, I can see us just being friends. Actual friends." He'd prefer the first, but this might not be the moment to analyze why. Or to push the topic. "What I can't see is either of us being happy pretending the other doesn't exist for the next four months."

"You don't know what you're asking."

Brittany sounded so confident, but her body language was much less so. Her knuckles were white where they clutched the portfolio. She couldn't stand still to save her life. And her eyes kept sliding away from his. Then back, yes, but she seemed unable to make it stick.

"Since I'm open to a variety of outcomes, I don't have to know what I'm asking right now. Especially since I'm not all that sure, myself." Killed him to say that, especially when, right now, he was getting more certain by the second. "We can figure that out as we go. Or not."

The only trait she really had in common with Kayla was her predilection for artistically torn jeans, which she hardly ever wore. Kayla had owned two or three casual sundresses, while Brittany seemed to have a dozen professional outfits and almost as many ways to pin up her long hair. Kayla's makeup seemed excessive, while Brittany's seemed fresh and impeccable.

But the biggest difference between the women was character. Brittany would never take a man's heart and trample all over it. Not like Kayla had done.

Brittany shook her head. "That sounds too open-ended for me, Mr. Ackerman. I like to know the purpose."

Treyan allowed his eyebrows to lift. "Friendship is a purpose. And I have it on great authority that it is a requirement as a solid foundation for a deeper relationship. Or so my brother says."

"I've been wondering about your brother."

Hopefully she didn't mean she had eyes for Mitch, not Trey. "His wife passed away about three years ago, when Hudson was a baby. She had cancer."

"I'm sorry."

"Me, too. Mitch and Lindsey seemed to have it all together, unlike Kayla and me. They lived out on the farm, while Kayla, Scarlett, and I lived in a rental in town. Kayla hated everything about the farm."

"That would make it difficult."

Somehow, Treyan managed to zip the question of whether Brittany liked farms behind his lips. Look at her, dressed for a New York office in her lavender skirt suit and perfectly manicured nails. She could not possibly like farms. They came with muck, mud, and smells. They came with blisters and calluses and heavy work.

Trey shook his head. "Forget I asked."

Brittany's eyebrows sprang up. "All this talk, and now it's forget it?"

He nudged his mouse and tried to focus on the monitor. It wasn't like he didn't have a ton to do today, such as narrow down the bids for the fire-hall construction to the top five for presentation to town council.

"I'm not Kayla."

"Somewhat obvious, Ms. Santoro." He wasn't looking at her, but caught her head shake in his periphery.

"She really did a number on you, didn't she?"

That didn't require acknowledgment.

Brittany set her folder down on the edge of his desk and waved a hand in front of his face. "I think you might need a friend more than I do."

He flicked a gaze at her face. "Are you offering?"

"Do you think we can keep it in the friend zone?"

Treyan leaned back in his chair just a little, partly to get further from her lingering fragrance, partly to feign nonchalance. "No promises, but we can see."

"More than friends is a really bad idea."

"I know, I know." The proverbial bucket of ice water dumped over his head. "You're leaving in the fall. Though I wouldn't be surprised if Ms. Kozak offered you a permanent position."

"If she does, I'll refuse it."

"Right. I know." But a man could hold out hope, couldn't he? "If friendship is what I'm offered, I'll take it."

"Okay. Friends." She reached across his desk.

Pretend she's Austin Sharp offering a business deal. He shook her hand with brisk firmness. "I have a question."

Brittany rolled her eyes. "Doesn't that just figure?"

At least she was talking to him. "What does being just friends look like for a man and a woman in their twenties?"

"You're not over thirty? You married young."

Treyan winced. "I was twenty-two, which should have been old enough. My thirtieth birthday is later this year."

"How much later? Will I still be around to throw you an over-the-hill party?"

He eyed her. "You would, wouldn't you?"

"Definitely. It sounds to me like it's one of the things friends would do. I'm an expert at events. When I was home, I arranged a girls' getaway weekend the week before my cousin's wedding. We've rented a cute Airbnb at Port Angeles on the Olympic Peninsula."

"Girls' weekend sounds terrifying."

She grinned.

Oh, how he'd missed her sunshine in the office.

"There will be a lot of movies and a lot of popcorn and a lot of hiking. Maybe some whale watching."

"Whales, huh?"

"I've always wanted to go in one of those Zodiacs and see what's out there."

"Yeah, me, too." He'd suggested that area for his and Kayla's honeymoon. She'd wanted Hawaii. He'd agreed. Of course, he'd agreed. But that left an exploration of the Strait of Juan de Fuca and Puget Sound firmly on his bucket list. "You'll have to take lots of pictures to show me. That's what friends do."

"Deal. I, uh... I should really get some work done."

"Me, too.

FRIENDS. What did mixed-gender friends do? She should never have agreed, but Treyan looked so woebegone. She couldn't handle puppy-dog eyes, at least not when they weren't faked.

Brittany stewed over the question for a few days. In the office, it was easy. They fell back into the way they'd discussed things back in April. She asked questions about Galena Landing. He answered them. Both of them revealed a few tidbits about their lives. She had certain things she kept locked away, but she'd been doing that for a couple of years now, and was pretty good at keeping the boundaries in place invisibly.

After hours, though? Wasn't that when friends would hang out and do stuff together? But that meant his brother knowing. Maybe he already did. It meant Gina and Chris knowing, then Aunt Connie and Uncle Matt. Which meant word would get back to Mom and the rest of the family in Bridgeview.

She should have said no. Held the line. Because even *just friends* was a slippery slope. He'd asked to take her out on a date but accepted less, so he'd be looking for opportunities to get closer.

Why, though?

Brittany knew she was pretty. She took great care in her appearance. She had a professional persona that impressed people.

But it was a mask. If she could only keep people at arm's length, they wouldn't see her insecurities. Her pain. Her secrets. Even Ava didn't know. Not all of it.

That meant she should be able to keep Treyan in the dark, too, right? It wasn't like they'd share an apartment like she had with her cousin. He wouldn't see her any old time of day.

A vision bloomed in her mind of a tousle-haired Treyan in a T-shirt and plaid pajama pants reaching for a cup of coffee. Her breath caught. The mental picture was endearing, really, whereas she looked dreadful when her hair and face weren't done. No one wanted a glimpse.

Married people saw each other at their best and worst. They saw each other's imperfections and loved each other anyway. Unless they split up, like Kayla and Treyan.

Brittany changed into capris and a soft fitted T-shirt and went up the stairs in her cousin's house.

"Hey!" Gina looked up from deseeding a red pepper in the kitchen. "I've been meaning to ask if you're doing the market this weekend."

"Yes, I was planning on a baking binge tonight and tomorrow night. Is that okay?"

"Sure. I really hate to presume, but is there any way you could watch Emma Saturday? Ethan has a soccer game in Wynnton, and my folks are out of town this weekend. We could take Emma, but she gets so bored."

"She'll be plenty bored at the market, too." Brittany had seen the days Treyan had Scarlett and Mitchell's boys there. They did run around the playground some, but one of the guys was constantly keeping an eye on them.

"We could drop her off to you at eleven and still get to Ethan's game on time. We'll be back by dinnertime." Gina glanced at Brittany as she chopped the pepper. "Actually, never mind. It will be fine."

Friends. Emma and Scarlett were friends. This could be okay. "You know, that might work," Brittany said as casually as she could. "The whole four-hour market is pretty long for kids, but we could manage half that time fine. Does she have anywhere she needs to be that afternoon?"

"No, her calendar is wide open." Gina gave Britt a fierce hug. "Are you sure? I don't want to take you for granted."

Brittany snagged a few slivers of red pepper. "I've been here two months, and this is only the second time. Taking me for granted would look like five times a week."

"Good to know. She'll be so relieved. She adores you, you know."

"Aw, that's sweet. She's a cool kid, and I kind of adore her right back."

"You'll be a great mom. You just need find a great guy and..."

Britt's smile faded. "Maybe in ten years. We'll see."

"Love has a way of sneaking up on a person." Gina smiled then pulled a package of chicken breasts close.

Must be stir-fry night. That was one of Gina's defaults. "Can I help?" Brittany crossed to the sink and washed her hands.

"Can you grab the mushrooms off the deck railing and chop those? Then I'm ready to start cooking."

"You are weird. You know that? Why are the mushrooms out there?"

"The Vitamin D in them is activated by sunshine."

"Right." Brittany rolled her eyes.

"Seriously. Ask Google."

"Don't think I won't." She rolled the patio door aside, grabbed the tray of upended mushrooms, and brought it back to the kitchen.

"Good. The Vitamin D dissipates again, so we should always sun our mushrooms just before cooking them for best results. Even twenty minutes helps, but a couple of hours is better."

"You're serious." Britt selected a sharp knife from the magnetic rack and set to work on the fungi. "Where on earth do you pick this stuff up?"

"Oh, I've taken a few one-day classes out at Green Acres over the years when something catches my eye. Austin Kestrel took the same workshop and started a small business growing mushrooms commercially."

"Where does he sell? He should be at the market."

Gina turned the element on under her wok and drizzled in some avocado oil. "I think restaurants in Wynnton take everything he can produce."

"Paula should talk to him, because that's the kind of unique vendor that will draw people to our market."

Gina smirked.

What? Oh, because Brittany was taking some ownership? That didn't mean anything. She was eating, sleeping, and breathing Galena Landing and their farm-fresh market until the end of September and then totally switching gears.

"So, about the mushrooms. There are lots of clouds. Does that mean the Vitamin D hasn't formed?" She might as well play along with her cousin's obsession.

Gina glanced out the window. "Wow, there must be a storm coming in! But I put the mushrooms out when I got home from work at two, so they've had plenty of time."

"Don't mushrooms freeze out there in winter?"

"Yeah. I use a sunlamp when it's too cold or overcast." She scooped the chicken into the sizzling wok.

"You're weird. You know that, right?"

"I prefer to think of myself as eclectic, but thanks, anyway. What do you think you'll do with Emma on Saturday after the market closes?"

Britt definitely wasn't talking to Gina about Treyan, though she'd find out soon enough. "Playground, maybe."

A crack of thunder reverberated through the house. "You might need a Plan B."

"I am the master of Plan B. Need me to set the table? Where are Chris and the kids?"

"The kids are next door, and Chris is mowing his mom's lawn. He should be back any minute. So should the kids."

"How's she doing?" Mrs. Zima was recovering from gall-bladder surgery.

"Better… but not up to a few hours of Emma on Saturday."

"Fair enough, but that's not why I was asking. She seemed in a lot of pain the other day."

"She really was."

The door crashed open and the kids burst through just as another clap of thunder sounded. Emma attached herself to Gina's waist. "Mom, that scared me."

"Hey, sweetie. I'm glad you're home." Gina hugged her daughter with one hand while stirring with the other.

"Here, let me." Brittany hip-checked her cousin away from the range and snagged the wooden spoon from her hand. "You've got everything ready for me."

"Thanks. You're a lifesaver." Gina offered a smile as she bent to gather up her daughter.

The sky had darkened considerably in the past few minutes and now split in two as torrents of rain gushed downward. Chris ducked into the house, his dark hair plastered to his head while his gray T-shirt clung to his torso. "Wow, that's crazy!"

"Get your mom's yard finished?"

"I did." He paused in the kitchen doorway. "Smells good, honey. I'll get into some dry clothes and be right out."

Brittany added vegetables to the wok while Ethan and Emma set the table and Gina dished rice from the multi-cooker into a serving bowl.

Family life wasn't so bad. Gina and Chris were happy. Their kids were well-adjusted. Gina hadn't had to give up her dream of nursing. Had working in an old-folks home been her goal all along? It seemed to be okay, though.

Why did Brittany think she couldn't have it all? A home, a family, and a fulfilling career in graphic design?

And why did Treyan and Scarlett lurk on the edges of her awareness the instant she thought of a family?

They were going to be friends.

Just friends.

That was all.

THIRTEEN

I t's not supposed to clear up until Tuesday." Mitchell loaded bins of hydroponic romaine into the back of his pickup under the shelter of the carport. "You can't till the garden in this."

"I know. The weeds are sure growing, though."

Mitch shrugged. "First rule of farming is that you can't do anything about the weather, so you just roll with it."

Treyan stuck the box with the receipt book and cash float into the backseat. "And that's why you're a better farmer than I am."

"Your cushy office job doesn't afford you as much experience as I'm getting."

"I should be helping more—"

Mitchell cut him off with a decisive hand chop. "We agreed to run the farm this way. Your job has helped a ton with cash flow around here."

Despite inheriting the hundred-acre farm from their grandfather, getting the operation into the twenty-first century had taken both elbow grease and greenbacks. Kayla hadn't understood why Treyan helped the farm out financially. She'd seen it as Mitch leeching off of them.

Kayla was gone, and Trey needed to excise her from his thoughts, which would be easier if he didn't see her every Friday and Sunday afternoon.

He waited until Mitch had checked off the loaded inventory against the list on his tablet. "Well, I'll find something useful to do this weekend." When Brittany had asked if he and Scarlett had wanted to hang out at the playground with her and Emma after market today, he'd reluctantly turned her down. The cut of hay came first.

Until the weather turned ugly with little warning. Then the hay waited until the ground was dry again. The thought of the playground still held no appeal. Not in this downpour.

"I don't envy you at the market."

Mitchell chuckled. "The canopy is waterproof, I'll attach the canvas walls, and I'll weight the corners. It will be fine. A little rain won't hurt the produce or me."

It might hurt Brittany's baking. She was using a newer canopy than that first day, but it couldn't be fun trying to keep the wind and rain off cupcakes. Maybe she'd cancel, after all.

Then they could spend all day together.

She wouldn't forfeit the market. That woman had a contingency plan for everything. Even a non-dating friendship. Why had he agreed to that nonsense, anyway? He was pushing thirty and had his daughter to think of. He should be dating for keeps, not allowing a woman to friend-zone him for months on end.

He'd date again after she left Galena Landing. Maybe. Unless she stayed.

He was stupid.

"Okay, well, I think I've got everything." Mitchell pulled his truck keys from his pocket and moved toward the driver's door. "Have fun with the kids, and I'll see you later."

"We might come by the market."

"In this weather?" Mitch's eyebrows tilted up. "Don't you see enough of her at work, that you have to come gawk there, too?"

"Funny guy."

Mitch jumped into the cab, started the engine, and drove off toward town.

Treyan turned back to the house where the kids were probably hanging from the rafters while they waited for pancakes and bacon. Instead, Scarlett was curled under the table while her cousins taunted her.

"Stop it, you two." Treyan scowled at his nephews. "What's going on?"

"Aw, we just want her to play. She can be the bad guy and we'll catch her and put her in jail."

Didn't that sound like a ton of fun for a little girl?

"The jail can even be under the table. She likes it there." And Lincoln sounded so reasonable about it, too.

Treyan needed his own home with a real place for Scarlett. Every time he thought about it, he remembered that he and Mitch depended on each other for childcare. Even with his own place, Trey would still need to be here on a Saturday morning while his brother was at the market.

Wasn't that what siblings did for each other? Helped them out in their times of grief and need?

The grief had dissipated for both of them. Sure, Mitch was no more likely to forget Lindsey than Treyan could forget Kayla, but pain's sharp edges no longer bit the same way.

A future where he and his brother wrangled their three teenagers with only each other to help loomed as gloomy as the heavy rain clouds above the farm. Things needed to change.

"Come on, Scarlett. Help me make breakfast, okay? You can flip pancakes."

Lincoln shoved in front of his cousin as she crawled out from under the table. "I want to flip pancakes."

"Scarlett is helping." Treyan fixed his nephew with a hard glare. "You go get some clothes on and then set the table. Hudson, you, too."

"Don't wanna."

"Do you want breakfast?"

The seven-year-old's gaze slid to the mixing bowl on the counter then back. "Pancakes? Yeah."

"Then do as you're told."

"You're not my dad."

"Lincoln Ackerman." Treyan kept his voice even and his gaze fixed on the boy's. Had he and Mitch been this much trouble for their parents? Maybe that was why Dad left. Maybe his absence had been an improvement over taking out his anger and grief over his brother's death on his sons.

The boy's shoulders slumped as he dragged out of the room, his little brother at his heels.

Whew. Treyan had won that one. Those boys harbored some serious issues with their mom gone. As did Scarlett, only in a different way.

She dragged a chair to the counter and climbed up. "I'll help, Daddy."

"Thanks, pumpkin. I'll put things in the bowl, and you can stir, okay?"

"Okay."

Trey kept an eye on the recipe while he cracked in the eggs and added the other ingredients. Left to his own devices, he'd have used a mix, but Lindsey had introduced Mitchell and the boys to the finer things in life, namely, food from scratch.

It wasn't that hard, and Brittany would approve of real ingredients. Not that he wanted to keep thinking about her. Which was about like telling the rain not to fall today.

He'd told her he couldn't hang out because he needed to cut hay. That wasn't happening anymore, nor was any outdoor activity. The thought of her coming over here made him cringe. This was so obviously a bachelor pad, plus he didn't want to share her with Mitchell and the boys. His space downstairs was even worse.

He and Mitch should talk again about him building. Or maybe hauling in a manufactured home. Those were far better built these days than the decrepit trailer they'd lived in with Mom way back when. There was a spot on the other side of the driveway that might work as a building site.

Maybe Mitch needed to hire a nanny for the boys. Maybe helping raise his nephews didn't have to be Treyan's job for the next fifteen years.

Yeah, there were definitely discussions they needed to have.

And the batter was ready to go. He started bacon frying in one pan and began heating the griddle for the pancakes.

"I miss going to the market," Scarlett announced, leaning over the counter.

"Oh? I thought it was boring."

"It is, but Miss Brittany makes the best cupcakes."

Trey chuckled. "You're right. She does." He'd eaten as many as Scarlett had. Huh. Maybe there was a different way this afternoon could go.

Brittany stacked the last of the boxes of baking on the kitchen counter. There had been way fewer customers at the market this morning than usual. She could hardly blame them for staying out of the rain, but she'd still way overestimated how much baking she'd sell.

The marketer in her considered an indoor venue, but where? It seemed presumptuous to secure a permanent location when the market was so small and new. Maybe in ten years or so if it built up to draw visitors to town.

She'd be long gone. It wouldn't be her problem. Her job was to set them up for success in the shorter term.

They were stuck with the weather.

Her phone buzzed as Emma ran down the hall to the washroom. Brittany glanced at it, and her heart hitched when she saw Treyan had sent a text.

How was the market?

Wet, she texted back. *And I didn't sell much.*

Scarlett and I can help you eat the leftovers.

Brittany laughed. If he only knew how much there was, he wouldn't be so optimistic. *You're welcome to try.* Then she snapped a photo of the remains and sent it to him.

Oh. Wow.

Exactly.

BTW it's too wet to cut hay.

Her eyebrows lifted. What was he really saying? While she considered a reply, another text bubble appeared.

Have plans for the afternoon? Turns out Scarlett and I are free after all.

Brittany looked around her cousin's house. They wouldn't be home for three or four hours — she spared a cringe for poor Ethan's soccer game. Had it deluged in Wynnton as it had in Galena Landing? *Come on over to Gina's house. Emma will be excited to play with Scarlett.*

And Brittany would be plenty okay with seeing Treyan, but she wouldn't tell him that. It didn't seem the sort of thing a friend would say. Although why not? Didn't friends acknowledge that they liked spending time together? Girl-friends, sure, but she'd never been friends with a guy before. Not since grade school. Every boy she'd met since puberty had been a potential crush. That had never seemed strange until this minute. Why would a girl be just-friends with a guy when she could have more? Friends with potential benefits?

Ava would be appalled at the way Brittany's brain tracked. Well, what her cousin didn't know wouldn't hurt her. And Brittany could *so* be just friends with a guy. She was going to learn how, starting now, today, with Treyan.

She had forty-nine reasons why more was a terrible idea. She'd wear her Statue of Liberty T-shirt this afternoon to keep the icon of freedom in mind.

"That's a lot of cake," Emma observed.

"It is. Thankfully, your mom has a lot of room in the freezer."

Gina had been clearing out last year's side of beef and vegetables to make room for this summer's bounty.

"Can I help?"

Brittany envisioned the little girl carrying boxes down the stairs. "No, it's okay. But listen. Scarlett is coming to play after lunch! What do you think of that?"

Emma's eyes grew round. "My friend Scarlett?"

"Yes!"

"Can we play Candy Land?"

"Sure, that sounds fun. I'll put the baking away, and you get the game out. How's that?" And she'd change while she was down there.

"Okay!" Emma called over her shoulder as she darted down the hallway.

Brittany left a box of cupcakes upstairs — Treyan and Scarlett both loved those salted caramel ones — and hauled the rest to the freezer. She'd have to sign up for next week's market again, though she hadn't planned on it. At least she wouldn't have to do much, if any, extra baking for it.

She'd just put on a pot of coffee — Redband Roasters, of course — when the doorbell rang.

"Scarlett's here!" Emma darted down to the foyer level and flung the door open.

And Treyan.

Just friends, Britt. She fingered the hem of her T-shirt. Freedom.

It was hard to remember when his gaze immediately latched onto hers, though she stood at the top of the half-flight of stairs. His gaze softened as he grinned. "Hey. Looks like you've dried off since the market."

"Come on in." The two little girls had already dashed up the stairs. "I've got a pot of soup *and* a pot of coffee on to warm me from the inside. That was amazingly cold for June."

His grin widened. "Welcome to northern Idaho."

"Thanks. I think." She stepped aside as he mounted the steps and brushed past her. Was he wearing different cologne than he did at the office? And was it okay to notice that on a guy who was just a friend?

"Is some of that coffee for me?"

Brittany chuckled. "Of course. Help yourself. How was the market for Mitchell?"

He reached for a cup from the wooden mug tree. "I didn't ask."

"You asked *me*." Which she shouldn't have said out loud.

Treyan shrugged but didn't turn. "You're my friend. Mitchell is my brother."

"Touché." She turned to the hallway. "Emma, the soup is hot."

"I just want a cupcake."

"Soup first, cupcakes after."

"Mmm, cupcakes," murmured Treyan. "I knew coming over was a good idea."

She shot him a mock glare. "That gives a whole new meaning to friends with benefits." Then her face flushed in two seconds flat. Why on earth had she said that? It would make him think she was predatory, and she'd fully decided not to go there. Not with Treyan. He'd been hurt enough, and there was his little girl to consider. "Sorry," she mumbled and turned to ladle soup into two bowls. "Want some tomato soup?"

"No, thanks. We had lunch before coming."

Thankfully, the girls burst on the scene right then, and the awkward moment passed. Brittany set the bowls on the table and buttered the toast that had just popped up. "Here you go, Emma." Then she set a plate of cupcakes in the center.

Emma gave the treats a longing look and dug into her soup.

Bribery worked. Good to know for when she had kids of her own in the vague and distant future.

"We're going to play Candy Land," Emma told Scarlett between slurps.

"I haven't played that."

"You haven't?" Emma's eyes grew wide. "It's my favorite game ever."

Gina and Chris didn't have many games suitable for pre-readers, but Brittany managed not to laugh out loud. She still couldn't resist the dig. "Maybe your daddy can teach you, Scarlett."

"You may have to teach us both." Treyan's voice dripped with amusement.

Whew. At least he wasn't going to call her out on the dumb friends-with-benefits comment. She glanced down at her T-shirt. *Remember the long game.*

Sometimes she didn't want to.

The thought parked in her mind and stalled her spoon from its next trip to her mouth. She didn't want to go to New York? Of course, she did. That had been her goal since high school. She hadn't been anywhere bigger than Seattle except for that trip to Los Angeles to see Disneyland when she was a kid.

Think of all the amazing things to see and do. The shopping, the museums, the Broadway plays, the parks, the subways, the everything. Yes, she absolutely wanted to move to New York City.

Or at least visit.

No, live there. It wouldn't be possible to really get the feel for the huge metropolis in a visit. It would take a lifetime.

Which meant keeping Treyan at friends-length. But hadn't she already decided that, like eighteen times? What was it about him that made her keep second guessing her decision?

As she finished her soup, she eyed his interaction with his daughter. She'd told Ava the truth. The man wasn't movie-star gorgeous like Jeff, but his looks were starting to grow on her. She could imagine running her hands through his hair. Would it even be possible to muss it up, as short as the strands were? And then there was his facial scruff, that purposeful unshaven look. What was up with that, and was it soft?

Treyan looked past Scarlett, his gaze catching hers.

She'd been caught staring. Again. By a guy she had no intention of getting involved with.

Seriously, though, what would a few dates hurt? He knew she was leaving town. If he wanted to go out in the meanwhile, why not? He'd guard his heart; she'd guard hers. It wouldn't get too deep.

She'd make sure of that.

FOURTEEN

Who would have guessed a simple, zero-strategy board game could be so much fun? Okay, Treyan wouldn't actually admit the game itself had been entertaining, but it had been a great way to while away an hour and enjoy the glee on Scarlett's face when she won a couple of rounds.

Watching Brittany groan dramatically every time she lost was worth the price of admission all on its own. If he didn't know better, he'd think she actually cared about the results of a game of chance for little kids. Emma had even offered her a conciliatory hug when Brittany had dabbed her eyes after her third loss.

It was all Treyan could do to hold in his laughter. Man, she was good with kids. She should give up graphic design to be a preschool teacher.

Or a mom.

Didn't that just wipe the smirk off his face? Because as great as she was with his daughter, he'd been so firmly friend-zoned that he wanted nothing more than to pack

Scarlett up and take her back to the farm when the girls tired of the game.

Which also wasn't accurate. He could think of things he'd rather do than go home. Things that might land in the friends-with-benefits zone, advantages beyond enjoying a couple of very tasty cupcakes.

"Come play with my Calico Critters!" Emma grabbed Scarlett's hand and dragged her down the hallway. Not that Scarlett was reluctant to follow.

Treyan scooped the game pieces together. "What's that?"

"You must be living under a rock." Laughing, Brittany set everything in the Candy Land box, and closed it.

"I don't know what I don't know."

"Calico Critters is only one of the most popular lines of toys for little girls that's ever been invented." She took a seat in the adjacent living room.

Treyan raised his eyebrows as he settled into a comfy chair across from her. Distance was good, but at least he could look at her.

She mimicked his expression. "Seriously? They're miniature animal families, complete with houses, cars, furniture, and every accessory you can think of."

"So... dolls that are animals."

"Sort of. But smaller and cuter. Go have a look, if you're curious."

"I'm not that interested."

"You should be. What does Scarlett play with on weekends?"

Treyan leaned forward with his elbows on his knees and considered his folded hands. "Her cousins?"

"What do they like to do?"

He winced. "Cops and robbers is the current favorite."

"Does she like it?"

Man, he was a terrible father. "Not really. But they spend a lot of time together." He tried hard not to look at Brittany, but she was so motionless in his periphery that he couldn't resist sneaking a peek.

"I'm sure you're busy with the farm and all."

Whew. She understood.

"And I get that you were raised with a brother. No sisters, I take it?"

"No sisters." Treyan shifted uncomfortably. "Where are you going with this?"

"Because I'm here to tell you, my sister and I played a lot differently than our three brothers did when we were little. Those who say it's all nurture not nature live in a bubble."

Scarlett truly was different from the boys, and he couldn't blame it all on his ex. He let out a long breath. "I know I've been letting things ride too much. I've depended on Kayla to provide the little-girl touches and figured that Scarlett would be happy just to hang out with me on the weekends."

"It's not too late. She's only four."

"Five. Her birthday was in March, so she's off to kindergarten in August."

"Ah, Emma turns five in July. I guess that's why I assumed."

"No worries. But you're right that I haven't really tried to figure things out. At first I thought Kayla would come back."

"Did you want her to?"

Treyan studied Brittany's impassive face. "Yeah, I did.

Because I didn't want to admit I'd failed her. Because kids need two parents. All that stuff."

"And because you loved her."

He shook his head. "Not like husbands should love their wives."

"We're so darn human."

"I know, right? But I could've done better. *Should* have done better, even when it was hard." How much better, though? Kayla'd had wandering eyes all along. He hadn't seen the signs at first, probably because he hadn't wanted to. Could he ever have loved her so much — so well — that she would have stayed true to him in return? There was no way to know from this side of their history. He'd picked the clues and scenarios apart many times in his mind, as objectively as he could, and he didn't think it would have made the difference. Of course, he might be deceiving himself.

Just like he was fooling himself now, trying to pretend being friends with Brittany was enough.

But it had to be enough. He knew all the reasons.

Treyan looked at her. Time to lighten things. "Three brothers and a sister, huh? You've met Mitchell, my one-and-only sibling. Tell me about your family."

"Well, Dominic is the oldest. He was never your average kid. He loved to study and do science experiments, so none of us were shocked when he decided to go into medicine."

"Your brother is a doctor?"

"He is. It's like he got all the brains in the family. Or half of them, and the other four of us had to make do with the remains."

Treyan laughed. "You're plenty smart."

She looked away. "Not like Dominic, that's for sure.

Anyway, he met a nurse when he was in med school in Seattle. He married her last year just after he graduated, and they moved to Spokane."

"And who's next?"

"Me. Dominic was a hard act to follow. I was as social as he was focused. What can I say?"

"But you have a degree."

"In graphic design. I can draw pretty pictures, but don't count on me to save anyone's life. That's Dom's thing."

Treyan was starting to understand. "The world needs beauty, too."

She shrugged. "I guess. Anyway, after me is Gabriella. She has one year of college left in accounting." She made a face. "Maybe she got most of the smarts left over from Dominic."

He bit his tongue on that one. "But you two played Candy Land, right? And your big brother didn't."

Brittany laughed. "We did, and we made up rules. Then we made up our own games."

"Let me guess. You drew them."

"Yeah. Anyway, after Gabby is Landon. He's in college now, studying agriculture."

Treyan straightened. "Really? That seems like an unusual choice for a city boy."

"Now who's making assumptions?"

He spread his hands and shook his head.

"A few years ago some of our cousins started Bridgeview Backyards, a CSA program in our neighborhood."

"Community-supported agriculture, right?"

"Yeah. They garden a whole bunch of yards the homeowners don't want to take care of, and people subscribe to their organic veggie box program. Anyway, Landon worked for them for several summers in high school. I guess he got hooked."

"Cool. I wish someone would do something like that in Galena Landing."

Brittany pulled back a little. "Isn't it too small a town? And besides, everyone has a garden of their own."

"Lots of people do, but not everyone. If there wasn't any demand at all, the farmers market would be a waste of time, too."

"True. Well, it's a business idea for somebody, I guess. Like Mitchell, since he's already growing a ton of veggies."

"That's what I was thinking. You should come by and see his operation sometime."

"Yeah, maybe. I'm curious why you work for the town instead of with your brother."

He held up one hand. "First, you've got one more brother, right?"

"Right. Mikey. I mean, Michael. Apparently, he hates being called Mikey. Or Pipsqueak."

"Poor kid. How old is he?"

"Fifteen? I think?"

"And what are his interests?"

"Nothing but basketball. Three-on-three, to be more precise."

He frowned. "What's that?"

"Just what it sounds like. Teams of three play against each other. It's such a big deal in Spokane that we even have a major festival for it the third weekend of June. Hundreds of teams compete in Hoopfest, including several Santoro teams in various categories." Brittany laughed. "Some of the cousins are upset because Ava's wedding is that weekend, but it was the only week her fiancé could take off work for a honeymoon until fall. They thought she and Seth should wait until then."

Treyan didn't much care about Brittany's cousin. "Do you play basketball?" She'd have to lose the suits and heels for that, wouldn't she?

"Of course. Doesn't everyone?"

He laughed. "I don't think so. Apparently, there are other sports. You may have heard of baseball or football or hockey. And then there's the crazy reality that a lot of people don't like or play sports at all."

"Heresy. Do you play any basketball?"

"A little." He wasn't admitting anything further. It had been ages.

"There's a hoop on the carport right outside." She said it like a challenge.

Treyan glanced behind himself out the window. "Have mercy. It's pouring rain."

"Some other time."

He'd take that, because it meant they were friends. And friends could become more, right?

Why couldn't he squelch the hope in his heart? Maybe because he didn't really want to.

THREE DAYS with her sister and her cousins along the ocean would be bliss if they would all just stay focused on the bride the way they were supposed to. But, no.

"Tell me everything about Galena Landing," begged Gabriella. "You must have met a cute guy or two by now. You've been there nearly three whole months!"

The four of them were sitting on a driftwood log looking out across Juan de Fuca Strait. Maybe they'd spot a pod of orcas or even a humpback whale. Right now would be great timing.

Which tack should she take? The over-the-top one. "So many cute guys!" she gushed. "Dozens or hundreds of them."

"Silly." Gabby tossed a handful of sand at Brittany's bare feet. "Anyone special?"

Treyan's face surged to the forefront. She'd almost managed not to think about him in the twenty-four hours since she'd left Idaho. She'd be gone another eight days, which should be long enough to forget him completely. Right?

"It's a temporary gig, remember? I'm not looking for a special someone. Sorry to disappoint."

"What about that guy you share an office with?" Ava kept her question bland.

Thanks, cuz. "Just friends."

"That's a great beginning."

"And also a great ending. Very few friendships end up at the front of a church."

Ava's younger sister, Dafne, laughed. "Isn't that the truth?"

"How about you, Daf?" Anything to turn the conversation.

"Don't look at me. I'm just trying to finish college in one piece. Then I need to find a good teaching position and move out of Mom and Dad's basement. *Then* maybe I'll see. What I do know is that Gavin doesn't need a parade of guys coming through."

Dafne was a single mom with a four-year-old. Her example had been a good reminder to Brittany to stay on the pill and not take any chances, especially after that close call with Duncan last summer. Of course, since the fiasco with Jeff, she'd been living like a nun in a monastery. She was still popping her daily tablet — they also kept her acne away — but it wasn't the necessity it had been.

"I hadn't heard about the guy in your office." Gabby sounded a little hurt.

They used to be so close, but Gabby was totally Team Charlie while Brittany was less enthused with Mom's new husband.

"There's nothing to tell, really. He's the town planner, he's divorced, he has a kid, and he lives on a farm."

Gabby laughed. "I can't see you dating a farmer, even for funsies."

"Exactly." Although, if she were going to, it would be Treyan. Because he was smart and funny and trying to be a good dad even though he was endearingly clueless. "How about you, Gab? Seeing anyone?"

"Study nights with Jonathan!" sang out Dafne.

Face reddening, Gabby elbowed her. "And that's all it is."

"Except now the school year is over, and you..."

Gabby pressed her hand against Dafne's mouth. "Have

you ever heard of parties? Over a dozen kids from our class got together to go bowling. It was not a date."

Sounded like Britt's sister lived in the same state of denial she did. Not that she'd admit that out loud... which was another layer of denial. La, la, la. She turned to Ava. "Just think. You no longer have a part to play in all this. Any misgivings?"

"About Seth? None." Ava's face glowed. "I'm absolutely certain I've met the man God has for me."

Dafne sifted a handful of sand between her fingers. "Do you think we all have one perfect match?"

"Yeah. I remember dancing with Seth at Alex and Marley's wedding. There was an instant connection I'd never felt with anyone else. I should have forgotten him by morning, but I couldn't get him out of my head."

"I'm happy for you." Gabriella studied Ava. "But that seems to put a lot of pressure on the rest of us."

Ava frowned. "How so?"

"Well, I'd been thinking about going to college in Pullman. Maybe by staying in Spokane, I missed meeting my one-and-only."

"Jonathan," whispered Dafne.

Gabby elbowed her cousin. "Shush. It's a valid question."

Brittany hadn't thought of it in those terms. Maybe because she was still complaining at God for Dad's death. Taking the idea further meant God had *willed* Dad to die so Mom could marry Charlie. That was all kinds of wrong. "I don't think so."

Gabriella turned to Brittany. "Then how do you explain that whole instant connection Ava experienced?"

Brittany squelched the thought she'd been instaattracted to Treyan Ackerman. Well, after he'd gotten over his obvious sulk at making room for her in his office. "I don't think it's that simple. It can't be. We all know people who were just friends for years who suddenly realized they were in love. Like Gina and Chris. They grew up next door to each other and played together as kids. They hung out in high school and did homework together. But they didn't start dating until Gina was away at nursing school and Chris realized he missed her as more than a study buddy."

"You're lucky, getting to know Gina better." Gabby sounded wistful.

"Yeah." Brittany smiled at her sister. She wasn't quite as annoyed that she'd been sent to Podunk Galena Landing as she had been three months ago. She'd been beyond annoyed and all the way to livid, while realizing she'd brought it on herself and should be grateful for a second chance.

Maybe because she was almost half done with her exile. But, if that were the reason, she wouldn't feel any pangs of regret that her time in Idaho was zipping by. As it was, the thought of leaving Treyan behind was disquieting.

Just friends. They'd agreed. She'd been good with that. Still was.

Just friends could fall in love. Gina and Chris had.

But not her. Gina had planned to return to Galena Landing anyway. Brittany's destiny was in New York.

Was her perfect guy there, too? The one she was destined to meet? New York didn't seem like a family-raising spot, which maybe was a silly thought. Obviously, millions of its residents were happily having kids and thriving there.

But in all her imaginings of the Big Apple, she'd never envisioned herself falling in love for real, getting married, having a family. She'd never envisioned herself growing old there.

All she'd dreamed of was the high-powered job, men at her beck and call, and being far away from her very moral family... like the three girls beside her on this log, each of whom she loved dearly.

Huh. Brittany frowned. How could her New York dream be shortsighted? It had lured her on since she'd been in high school and discovered that graphic design was, in fact, a career she might be suited for.

"Britt?"

She blinked and turned to her sister. "Hmm?"

"You're far away."

"Sorry."

"We're heading back to the condo for lunch." The other three gathered their packs and water bottles.

Brittany surged to her feet. "Good idea. I'm starving."

And it wouldn't be a good idea to let this group catch a hint of any misgivings she might be experiencing before she'd had a chance to squelch them.

Squelch them she would, right? Because Galena Landing was not her future. Treyan was not her future.

Friends only.

CHAPTER
FIFTEEN

Brittany definitely had a smile for occasions such as her best-friend-slash-favorite-cousin's wedding. She was genuinely happy for Ava and Seth. She'd never let her misgivings about her own life show on someone else's big day.

She turned gracefully at the front of Bridgeview Bible Church as the music changed and the friends and family rose to honor Ava as she entered, radiant on Uncle Dino's arm.

Brittany scrunched her eyes shut, willing her tears to dissipate without dribbling down her cheeks. Who was going to walk *her* down the aisle? Would Charlie think he had the right to give her away?

That was old fashioned, anyway. The practice assumed a girl belonged to her father as though she were an object, and that he could hand the responsibility to some other guy. That it was a father's right.

So, she'd walk herself down the aisle. It wasn't unheard of in this day and age. Dixie Ranta had walked alone. So had the brides of a couple of Brittany's guy cousins. Of course, none of those women had a real family at all, not like Brittany did.

She blinked a couple of times. The tears seemed to be staying put. At least as much as anyone else's. It was okay to cry at weddings, just not buckets of ugly tears.

Then her gaze caught on her mother and Charlie standing a couple of rows from the front as they watched Ava and Uncle Dino's approach. Charlie had his arms around Mom from behind, whispering in her ear as she leaned back against him. Mom turned slightly and smiled up at him, her eyes so full of love that even Brittany couldn't miss it from twenty feet away. He kissed Mom's hair and refocused on the bride.

Mom had the capacity to love well. Just because she loved Charlie now didn't mean she hadn't loved Dad with her whole heart. Didn't love him still.

Britt *knew* that. Then why did she feel like she was the one personally responsible for keeping Dad alive in their family?

Her older brother had married Charlie's daughter. Obviously, Dominic was Team Charlie. Gabriella had been won over. Easygoing Landon thought their stepdad was chill. Young Michael had accepted Charlie, though it had taken longer than the other three. Brittany was the sole holdout.

Yeah, she'd said all the right words of acceptance when they first got serious. She'd hidden her feelings, not wanting to hurt Mom. But when the reality had sunk in, she'd pulled back.

Did Charlie deserve her snub?

He didn't. Not really. How could she blame him for falling in love with her mother? He'd been divorced for over a decade when they met through Dominic and Katri. He hadn't been on the rebound or even looking for a relationship at all. Neither had Mom.

Love had found them, not the other way around.

Charlie treated Brittany with the same affection and respect as he did her siblings. He'd cheerfully brought his coffee truck to Galena Landing three times this spring — the first occasion with no lead time. He'd made it happen for Mom's sake.

And maybe a little bit for Brittany's.

At the front of the sanctuary, Uncle Dino placed Ava's hand in Seth's and retreated to his seat beside Aunt Betta and Nonna. Ava beamed as the couple mounted the three steps to the platform. She passed her gorgeous bouquet of gardenias and roses over to Brittany then turned to grasp her groom's hands with both of hers.

Britt closed her eyes for a few seconds to absorb the bouquet's fragrance. Yes, a few sprigs of juniper had been tucked inside here and there, a reminder of their decision to choose joy and each other.

Back in February, their cousin Basil's bride's bouquet had contained shoots of aromatic thyme, an herb that represented the courage they'd embraced in going public with their secret past.

What symbol would she and Treyan pick?

Nothing. They weren't a couple, they weren't getting married, and they wouldn't have a semi-secret little motif.

Right?

Right.

But the notion wouldn't leave her mind. There had been way too many weddings in the past few years, many of them right here in this church, as her cousins fell in love, tumbling like a row of dominoes. Then there had been Mom's wedding to Charlie.

Brittany shot another glance at them, sitting with Dominic, Katri, Landon, and Michael. Her big brother shared a private smile with his wife. Charlie's arm was around Mom, his hand gently caressing her shoulder as they both listened to Pastor Tomas's instruction.

Why had she been thinking the single, carefree life was the only one for her? Was it wrong to belong with someone? Not belong *to* them, but *with* them. To share little glances and caresses and, yes, semi-secret motifs that represented their love.

Charlie must have felt her gaze upon him, because he met it. His face softened and his eyes warmed as his mouth curved into a gentle smile. For her. The stepdaughter who accepted his help with the big things but refused to let him in close.

It wasn't Charlie's fault Dad had died. Charlie's friendship with Mom had begun completely innocently when she bought a salted caramel latte from his coffee truck every week at the market. They'd done nothing but exchange social pleasantries over the counter before Dominic had asked Mom to invite his girlfriend's dad for Thanksgiving. Planning Dom and Katri's wedding had pulled them together, and they'd beat their offspring to the altar.

Not that a Florida beach had an altar, exactly.

Keeping Charlie at arm's length couldn't bring Dad back. Brittany knew that. Maybe it was time to let go of her resentment. Her mind slid back to that time in Junior High when she'd been so angry with one of her friends for betraying her trust. Jessi had apologized in tears, but Brittany had refused to forgive.

What had Dad said? That holding onto her bitterness was like drinking poison and expecting Jessi to die.

Dad hadn't been one to hold grudges. Was it even possible he smiled down at Mom and Charlie from heaven? That was a seriously weird thought.

Charlie still held Brittany's gaze, his smile for her small but steady. He was waiting for her.

Pastor Tomas's voice filtered into Brittany's consciousness as he read from 1 Corinthians 13. "Love is large and incredibly patient. Love is gentle and consistently kind to all. It refuses to be jealous when blessing comes to someone else. Love does not brag about one's achievements nor inflate its own importance. Love does not traffic in shame and disrespect, nor selfishly seek its own honor. Love is not easily irritated or quick to take offense. Love joyfully celebrates honesty and finds no delight in what is wrong. Love is a safe place of shelter, for it never stops believing the best for others. Love never takes failure as defeat, for it never gives up."

It refuses to be jealous when blessing comes to someone else.

Those words stabbed Brittany in the heart. It wasn't only her stepfather she was hurting by her refusal to fully accept him. It was her mom. It was herself.

Let it go, Britt.

She offered a tremulous smile to Charlie, and his grin widened as though he understood her message.

"I, Seth Jonathan Donahue, take thee, Ava Elizabeth Santoro, to be my lawfully wedded wife..."

Brittany's cousin was minutes away from becoming Ava

Donahue. She'd forged a relationship with a man, whom, though he had a past, had found forgiveness and joy in Christ's love. Charlie had a past, too. He'd been divorced from Katri's mom for over a dozen years.

Treyan Ackerman had a past. Like with Seth, that didn't make him a terrible man. Everyone made mistakes.

And Brittany was no innocent herself. She was worse. She'd known Jesus and still gone her own willful way.

"I, Ava Elizabeth Santoro, take thee, Seth Jonathan Donahue..."

Britt had better start paying attention or she'd miss her cues.

"Wasn't that a beautiful wedding?" Gabriella kicked off her heels and flopped back on her bed dramatically.

"It was." It'd been a long time since Brittany had shared a room with her sister, but there wasn't much left at the apartment she'd rented with Ava. A charity would pick up the last of the furniture stacked in the living room on Monday, and that would be that.

A chapter closed.

Tonight, Brittany was on a camping mat on the floor of her sister's room. Her own previous bedroom on the main floor of her parents' house had been demolished to make way for an expanded master suite when Mom married Charlie. Her brothers had moved to the walkout basement years ago.

Britt slid out of the poufy dress she would never wear again and hung it in Gabby's closet. She changed into basketball shorts and a T-shirt while her sister got ready for bed, too. They'd both scrubbed the makeup off their faces, but a shower was going to have to wait until morning.

"I've missed you, Britt."

"Back atcha." It wasn't completely true. She'd separated from her kid sister when she moved in with Ava three or four years ago. She could almost feel sorry for Gabs not having a girl cousin to share an apartment with. Dafne was planning on staying put with her parents until she was through college and had a job. She needed their help with Gavin.

Brittany brushed her hair out of its 'do and pulled it into a ponytail. She sat cross-legged on the mat. "Tell me about Jonathan."

Gabby rolled her eyes. "There's nothing to tell."

"You sure? It's okay if there is, you know."

"Right. But there isn't. Just like there isn't with you and the guy in your office. Unless you were lying about that."

Busted. "Can you just see me as a stepmom?" Brittany forced a chuckle.

"Sure, why not? You're great with kids."

"I love turning kids back over to their parents, too. I've babysat Gina's kids a few times, and they're fun. But Gina and Chris make the rules and enforce them. I can simply be the fun aunt."

"How old is the office guy's kid?"

"She's five. One of Emma's friends, actually."

Gabby dropped to the other end of the temporary bed and hugged a pillow to her chest. "Mom said he's cute."

Seriously, had Mom told everyone? Was denial worth the effort?

"She's met him, right? When she and Charlie came to your market?"

"Yes..."

"She thinks there's something there."

"Friends. Just friends."

"Famous last words."

Britt leaned forward and skewered her kid sister with a look. "About Jonathan. Why does Dafne think there's more than you admit?"

If Gabby's sudden facial flush didn't tell the story, nothing would. "She sees romance under every rock. You know her."

"I do know her... and that doesn't sound accurate. She was burned pretty bad."

"Okay, well, you know what I mean." Gabby bounced to her feet. "I'm going to have a shower tonight after all. I can't stand five pounds of product in my hair."

Brittany chuckled as her sister fled. In the quiet room, she realized she was hungry. She'd been too busy with the wedding reception and dance to eat much, though there'd been plenty of food. Probably Mom had some cookies or muffins stashed away.

She padded down the hall in her bare feet and crossed the living room. She angled into the kitchen and stopped at the sight of her stepfather fixing a sandwich at the counter.

"Hey, Brittany."

"Hey." She didn't want to look at the man in plaid lounge pants and a Redband Roasters T-shirt as though he belonged in this house wearing pajamas.

"Hungry? I'm happy to make you a sandwich. This one is roast beef — if you like mustard, here you go, and I'll fix another."

There was no time like the present. "Charlie?" She leaned against the cupboard and crossed her arms.

He glanced over. "Yes?"

"I'm sorry."

"You don't like mustard?" He pulled the fridge open and peered inside.

"I do. That's not what I'm sorry about."

Charlie set the roast beef, mayo, and mustard on the counter and began assembling a second sandwich. "I forgive you."

She huffed a laugh. "You don't even know for what."

"It doesn't matter."

"It does. I've resented you for being here in this house, the one my dad bought for my mom. For being in my mom's life."

He turned to study her, compassion on his face. "I know, Brittany. Sometimes life just isn't fair. For your sake, for your siblings' sakes, I wish your father hadn't died. It sounds terrible to say that it worked out for me, but that doesn't help you any."

"Mom loves you." How the words hurt to say.

He nodded. "She loves you, too. She has a great capacity for love."

Brittany considered that. It was true. "Anyway, I've basically punished you for my dad's death. It wasn't your fault in any way, and I'm sorry. I know you make my mom happy, and I know you're a nice guy. Forgive me?"

"Absolutely." Charlie shifted slightly, just enough that Brittany knew he'd hug her if she made the first move.

So she did. She stepped into her stepfather's arms and accepted his quick embrace. "Thanks, Charlie."

"Want to sit and talk while we eat our sandwiches?" He layered roast beef in between two more slices of bread. "Because I think there's more to the conversation."

Hadn't he said he forgave her? And it felt like he had. So, what was all that about? She nodded cautiously. "Okay."

Charlie set both plates on the kitchen island and pulled out one of the stools while she took the other. "Your mom might like to hear this, too. Maybe tomorrow. She's soaking in a bubble bath right now."

Brittany didn't want to think about that. "You're right."

He took a big bite, chewed, and swallowed. "But one more person."

She angled a look at him.

"Jesus."

Oh. She tried to keep her face from showing her thoughts on the subject change, but it likely didn't work.

"Because, I think, if you resented me for stepping into your father's place, then you've probably also been angry with God for allowing him to die in the first place."

Brittany let out a shaky breath. She wanted to deny Charlie's words quickly and forcefully, but it was already too late for that. Also, angry didn't begin to cut it.

"I'll be the first to tell you I don't understand how God works. I know what it says in Romans 8:28, but that seems overly simplistic, doesn't it? I read it in The Passion Translation the other day: 'So we are convinced that every detail of our lives is continually woven together for good, for we are his lovers who have been called to fulfill his designed purpose.'"

We are God's lovers?

Brittany blinked.

"There's so much we don't comprehend. My divorce is easier to understand. I didn't know Jesus. I was a terrible husband and father, never home, throwing money at every problem. But Christians have big, deep issues, too. Good people die, like your dad. It doesn't mean God doesn't love us. Doesn't care."

"It seems like it."

"I know." Charlie offered a compassionate smile. "You've flown a few times, right?"

She nodded. He knew she had. He'd bought her and her siblings plane tickets to Florida for his wedding to Mom last year.

"And you've taken history in school. All about Lewis and Clark seeking the way through the mountains to get to the Pacific Ocean."

Where was he going with this?

"They didn't have maps. They didn't have a birds-eye-view. They did have guides, though."

"Uh-huuuh."

"But when you fly over the Rockies, it's easy to see where the best routes are. The box canyons and dead ends become clearly visible." Charlie studied her for a minute. "So do the passes."

"You're saying..." She tried to follow his train of thought. "You're saying that we're stuck and can't see the way through. We keep running into blocks because we can't see the big picture?"

"Except for the expedition had guides, like Sacajawea. They wouldn't have made it without her."

She mulled that over.

"Jesus is our guide, Brittany. We can't see the big picture any more than Meriwether Lewis and William Clark could. Like them, we know there is something worth experiencing on the other side of our trials. We could deny needing help. I know I did for many years."

Brittany stared at the sandwich in front of her with two bites taken out. She wasn't so hungry after all.

"We don't need to live like that," Charlie went on gently. "We have a guide, and He sees the big picture. To Him, the obstacles aren't fearsome and large. He knows the way. We just have to follow."

"How did you get so wise?" Her voice sounded shaky.

He let out a rueful chuckle. "Trial and error, Brittany. Trial, error, and the grace of a loving God."

Brittany slid off the tall stool. "I wonder if Gabriella is hungry. She might want some of this sandwich."

"Good night, honey."

Her stepfather's term of endearment didn't even bother her as she made her way back to Gabby's bedroom.

SIXTEEN

On Monday morning, Treyan let himself into the quiet building twenty minutes before office hours officially began. Would Brittany come in early, too? Or would she have a meeting with Paula or the mayor this morning and be in later?

All he knew was that the week she'd been away had seemed interminable in a way that the half-dozen texts they'd exchanged couldn't begin to assuage.

He set a bouquet of flowers on her desk and wiped away imaginary dust. The janitor had been through on the weekend, of course. Even the window above her workspace glistened as it revealed the lush green magnolia tree just outside. A few songbirds flitted among the branches.

His computer ran through its boot-up sequence, and Treyan settled into his chair. Then bounced back out of it. This was ridiculous. He shouldn't have come early. What could he do for the next few minutes? There really wasn't any point in logging extra time on the day job that he wouldn't get paid for. Nor would he get off early for starting now.

He paced back toward the window.

A sound in the corridor gave him a half second to pivot just as the door swung open. There she was, eyes wide as she stared back at him.

"Hey, Brittany." Had he managed to sound casual? He doubted it.

"Hey, yourself." She blinked. "You're here early."

"You, too." He grinned. Maybe it looked like a grimace. This was too awkward.

Her gaze shifted past him to the flowers on her workstation. "Those are beautiful." She glanced at him. "Where did they come from? Do you know?"

"I, uh, brought them for you. Do you know Arleigh O'Neill? She's growing flowers for sale, and I thought you might like these."

"She's the daughter of Mrs. O'Neill downstairs, right? Young, pretty, single?"

"Uh..." Arleigh was, in fact, all those things. "Not as pretty as you."

Brittany chuckled. "Smooth, Mr. Ackerman."

He dared to breathe as she crossed the space and buried her nose in the blooms. He hadn't lied. She was gorgeous with her dark hair pulled into a fancy bun on the back of her head, her usual blazer paired with a more casual floral skirt.

"I missed you." Wait, had he really admitted that? Was it okay in a friends-only world? "I mean, the office was so quiet this week I could hear..."

His voice petered out as she turned to face him, her dainty eyebrows hiking up. "Are you calling me noisy?"

She'd given him an out. "Chattering all the time. So loud."

"So annoying."

Treyan held up both hands. "Don't put words in my mouth, Ms. Santoro."

"You've changed your mind about that?"

"A long time ago. Annoyance lasted only a week or two."

"A month or two."

He shook his head. "Nope." By then, he'd been falling under her charms. Maybe best not to say that, though. Friend zone.

Brittany set her messenger bag down on her swivel chair and pulled out her laptop. "I've got a meeting with Paula tomorrow. We've got some strategizing to do for the future of the market."

"You've done wonders."

She shrugged and didn't turn to face him.

"No, really. That new sign is a huge start. Plus, you got the town council to approve three canopies and five tables for vendors to rent."

"The next big wind would have lifted the old canopies and sent them to North Dakota like untethered hot air balloons."

"That is true. However, Paula didn't think the council would approve improvements, so she didn't even ask. That didn't stop you."

"It's my job to be annoying. Like you said."

Treyan bumped the door closed with his foot and took a few steps closer, where the scent of her gardenia perfume intensified the aroma of the bouquet. "You're not annoying. You're driven. Passionate about what you do."

Friends-only was not going to work. Not when he

wanted so desperately for that passion to be directed at him. He stumbled a step back.

"Thanks." Her glance bounced off his. "Anything new on the fire-hall front while I was away?"

"I'm just preparing more propaganda ahead of the referendum."

"Propaganda, huh?" A little smile teased at her lips.

"That's what Nolan Leask and company call it. Everything they say is the truth, of course. It's only the town who's trying to hoodwink people. Never them."

"I've never met the guy."

"May it ever be that way. He's a loser."

"So I hear." Brittany set her messenger bag and purse under the desk and flipped open her laptop. "I've got a lot to do."

"Still five minutes before starting."

"You never did tell me why you're here so early."

"To be here when you arrived. To give you flowers as a welcome-back gesture."

"That's not what friends do," she said softly, not looking at him.

"I know."

Her gaze flew to meet his then down to her lap where her hands fisted together. "Treyan, I'm leaving in three months. You know that."

Here went nothing. "Maybe I can change your mind."

"We agreed to be friends."

"I only agreed under duress."

"Treyan, please don't..."

His heart plummeted. Why had he assumed a week apart would make her look at him differently? Why was he so fixated on someone who was temporary? Because that was safer? But it would kill him when she left.

"Arleigh's really nice. She had a booth next to mine a couple of weeks ago and we chatted some in between customers."

"Why are we talking about Arleigh?"

Her fingers tapped away on her keyboard. "You brought her up to start with."

"Because you asked where the flowers came from. I bought flowers from her *for you*."

"She's single, young, and pretty, remember?"

"I remember. But I'm not attracted to her."

"Mr. Ackerman." There was a note of censure in her voice.

"Yes, Ms. Santoro? I have a strong need to be truthful in everything I do. And so I feel compelled to tell you that I am, in fact, attracted to you."

"Friends," she whispered.

"I'll take that for now. But please remember that friendship isn't my end game. That's not what I'm really shooting for."

"I really need to get some work done..."

"Are you going to Spokane next weekend for the Fourth?"

She bit her lip and stared past her monitor. "No. I signed up for the market. Besides, Spokane is too far to drive back after the fireworks, since the fifth is a workday."

"Want to hang out? The town puts on a pretty good Independence Day celebration."

"I'll have to get back to you on that."

He'd pushed too hard.

"Let's walk down to Bella's instead." Paula rose from the shaded picnic table near the beach. "It's way too hot out here."

"You're right. I wasn't thinking." Last time Brittany had met Paula here, it had been a lovely spring day. Now it was blistering. She shifted her messenger bag to allow a little air between it and her body.

Paula fell into step beside her. "You know I didn't think the town needed to hire someone to take the market to the next level."

Brittany held back her grin as the manager dove into her usual speech.

"...but I'm so glad they brought you in. I don't know what we'll do without you."

"You'll be fine. Besides, I'm not going anywhere for a few more months. We've got time to get your feet under you."

Paula held the door to the bakery.

Brittany felt the welcoming blast of air conditioning begin to dry her perspiration. So much better.

Rylee, the owner's niece, smiled at them from behind the counter. "Hi! What can I get you today?"

"I'll take an iced tea and a Danish, please." Brittany stepped aside. "Paula? This goes on my expense account, remember."

"Um, I'll have the same. Make my tea unsweet, please."

Rylee rang it up. "Go on and find a seat. I'll bring that right out to you."

Half the tables were occupied. Probably the two of them weren't the only ones seeking a cool place to visit. Paula led the way to a small booth near the back and slid in, setting her large purse on the padded bench beside her. "I've been thinking..."

Brittany settled across from her. "Thinking is good."

"If we had a place to host it, I bet a fall market — right through to Christmas — would do well."

"Hmm." Visions of wreaths and handmade gifts and gingerbread cookies and Zadok Shirkowski singing Christmas carols streamed through Brittany's mind. "It would. Any ideas where? Most of the managers I've been in contact with have a permanent indoor space if they're stretching the season."

"I know. I keep thinking about it, but nothing comes to mind. I don't think the church is an appropriate location, but I'm also not sure it's big enough. There's the arena, but it's pretty booked with hockey games."

Britt nodded as her mind ran up one street and down the next, envisioning the various buildings. "The seniors' hall?"

Paula shook her head. "They play bridge on Saturdays."

"There has to be someplace."

"I haven't come up with anything. I almost didn't mention the idea to you because it seems dead in the water before we even get started."

Rylee deposited two tall glasses of iced tea and two Danish pastries on the table.

"Thanks." Brittany stirred her straw through the clinking

ice cubes. "There has to be someplace where the fall months are quiet."

"Someone's hay barn? But that probably wouldn't be warm enough."

"That's not a bad idea. Except wouldn't it be the most full at that time of year?" And wouldn't it stink of animals? Maybe not. She was no farmer, so how would she know?

"Probably." Paula sighed. "I knew it was a bad idea."

"We could ask around and see if anyone else has a thought." Treyan, maybe. Or Gina. "Maybe one of the vendors knows a spot. How about at Green Acres Farm?"

Paula broke off a piece of her pastry and ate it before shaking her head. "I don't think so. People don't like driving that far in winter. I mean, I know it's not actually far, but one of the nice things about our location in the park is that most residents can walk there."

"Yeah, Claire mentioned something to me about the distance being a deterrent when they experimented with their farm stand."

"The Ackermans have a big barn, but it's not much closer to town. And I think we decided a barn wasn't the best, anyway."

"Mitchell Ackerman also has a pretty big greenhouse."

"Which is still out of town." Paula sipped her iced tea. "But wouldn't fall be kind of a downtime for greenhouses?"

"Maybe? Probably." The location was still a deterrent. Brittany had a bite of the pastry. If that didn't make her homesick, nothing would. The bakery back home made way better Danishes and everything else. She'd only tried the cinnamon roll here once. No, thank you. Not when she could indulge on every trip back to Bridgeview. She'd have to bring one back for Treyan next time, though they were best fresh.

Maybe Treyan would visit Spokane with her sometime. Or not.

"Anyone else have a greenhouse?" She needed to divert her thoughts.

"Arleigh O'Neill has a small one."

"The flower grower."

Paula nodded. "It's still out of town, but a lot closer since it's just across the bridge. But I don't know if it's big enough, or if she even bothers to heat it at that time of year."

Brittany had a vague memory of passing it on her rare trips north of town. "We could charge more per vendor to pay for heat. That's if she's at all amenable."

"The vendors wouldn't pay—"

"They would, actually. Think of how much Christmas stuff they could sell with a fall market season. Think of the craft vendors we could lure in. There's that author guy who almost never comes because the weather has to be exactly perfect so his paperbacks won't get damaged from rain or wind or sun. All kinds of people might prefer an indoor market."

"True."

"It's definitely worth pursuing before we decide to abandon the idea."

"I suppose." Paula twisted her straw around and around in the glass.

The verse, *you have not, because you ask not,* was written for people like Paula. "You should swing by Arleigh's place and scope it out. Talk to her and see what she thinks."

"You should."

Brittany shook her head. "You're the market manager. I'm here to give you background support."

She wasn't going to be here when the fall market lifted off. She'd be in New York. Maybe if she flew home for Christmas, she could drive up on a Saturday and see the vision come to life. The whole thing had already formed fully in her mind, like one of those kids' books where a 3D scene unfolded from the page when you turned it.

She turned the mental page again, and the scene folded away. New York was going to be awesome. She wouldn't give Galena Landing more than a passing thought every few weeks once she was there.

Right. She was rarely going to think of Treyan Ackerman. She'd go from twenty times an hour to twice a year in the blink of an eye.

Paula laid a steno pad on the table and clicked a pen. "Okay. Help me think of all the things to talk to Arleigh about. All the things I should consider if we're really going to do this thing. Do I need to ask the mayor?"

Brittany yanked her mind back to Bella's Bakery in Galena Landing, Idaho. It was July, not September, and not Christmas. "We do need her stamp of approval, but she'll be most likely to give it if we can present a fully formed idea with all the logistics in place."

"That makes sense." Paula turned to a fresh page in her notebook and wrote *Fall Market* across the top. Below that she jotted *WWWWWH*.

Brittany squinted at the upside-down page. "What?"

"Yes." The other woman grinned. "Who, what, where, when, why, and how."

"Gotcha." Brittany let her mind drift through a typical

189

Saturday market. "Any of our current vendors unlikely to participate?"

Paula's pen tapped. "Mitchell Ackerman? Although produce vendors might have late-season vegetables. Otherwise, it seems like everyone could benefit from an extended market. So, the who seems to be all our current vendors and probably a few extras."

"And the what is an extended indoor market."

Paula made a note. "When is every Saturday until Christmas." She pulled out a day planner and counted. "Twelve additional weeks."

"Why is easy. To provide the vendors with more opportunities to sell goods, and to provide the community with more chances to buy local."

"That leaves where and how."

Brittany ate another bite of her Danish. "I think the how depends on the where, if that makes sense. Like, if the location is a greenhouse or"— she waved a hand —"I don't know, the seniors' center, the logistics look quite a lot different."

"Right." Paula flipped to a fresh page. "So what do I need to discuss with Arleigh?"

"Well, first find out if it's even a vague possibility. It might not be. You might be more knowledgeable than me, but I don't know much about the flower business. We could be way off base."

"So, I will probably need a backup plan."

"One step at a time. Talk to her and let me know what she says. We can hammer out the details with her or brainstorm a new location after that."

"You've got it." Paula snapped the notebook shut and

took a long sip of her iced tea. "Are you riding the town's float for Independence Day?"

"Not me. I'm a temp, remember?" She'd heard a bit about the mayor's carriage that would be hitched to two Clydesdales. Let Ms. Kozak smile and give the royal wave while her footmen tossed candy.

"But you're coming, right?"

"I wouldn't miss it for anything. At eleven?"

"Yes. It starts at the fairgrounds and finishes at the park. I keep thinking we should have entered a float, too, but it's too late now."

"Maybe next year. Add it to your planner."

Paula tapped her pen and nodded. "Even Rome wasn't built in a day."

A fully decked out Farm Fresh Market wagon pulled by a John Deere tractor sprang to Brittany's mind.

Too bad she wouldn't be here to implement her vision.

CHAPTER
SEVENTEEN

Daddy! There's Emma!" Scarlett tugged on Treyan's hand amid the throng lining Main Street. "I want to watch the parade with her."

Emma Zima stood across the street with her family... and, yes, that included Brittany.

Trey's heart skipped a beat. "Are you sure? We've got a better view here." He'd claimed a curbside spot well in advance.

"Yes! Emma's my best friend."

Who cared about watching a parade, anyway? Not him. Not if he could spend half an hour with Brittany away from the office instead. "Okay, if that's what you want."

She dragged him onto the blocked-off street. "Come on, Daddy."

Brittany saw them coming long before they arrived, and she offered a hesitant smile.

Emma and Scarlett hugged and jumped and chattered. Chris Zima chuckled. "Kids, right? Good to see you, Treyan."

Trey shook Chris's hand then Gina's. "Happy Fourth."

Then he extended his hand to Brittany. "Hey. Long time no see."

"Hi." Her hand was warm in his, but that might be weather-induced.

Still, this was definitely the most casually he'd seen her dressed, in a pair of navy shorts and a red-and-white striped T-shirt. "Patriotic outfit." He grinned.

She pulled away and gave a sidelong glance at her cousin. "Nothing less for a Santoro."

"Hey, I hear you're a failure at Candy Land," Gina offered, glancing between them.

Treyan groaned. "It's a game of chance. No skill involved. No odds."

Brittany's cheeks pinked.

Interesting. Had her cousin been ribbing her about inviting Treyan and Scarlett over that day? Although it had mostly been his idea... and he needed more of them.

"Emma's birthday is in a couple of weeks. She's hoping Scarlett can come for her party."

He focused on Gina. "If it's on the weekend, she'd love to. Otherwise, you need to consult Kayla."

"You got a special dispensation for Independence Day?" Chris brimmed with sympathy.

Treyan sighed. He really didn't want to talk about Kayla in front of Brittany. "It was hard going, but in the end, she took a few days to go visit her parents in Lewiston."

Chris's eyebrows rose. "Without Tyrell?"

"Apparently. She wanted to take Scarlett, but I argued my rights." See, he was crazy for even thinking of pursuing Brittany or any other woman. Kayla and her whims would always be in the picture.

"That's tough."

There was no real reply to that, but Treyan didn't miss that Gina had slipped her hand into Chris's while they talked.

A siren sounded from over by the fairgrounds, and a cheer went up from the crowd lining Main. Looked like the entire county had converged for today's celebrations.

Treyan took Scarlett's hand, sidled in next to Brittany, and racked his brain for an icebreaker. Which was all kinds of ridiculous. He poked his chin down the street. "Now you get to see the joys of a small town in action."

She flashed him a smile and focused on the police car idling at the head of the parade while the chief, Jared, waved out the window. Several businesses came next with decked-out pickup trucks, some pulling trailers. The high school marching band followed, then Green Acres Farm's float, pulled by their Percheron team.

The mayor came toward the end, followed by the fire engine. Big signs plastered on both sides read *Vote YES for a new Fire Hall!*

If only it were that simple, though it did seem as though the tide had begun to turn in favor of the project. The referendum would be held in late August, after school was back in session and most residents back from whatever vacations they'd taken.

Treyan spared a thought for how upset Kayla's parents likely were that she hadn't brought Scarlett on this trip. He could almost hear them all grouching about how unreasonable he was, in this and every way. They'd never really accepted him, but he doubted they liked Tyrell Burke much better.

Brittany's shoulder brushed against his arm as the tail end of the parade made its way past them. The din of the crowd deepened as many followed the final float. "What happens next?"

She was asking him? "The Lions Club is grilling hot dogs and burgers as a fundraiser down in the park. Want to get some lunch with me?"

Brittany bit her lip. "I'm with Gina and Chris."

He leaned a little closer, taking in her fragrance. "May we hang out with your family? Scarlett would be more than willing." And he'd guess from the sneaky smiles between the Zimas that they wouldn't be against it, either.

"If you like."

"Friends, remember?" It pained him to remind her.

"Right." She flashed him a smile, but it was gone in an instant.

Where was the confident Brittany he'd come to know at town hall and at the Farm Fresh Market? Was it simply the fact that there were onlookers? She'd been quieter all week since she'd been away for her cousin's wedding. Maybe she'd been having second thoughts.

He wasn't. Every thought of her led him deeper into her spell. He didn't even want to be free of her anymore. He'd give up half his office forever. Half of anything she wanted. More than half.

Treyan fell into step beside her as the two little girls swung their joined hands. Brittany wouldn't go for that. Not yet, if ever.

"Saturday's good." Gina's voice came from the other side of Treyan.

Saturday? He looked at her, trying to make sense of the comment.

"For Emma's party, so Scarlett can come."

"Oh. That's great. What time?"

"What works best for you? But it's still a few weeks away."

"For me? It's your party. I'll make it work."

"How about right after the market? That way I can put my cousin to work." Gina peered past him at Brittany.

"I'll make the cake," Britt volunteered. "I bet she's a confetti cake kind of kid."

"You've got it." Gina shook her head. "Mermaids and glitter are what my kid ordered."

Treyan tried to imagine a life like that and failed. But he'd attend a mermaid party if he got to see Brittany that way. "Do you or Chris need a hand with anything?"

"You could supervise the Candy Land round-robin," deadpanned Brittany.

Gina snickered. "You could... but I'm sure Chris wouldn't mind company at the grill."

"Whichever." He bumped Brittany's shoulder. "Anything to learn how a girly-girl party should go. So far, I've abdicated." He'd figured Kayla could handle those, but Brittany had been right a couple of weeks ago. He needed to focus more on Scarlett and what she really wanted. They'd started with her riding on the tractor with him while he'd tilled the market gardens. Surprisingly — at least to him — she preferred that to playing with her cousins.

"Well, we can definitely handle another adult around, though I think it will be a smaller crew than some years.

Probably only fourteen girls." Gina rolled her eyes. "Emma's been badgering for a sleepover party, but I am so not ready."

"Only fourteen?" Treyan's voice caught as he glanced at the two little girls and multiplied them by seven. Ramped up the excitement and glee by seven. The glitter and sparkles by seven. He looked across Gina at Chris. "How do you survive this?"

The other man chuckled. "It comes with the territory of being a girl-dad. I can put up with a lot to make my daughter happy. Then Ethan and I escape outside and shoot hoops or something to keep our man cards."

"Having second thoughts, Mr. Ackerman?" asked Brittany.

He looked down at her, inches from brushing against him. "Not at all, Ms. Santoro. A good planner makes himself aware of all existing parameters and extenuating circumstances."

"Ooooh, so formal," Gina teased with a giggle.

But Treyan remained lost in Brittany's eyes until she looked away.

Scarlett tugged on his other hand. "Daddy, me and Emma want to play on the teeter-totter. Will you help me?"

"Wouldn't you like a hot dog first?" Although the lineup already snaked halfway around the park.

She shook her head. "Please?"

Brittany reached for Emma's hand. "Come on, honey. Let me help."

Suddenly helping his daughter looked a whole lot more interesting.

How had Treyan managed to attach himself so firmly to her family? She could try to blame it on the little girls' friendship, but she knew better. Emma and Scarlett had seen half a dozen of their preschool friends while playing and then, finally, waiting in line for their picnic lunch. Yet, they were still glued at the hip as they munched on their potato chips and hot dogs. Which meant Treyan was still sticking close to her.

Friends. He could say the word, but that didn't mean she believed him. By the appreciative gleam in his eyes, he didn't believe himself. And Brittany doubted Gina or Chris had fallen for the ruse, either.

Tell yourself what you need to hear.

Yeah... she wasn't sure anymore that friendship was truly what she wanted from him. It was terrifying admitting that to herself, let alone anyone else. New York. She'd always wanted to live in the Big Apple. The hustle, the bustle, the culture, the... everything.

The crime.

Well, no, not that, of course. But it did come with the territory of big cities. Not in Galena Landing. The police report in the Galena Herald talked about landlord-tenant disputes, altercations where a woman had allegedly thrown a pot of pasta at her husband, and underage drivers chasing deer across a pasture in a pickup. None of those would make headlines in New York.

Brittany swallowed her last bite and leaned back on her outstretched arms. The lake glistened nearby, the hills beyond garbed in evergreens. Across the creek, the gently rolling valley stretched northward.

It was a beautiful place. Not showy, just pleasantly satisfying on a July afternoon. The temperature hadn't tipped 100 degrees yet this summer, but today might change that. Kids and grownups alike splashed in the lake, while a few boats pulled water-skiers along the placid surface.

"Want to swim?"

Treyan's voice came from close beside her. She shook her head. Not a chance was she wearing a swimsuit around him. Not with her pudgy thighs.

"We're going to." Chris rose and pulled his muscle shirt over his head. "If you're not going in, here, stick my wallet in your humungous bag." He tossed it at her.

Gina had said something back at the house about wearing her tankini under her clothes. Now she stripped out of her clothes and laid them beside Brittany. "You kids coming?" She held out her hands.

"Can I, Daddy?" begged Scarlett as she wiggled out of her sundress to reveal a pink swimsuit.

"Sure."

And, in the blink of an eye, most of their group jogged toward the water, leaving Brittany sitting beside Treyan Ackerman wondering what had just happened.

Treyan couldn't have planned that better had he tried. He angled a glance at the sky. They'd have half an hour or so before sunshine invaded their shady spot. Then he looked over at Brittany. "Well, hi."

She sat forward, drawing her knees to her chest as she chuckled. "I think we've been abandoned."

"Sure you don't want to swim?"

"Quite sure."

He plucked a piece of grass and tore it into tiny pieces. "So, Mitch and I have been talking."

"Oh?"

"And I'd like your opinion. As a friend." He hurried on.

"Now I'm curious."

"Well, his wife passed away about three years ago. Kayla and I were living in a rental in town at the time, and as you may recall, our marriage didn't last much longer. When she left me, I moved into Mitch's basement. We figured we could help each other with childcare and the farm and... life." He shredded another piece of grass.

"Makes sense."

"You made me think about what that does to Scarlett when she's over for the weekend. There's nothing about the situation that feels like home to her."

He saw Brittany nod in his peripheral vision.

"This was never meant to be a permanent solution, but it's been easy to put off making decisions about it." Treyan shook his head. "And it's been Scarlett that's suffered the most for that."

"What are you thinking of doing? Moving back to town?"

"What?" He swiveled to look at her. "No way. I love the farm. Mitch does most of the work in the greenhouse. We both take care of the cows and chickens, but the field work is mine. The hay and all that."

"Do you grow wheat? Like, for flour?"

"Uh, no. Hay is dried grass for animals to eat over the winter."

She waved her hand dismissively. "Why not grow wheat?"

He blinked and stared at her. What on earth? She might as well have two heads for all the sense she was making. "Why would I do that? We're already growing hay."

"But people use wheat for bread. Wouldn't you make more money?"

"Not necessarily. We already have a business model and the equipment for it. We grow hay and sell what we don't need for our own animals."

"Okay, sorry. I derailed you. You and Mitch were talking, but you're not moving to town. What did you want my opinion on?"

"I've been debating building a house on the farm. There's a spot across the driveway from Mitchell's place. Oh, sorry, I forgot you haven't seen our place yet."

"I drove by once when I went out to Green Acres, so I think I know where you mean."

Treyan was going to let that pass. It wasn't like the Ackerman Farms sign on the greenhouse was small. "Now that I have the idea in my head, I don't know that I want to wait for a house to be built. There's a guy down the road — Brent Callahan, at Green Acres — who really builds awesome houses, but he's pretty backed up. It'd take a couple of years to get on his list."

Besides, Brent had built Tyrell Burke's house. That, right

there, was enough to make Treyan want a completely different style.

"Still not hearing a question."

Treyan rolled his eyes. "Or, I was thinking about buying a manufactured home. There's a place in Wynnton that has some in stock. I just don't know if they're built as well as a regular house."

"Do you mean a trailer? I'm not really familiar with them, honestly."

Of course. In cities like Spokane, modulars were only allowed in designated mobile-home parks. "They're not called trailers anymore, and they're built a lot better than they used to be. A manufactured home is meant to be moved once, to the site, and that's it. But I don't want to make a mistake just because I'm in a hurry."

"You've been living there for three years. What's the big rush now?"

"Scarlett." At least, she was the reason he'd give out to the public. And to his brother. Inside himself, though, he knew it was because he was finally, after three years, able to look at the future with some kind of hope and confidence again.

Of course, that would likely dissipate when Brittany's term position with the town ended. But, meanwhile, he kind of liked the idea of living in hope, and if he and his little girl got a real home out of the deal in the meanwhile, that wasn't all bad, was it?

CHAPTER
EIGHTEEN

Of all the things Brittany thought she might do on a sunny July Saturday, driving to nearby Wynnton to tour manufactured homes had never been on her list. Treyan had voiced the thought that they should take a weekday off work instead so they could go without Scarlett, but his workload was too great as the fire-hall referendum neared.

So here they were, his five-year-old in her booster in the backseat with headphones firmly clamped over her ears while watching a cartoon on Treyan's tablet.

Treyan glanced Brittany's way, both hands flexing on the steering wheel. "Thanks for coming with me."

"You're welcome. For like the eighteenth time."

"Well, I really appreciate it."

"Nineteen."

He cracked a grin. "I don't know what to look for in these things."

Brittany raised her eyebrows at him. "Isn't the most important thing how it's built and all that kind of stuff?"

Two of her uncles were in the construction trades. She'd overheard more than one conversation over building codes.

"Well, yeah. Of course. But both these companies have good reputations established over multiple years. Decades. I'm sure their houses are well-constructed."

"Fair point."

"Thus, my question remains. How will I know if I've found a good one *for me*?"

"Um. How many bedrooms do you want?"

He shot her a sideways glance. Was that a tinge of red beneath his scruff? "Three or four?"

"Planning on having more kids?" Her question, meant to be lighthearted, hung in the air awkwardly.

"If I ever remarry, yes, I'd like to."

She tried to imagine Treyan with a pregnant woman next to him, but that woman just turned into Kayla. They both folded their arms and stepped apart, glowering at each other. That was fine. Brittany couldn't fathom the two of them getting back together, anyway.

What kind of woman would he go for? She tried to picture him with a willowy blonde. Maybe someone with short, curly hair and an hourglass figure. A cute wisp like Arleigh.

Nope.

"At least, I don't want to get a new house and then regret the size or layout if God answers my prayer."

Whew. "Praying for a wife, are you?" Maybe this time she'd mastered a light, teasing tone.

"Yes." He looked her way and held her gaze for long enough that she worried about the truck staying on the highway. Those dark eyes of his seemed to burn right through her.

No way. He'd been okay with friends. He knew she was leaving. He could not possibly still be having those sorts of thoughts about her. Could he?

Not that she hadn't done a little daydreaming of her own, but she wouldn't act on it. She had a game plan, and it didn't include Treyan Ackerman and his adorable child. It didn't include Galena Landing.

The highway paralleled the river as they approached Wynnton.

"Have you ever seen the rapids here?" Treyan flipped on his signal light. "I'd like to give Scarlett a minute to stretch her legs and use the restroom before we start touring."

Brittany took in the small parking area, surrounded by trees. "No, I didn't know there was anything here worth seeing."

"Are we there, Daddy?" Scarlett tugged the headphones off of her head. "I don't see any houses."

"This is a chance for you to go potty first. And we'll go for a little hike, okay? The river is pretty here."

"Okay." She dropped the tablet to the seat beside her and reached for her seatbelt as Treyan put the truck into park.

"Do you want me to take her?" Brittany slid out of the truck, absorbing the humid heat of the thickly overcast day.

"I've got her, but thanks. The restrooms here aren't so fancy anyone would care."

A few minutes later, she squeezed hand sanitizer on everyone's hands. As they rubbed it in, Treyan tipped his head toward a wooden sign. "It's just a few minutes' walk to the river. Hear it?"

She nodded. Rivers were Brittany's thing. They'd had a great view of the Spokane River from the house where she'd grown up as well as the apartment she'd shared with Ava. The Galena was a lot smaller than the Spokane, and the trail was only a row of gravel strewn amid roots and rocks. She'd need to watch her step.

"Give me a piggyback ride, Daddy," begged Scarlett.

"You need to stretch your legs, pumpkin."

"But I don't want to."

Brittany reached for Scarlett's hand. "I'll walk with you." It might get dicey in some spots, but she could try.

"Okay, but I want to walk with Daddy." Scarlett reached for Treyan's hand as well.

Great. Now they looked like a little family. What did it matter? They weren't one. She was just a friend helping out for the day. If she happened to have a connection with Scarlett, what of it? Brittany swung Scarlett's hand, and the little girl beamed up at her as she swung her dad's, too.

Chain reaction. Like so many things in life.

Brittany glanced at Treyan across the open space above Scarlett's head.

A little smile flashed across his face and disappeared again, but the intensity of his gaze didn't dissipate. Man, she could get lost in there.

She rammed her sandaled toe against a root and stumbled. Ouch, that hurt.

"You okay?" His voice was soft.

"Yeah, I think so. I better watch where I'm going."

Treyan chuckled softly. "Probably a good idea."

The trail wound through the trees for two or three

minutes then emerged alongside the river, with its bubbling rapids. "This is pretty."

"Can I play in the water, Daddy?"

"No, baby. It's dangerous.

"Can we throw some rocks?"

"How about a stick?"

Scarlett let go of their hands, picked up a stick, and hurled it forward. It fell inches in front of her.

Treyan's eyes danced, but he said nothing. He picked up a broken branch and whipped it into the river. The branch bumped against rock after rock while the current carried it through the rapids.

Brittany shaded her eyes and looked downstream, where the rapids churned all the way around the next bend.

Playing in the water was dangerous. As was playing *with* the water. She could lose herself in Treyan's eyes, but she needed to remember the branch. Likewise, her heart would bounce and crash down the river of romance if she allowed it to jump in. Nothing good could come of it.

The trouble was, her heart had already made the leap without asking for permission. She could only hope it would find a quiet pool along the bank to escape the churning rapids. Or it could bubble all the way to the next lake, where it would be calm and peaceful again.

Could love ever be calm? Or would it always be unsettled and pushing somewhere? Somewhere that wasn't New York City?

After Scarlett flung another stick with not much better results, her daddy crouched beside her and helped loft a third one into the middle of the rapids. The little girl clapped her hands in glee as the branch bobbed back to the surface, twirled around, and made its way downstream.

"You should try!" Scarlett grabbed Brittany's hand.

Brittany shook her head. "It's okay."

Treyan met her gaze. "Let's get going. We'll go tour one set of houses and then go to the Bluebell for lunch."

"Sounds like a plan."

"I'M pleased to meet you, Treyan, Brittany. My name is Wilf." The salesman shook their hands then crouched. "And who have we here?"

Scarlett burrowed behind Trey's leg.

"My daughter, Scarlett."

Wilf rose and looked between them. "We have three display homes here at the moment, although we have a pending offer on one of them. It's a two-bedroom, but I'd like to show it to you anyway, since we have a very similar model with three. This will give you an idea of the basic layout, especially the kitchen." He nodded to Brittany.

Treyan bit his tongue. He'd introduced Brittany as his friend, but clearly Wilf had understood that to mean girl-friend at least and live-in at most. There probably wasn't any need to correct the man unless his assumptions got out of control.

Brittany took Scarlett's hand and smiled at the salesman. "Lead the way."

Okay, she didn't look too perturbed. Treyan managed a

deep breath as he followed them into a modern interior with dark wood floors and pale gray walls. Beyond, glimpses of white cabinetry and black appliances offered a peek into the kitchen.

Wilf turned to him. "You mentioned this would be going on private property, not in a park, right?"

"Yes, my brother and I inherited the family farm."

The man's eyes crinkled. "And he got the house?"

Treyan tipped his head. He didn't need to explain everything to this man.

"If you have the space, some would consider adding a mudroom off the utility room. I imagine all sorts of things get tracked in on a farm."

The man's imagination would likely be correct. Mrs. O'Neill lived in a mobile home and had told Trey each room was plenty big enough to fulfill its purpose. The problem was more that there wasn't much space for storage or hobbies. Apparently, a place to kick off muck boots fit into that category, as well.

He didn't love this home. The dark floors would show every speck of dust and every puppy footprint if he decided to house-train one of the farm pups. A mudroom would only help so much. And the starkness of the kitchen with black and white really wasn't his aesthetic.

"Very nice." Brittany peeked into the ensuite and nodded.

Really? She liked it? Trey tried to imagine this home with her inside it. She always looked amazing, but today she wore a hot pink sundress that flared around her knees. So much more casual than what she wore to the office, but a far cry from what the average town woman wore on a Saturday. Maybe this home really did seem attractive to her, but could he live with it? He cleared his throat. "I'd like to see the next one, please."

"Certainly. It's right over here." Wilf led the way.

The layout was a little different — this one had a fourth bedroom that could double as an office — but the color palette was the same. He could probably order it with custom finishes, but wouldn't that add to both the timeline and the price?

Treyan heaved a sigh of relief when they headed to the Bluebell.

"See anything you liked?" Brittany, sitting in the passenger seat, played with the hem of her dress.

He'd keep his gaze averted. "A bit modern for my taste."

"It was fairly stark." She glanced at him. "My mom has an oak kitchen. Charlie updated the countertops but she wouldn't let him replace or refinish the cupboards. The apartment my cousin and I shared had butter-yellow painted cabinetry and ancient white appliances. And you've seen Gina's kitchen. Basic white but with plenty of warmth."

He nodded. The Zimas' house was fairly typical of something built forty or fifty years ago. "What would you go for? If the decision were yours?"

"It's not." Brittany stared out the windshield as he navigated into the Bluebell's parking lot.

"I invited you along for your insights."

She shot him a glance as she reached for the door handle. "I've never really thought much about having my own home."

As soon as he put the truck in park, she slid out and straightened her dress. What was all that about? Could someone as creative as she was reach adulthood with no opinions? She stood with her arms crossed and her shoulders hunched as though she huddled against an icy wind, not a blistering July day.

Treyan let Scarlett out of her booster and took her hand as they crossed the parking area and entered the restaurant. Then he ushered them both to a booth beside a window.

The server dropped off two menus and a coloring sheet, promising to return with iced tea in a minute.

Brittany glanced through hers then closed it.

He hadn't even scanned his yet; he'd been so busy watching her. "What're you having? My treat, remember, as thanks for coming along."

"Gina said they make a great burger." She pulled her pouch of sparkly gel pens from her large bag and slid them across the table to Scarlett.

His little girl brightened as she pushed the four tiny crayons aside.

"A burger sounds good."

Scarlett would want chicken fingers, as always.

After they'd placed their orders, he sipped his tea and tried to keep his attention on Scarlett's careful coloring.

Brittany's voice was so quiet he barely heard it. "Is this really what friends do?"

His heart leaped in his chest as he focused on her. "Sure. Why not?"

"I don't know what the rules are. I've never had a guy friend before." Her face reddened. "I mean, other than a boyfriend."

Scarlett's head remained bowed over the paper. She didn't seem to be paying a lot of attention. Good.

"The rules are whatever we make them."

"That's kind of a problem."

He knew exactly what she meant, but he couldn't let on. "How's that?"

"I like rules that stay put, so you know if you're breaking them or not."

"We could throw out the rules."

"That feels even more scary."

"I know we don't have a lot of time, but I'd rather just see where our friendship took us instead of trying so hard to keep it defined."

"Emma is my friend," Scarlett put in conversationally.

And this was why Treyan needed to spend more time with Brittany on weeknights, when Scarlett was with Kayla. Even when his little girl appeared preoccupied, she missed very little.

"Having friends is really nice." Brittany focused on Scarlett, but Trey was pretty sure the words were meant for him.

They were distancing words, so he ought to feel them that way. But instead, they proved it wasn't so easy for her to pretend the attraction didn't exist between them, either. While she was fighting it, there was hope.

Did he really want there to be hope?

Brittany picked up a bronze gel pen and began doodling a scrolled border along the edge of Scarlett's paper. Her dark hair had been pulled into a knot low on her head, and her impossibly long eyelashes brushed her perfectly made-up cheeks as she focused.

Yeah. He wanted there to be hope. Not only was she beautiful, especially in this flirty dress. Not only was she great with Scarlett. Not only was she quick-thinking and imaginative, but she was funny and nice. She made the office bearable. She made the market more entertaining. And she attracted him to the core of his being.

"Having friends is good," he said at last. "It should be a base for everything, really. Couples I've met who didn't have a foundation of strong friendship didn't have anything at all when the initial rush wore off." Take him and Kayla for instance, not that he would name Scarlett's mom in front of her.

Brittany shot him a quick look as she switched to a chocolate brown gel pen and added leafy shapes between the waves. "I'm not very good at friendship."

"You just need to share nicely," Scarlett informed her. "Taking turns is important. And saying sorry. You also need to be kind."

"You're really good at being a friend." Brittany picked up a warm tan pen.

"It takes practice."

"That's true."

"Are you friends with Daddy?"

"Um, sure. We work together."

"Do you share and take turns?" Scarlett set down her teal pen and studied Brittany.

Treyan held his breath. Should he stop his kid? Burst out laughing? Cheer her on? All three responses elbowed for the chance to erupt.

"Well, your daddy shares his office with me. I don't have one of my own to share back."

Scarlett nodded. "I share with you, too. Because my coloring table is gone."

"I understand. Thank you."

She was so good with Scarlett, having a real conversation

with her like Treyan himself rarely did. Being friends with Brittany Santoro wasn't going to be enough. Not when she made his daughter feel heard and made his own heart sing.

This was beyond friendship. Beyond attraction. He was falling for her, little bit by little bit. His task over the next ten weeks was crystal clear. He needed her to fall for him, too.

He needed her to choose Galena Landing.

He needed her to choose *him*.

And wasn't that a scary thought?

CHAPTER
NINETEEN

Coming on this excursion with Treyan and his daughter had been a mistake. Somehow, Brittany had thought having Scarlett along would help keep a distance between them.

She could see her assumption had been all kinds of stupid. She was attracted to the guy. He bumbled as a father, but he'd made great strides in the past couple of months. He was really trying to focus more on providing the best possible environment for Scarlett.

But he hadn't been above inviting Brittany to more than friendship in front of a five-year-old. She'd never been so relieved to allow a small child to school her in the ways of friendship and hijack the conversation to less grownup topics.

"Come on, pumpkin." Treyan slid out of the booth and stretched his hand toward Scarlett.

The little girl held the coloring page toward her dad. "Can you put this on the fridge?"

He hesitated, probably imagining his nephews folding it into a paper airplane.

"Please? It has Miss Brittany's pretty drawing on it. I want to keep it forever."

Treyan shot a glance at Brittany as she rose from the end of the bench on her side. His eyes warmed as his gaze met hers. "All right. It's up to you to keep it from getting crumpled in the truck, though."

"Okay! Thank you, Daddy."

Brittany swung her bag to her shoulder, reached for Scarlett's free hand, and led her outside while Treyan stopped at the hostess desk to pay for their lunch.

A little hero worship went a long way. This kid... she was simply the sweetest thing. Scarlett reminded Brittany a bit of her cousin's daughter, Tieri, when she'd been five, back when Brittany used to babysit her and her little brother from time to time. Only Tieri's mom and dad had a strong marriage — from what outsiders could tell, at least — unlike Scarlett's parents.

At least Kayla hadn't walked away from her daughter. Wasn't it common for one parent to concede completely in a divorce case? Brittany didn't actually know, since most of the couples around her had worked out their problems and stayed together. One of her cousins was married to an attorney who specialized in family law. There wouldn't be a need for Sadie's work if everyone had their children's best interests at heart.

Treyan would be linked to Kayla for the rest of his life, but especially while their daughter was a minor. Could Brittany handle being the other woman in that scenario?

Whoa. Coworkers. Friends. A little harmless flirtation. No

way was she considering anything long-term. New York, remember?

Scarlett tugged on her hand, bringing her back to the café parking lot. Galena Landing was a lot prettier than Wynnton with the river winding through the lake and the entire landscape. The wide valley lay patchworked with assorted crops in various degrees of ripeness. It had a peaceful ambience unlike Spokane. Definitely unlike New York. When had that become a good thing?

Brittany heard the door behind them swish. She glanced back to watch Treyan approach, jiggling his keys.

His gaze was trained on hers, a soft smile lurking amid his light stubble. When had she ever thought him plain looking? There was something about his eyes. His smile.

She gave her head a shake as Scarlett dashed to her dad. Treyan tossed her over one shoulder, and the little girl giggled.

Brittany should keep her distance from this duo as she'd decided three months ago. But... why, again, was that important? Would it be so terrible to change her mind? It wasn't just location, though. It was lifestyle. She didn't want to be stuck with people, like her entire family, who wanted to follow God.

Not that Brittany had anything against church. And she had to admit the sense of community surrounding Bridgeview Bible Church, where she'd grown up, and Galena Gospel Church was quite attractive. People seemed to be happy loving God. Contented. They worked on their relationships together.

"You seem far away," commented Treyan.

Suddenly, he seemed so close. Brittany backed up a step.

"I was just thinking."

"Good thoughts, I hope." His dark eyes warmed.

Had they been? Well, they hadn't been horrible. Maybe if she kissed him, she'd know if she should stay or go. Maybe that would prove there was no chemistry.

Unlikely. Also a dumb, dumb idea. Treyan wasn't the kind of man she was attracted to.

He touched the small of her back and nudged her toward the truck as he beeped the locks open.

That tiny contact made her entire body zing.

A kiss would curl her toes. She wanted her toes curled.

Scarlett tugged the truck door open, her back to them.

Brittany turned into Treyan, stretched a little, and brushed her lips against his before stepping away.

He caught her hand, his deep eyes probing hers. "To what do I owe the honor?"

She squeezed back. "I may have changed my mind, but I'm not sure."

A slow smile creased his cheeks. "We'll have to explore that concept further. Later."

Was she really ready for that? But if not now, when?

"Daddy, can you shut my door? I can't reach."

"Can do, pumpkin." And he closed the truck's back door as he opened the front passenger one for Brittany.

She clambered in, her gut in a turmoil. What had she done? Was she sure?

No. Not completely. But she owed it to herself to give Treyan a chance. Guilt poked. Did she owe it to Treyan? What did he see in her, anyway? Only the facade she'd carefully constructed. He wouldn't be so interested if he knew why she was in Galena Landing to begin with, but all that information could come later, if at all. There was no point in laying all her cards on the table until she knew the outcome of the game.

Brittany blinked as he navigated the highway through town toward the second modular home dealer. Wow, she was seriously mixing her metaphors. Besides, no one actually knew if they'd won until or unless every player had all their cards laid out. She could think she'd won and still lose.

She angled a glance at Treyan as he shoulder-checked, flipped on the signal light, and angled the truck into the left-turn lane.

Did he have skeletons in his closet, too? Besides the obvious ones of his failed marriage. He hadn't pretended the breakup was all Kayla's fault. He'd hinted at some of the issues they'd faced. So far, any further information hadn't been any of Brittany's business. Was it now? She'd kind of agreed to explore the idea of something more than friendship.

Okay, it was more than *kind of*. She'd kissed him in a not entirely platonic way. It also hadn't been satisfying in the least. It had only teased her senses and made her wish to sink into his embrace.

Was more kissing — better kissing — part of the further exploration he'd offered?

Maybe. She'd need to remember where to draw lines, though. She hadn't been involved with a Christian since her teen years. There'd been Duncan, but he'd only worn a church mask. Brittany was pretty sure Treyan's faith ran a whole lot deeper than Duncan's.

With a start, she realized the sound of the motor had cut out. A middle-aged woman came down the steps of a small building marked *Office*, and several homes sat in an arc nearby.

Treyan's hand enveloped hers on her thigh. "Ready?" he asked quietly.

Not at all. And yet... strangely, yes.

Brittany offered a fleeting smile. "Let's do this."

His fingers squeezed hers as he offered a lopsided grin and reached for his door handle.

Ms. Jennings led them into the first home, chattering a mile a minute as she explained how their construction standards were top in the industry and designed for the harsher northern winters.

Treyan rested his hand on the small of Brittany's back as she preceded him into the great room, Scarlett's hand nestled in hers.

She stopped short, and he ran right into her. A second later, he realized why.

"Miss Brittany, look. It's just like your drawing!"

And it was. The floors were of a warm wood tone while the walls had been painted a hue somewhere between beige and tan. A copper-toned abstract border ringed the room.

Brittany crossed the room with purposeful strides toward the kitchen. He followed her into a warm but streamlined space with a large window. He could practically see his hay fields outside the window already.

"Do you like it?" Ms. Jennings glanced between them.

She'd probably picked up that Scarlett hadn't called Brittany Mommy, so she wasn't certain which of them to focus her sales pitch on.

Treyan turned slowly, taking in the kitchen and breakfast nook. "I do like the style and palette. What are the bathrooms like?"

"Right this way." The saleswoman pointed them toward the master suite.

The ensuite featured a jetted oval tub and natural-looking finishes. Treyan could see himself and Brittany getting ready for a busy day in this space.

Whoa. He was definitely getting way ahead of reality. Could he face this home day after day, year after year, if she left him for New York after all? He couldn't think about that. He had to convince her to fall in love with him before that happened.

Lord, please. I know Your desire is to give good gifts to Your children. Brittany would be an amazing gift to Scarlett and me.

He'd pray more, harder, deeper, later. For now, he followed Brittany through the other bedrooms, bath, utility room, and a nook off the great room that could make a decent office, even without a separate door.

Treyan was ready to sign on the dotted line, but he had to think for at least a few minutes. He'd already prayed about this direction, but was this home really the best possible spot for him and Scarlett? And, Lord willing, Brittany?

"THAT WAS A PRETTY HOUSE." Scarlett swung Brittany's hand as she made her announcement.

Brittany glanced toward Ms. Jennings as they exited the first home and made their way toward the second. She didn't want to give the saleswoman false hope, but surely the woman was smart enough to know five-year-olds didn't sign legal paperwork. The more important thing was what Treyan thought. He was deep in conversation with Ms. Jennings, so Brittany didn't have much to go on... although she had noted his pleased smile a time or two.

They toured the other two homes more quickly. They were okay, decorated in similar tones, but lacked the perfect layout of the first. Not that Brittany was the one who would decide what was ideal and what wasn't. Having all the bedrooms grouped in one wing had both pros and cons, after all.

They came to a stop beside the small office building, and Treyan turned to the sales rep. "Mind if we take a few minutes to go back through on our own?"

Ms. Jennings smiled. "That will be fine. Come on in when you're done."

Treyan reached for Scarlett's free hand, and the three of them turned to the first house together. As soon as they entered, Scarlett let go and dashed into the nearest bedroom. "I can see trees from the window!"

Brittany chuckled. She wouldn't be the one to remind the little girl that the view would be different if this home were delivered to Ackerman Farm.

Treyan closed the gap left by his daughter's departure and twined his fingers around Brittany's. "What do you think of this one?"

She leaned into him, just a little. "It doesn't matter what I think."

"It does matter."

Even if they wound up not together? Which was the likeliest outcome, but it caused a little chill to ripple over Brittany.

"Tell me what you think of the layout. Is the kitchen decent for cooking or baking?" He guided her into that space, out of sight of the doorway to the room Scarlett had claimed. Then he turned and held both Brittany's hands.

She walked her fingers up the placket of his short-sleeved shirt. "Sneaky."

"Maybe." He grinned at her but didn't gather her closer. "I really do want your opinion."

Brittany fingered his collar for a few seconds then sighed. He was right. Besides, Scarlett could run in at any instant. She turned to look at the space. "Well, this cupboard by the dishwasher is where you'd keep plates and bowls. And there are drawers for silverware and containers nearby."

Treyan stepped closer behind her, his hands resting on her hips. "That sounds good."

Not as good as his breath on her neck felt. She forced herself not to pivot into his arms. "So, over here... this is where I would put baking and cooking supplies. Coffee pot right there."

"Only Redband Roasters beans on hand."

"Of course." She held her breath as she absorbed the gentle warmth on her hips and the awareness that he was only a breath away. "There are some shelves in the utility room that could be used for bulk groceries like extra bags of flour. Or wheat ready to be sprouted and ground."

"You really think I should grow wheat?" His breath tickled her ear.

Brittany shivered. "It's a sustainable business model for the future."

"The future sounds like an intriguing place."

"Trey—"

"Where are you, Daddy?"

"In the kitchen, pumpkin."

His hands dropped from her hips, and she took a few steps forward to open one of the cupboards. "Oh, nice. Adjustable shelves."

Treyan chuckled as Scarlett bounded around the corner. "Hey, baby girl. Do you like this house?"

"I do!" She nodded vigorously. "The trees out the window are so pretty, and I saw some birds."

He crouched in front of his daughter. "If we bought this house, we would take it home to the farm. Then the view out the windows would be of Uncle Mitchell's greenhouses, and the barns, and Thompson Road, and the hay fields."

Scarlett's eyebrows pulled together as she contemplated his words. "Okay."

"So tell me what you like about the *inside* of the house."

"The windows."

Brittany couldn't help grinning at Scarlett's stubborn insistence. She turned and leaned against the countertop, watching father and daughter.

"But I told you—"

"But, Daddy, the windows aren't high up. I can see outside without climbing on a chair."

Treyan closed his eyes and pulled Scarlett into a hug. "Like upstairs at Uncle Mitchell's house."

She nodded vigorously. "Not like the basement."

"Right. But all the houses we saw today had nice windows, right?"

"Yes, but this one looks like Miss Brittany's drawing."

The little girl wasn't wrong. "It does, doesn't it?" Treyan looked up at Brittany from his spot near the floor. "It is pretty, I agree."

Was he calling Brittany pretty? That wasn't what he'd said, but the expression on his face definitely added another layer to his words.

"Any negatives? Anything one of the other houses did better than this one?"

"I can't think of a thing." Brittany couldn't tear her eyes away from his. She couldn't think at all, let alone about the house. Not with that intensity in his gaze.

"Okay, why don't the two of you go for a little walk, and I'll talk to Ms. Jennings for a bit? I think we passed a playground a couple of blocks closer to town. Can I pick you up there?"

"Yay!" Scarlett clapped her hands.

"Sounds good." Brittany swallowed hard. She needed out of range of Treyan's focus in the worst way. "I've got my phone, so give me a call if you need to."

What she really wished was that she had the right to sit in on the financial discussion sure to be taking place shortly. But she had nothing to contribute. No claim. No rights.

Was that about to change? Did she want it to? Wait, she'd already decided to see where this took her. She'd decided to be open to the possibility of a permanent relationship with Treyan. She wasn't going to chicken out now before they'd ever gotten started.

CHAPTER

TWENTY

Brittany let herself into Gina and Chris's house late that afternoon, wishing she truly had a place of her own to savor the day in solitude. She glanced up the half-flight. Maybe she'd been quiet enough to disappear down—

"Britt?" Gina appeared around the kitchen corner. "Did you have a good time?" She studied Brittany for a few seconds while a slow smile spread across her face. "Oh, my goodness. He kissed you!"

"You're a terrible guesser. He did not."

Gina's eyebrows shot up as she tilted her head.

Was the change in their status this clear? It must be. But it was true Treyan hadn't kissed her. *She'd* kissed *him*... so briefly he hadn't had a chance to react before Scarlett would have taken notice.

"But he did sign a sales agreement for a really nice three-bedroom house. Scarlett thought it came with the view out the window, but I think he convinced her the view would be of Ackerman Farm instead."

Gina chuckled. "Where on the farm is this going?"

"To the left of the driveway, he said."

"Oh, that makes sense. How soon can he move in?"

"They'll deliver it at the end of August. That gives him time to get the utilities in place."

"By the way, I think you lost our bet."

"Our bet?"

"That you'd never date a farmer, because you could spot them a mile away."

Brittany would like to argue that one. She'd fallen for the well-dressed guy in her office, not the guy who wore muck-covered rubber boots while driving a tractor around a field.

She'd also like to argue that they weren't dating, but he had asked her to dinner tomorrow evening, after he returned Scarlett to Kayla, and Brittany had agreed. All the requisite fluttery feelings for a first date were in place, even though she knew where it wasn't going.

This was a bad idea. But also a good one.

Gina laughed. "All that silence while you stare at me like a deer caught in the headlights. I was just teasing, cuz. I'm really happy for you and Treyan. You both deserve someone fabulous, and I'm tickled pink you've found that person."

"It's early days." Brittany needed to cling to all the caution.

"Getting through the early days is the only way to get to the good parts."

"You're smarter than you look."

Her cousin fluffed her hair with a vapid smile. "I'll pretend that's a compliment. Seriously, though, I'm happy for you."

"Thanks, but—"

"But it's early days. I get it. Hey, do you have a few minutes to brainstorm Emma's party with me? It's next Saturday. I'd been thinking of going to the beach, but I'm not sure I can watch fifteen five-year-olds adequately, even with Chris's help. My mom will come, but she's not a strong swimmer, and it's not really Dad's thing."

Brittany couldn't remember ever seeing Uncle Matt in swim trunks. Or, honestly, any of her uncles. Dad had a few times when they'd all visited Grandma and Grandpa Kuyper in Fort Myers. Those had been the days. The five kids had dashed in and out of the waves, watching for dolphins and picking up shells. Mom and Dad had walked hand-in-hand with the warm Gulf water lapping at their feet.

It had sure been a lot different on their most recent visit last spring when Mom had married Charlie on that same beach. But Brittany had forgiven Charlie, remember? Accepted him. Obviously, that, too, would be a journey. She had no clue how many journeys she was on simultaneously. A faith journey, too? If she were going to keep seeing Treyan — and she was, right? — then she owed it to him to honestly examine her belief systems.

Maybe she owed it to herself, either way. Her two strongest arguments were that God was against her having fun, and that He purposefully punished people, even those who loved Him and followed Him.

There might be a flaw or two in her thought process.

"Britt?"

She'd spaced out again in front of Gina. Her cousin would never believe she wasn't just daydreaming of kissing Treyan. Because she was definitely not doing that.

Much.

"Sure. Let me just drop my stuff off downstairs, and I'll be right up." Brittany jogged down to her room, then changed out of her sundress and into shorts and a tank top before returning.

Gina sat at the table, tapping her pen against the notebook open in front of her. Really? Someone besides Paula still used old-school pens and paper for brainstorming?

Brittany poured herself a glass of ice water and settled across from her cousin. "Where are Chris and the kids?"

"They've gone to buy Ethan a new pair of soccer cleats. I kid you not, that boy's feet grow a size every week."

Brittany chuckled. "You might have to stop feeding him. He's a busy, growing kid."

"Next stop, groceries. Again." Gina jotted something in her notebook. "How many hot dogs will fifteen kids eat?"

"You're the expert, but probably twice as many as you think."

"No doubt." Gina shook her head. "Oh! I was down at the market this morning to buy some eggs and fresh produce. At least half a dozen people stopped me to ask where you were today. They'd come for cakes and cupcakes and seemed super disappointed not to find you there."

"That's nice. What did you tell them?"

Gina smirked. "You mean, did I announce to everyone that you were off in Wynnton looking at mobile homes with Treyan Ackerman?"

"You didn't." Brittany raised her eyebrows and nailed her cousin with a look.

"You're right. I didn't, but it was tempting. I'm pretty sure Rosemary Nemesek would be cheering for that outcome."

"Who's that again? Sounds familiar, but I'm not coming up with a face."

"Her husband, Steve, is the man with the walker. Two of their kids and a pile of grandkids live out at Green Acres Farm."

"Oh, right. I remember now. They both seem very nice."

"They are. Rosemary is a bit like our nonna, invested in everyone in this town. I'm sure she knows every single person and prays for them by name."

Brittany managed a smile. "That does sound like Nonna. But I'm sure Rosemary doesn't care about me."

"You'd be wrong. She was one of the people who'd come hoping for cupcakes. She also asked if Galena Landing had won you over yet so you'd stay here."

What was it with small towns? Brittany forced herself to relax in her chair and have another sip of water. "I'm impressed I haven't had more pushback for the prices I've set on baking. That other table doesn't have as much, but what they do have is half the price."

"Jean Stedman. She does sell out most days, even so. But her stuff is basic, like regular chocolate chip cookies. At any rate, if you decided to stay in Galena Landing—"

"I'm not." Brittany hiked her eyebrows.

"—you could make a great little side business out of that market."

"I'm just there to give myself an excuse to keep an eye out on Paula and how she's running everything."

"Oh, because you hate baking and socializing and making a little pocket change?"

"Totally." The return from the market was padding Brittany's New York nest egg.

"You said yourself the market needs a more diverse base of committed vendors."

"When I leave town, you can take over my niche. Your baking skills are on par with mine."

Gina laughed. "They are *so* not. Also, you may have forgotten I have a full-time job and often have to work weekends. What are you planning for Emma's cake?"

"I'll never tell."

"Right. Will you have time to do that as well as the market that weekend?"

"That's what Friday evening and early Saturday morning are for."

"For someone with no social life…"

"Exactly." Treyan spent weekends with his daughter, which made them less ideal for dating. "Don't worry. I've got the cake under control."

"I wish you did have a social life. Nothing new on that front after today?" Gina raised her eyebrows.

Brittany rose to her feet and refilled her glass. "We might be going out for dinner tomorrow after Scarlett goes back to her mom's."

Gina's whoop almost sent Brittany's drink of water down the wrong pipe.

Treyan escorted Brittany into The Sizzling Skillet. He could barely take his eyes off her in a floral skirt and blue top. Today her long hair flowed over her shoulders, and — was that a different scent than the gardenia she usually wore? He shifted a little closer. It was different, but he couldn't place it.

The hostess came over. "Do you have a reservation tonight?"

"Yes, for Ackerman." Though it was a bit of a laugh, since the dining room wasn't even half full.

"Right over here." She turned and led the way to a nook with a lake view.

That gave Treyan an excuse to rest his hand on Brittany's back as they followed. Mitchell had reminded him of all the reasons he'd once announced why he wouldn't pursue this woman, but none of them were worth mentioning. Not anymore. Not since his head had decided to follow his heart and see where it led.

In this perfect moment, it was easy to ignore the negatives poking for supremacy. This seemed very different from the previous time they'd been here.

The hostess set down the menus and promised their server would be with them in just a minute, but that wasn't enough incentive for Treyan to peruse the folder. Not when he had permission to simply sit and drink in the sight of Brittany as she tucked her hair behind her ear and opened the menu.

She glanced up. "Is something wrong?"

He shook his head. "I'm just sitting here thinking about how lucky I am."

"Oh. That." She looked down and took a deep breath. "I'm pretty sure there's nothing quite that remarkable about me."

"You might be wrong about that."

"But probably not."

He covered her hand with his. She was still for almost long enough to freak him out before she flipped her hand over. "Thanks. I doubt you'll convince me, though."

With sudden clarity, he could see that her reluctance to believe in her own worth was linked to her desire to leave Galena Landing. If he could convince her she deserved love... wait, what? He meant *God's* love, of course. On the other hand, falling all the way in love with this woman didn't seem like an impossibility.

It wasn't that long ago that Kayla's rejection had done a similar number on his own self-worth. "Who's the guy who hurt you enough that you don't believe in yourself?"

Her startled gaze snagged on his. She opened her mouth then closed it again before she mustered a small laugh. "You're reading into things."

If anything, her response confirmed his guess. "I've been there."

"Kayla. Right." Brittany looked down at their joined hands but made no effort to pull away.

He'd take that as a win. "Your parents loved you, so I don't think it was them."

"Even Charlie's not so bad." She managed a smile.

Treyan nodded and waited.

Clink. Two glasses of iced lemon water landed on the end of the table. "Can I get you something else to drink?" The server looked down at their hands. "Wine, perhaps?"

"Not for me, thanks," Treyan responded.

"Water's good for me." Brittany glanced up. "Thank you."

"Ready to order?"

"Can I get the salmon on zoodles, please?"

She'd obviously had a glimpse of the menu, which was more than Trey had managed. Whatever. They made good steaks. He ordered one.

Brittany gathered her hair and tossed it back over her shoulder. "Are you still available to help supervise Emma's party next Saturday afternoon?"

"Totally. What's the plan?"

"Mermaid everything. That means we're meeting over at the park." She motioned out the window. "Swimming and mermaid games, then a hot dog roast — Chris is bringing down their camping grill — and then a mermaid birthday cake, of course."

Treyan's eyebrows rose. "Of course." He waited a beat. "I'm trying to imagine that."

"It'll be tall with shades of watery blue frosting. I'm making shells out of fondant, and there will be a mermaid tail sticking out of the top."

"Flavor?"

"Vanilla with blue confetti inside."

His thumb caressed her palm. "That sounds impressive, but a ton of work."

"I'll do the shells tomorrow evening. Bake the cake Tuesday when I start the baking for Saturday's market."

"You're amazing."

"You keep using that word. I do not think it means what you think it means."

He grinned. "We should totally watch *Princess Bride* sometime. Do you think Scarlett would like it?"

Brittany grinned, and he could practically see her relax. "How could she not?"

Now her thumb was stroking his. Was she even aware of

the action? Did her whole body hum with awareness like his was doing, or was she immune to his charms? He chuckled, drawing a startled look from her.

"What's so funny?"

As though he had any charms to his name... but wasn't that the attitude he'd rejected in her? He had an excuse, though. Kayla. And Brittany must have a similar one, even though she'd never been married. Not unless she was keeping secrets much deeper and darker than he suspected.

The server delivered two bowls of Caesar salad just then. Treyan hated to lose the contact with Brittany, but he'd make quite a mess eating with his left hand. He could handle a few minutes of not touching, right?

First, though, he laid his other hand on the table, palm up. "Let's pray."

Brittany bit her lip, placing her hand in his as she bowed.

"Father, I thank You for tonight. I pray that You'll bless this food, and that You'll also bless our conversation as we get to know each other. In Jesus's name, amen."

He felt like he knew her pretty well. They'd shared an office over three months, after all. Of course, she'd guarded herself carefully for the first while, at least for anything other than the market.

Their entrées arrived just as they finished their first course, and talk turned to the office and town doings. Treyan shook his head. "Wow, don't we get enough of that at work? Tell me one thing about you that I don't know."

Brittany blinked, her fork pausing halfway to her mouth. "I have a meddling grandmother."

He laughed. "Okay, that was random."

"Like your subject change wasn't."

"True. So tell me about your grandma."

"Nonna came from Italy when she was a girl, after the war. She married my nonni when she was still a teen. I never knew him — he died before I was born."

"Did she remarry?"

Brittany shook her head. "A couple of years ago we thought she might be getting sweet on Kenji Ito, an elderly Japanese man in our neighborhood. Turns out he and Nonna had been interested in each other before she met Nonni. But, to everyone's relief, she and Kenji are just friends."

"How old is she? Maybe she's not too old to marry again."

"Eighty-two. I'm sure some have remarried at that age, but I doubt Nonna will. She's been a widow for over twenty-five years. If she was going to go for it, I'd think it would have happened a long time ago."

"Maybe she just hadn't met the right man."

"Kenji and his wife lived four or five blocks away for sixty-some years, and his wife passed away a dozen years ago. So... I'm thinking no. But it's nice she has a good friend."

"She's focused on her family?"

Brittany nodded. "Five sons. A pile of grandkids. And now the greats are well underway. Being the matriarch of a clan like that takes quite a lot of time and interference."

Treyan chuckled. "Interference, huh? Is she a believer?" Seemed like he knew Brittany's mom and stepdad were.

"Yes."

"So time, meddling, and praying, maybe?"

"I guess."

"What do you think she prays for you?"

She shrugged. "Same as she does for everyone else, probably. Making wise decisions, living for Jesus, and all that."

Something about the way she said it caught Treyan's attention. "They sound like good prayers."

"I'm sure they are. But she also thinks she knows what's best for everyone, and she's not afraid to be blunt about it."

"I think I'd like her." Would Britt's grandmother like *him*? Would he ever get a chance to find out? He had some praying of his own to do with that in mind. Because, as he got to know Brittany, he wondered what held her back. He also wondered why he was so drawn in that he'd take a chance on someone who didn't want to stick around.

He kind of didn't want to stay himself, but as long as this was where Kayla lived, he didn't have many choices. He wasn't going to give up his weekends with Scarlett, especially now that he'd made a hefty deposit on a home to be delivered in five weeks, right after the referendum on the fire hall.

Maybe he should have waited until after that. What if the whole thing went south and the mayor fired him in favor of someone who could make things happen?

It wouldn't get that bad. He and the others had a plan for getting the voters on their side.

He was going to stay in Galena Landing for a long time.

Would Brittany?

CHAPTER
TWENTY-ONE

Could she be happy here? Was Treyan Ackerman worth giving up her dreams for?

In this moment, the answer seemed to be a quiet, settled yes. They walked hand-in-hand down the lakefront path, having left The Sizzling Skillet and the nearby park, beach, and marina behind. The evening sun angled through the band of trees, then glistened off the far side of the lake and illuminated the conifer-covered hills on the water's eastern flank.

A gentle breeze stirred the air, just enough to alleviate the day's stifling heat. It brought with it whiffs of a riot of flowers from the yards adjoining the path. Occasional voices conversed in those same yards, but not loudly enough to intrude on their cocoon.

Was this what contentment felt like?

Had she ever experienced it before? Not like this. Tonight, the universe seemed aligned — well, Mom would say God was smiling down on her and giving her a little glimpse of His love.

She'd once felt that on a regular basis. Not since Dad died. Not since long before, honestly. She'd been drifting quite a while.

This was no time to think about God stuff. Not when she could be soaking up Treyan's rough palm against her own. His arm brushing against hers. His musky cologne melding with the floral scents.

He sighed and squeezed her hand.

Brittany bumped him lightly. "A penny for your thoughts?"

"It's so peaceful. I have so much to be thankful for."

"Oh, yeah?" She couldn't help the tease in her voice.

"Yeah. Look around you. Sometimes living in a small town seems constricting. Other times I can't imagine being anywhere else."

If that wasn't a lead-in, she didn't know what was, but she couldn't afford to fall for it. "It's nicer than I thought it would be."

"Oh, yeah?"

She elbowed him for his mimicry. "I came on April first. There were still piles of dirty snow stacked in the corners of parking lots. There wasn't much to recommend the place, honestly."

"Mud season comes after second winter and before first spring."

Brittany chuckled. "That's the truth."

"Full disclosure. It's even worse on the farm at that time of year. Now it's pretty idyllic... you haven't come out for the grand tour yet."

Should she remind him how new this relationship was? It wasn't like she'd been going to drop in on him and his brother when Trey was only the grumpy guy from her office. It'd been a long time since she'd thought of him that way, though.

"I'd like to see it sometime. Especially where you plan to put the house."

"The guy from the county is coming by on Wednesday to confirm or deny my preferred location. After I get his approval, it's full steam ahead."

That probably meant Treyan would be leaving work early on Wednesday. She'd miss him in the office. Maybe it would be a good time to schedule a meeting with Paula. She'd slacked off on regular meetings with the market manager since things seemed to be running pretty smoothly these days. But she needed to work with Paula for future visioning, not only the Christmas market but next spring as well.

"Maybe sometime next week, then. I'll be pretty busy this next week baking for the market and for Emma's party. You're still in, right? Did I mention it will be at the beach? Gina's rented the picnic shelter for the afternoon."

"Wouldn't miss it. Mermaids are totally my thing."

Part of her wanted to laugh at his absurd claim, but humor was lacking in his intense gaze. There was no way it was true, of course. But maybe... maybe he was thinking about seeing her in a swimsuit? Beach visits had definitely contributed to her clandestine relationship with Duncan last year. He'd claimed he couldn't keep his hands off her.

In her admittedly limited experience, that was a failing of most guys, if not all of them. Her cousin Ava had insisted Seth wasn't like that, but evidence proved otherwise. His son, Leo, wasn't a product of immaculate conception. How about Brittany's cousins? She knew Basil hadn't abstained, but what about Peter or Alex or Tony? She wanted to believe they would never have taken advantage of a woman.

Duncan hadn't really, either. She'd been a willing participant, and she would be again. But not in Galena Landing. Not with Treyan. She was only here short term, and he was a nice guy with a little girl. She wasn't going to take this too far.

Did she have a conscience, after all? Apparently. A girl didn't grow up in a Christian home and get taught that her body was the temple of the Holy Spirit without absorbing some of that morality.

For the first time in a long time, she kind of wished that philosophy had stuck. That Jesus had stuck. Treyan might have messed up a time or two — he'd admitted as much to Brittany — but he seemed to truly be devoted to being a good Christian, a good dad. He deserved better than Brittany, that was for sure.

Out on the lake, a little splash signaled a rising fish.

Brittany clung to that connection to the present. She was totally overthinking all this. Treyan knew she was almost certain to leave in September, and he wanted to date her anyway. He wasn't thinking long-term, even though he'd asked for her opinions on the house.

But Treyan didn't know how weak her faith was. How little she strove to regain the connection she'd once had. No one really knew, though Ava may have guessed.

She wasn't ready to announce it. Probably never would, not if it meant facing Nonna's displeasure. And it seemed silly that Nonna's opinion came to the forefront of her mind.

Brittany shivered.

"Are you cold? We can head back if you like."

"No, I'm okay. Thanks, though."

Treyan turned toward her, capturing her other hand as well. "You sure? There's a bit of a breeze now."

"It feels good." She smiled at him, keeping her face as open as possible. No way was she ready for the evening to end. Not yet. Not like this.

"*You* feel good." His hands shifted to her hips, slowly drawing her closer as his eyes searched hers as though for permission.

Brittany slid her hands up the placket of his button-up then around the back of his neck. "You do, too."

"You sort of kissed me yesterday."

"Yeah? You want a little more of that?"

"If you're offering." His warm hands enfolded her, one tucking around her waist and one behind her shoulder blades. Then he pulled her flush against him.

She drove her fingers through his short hair, pulling his head closer to hers. For a long moment they stared into each other's eyes from a space of only an inch or two, then Brittany released a tiny sigh and closed her eyes.

Treyan's lips touched hers gently, sparking a flame that coursed through her entire body. A fire that wouldn't be quenched tonight or any time soon, and that had to be okay.

She parted her lips and welcomed his deepening kiss as his fervor increased.

This. How she'd missed being kissed so thoroughly. And there was, remarkably, something freeing about immersing in a kiss that wasn't going to lead to more. She respected Treyan too much. Her future plans didn't include him. Didn't include Galena Landing.

But it was hard to remember why.

Treyan lounged on the beach on Saturday afternoon. He'd known this wasn't a time to explore things further with Brittany, and his assumption had been correct. She and Gina had been out in water up to their waists for the past hour or more, playing water games with fifteen little girls, including Emma and Scarlett. Brittany was so good with kids.

Chris checked his watch. "They'll be ready for food in a few minutes. Give me a hand?"

"Sure." So far, he'd simply felt like a fifth wheel, though he knew his purpose was to assist in case anything didn't go according to plan, like if a little girl submerged and didn't pop back up. Not that he was a trained lifeguard, but they weren't in deep water, either.

"Grab the other end of this tablecloth." Chris flipped a long piece of fabric toward him.

Treyan caught it reflexively and helped spread it out. He raised his eyebrows. "Tie-dyed? Did Gina make this just for Emma's party?" Way to remind him he was failing as a parent. He'd taken Scarlett to the diner for burgers and expected applause. To be fair, his daughter had been thrilled... and Kayla had hosted an actual party for Scarlett's friends.

Chris laughed. "She did, but next week it will turn into a duvet cover for Emma's room. Apparently, we're redoing the whole space in a mermaid theme."

"That's a thing?"

"It is, bro. We redid Ethan's last year to look like a log cabin in the woods. There are beavers and moose and trees everywhere."

"Huh." Trey tried to imagine the room Scarlett had claimed in the new place done up in some girly way. What did she even like besides Disney princesses? He had no idea, but he couldn't imagine existing in the same house as a pink, poufy room.

It's not all about you, Treyan.

He knew that. He did. But pink and sparkles? Mermaids would be a definite improvement over princesses. Blue was more soothing. More natural and neutral. But he could do pink if he had to. Curtains and a duvet cover, at least.

"I'm gonna grab the portable grill from the back of the truck."

Treyan focused on Chris. "Do you need a hand?"

The other guy shook his head. "Nah, it's not that heavy. You could open up the coolers and lay out the food, though."

There were several coolers. He opened the smaller one first. Whoa. That cake was totally professional. Shouldn't surprise him, considering the way Brittany's market booth looked. But she'd definitely kicked it up a notch for her cousin's daughter. She'd worked a forty-hour week, had a full table at the market this morning, and somehow managed to pull off this masterpiece.

He closed that cooler, opened the other, and busied himself setting out the condiments. Then the containers of chilled, cut veggies — baby carrots, sugar snap peas, mini cucumbers, and more. Those veggies looked like they'd come straight from Mitchell's garden. It was quite possible.

By this time, Chris had set up the portable grill and

connected a cylinder of propane. He pulled several packs of hot dogs out of the cooler. "Gina cut the buns ahead of time. Mind setting the stack of plates at the end there and then everything in a sort of logical order?"

"Sure." Treyan moved the bags of chips off the top of an open box. "Wait. She brought real dishes and silverware?"

"Yeah?" Chris glanced over. "She always does."

"I thought everyone in the world used paper plates, at least at picnics."

"It's not like we need to create more trash. The planet is covered in plenty as it is."

Then a little more wouldn't make a noticeable difference, right? But Treyan was smart enough not to say that out loud. "Most people I know would be happy not to come home from a party this size and do the dishes."

"That's what dishwashers are for. Ethan and I will get it loaded."

"Where is he, anyway?"

"He's out at Green Acres, hanging out with his buddy Ash. I'll take Zoey and Lucy home and pick up Ethan after all the other kids are picked up here."

Treyan set the stack of plates on the table. "I should really set up some play dates with those girls for Scarlett. They live so close, and she likes both of them just fine."

"You don't do play dates?"

He ignored the other man's questioning glance. "I haven't, really. The weekends seem to go by so quickly. It feels like I barely get any time with her as it is."

"Kids need friends, too."

"Yeah, well, I'm trying to do better."

"Sorry. I shouldn't offer advice."

Giggles and squeals drew Treyan's attention to the fact that the gaggle of little girls had emerged from the lake, having traded imaginary mermaid tails for regular legs and feet. "Here they come."

Chris snapped his tongs together twice. "On it." He filled the grilling surface with frankfurters while the kids grabbed towels and surged toward the picnic shelter.

Treyan's gaze lingered on Brittany as she tied a towel around her waist, chatting with Gina. He didn't know too many women who'd go to all this effort for her cousin's daughter's birthday party. It wasn't like Gina was paying her.

Or him, for that matter. Mitchell had wanted help with the market garden this afternoon, and Trey had felt bad when he refused. The whole thing his brother was trying to do was a big job for one guy, let alone a man with two rambunctious and inventive kids like Lincoln and Hudson. The farm could probably afford to hire someone part time, though. He should suggest that to Mitch. Some high-school kid would probably enjoy working out there over the summer months. Ackerman Farm was close enough for riding a bike to town. Of course, they needed the help during parts of the school year, too.

Brittany slid her sunglasses to the top of her head as she entered the shade by the pavilion. Her gaze warmed as it caught on his.

Not that he could do anything about it. The cacophony of over a dozen starving children clamoring around him saw to that. But those kisses last Sunday were much too far back in history for his liking.

There'd been no smooching at the office — they hadn't

talked about it, which meant they were both in complete agreement. Work hours were for work, which hadn't stopped him from getting distracted when he looked past his monitor to see her profile, lit from the window in front of her. But the weight of the upcoming referendum kept the diversion from playing out. The *say no* committee had only amped up their propaganda as the date drew near. Tyrell Burke was in the thick of it. Blast the guy anyway.

Brittany leaned over the table beside him, her arm brushing against his as she plated buns and handed them to little girls.

He could live with that tantalizing touch, though it drove him crazy. He pressed a little closer, drawing a grin from her, before noticing Gina lifting a juice dispenser out of yet another tote. He could help with that... and get out of Brittany's space at the same time. Not that he wanted out, but he couldn't exactly gather her in his arms right here, right now, and kiss her in front of all these kids, to say nothing of Scarlett.

Chris began setting grilled franks inside the waiting buns. The Zimas were handling this whole thing like old pros. Treyan should be taking notes.

A little girl dropped the ketchup bottle, and he swept in to help out just as the cell in his pocket rang. Who'd be calling him on a Saturday afternoon? Maybe Mitch needed something after all.

Treyan pulled his phone out. *Kayla.* He should just let that go to voice mail. It was the weekend, his time with Scarlett, and Kayla had no right to interfere. But what if there was something he needed to know? It wasn't like she called him often.

"I need to take this." Not that any of the other adults present seemed to hear him, even Brittany. He stepped aside. "Hey, what is it?"

Kayla sniffled into the phone.

He hardened his heart. Whatever her problems were didn't affect him. Not one little bit. Even if they affected Scarlett? But they didn't. Couldn't. His little girl was right there beside the picnic table, accepting a glass of blue juice from Brittany.

"Kayla?"

"Trey... it's Tyrell."

He rolled his eyes. Like Tyrell Burke was his problem. Nope. He was all Kayla's. "And?"

"He... he hit me."

Trey's jaw tightened. "Leave him."

"I can't. I have nowhere to go."

As far as Trey knew, there wasn't a women's shelter in town, but then Tyrell wouldn't actually follow her and create trouble, would he? Nah, the guy was too well known in the community to risk anything like that. It had likely been an aberration. Kayla had probably mouthed off to him.

He shifted uneasily. Wasn't that the old narrative boys had been taught to believe? That girls brought that kind of thing on themselves? But it wasn't always true. Maybe it wasn't even true *often*. "Look, it's not okay. You must have a girlfriend you can stay with. Scarlett can stay with me until you figure things out."

"You're not getting Scarlett."

"I'm not talking permanently." He clenched the phone and strode toward the lake, away from the party. "Just until you get settled again." Which would mean he'd need to find daycare ASAP. School didn't start for a couple of weeks. Maybe he could take some vacation time. He hadn't used up all that was due him.

"I could come to the farm."

"The farm? You're on a farm." She wasn't making any sense, not that she ever had.

"Ackerman Farm."

"No. I'm sorry if things aren't working out with Tyrell, but you're not coming back to me. There's just no way."

"For Scarlett's sake."

"No."

"I thought you loved me."

"I did, but not anymore. Kayla, you left me for that joker three years ago. You're carrying his child."

"He blames me for being pregnant. He never wanted to be a father."

Treyan didn't want to know that. He rammed his fingers through his hair. "Kayla. Get help, but not from me."

"But the grapevine says you're getting a new house. You have room for me."

Oh, the grapevine, was it?

"For one thing, I'm not moving in until the end of August. For another, you hate the farm. But most importantly? Do I have to remind you that we're divorced? You don't get to just say, 'oops, my bad,' and waltz back into my life."

"What would it take?"

She couldn't be serious. She just couldn't.

He pivoted and faced the now-distant picnic shelter. Brittany sat between Emma and Scarlett, both girls looking up at her and giggling. Then she seemed to notice him watching and smiled his direction.

Treyan looked away. "Kayla, we're over. Totally, completely, forever over. Find a place to go. Get things figured out. Let me know when you've got a safe place to bring Scarlett home again. Until then, she's mine."

"I have primary custody, Trey. You can't keep her from me."

Watch me. But he didn't dare say that out loud.

"We were good together, babe. Please—"

"No. Call me when you've moved out, and let me know where you are." He tapped the *off* button, shoved the phone into his pocket, and strode closer to the water.

He had no right to play at a relationship with Brittany Santoro or anyone else. Not when he wasn't free of Kayla. Because of their daughter, he never would be free.

Brittany was better off without him. Better off in New York.

Treyan had nothing to offer her.

CHAPTER
TWENTY-TWO

What on earth was going on with Treyan? Brittany couldn't figure the guy out. He'd brought Scarlett to Emma's birthday. He'd hung out with Chris on the beach and helped set up the entire picnic. But then his phone had rung and he'd turned away to take the call, and now he was nowhere to be seen.

They'd served the mermaid cake. To say Emma was thrilled was a massive understatement. All the little girls were completely enthralled and starry-eyed, and Britt had been so proud of herself.

Trey hadn't even seen the cake. She had photos she could text him later, but that wasn't the same thing at all. He'd just disappeared, leaving Scarlett behind.

Half of Emma's friends had already been picked up. Denise Sommers had oohed over what was left of the cake and asked if they could talk about her daughter's birthday in a couple of weeks. But Treyan hadn't been there to share this little triumph.

She was starting to get worried.

"Where'd Treyan go?" Chris asked quietly.

"I don't know. He took a phone call." Brittany shook her head.

"There come the last of the parents now. Besides Trey."

She glanced toward the parking lot. "His truck is still here, so he'll be coming back. I'll hang out here with Scarlett and wait for him."

"Something serious must have happened."

"Yeah, must've." And it involved his ex, because he'd said her name before moving out of easy hearing range. But walking away to take a call in privacy was one thing. Not coming back was something else entirely.

"I need to take Lucy and Zoey out to Green Acres. Call me if you need me, okay?"

"Thanks. I can walk home from here easily enough."

Maybe Treyan hadn't wanted Brittany to overhear his conversation with his ex.

What would he and Kayla be talking about if that were the case? Getting back together? The thought knifed Brittany's gut. That would probably be a good thing for Scarlett. A kid deserved both parents. Brittany had been out of her teens when Dad died, so she couldn't really imagine her parents splitting up when she was a preschooler, but she did know the hole Dad's loss had been in her life. Would that be any less in a little kid? Most likely it would be more.

Not that Scarlett had lost her father. Treyan was still around. Not at the moment, of course, but in general. The little girl's life had been turned upside down.

"Where's my daddy?"

"He'll be back in a few minutes." Brittany poured all the

confidence she could muster into her voice. "Would you like me to push you on the swing until he gets here?"

Chris hauled a cooler to his truck while Gina carried one of the boxes, much lighter than it had been earlier. Treyan's vehicle was the only other one still in the parking lot.

Scarlett slid her hand into Brittany's. "Can mermaids swing?"

"I'm sure they can. You don't need to be able to move your legs separately to swing."

"I like playing mermaids." The little girl leaned on Brittany's arm.

Britt crouched. She'd shed the towel earlier and pulled a short, flared skirt on over her swimsuit. "Is it more fun than princesses?"

Scarlett stifled a yawn. "Maybe. But mermaids can be princesses, too. Can wolves be?"

"Can wolves be what?" Sometimes it was hard keeping up with the brain of a five-year-old.

"Can wolves be princesses?"

"Um. Only in pretend, I think. Real wolves live in a pack, and there is only one boss."

"The daddy."

That worked. Brittany nodded. "But a wolf mermaid would look pretty funny, don't you think? Would she have a furry fishy tail?"

Scarlett giggled and leaned heavier against Brittany. "That would be silly. Do wolves like to swim?"

No clue? "Not as much as little girls do."

"Oh." Scarlett rested her head against Britt's shoulder. "I love you, Miss Brittany," she said sleepily.

Oh, man. Talk about a melt-the-heart moment. Brittany

glanced around, but Treyan still wasn't in sight. She gathered Scarlett into her arms, carried her over to the picnic bench, and settled on it with the child snuggled against her.

Ava had told her she loved Seth's son, Leo, like she'd given birth to him herself. Britt had managed not to roll her eyes. There was no way that could be true. Maybe blood wasn't everything, but it was something. Maybe more important was knowing the child from birth.

Scarlett was five years old.

There was no way Brittany could love the child as though she was her biological mother. She thought of Kayla. It might be possible to love Scarlett as much as Kayla did, though. The other woman used her child as a pawn with Treyan. That wasn't love.

"Do you love me?" whispered Scarlett, her eyes shut.

How could Brittany deny the warmth in her chest and the tears pricking her eyes at the thought of this precious child? "I love you, Scarlett."

"Mmm." She snuggled closer, and Brittany tucked a towel around her.

It must have been a late night at the Ackerman residence. This kid was all but out cold.

And her daddy was still nowhere to be seen.

There was something soothing about a small child nestled trustingly against her. Brittany smoothed Scarlett's tangled hair, still slightly damp from the lake, away from her face. The little girl's lashes spread across her rosy cheeks, and her hand rested on Brittany's swimsuit strap.

All was well with the world. She and Treyan were building something surprisingly beautiful here in this small town. This child was part of that. Could Brittany be a good stepmom? She wouldn't be able to — wouldn't want to — replace Kayla. It would be a different relationship.

Charlie knew all about that. He'd loved Mom without reservation, and offered himself to each of the kids. Dominic had been easy. He'd already been engaged to Charlie's daughter. But for all of them, Charlie had been smart enough to know he couldn't replace Dad. He hadn't tried to. He'd just been there, ready and waiting, to forge a new relationship with each of them when they'd been ready.

Brittany was glad she'd opened up to him when she'd been home for Ava's wedding. Dad's death had nothing to do with Charlie. She'd known that all along, but she hadn't been ready to accept Charlie into her childhood home.

Charlie had his own house, bigger and fancier, but he was letting Dominic and Katri live there, because his teenage stepson — Mikey — hadn't wanted to move away from his friends. He'd had the master bedroom suite renovated and made a few other updates to the house.

He was a wise man. Brittany could learn from him. Kayla wasn't dead but had primary custody. Being in Treyan's life meant being in Kayla's. Well, Britt wasn't afraid of her. Hadn't she convinced Kayla to switch to a different yoga class than the Friday afternoon one? Kayla had likely agreed because she didn't want Scarlett spending that hour with Brittany every week. Whatever the reasoning had been, Brittany's intervention had the desired effect.

She could manage Kayla long-term if she needed to.

Treyan was worth the sacrifice.

Brittany shifted on the hard bench, and the little girl in her lap let out a contented sigh.

Was she in love with Treyan Ackerman? Not likely. A person didn't fall in love in three and a half months.

Although Ava had. So had Mom. And Jasmine and some of the other cousins.

Okay, scratch that. Love could be quick.

Acknowledged.

That didn't mean Brittany was in love. Love was patient, kind — what all did 1 Corinthians 13 claim? Was it even about human love or about God?

She didn't much want to think about God's perfect love. She'd been pushing that away for a long time.

Like she'd pushed away her stepdad. Only God had far more right to her love than Charlie did. God had created her... yeah, she wasn't walking the walk or talking the talk right now, but that didn't mean she didn't believe the basics.

So... why was she so stubborn about going her own way?

It was a whole lot easier to stay on the path than admit she'd been wrong and get herself turned around.

TREYAN PAUSED AT THE WATERFRONT. He'd been gone longer than he'd expected, trying to jog off his frustration. He hadn't expected the party to be over and the pavilion cleared out except for Brittany and Scarlett.

He took a deep breath and drank in the sight of them. Both seemed to be asleep; his baby girl cuddled close in Brittany's arms, her messy curls half out of their ponytail and strewn across Brittany's chest.

If only.

But it was not to be. He couldn't ask Brittany to enter the mess that was his and Kayla's. She might — or might not — be tempted to give up on her dream of taking New York City by storm, but he couldn't let her. Six months in, a year at most, and she'd be sick of Kayla's drama and wishing she'd followed her original plan.

He wasn't worth it. He knew that. He'd known before Kayla told him so a hundred times. He didn't deserve happiness. His only goal in life was to make sure Scarlett didn't suffer too much for her parents' broken marriage.

Watching the two of them wasn't doing his heart any good. Treyan took a fortifying breath and strode across the sand, then the grass, coming to a stop beside them.

"Sorry about that. I've got her from here."

Brittany blinked up at him, her eyes quickly focusing on his. Her hand caressed Scarlett's back. "You okay?"

He glanced at his daughter. "She's got a mess. She said he H-I-T her." He spelled out the word just in case Scarlett wasn't as asleep as she looked.

Brittany's eyes widened. "No way."

"That's what she claims. Says she has no place to go."

"There's always somewhere."

"You'd think." He scrubbed his hand through his hair. "She's trying to drag me into it."

"You don't have to let her."

"That's true to a point."

"I think your responsibility to her ended with the divorce."

"Except for..." He poked his chin toward his daughter.

"Responsibility for your child is not remotely the same thing as responsibility for your ex."

Brittany's voice had risen. Scarlett stirred then nestled in deeper.

"No, I know it's different."

"Then...?"

She was waiting for him to say Kayla's problems had been hers to make and were hers to solve. And that was all true, but... but, what?

He didn't want to talk about this over his daughter, whether she was awake or asleep. He didn't want to talk about this at all. He didn't even want to live this life.

Should've thought of that a decade ago, buddy.

Yeah, yeah. Just like Kayla had made her own mistakes, so had he. Mostly different ones, not that it mattered in the end.

"How are you planning on helping her?" Brittany's eyebrows peaked, and the gentian blue of her eyes looked somehow colder than it had for quite a while.

"I told her I'm keeping her"— he poked his chin toward Scarlett —"until she's settled again somewhere else."

"What kind of someplace else are we talking?"

Treyan shook his head. "I don't know." But it was a good question. Would Kayla stay in Galena Landing, town of two exes? She hadn't married Tyrell Burke, but she'd been with the narcissistic loser for three years. She couldn't just leave town, though, not without the court's permission. They had a custody agreement that outlined when each of them was the parent on deck.

Legal agreements could be changed. Would Kayla try?

Would he let her? He should never have agreed to the one they had in the first place.

His gaze fell on his little girl, and he reached for her. Brittany didn't let go quickly, and they nearly had a tug-of-war over Scarlett. But then his sleepy child was in his arms, her little arms settling around his neck.

"I love you, Daddy."

"Love you, too, pumpkin."

"I'm not a pumpkin. I'm a wolf mermaid."

What on earth? Chuckling, he rubbed her sweaty back, and she pressed against him. Yeah, he was going to do whatever it took to protect this sweet, amusing child.

Brittany rose to her feet, still looking at him from unreadable eyes. "I need to get back up to the house and help with the cleanup."

Should he tell her Chris said he and Ethan would be covering that? She'd find out. "Thanks for staying with Scarlett."

"You're welcome. It wasn't a long time, and she slept most of it. She must've had a late night."

Was that a dig at his parenting? "A bit. Mitchell's boys were running around upstairs until ten o'clock. They sounded like a herd of elephants."

"Guess you can't wait to get into your own place, then." She looked just past his shoulder.

"Yeah, it will be nice." For an entire week, he'd been dreaming of sharing it with her, but that pleasant vision had dissipated with a poof half an hour ago.

Thanks for ruining my life a second time, Kayla.

Was it fair to blame her? Sure, it was. She'd reminded him that she'd always have the power to derail his plans.

Brittany shifted from one foot to the other. "Well, I'll see you around. At the office Monday?"

She was getting the hint. He'd come right out and say it more clearly if Scarlett wasn't here. Wouldn't he? Yeah, they'd be hard words, and it would be better not to have the conversation in Town Hall. "We need to talk. We could meet tomorrow evening."

Meet. What a dumb word. Last week it had been a date. Now it was a meeting? Lame.

"I'm headed home for the rest of the weekend."

Had she told him before? His heart sank. He'd bet anything she'd just made the decision right this minute. "Okay, well, have a good visit."

"Thanks." She turned away.

He should offer to drive her back to Gina's, but it was only a few blocks, and she'd be fine. Ms. Independence was always fine.

"Text me when you get there."

She waved a hand over her shoulder as she strode across the grass.

Had that been a yes? Would he hear from her?

Probably not. Probably not until he'd evicted Kayla from his life, once and for all. So... never, then. He couldn't do that in good conscience.

His chest tightened in loss as his gaze followed Brittany, memorizing every line. How her tanned legs disappeared into that short, flirty skirt. How her long, dark hair had been twisted up into a clip, exposing the back of her racer-style swimsuit. She was gorgeous. She was smart. She was everything he'd ever dreamed of.

And he had to let her go.

"Daddy?" Scarlett whispered against his neck.

Enough staring at what might have been. He turned and grabbed Scarlett's towel from the nearby picnic table. It looked like that was everything. Just him and his baby girl. "Time to go home, pumpkin."

"To our own new house?" She straightened a little, looking at him.

"No, it's not coming until after school starts, remember?" Should he tell her she'd be staying with him for at least the next week or two? He hesitated. Not yet. He'd confirm with Kayla tomorrow afternoon and see how things were going. Maybe she'd get her life arranged by then.

He doubted it.

But she'd moved out of their apartment in town hastily once she'd decided to, so she had that sort of decisiveness in her. This would be a good time to exercise her gift.

And he'd be there to pick up the pieces she left behind, like their daughter's crushed heart.

It was what Treyan did best.

TWENTY-THREE

Brittany should feel some guilt for letting Treyan think she was headed to Spokane. The idea had flitted through her mind, but she didn't actually have a home there anymore. Not since she and Ava had given up the apartment in June. She could go to Mom's, but no. There'd be too many questions, and she had too few answers.

Gina and Chris's house was home for now, right? She hadn't actually lied.

She let herself into the house. Low murmurs came from upstairs.

"Need a hand with anything?" she called from the landing.

Gina appeared in the kitchen doorway. "Chris will be home soon to finish the cleanup. Thanks for all your help, by the way. The games and especially that cake. It was a huge hit."

"You're welcome." Brittany forced a smile. "It turned out pretty well, I think. One of the moms will probably order something similar for her daughter's birthday in August."

"You could launch a complete custom cake business!"

Play it cool. Brittany shrugged. "I'm just goofing around for the summer, remember?"

"I was hoping you might change your mind. Treyan—"

"Yeah, well, that's not happening. In fact, I've got some résumés to send off tonight, so if you don't need me for anything..."

Gina made a moue of disappointment. "Aw, so soon?"

"There's only two months left. I'd like to see if I can get a few interviews for when I fly out for a couple of days."

"You're serious about New York."

Brittany raised her eyebrows. "Haven't I been saying that all along?"

"Well, yes, but I hoped and prayed you didn't really mean it. I was sure you'd fall in love with Galena Landing."

No, but she might've fallen in love with one tall, kinda cute farmer, given a bit more time. Good thing she'd figured out his ex-wife would always come first before it was too late. Kayla was Scarlett's mother, so it made sense.

No, it didn't. There was something Brittany was missing.

She took a deep breath. "It's been a busy day. I'll be downstairs if you need me for anything."

A troubled frown crossed Gina's face, but she nodded.

Brittany took the downward steps at half the speed she usually did. Whether it was all the sun and water and excitement or the downer of the unsatisfying talk with Treyan when he finally returned, she didn't know, but she was tired. Definitely too tired for a three-hour drive.

Treyan hadn't exactly been speaking clearly in his attempt to keep Scarlett from comprehending what he said. Which meant Britt couldn't be completely sure, either.

What she did know was that there had been a pleasant, carefree man hanging out with Chris while the girls played mermaid games in the water. That man was still there while the kids were loading their plates, but he'd vanished — literally and then figuratively — when his phone rang. A very different man, guarded, dejected, had come back an hour later.

A man who didn't feel inclined to explain his train of thought.

Not that there was much he could say to soften the realization he still felt such a deep loyalty to Scarlett's mother. He'd been married to her for how long? Three or four years? Possibly longer. Just the fact that he still lived in his brother's basement and shared kid duties should have been all the clues Brittany needed. The man was still in limbo.

He'd bought a house, though. Didn't that prove he was moving on from Kayla? It had seemed like he was envisioning Brittany there, not his ex. But she'd obviously been wrong.

Brittany had been some sort of summer fling to Treyan. He hadn't seemed the sort, but evidence was evidence. To be true to the idea, he should have let it go a little longer and then waved goodbye when she left for the East Coast. As it was now, things were going to be mighty awkward in the office for the next couple of months.

Well, she'd figured out once before how many of her work hours she could spend elsewhere. There'd be meetings galore; she'd make sure of that. She wasn't a regular employee, so the mayor allowed her quite a lot of flexibility in her schedule. Brittany wouldn't be able to avoid Treyan completely, but she could cut contact by an easy fifty percent if not more.

Was it possible she was reading into this?

Maybe?

But probably not. His words — his distance — had felt like a bucket of icy water in her face.

Jeff's face superimposed on Treyan's. *Sorry, babe. Jenna and I are working things out. It's been fun.*

She hadn't guessed Jeff was married. Turned out he hadn't even been separated, just getting the cold shoulder at home. Why hadn't she ever thought to wonder why he never took her back to his place? She assumed it was for the same reason she hadn't invited him to the apartment: because she had a roommate. Only she hadn't been *married* to her roommate. Secretive trysts in Coeur d'Alene had seemed so romantic. At least until her boss found out she'd been sleeping with a client. Until Jeff chose Jenna and hung Brittany out to dry alone.

Brittany had been so stupid last winter. But she'd also been foolish this spring and summer. She'd had a plan, and she'd swerved from it. She'd fallen for the first man to give her a second look like some kind of giddy schoolgirl. A *farmer* of all things.

She dropped back across her bed and stared at the ceiling. She had no business falling in love with anyone. She'd been ricocheting from one relationship to the next for an entire decade. How did the song go? Looking for love in all the wrong places.

That was pretty much her theme song. She should get it tattooed on her body, likely in an unmentionable location so she'd be reminded not to strip down ever again. Not that

Treyan had hinted at that. He was one of the good guys, or at least he would be if he'd only quit trying to solve Kayla's self-inflicted problems.

That sounded mean, even in the privacy of Brittany's head.

Treyan was a fixer. That wasn't a bad quality, really. But it meant he was still trying to absolve himself from the guilt of his failed marriage.

She wasn't one to talk. She'd accepted a six-month banishment to cover up her own indiscretion and protect her reputation. So Mom and Nonna and Ava and all the rest wouldn't find out what a loser she was. And to get a good reference instead of being fired.

"I know this isn't who you really are, Brittany." Janice had leveled a look at her. "You have so much potential. Do you really want to throw aside a promising career with such thoughtlessness?"

She'd hung her head.

"I'd be completely within my rights to fire you."

Hope warred with dread. Had she mistaken the tiny hint of an unspoken *but*?

"But I think you may have learned your lesson. I'm willing to give you a chance to prove it."

Brittany had looked up at that. "Ma'am?"

"My sister is the mayor of a small town in northern Idaho that no one has ever heard of. Galena Landing. They're trying to invigorate a long-dormant farmers market there, but no one has the time or the skills to tackle the project. Really, the entire town needs to be put on the map. It's quaint and rather sweet, if you like small towns."

Clearly, Janice and Brittany were both on Team City, but

why this town had been inserted into Britt's dressing-down was unclear. It couldn't be accidental, though. Janice Durant was too sharp for that.

"She's been asking me for some marketing support, but there's not much I can do from here." Janice straightened folders on her desk then met Brittany's gaze. "That's where you come in. I'm offering you a deal."

Brittany wasn't sure where this was going. It sounded a bit like hope... but also like banishment. "Ma'am?"

"You have a choice, Brittany. You can go to Galena Landing — I believe you even have some extended family there — and work for my sister for six months. You will pull a salary from the town and you will do your very best work. If she can give you a solid reference at the end of that time, I will do the same."

That dinky little town she'd only seen a handful of times? Her relatives usually attended family events in Spokane, so there had been little need to visit. Protests formed on Brittany's tongue, but she'd been smart enough not to voice them. "Where's the choice in that?"

Janice nodded. "Or I'll let you go, along with the reasons for it. At that point, you'll be free to sink or swim completely on your own merits."

So... everyone would find out Brittany had slept with a client. Not just any client, but a married one. Her protests that she hadn't known wouldn't have absolved her. Even without that added nail in her coffin, it looked bad. It looked bad because it had *been* bad. She'd acted selfishly. Immaturely. There were no two ways about it.

"Six months in Galena Landing... and a good referral at the other end?" New York would be far enough away from

Idaho and Washington. She could start over where no one knew anything if only she had glowing references.

Janice smiled. "I thought you'd see it my way. You can drive out this weekend and start Monday."

Now, Brittany stared at the ceiling in Gina's spare bedroom.

When was she going to learn not to let her heart wander around and fall for just any dude who gave her a second look?

THE HOUSE WAS FINALLY QUIET. Scarlett lay asleep in her basic beige basement room, and Mitchell's boys' running footsteps had stopped a bit ago.

It was time to face his brother.

Treyan didn't want to. His life was a mess, and he didn't really want to listen to his big brother's platitudes. But they were a team, and everything one of them did affected the other.

He peeked into Scarlett's room, where she lay sprawled on her back only half covered by a blanket, her tangled hair across her pillow. He sent up a silent prayer for his little girl, for wisdom, for... everything. He couldn't dwell on the hurt in Brittany's eyes this afternoon. He couldn't drag her into this mess with Kayla. She was young and innocent and didn't deserve it. It wasn't her series of mistakes. It wasn't her fight.

Mitchell stood at the kitchen sink washing up the pots

from dinner hours ago and glanced over when Treyan exited the stairwell. "Hey."

Treyan grabbed a tea towel and reached for one of the saucepans. "Hey."

"What's up? You've been really quiet since the party Scarlett couldn't stop talking about."

"She had a good time. What she doesn't know is that Kayla called me." He glanced toward the hallway to the boys' rooms, but it was still quiet.

"Kayla calls all the time."

"Not *all* the time."

Mitch angled his head in acquiescence. "It's not exactly rare. What did she want?"

"She said Burke hit her."

Mitch let out a low whistle. "That's bad."

"Yeah. I told her to get out of there."

"Let me guess. She thought that was an invitation."

"Pretty much. She didn't take it well that she's not welcome here. I mean, she never liked the farm even when she pretended to love me. She certainly isn't going to like it any better now."

"She's been living on Burke's farm for three years."

Treyan clunked the pot down in the cupboard. "Okay, you're right. It's me she hated. The farm was just a handy cover."

"Bro." Mitch rested his hand on Treyan's forearm. "You can't save her. She has to save herself."

"What if she won't? Can't?"

"That's on her. Look, I know that sounds terrible, but it's still true. You guys are divorced. She chose Burke. You have no right to go in there and whisk her away. She has to do it herself."

Treyan met his brother's gaze. "What about Scarlett?"

"What about..." Realization swept Mitchell's eyes. "Oh, man. I wasn't thinking of her."

"I get it. I get that Kayla has to figure things out on her own, but there's two things happening here. One, she *did* reach out for help by calling me. Does that mean I have any right or responsibility to interfere?"

Mitchell opened his mouth.

Trey held up his hand. "And two, what if Burke takes out his frustration on my daughter? I can't let her go back to that house, knowing he's volatile. What kind of father would I be?"

"Did Kayla say if this was ongoing or a one-time thing?"

"Does it matter?"

"Well, kind of. I mean, these things tend to progress. Lindsey had some counseling training, if you remember. It usually starts out occasional, with profuse apologies, but it often escalates. So, my question is, what stage is she at here?"

Made sense. Treyan tried to recall the conversation's details. "She didn't say. She spent most of the call trying to convince me she should crash here for a while. She'd heard I bought a modular as though that was some kind of special invitation to her."

Mitchell grunted.

"And then arguing with me when I said I was keeping Scarlett until she left Burke."

"You have a nine-to-five job, bro."

"I know it. But what else am I supposed to do?"

"You haven't thought this through."

Treyan leaned back against the counter and skewered his brother with a look. "Okay, wise one, what do you think I should do?"

"Pray."

"I'm doing that."

"Wait."

He shook his head. "I can't wait. Either I hand Scarlett back to Kayla tomorrow as I do every Sunday at five, or I don't."

Mitchell huffed. "Look, I'm willing to help you out. You know that. But I can't add watching Scarlett for forty hours a week while you're at work."

"I've got some vacation time coming to me. And then school starts in a couple of weeks. It will work out."

"You told me yesterday you were swamped with preparations for the referendum."

And wasn't that the truth. "The timing is less than ideal, I'll grant you. But, seriously, what are my options? I can't take the risk Burke will let his frustrations with Kayla dump out on Scarlett. I can't."

Mitchell turned back to the sink and chewed his lip while he scrubbed out the last pot.

The silence was rather welcome, since Mitch had quit arguing and was contemplating real answers. Trey wiped a couple of knives dry and snapped them to the magnetic rack high on the wall.

"Did you talk to Brittany about it? Get her perspective?"

Why had Treyan ever trusted his brother with the acknowledgment he found Brittany attractive? "There's no real point." Somehow, he got the words past the lump in his throat.

"She's your girlfriend." Mitchell studied him for a second as he pulled the sink plug. "Isn't she?"

"I can't drag her into this thing with Kayla. That's not fair to her."

"Her words or yours?"

Treyan would ignore the sarcasm there. "Look, I'm no catch, okay? Just ask Kayla. I'm not worth sticking around for. Brittany wants to move to New York. I'm just a summer diversion for her."

"Her words or yours?"

"Shut it."

"Okay, here's the thing." Mitchell glanced at the clock. "You've got about twenty hours before you're supposed to show up for the hand-off. You need to ask people to pray for wisdom. The prayer chain at the church is a good place to start."

Treyan shook his head and snorted. "Right. And tell everyone Burke is abusing Kayla? If she denies it — poof — it becomes slander."

His brother's shoulders slumped. "And she's likely to deny it."

"Bingo."

"I don't like this whole thing, bro."

"You think I do?"

"We gotta pray."

Trey had been. He'd do more, but it didn't feel like enough. And was there any reason God would answer this prayer?

TWENTY-FOUR

O n Sunday morning, Brittany feigned a headache, which wasn't a complete lie. The Zimas headed off to church without her.

She drove down to the gas station convenience store and stocked up on all the artery-clogging food she could find. A ginormous cherry-flavored fountain drink. Bags of chips and candy and crappy cookies. A dozen breaded, deep-fried wings and a box of greasy fries that would probably be cold and congealed by the time she got back to the house.

Then she holed herself up in her basement room with her laptop open. Time to get serious about finding a job in the Big Apple.

Yeah, it was a bit early, since she wouldn't be free to accept a position for two months. Maybe the right firm would wait for her.

Probably not. It wasn't like her credentials were *that* amazing. But she could put a favorable spin on her résumé. Maybe she should do that first. She didn't really have one at all, since she'd interned with Janice Durant in college and been offered a full-time right afterward.

Brittany ran a search for templates, found one that seemed to hint at graphic design instead of financial consultant, and began filling in her own details.

It wasn't impressive. Not really. She'd done a lot of excellent work for Jeff's commercial construction company, but she couldn't very well use him as a reference. Yeah. She should've been thinking more clearly back then. Thought about how embracing his advances would affect her career. If she'd kept things professional, she'd still be working for Ms. Durant.

She'd be out a roommate, though. Ava would still have married Seth.

Brittany leaned back in her chair. Maybe Gabriella would have moved in with her after Ava's wedding, though she seemed content living with Mom and Charlie until after graduation. What would Britt have done?

It didn't matter. She'd made all the stupid choices and none of the good ones. As far as Mom knew, Brittany was here to pad out her résumé because Janice Durant liked her well enough to pave the way to a more rounded portfolio to help her get to New York.

Mom knew nothing of Jeff. Knew nothing of Brittany's lifestyle that had led to banishment, rather than opportunity.

But Jeff wasn't the problem here. Treyan was. And Mom had met him on several occasions when she and Charlie had brought the coffee truck up on a Saturday. Did Mom know her daughter was falling for her office-mate? Mom was astute. She'd probably guessed.

So, the question was, could Brittany dump these issues on Mom and get some wisdom without delving into the real reasons she'd left Spokane four months ago to start with?

Maybe. But the God talk was going to come regardless. Faith was the foundation of Mom's life. Her first question would be whether Brittany had prayed about the situation. If not, she should do that. If she already had, then what had God shown her?

No point talking to Mom. Not if Brittany already knew what Winnie Kuyper Santoro Jalonen would say.

Prayer.

Brittany stared at the ceiling, her eyebrows raised.

Was God really there? And if He was, did He care? And if He cared, was He mean enough to figure she should sink or swim on her own merits?

The ceiling tiles mocked her.

According to Dad, God would never ridicule her. He'd told her so many times that as much as he'd loved her, God loved her far, far more.

I miss you, Daddy.

Tears dribbled down Brittany's cheeks. How could it have been okay with God to let Alberto Santoro get hit by a drunk driver and then die a few days later? To let five kids finish growing up without their beloved father? To let a woman grieve the loss of her husband?

Mom hadn't mourned long enough, and that had hurt, too. That part, Brittany was mostly over. Charlie was a good guy. He'd been nothing but steady in his love for Mom. He'd given the five of them room to grieve and then accept him however they could.

Michael had been the most opposed at first. The poor kid

had seen Dad's crushed truck minutes after the accident, before the emergency teams had descended on the site. But once he'd accepted Charlie in Mom's life, he'd been all in. The two of them had forged a strong bond since.

Maybe Brittany was a little jealous of that. Of Gabby's relationship with Charlie, too. But she'd made her own tentative offer of acceptance a month ago, so her problem wasn't with Mom or Charlie. Not anymore.

No. It was *God* who'd deserted Brittany. Deserted all of them, even though it seemed only Brittany still held a grudge.

She'd looked for acceptance. Looked for love. She'd only found sex. Duncan. Jeff. Where would it end?

Treyan didn't fit that profile. He was a Christian. Yeah, he struggled more than what most believers seemed to, but like Mom, he clung to faith.

Why was that so attractive?

She shouldn't be thinking about Treyan Ackerman. Not after he'd withdrawn so totally yesterday afternoon with no indication of any relationship at all moving forward. He was just another example of someone who'd seemed to care for her when convenient and then changed his mind.

Brittany wasn't worth loving. That's what all the evidence pointed to. The problem was with her.

Okay, fine, she could hear Mom's voice in her head. Could hear Ava's. If they knew the whole story, they'd say the problem wasn't her, intrinsically, but with the fact that she'd shut God out. That if she repented and renewed her relationship with God, everything would be a-okay.

But Dad had still died, even though Mom had hung onto her

relationship to God with everything in her. Even though Dad had been the best Christian on the planet, constantly sharing his faith with everyone who paused long enough to listen.

It had been a bit embarrassing at times, honestly. Even when she'd believed in a loving God herself.

Mom would point to the dozens of Dad's friends and acquaintances who'd become Christians after his death. As though that made up for Dad being gone.

Brittany counted the ceiling tiles. They represented that many layers between her and God. Yeah, He existed. She'd give Him that. The world was too hard to explain with the absence of a deity.

But loving?

She'd had some glimpses of hope in the past few weeks, talking to Charlie that night. Watching Treyan's faith in action.

But now? She just couldn't see it.

There wasn't anyone she could depend on. Not a man, clearly, not even Treyan. And also, not God.

It was all up to Brittany Lina Santoro to take care of her own interests.

And that meant she'd better make that résumé of hers as inviting as she could, because New York City was calling her name.

"Where are you?"

Treyan winced at the harsh tone in Kayla's voice over the phone. "Where are *you*?"

"Don't play games with me, Trey. In case you've forgotten, it's Sunday afternoon at five o'clock, so *of course* I'm at Lakeside Park to pick up my daughter."

"Where are you taking her?"

"Treyan."

He could almost hear her eyes rolling over the wireless connection. "Kayla." He mimicked her tone as he wandered into the other room, away from where Scarlett was coloring mermaid pages he'd printed from some site online. "We talked about this yesterday."

Kayla huffed. "I shouldn't have called you."

"Does he do it often?"

"Of course not! He wouldn't."

"But he did it once."

"Well, it was probably a misunderstanding. I knew he didn't want—"

"There's no excusing it, Kayla. A man who would hit a woman—"

"I told you. It wasn't a big deal. I'll be more careful."

"You shouldn't have to be more careful." Treyan pinched the bridge of his nose. "Lindsey worked with battered—"

"I'm not battered. Seriously, Treyan. Bring Scarlett to me now."

What was he supposed to do? It was Kayla's word against his, and she would deny having ever mentioned the abuse. Maybe... maybe she was right? It was a one-time thing?

He doubted it, though. Or maybe it had been... so far.

The loser wouldn't hurt a child, would he?

By driving Scarlett into town, Treyan was gambling that

Tyrell wouldn't touch her. He may have hit Kayla — Treyan would stake his life that his ex wasn't lying about that — but Kayla had probably challenged him. She was like that.

Scarlett would be safe.

Right?

But if Kayla reported him to the courts as though he'd abducted their child by refusing to return her, then Treyan could lose the access he had now. He'd chatted with Jared after church, and the police chief had cautioned him about evidence.

"Kayla, I don't like the situation."

"Me, either. You're supposed to be here. I can't hang around and wait much longer. Tyrell expects me home in a few minutes."

That got his attention. "What will happen if you're late?"

Silence.

Which explained everything, and yet nothing.

God?

But there was no clear answer from above, either. Which meant Treyan had to make a quick decision and stick with it. What was the lesser of all possible evils? "Okay, I'll be there in fifteen minutes. But you have to promise me you'll protect Scarlett. You have to promise me that you really are looking for a way out of Burke's life."

She huffed. "Ten minutes is all I've got. Move it."

The call ended.

He'd made a decision, but he hated every bit of it. It felt like he was sending his precious child into enemy territory.

He'd talk to Scarlett every evening. He didn't usually do that. Didn't usually interfere in Kayla's time with her, but he would this week. Maybe in the guise of reading her a bedtime story on FaceTime or something. Then he'd be able to see her. Get a sense of her comfort levels.

Kayla was going to hate it, but then she shouldn't have dropped her little bomb on him yesterday. But, if it was true, he needed to know. It *was* true. It had to be. Kayla wouldn't lie about something like this... but she'd lie to cover it back up.

"Okay, Scarlett. Time to go meet Mommy!" He forced as much enthusiasm as he could into his voice.

She peered up at him. "Can I take my coloring sheet?"

"Of course. Do you have gel pens at Mommy's?" He'd picked up a twenty-four-pack in Wynnton last week. Not as attractive as Brittany's cool one hundred, but the best he'd been able to find.

Scarlett shook her head with a most pitiful expression on her face.

Treyan should have bought two packs. "You can take these with you and bring them back next weekend, okay?"

She brightened. "Okay." Then she scrambled off the chair and sat on the floor to put on her sandals.

Treyan grabbed her backpack and tucked the package of sparkly pens in down the side. A minute later they were headed to the truck, Scarlett clutching her paper.

This was a mistake. A huge mistake.

But what else was he supposed to do?

A few minutes later, he watched Kayla closely as Scarlett dashed across the parking lot into her mother's waiting arms.

Was Kayla wearing more makeup than usual? It had been a long time since he'd really paid attention to that sort of thing. Kayla wore capris — that was normal, right? — and an unzipped hoodie over the T-shirt that covered her bulging belly.

Treyan couldn't imagine a man willing to abuse the woman carrying his baby, whether he particularly wanted to be a father or not. But how could he not? This was a mystery too deep for him.

"What are you staring at?" Kayla scowled at him with Scarlett pressed against her side.

"Just checking."

"Checking me out?" She cocked an eyebrow then a hip.

"As if." Treyan shook his head. "Just making sure you're okay."

"As you so eloquently put it, it's none of your business."

"Until you dragged me into it."

Scarlett looked between them.

His little girl didn't need to watch her parents argue, even though Treyan could barely manage to let it go. He nodded stiffly at Kayla. "Call me if you need to. Got a hug for Daddy, pumpkin?"

Scarlett dashed over as he crouched. She flung her arms around his neck. "I love you, Daddy."

He squeezed her tightly. "I love you, too, baby. See you Friday. Be good for Mommy."

She pushed away and rolled her eyes.

Kayla took Scarlett's hand and led her to the waiting car without a backward glance.

He hadn't talked to her about FaceTiming with a story. He'd text her later. Or should he just leave well enough alone? Would Tyrell suspect something if Treyan changed his habits now? How should he know?

The car pulled out of the parking lot.

Still, Treyan stood there on the gravel, feeling more bereft than he had since the early days. He'd never liked Tyrell Burke, even before the beekeeper had caught Kayla's eye. He didn't much like Kayla, either. But he'd become accustomed to the situation over the past three years. The twice-weekly hand-offs were part of the rhythm of his life.

He had no reason to hurry back to the farm. He didn't want to face his noisy nephews or his brother's questions.

But this park was filled with memories of Brittany as well. Of the farmers market she was helping rejuvenate. Of their dinners at The Sizzling Skillet across the way. Of the mermaid birthday party on the beach.

He couldn't drag Brittany into this whole thing with Kayla. He'd told her too much already. He'd dreamed too much.

Brittany had barely given him a scrap of hope that she'd remain in Galena Landing after September. He was just a temp boyfriend to her; someone to while away a few months while waiting for her *real* life to begin. She was a city girl, Spokane born and raised, and only headed for bigger places. Bigger dreams. A life that didn't include him.

He shoved his hands into his shorts pockets and strode for the lakefront pathway they'd strolled only a week ago.

How could he keep falling for the wrong kind of woman? He should have seen the signs with Kayla. He *had* seen the signs with Brittany but duped himself into moving forward anyway.

That took a special kind of stupid.

Or maybe, deep down inside, he knew he wasn't worthy of love. His mom had left. Kayla had. Brittany would.

Maybe he was sabotaging himself.

Really? That was the best he could come up with?

Treyan broke into a jog. He needed to pound some of these negative thoughts out of his body. If he had a punching bag, that might work, but he didn't. So he'd run.

Run and pray. He didn't run often, so it wasn't like he could pray out loud. Just breathing would be all he could manage. Besides, who knew when someone might be lurking nearby and overhear him? For true privacy, he needed his tractor cab out on the back forty.

For now, the prayers would be silent, but he had a lot to say, even so.

Lord? Are You there? Do You care about me or am I just a bumper in a pinball machine? A pawn in a celestial chess game?

No. God loved him. He knew that, at least at one level. He needed to anchor himself in fact, not feelings. But, oh, wasn't that easier said than done?

Where were the verses about God's love? John 3:16: *for God so loved the world that He gave His only begotten Son, that whoever believes in Him should not perish but have everlasting life.*

But that wasn't super personal. It spoke of God's love for everyone in a generic sense. God created humankind, after all. Genesis was pretty clear about that.

Treyan slowed to a walk. Wasn't there something in one of Pastor Ron's recent sermons this spring? There'd been a lot about contentment. Treyan had tried to tune it out, because it hadn't seemed all that applicable. How could he be content within this mess with Kayla?

He thumbed open the Bible app in his phone. The reference he was trying to remember was in Psalms somewhere. Psalm 18, maybe? David had been struggling — man, that guy's problems put Treyan's to shame, and yet David had kept looking to God in ways Treyan sure hadn't. David felt surrounded. Doomed. And what did the guy do? Sing a song to God!

Here it was, the part Treyan had tried not to remember, starting in verse sixteen: *He rescued me from the mighty waters and drew me to himself. Even though I was helpless in the hands of my hateful, strong enemy, you were good to deliver me. When I was at my weakest, my enemies attacked — but the Lord held on to me.*

Ah, here was the kicker in verse nineteen: *His love broke open the way, and he brought me into a beautiful, broad place. He rescued me — because his delight is in me!*

A beautiful, broad place.

Treyan thought of Ackerman Farm. The entire Galena Valley, really. It was that sort of a place.

There were cross-references in his app. He flipped from screen to screen, scripture to scripture, translation to translation until he landed on Psalm 119:45 in The Message. *And I'll stride freely through wide open spaces as I look for your truth and your wisdom.*

Was there anything more loving that God could do than place Treyan in a wide and pleasant place? It was here. It was now, regardless of Brittany or Kayla or anyone else.

If David could say these words while on the run from King Saul, how much more should Treyan be able to say them when his life was fairly close to picture perfect?

So, he didn't have a wife. Kayla hadn't wanted him. Brittany — he'd pushed her away, but she'd be leaving soon anyway, so it was for the best.

From here on in, Treyan Ackerman was going to focus on

his relationship with God. He was going to be thankful for the wide, pleasant places he found himself in. He was going to give thanks even when things weren't quite so wonderful.

He was not going to be distracted by a woman. Not by Kayla's mess with Tyrell, though he'd pray for her and be ready to step in if Scarlett needed him.

And he wouldn't be distracted by Brittany. That was going to be a lot harder, since she'd managed to worm her way into his heart in four short months.

Contentment. Basking in God's love. That was his calling.

CHAPTER
TWENTY-FIVE

Treyan was in meetings with the mayor and members of the town council all day Monday.

That should have been a relief, but it wasn't. Sure, Brittany had a pile of stuff on her own plate, as well, but apparently, she'd held out hope that there'd be a word of apology or explanation or, well, something. Anything.

She tried to focus on tomorrow's meeting with Paula. The market manager had chatted with most of the key vendors to gauge interest in an indoor fall market. Some were avidly eager, like the folks at Green Acres Farm. Others were cautiously interested. No one had told Paula it was a stupid idea, unless that person had come along since Paula had last emailed Brittany.

They needed a location in the worst way. Brittany knew it was too early in the grand scheme of the revitalized market to plan for a permanent location, but she couldn't help it. Wouldn't it be amazing if they had a place they could open wide to summer breezes and close off in inclement weather? Something like that would cost a pile of money.

Maybe there were grants available... but the Farm Fresh Market would need a track record first. They didn't look great on paper. There'd been an attempt over a decade ago but, with no clear leadership, squabbles had overtaken the vendors until the whole effort had dissolved.

Brittany drummed her fingers on the edge of her desk and stared out the window at the heavily leafed magnolia tree. Now, here they were again for a second try. With the town involved and Paula leading, this time they had clear, neutral management and a decent, if fair-weather, location. The number of vendors had doubled since last year, according to Paula's records, and there was considerably more bustle on a Saturday morning than a few months ago. But it was going to take more than two successful seasons to feel like the whole thing couldn't dissolve in a heartbeat.

And, if it didn't look solid on paper, it wouldn't look solid on Brittany's résumé, either. Yes, Ms. Kozak would give a good recommendation. Following that, Ms. Durant would, as well. But wouldn't it look best if the market itself was clearly a happening thing?

A bird flitted in the tree outside.

That was what Brittany wanted to do. Some flitting. It was time to leave Galena Landing, even while part of her wanted to stay. Okay, a lot of her had settled in, at least while she could dream of a future with Treyan. Now?

The market needed to look good to launch her to the next level. She'd done great work on the graphics. She'd gotten the market on the map, both in the valley and as far away as Wynnton... but would it stay visible and thriving after she stepped away? Paula was fine at the day-to-day stuff, but vision wasn't her strong point.

It was Brittany's.

Was she a control freak, or would Paula actually be okay without Brittany around?

She pulled to her feet and paced the small open space in the office.

Control freak.

Paula had more tools now. She'd dreamed up the fall market on her own. She'd be fine. The Farm Fresh Market would be fine. Galena Landing would be fine.

Treyan Ackerman would be *fine*.

No one needed her. But hadn't that been the whole idea? To swoop in like a fairy godmother, grant a few wishes with a bippety-boppity-boo, then swoop back out, leaving a better market behind her?

She'd found plenty of openings in New York City yesterday. The better ones required a minimum of five years' experience. She had three. While better than zero, it was definitely not the same thing as five.

And some of the possibilities didn't pay that well, considering the cost of living in the Big Apple. She'd scrounged through some rent-share ads online and... no thanks. She'd had such a great apartment with Ava. They'd actually each had a bedroom. Their kitchen, while half the size of Mom's, had been adequate, especially compared to the motel-style kitchenettes some of the New York flats had.

How would she ever go on a baking binge in a space like that, shared with three or four roommates?

She hadn't gone off the rails baking up a storm since coming to Galena Landing.

Brittany dropped back into her chair with a thump. It rolled a few inches. What was different here? In

Bridgeview, she'd rarely gone a month without spending an entire day baking all manner of cookies and cakes and muffins and whatever. Far, far more than she or Ava could ever hope to eat, even if they didn't mind gaining five pounds a week.

The sight of her overloaded car had been a regular enough sight at the Blessings Under the Bridge drop-off that Jessica and Mike had just grinned and helped her offload while they thanked her profusely.

What was different here?

The stress level, for one thing. That had all started with the boyfriend before Duncan. Intensified in Duncan's era. Rocketed in Jeff's era.

And now she'd settled into a rhythm of baking for the market every second week. That had taken the edge off her need to create, as well as padding her New York fund.

Which brought her right back to where she'd started from. Her reserve was negligible when placed against entry-level wages and apartments shared with strangers. She'd be lucky if her nest egg lasted a year. Would that be long enough to impress her new boss and earn a decent raise? Or were there so many hungry graphic designers out there that she could be easily replaced?

Grr. She poked at her mouse, reactivating her monitor. What had she been doing, again? Right. Prepping for a meeting with Paula tomorrow. They needed to find a location for the fall market. They needed to think outside the box.

Brittany pushed her chair away again. It was half an hour until quitting time, but her hours were more flexible than most because she attended meetings and the market outside general office hours. She'd take off now, which would prevent an awkward run-in with Treyan.

How had life come to this? Their relationship had seemed so promising a week ago.

Whatever. She'd weathered Duncan and Jeff and moving to salvage her reputation. She might've given those guys her body, but not her heart.

With Treyan, it was the opposite. She'd lost her heart. She huffed. Lost her *head*, more like.

This would never happen again. She'd move on in two months — a seemingly eternal two months — and be strong on her own. If not in New York, somewhere else.

Huh. That had never entered her thoughts before. Where else would be far from home, be cutting edge on the graphics design front, and still be an affordable place to live? That bore some thought.

For now, she needed to escape the office, escape from Treyan, escape from Gina, and from anything or anyone that made her question her decision to leave Galena Landing in her rearview mirror.

Could his week get any worse?

It was five o'clock on Thursday. He'd seen Brittany for all of ten minutes this week. She was just as adept at avoiding him as he'd been at avoiding her. It should have soothed his soul a bit to not be constantly reminded of what he was giving up, but instead, he just plain missed her.

Kayla had brushed aside Trey's repeated requests to FaceTime with Scarlett. He'd get his little girl tomorrow for the weekend, but did he dare ask a five-year-old pointed questions about her life with Mommy and Tyrell? He wanted to, but Jared cautioned him on planting ideas.

One more week until school started, and then she'd be in kindergarten. Then his new home was coming in just over a month. He still needed to finalize all the utility permits and hire someone to prepare the location. He could manage the site prep himself if it weren't such a busy season at the office. He did have accrued vacation time, but he couldn't, in good conscience, take it before the referendum had clarified the town's future plans.

And the referendum was two and a half weeks away. Every passing day, the load in his inbox from the naysayers increased. Yes, multiple emails a day were from the same group of a dozen or so loudmouths, but it still took time to sort the inbox to determine if there was anything new that needed to be addressed.

The proposal for the second stoplight was on hold until the final results for the fire hall were in place. Treyan had only so much brain power in a forty-hour week.

Now he exited town hall, ever-present briefcase in hand, and turned toward the parking lot. He stopped short at the sight of a wall of waving placards. *Vote No.*

Treyan took a deep breath as his gaze landed on Nolan Leask, who stood just a little ahead of the others, a smirk on his face. Didn't the man have a farm to run? Why was this much-needed project such a thorn in the man's side?

He'd never understand people. Leask might live ten miles north of town, but who, exactly, did he think would come to his rescue if flames engulfed his house or barn? Galena Valley Fire Department, that was who.

"Good afternoon, folks." Treyan forced a smile and took a few steps toward his truck.

The group closed the gap in front of him.

Where was the mayor, anyway? Or Mrs. O'Neill? Or anyone else from the offices on the second floor? Not that Treyan wished this group on anyone else, but it would be nice to feel a little less alone out here.

"Just call off the project already," one man said.

"We can't afford higher taxes. We're on a fixed income." That from an elderly lady.

Don't engage. No matter how badly he wanted to explain that higher insurance rates would likely be next down the pipe if a new and improved fire hall wasn't coming, Mrs. Shirka had already been told that, and she was here, anyway.

"Excuse me, please." Treyan took a few more steps. "Excuse me."

The group of maybe thirty people shifted back.

He pressed forward again.

"Don't you have anything to say for yourself?" Leask challenged with a sneer.

"Not today." Treyan met the older man's gaze squarely and took another couple of steps.

Mrs. Shirka gave him room, and he took it. It wasn't far now to his truck, the only one left in the lot. That answered that question. Everyone else had either left before the protestors grouped, or they'd been allowed passage. It was the head of the planning department they were targeting.

Would they barricade his truck in, too? Would he have to call Jared? He hoped not.

"You're just like every other politician." Leask puffed out his chest. "Just out to suck money from the people who are barely breaking even and do what you want with it."

"Mr. Leask, you've had your say, and you'll get another chance to do so publicly in a couple of weeks. May I ask you to reserve your words for that venue?"

"Well, I..." The guy turned his eyes on the rest of his group. "Nobody's listening to us."

"We're listening." Didn't he reply to every single email? Yes, they were rote replies, but hey, he looked at them all.

"Don't seem like it."

"I'm not going to explain myself or the town to you, yet again, here and now. You've had your public meetings. You've presented your case to council. You're had your articles in the Herald. You've got your way — a referendum. I suggest you line up your arguments and present them well that day to the community, and then accept the results."

"Will you?" Leask's chin came up in a belligerent gesture.

Treyan frowned. "Will I what?"

"Accept the results when we win, and you have to put your tail between your legs and skulk out of town?"

He blinked. "The people will choose. We'll *all* accept that decision when it comes down." And if this motley crew won, Treyan was *so not* going to take it personally and run from the results. He'd wait his two years, buckle back in, and try again. The longer this went on, the higher the cost of construction would rise, and the greater the chance their current structure wouldn't pass basic health protocols in the meanwhile.

Why didn't Leask and his cohorts understand how inevitable, how necessary, the new structure was? It wasn't like Treyan and the council hadn't laid out the pile of reasons why they were on borrowed time with the building that probably hadn't even met the building standards in 1952 when it had first been built.

"Excuse me, please."

This time, the protestors shifted out of his way and allowed him to reach his truck. He started the engine and watched in his rearview mirror as they huddled by the town hall steps. Leask waved his arms and nearly hit Mrs. Shirka in the head with his placard.

The drive home wasn't long enough to bring his heart rate down. Treyan was still fuming when he parked beside his brother's vehicle.

Mitchell came out of the greenhouse, followed by his two small shadows.

Treyan took a deep breath as he slid out. "Hey, guys."

"Hi, Unca Treyan!" shouted Lincoln. "The melons are ripe! We are having watermelon for supper!"

"That's great, buddy." Too bad the kid couldn't keep his shrill voice down. The headache that had barely stayed in check all week threatened to erupt. Treyan loved watermelon as much as the next guy, but he sincerely hoped there'd also be some solid protein with the meal. A bit of peace and quiet would not go amiss, either.

The boys elbowed each other as they dashed into the house.

"Those two." Mitchell shook his head at Treyan with a grin. "How was your day?"

"It could have been worse, but I'm not entirely sure how."

Mitch's eyebrows shot up. "Oh?"

"It was rough, and then Leask led a protest at town hall as I was leaving. Who put a burr under that guy's saddle, anyway?"

"Was Burke there?"

Trey shook his head. "Thankfully, no. He may support the 'no' campaign, but he doesn't stoop to actually align himself with Leask."

"Small mercies."

Treyan squished his thumb and finger together. "Very small."

"Do you think they've swayed the community?"

"I don't know. I hope not. They'll only be putting off the inevitable."

"Maybe the fire hall needs to host an open house before the referendum so that folks like Leask and Burke can actually see for themselves what they're putting their trust in."

"Not a bad idea. But they say their trust is in the firefighters, not in the building."

Mitchell huffed. "The volunteer crew is topnotch."

"It is. They're amazing, considering the space they have to work with. But I'll talk to the mayor and the fire chief and see if they think an open house might help the cause." Treyan jabbed his brother's shoulder. "Thanks."

"How're things with Brittany?"

He glared at his brother. "There are no *things* with her."

"I'm sorry."

Treyan's frustration faded slightly. "Not your fault." It was his own. He'd known better, but he'd still fallen under her influence. This time, walking away was on him... though he knew she planned to herself, so he was only hastening the inevitable.

Too much pressure. Work. Kayla. Brittany.

Mitchell thumbed toward the market garden. "Have time to till the gardens tonight?"

Sure. Why not? Add the farm to the pressure cauldron, but at least it would give him plenty of time to think while he drove in circles.

Thinking could be painful.

TWENTY-SIX

P aula tapped her pen against her ever-present notebook. "I don't think Arleigh's greenhouse is ideal."

"But we haven't found anything better for this season." Brittany took a sip of her iced tea and glanced around the crowded bakery. It was probably only this busy because it was air-conditioned, and the August heat hadn't let up yet. "The only ideal space would be one we designed for this purpose."

This town needed more than a market venue. How about a dedicated coffee shop? Sort of like the Bridgeview Bakery and Bistro, which was the heart of her neighborhood back home.

No. Not home. The place where she'd been born and raised and where most of her family still lived. That set of owners had created a vibrant hub, unlike this rather tired, outdated bakery in Galena Landing.

Her cousin should open a coffee shop here. Except Gina

was a nurse who loved her job with the elderly town residents.

It would probably cost a ton of money to start a business, anyway. Probably as much as the market building she'd doodled in her long, boring evenings this week. But her stepdad was pretty rich. Would Charlie invest if she asked him?

It didn't matter. Brittany was going to leave in six weeks, and there wouldn't be any real reason to return. She'd managed just fine for twenty-four years, visiting her uncle and aunt's home only a handful of times. It would be even easier to avoid in the future, since she was no longer a dependent being told to get in the backseat because they were going somewhere.

Maybe she'd drop off her sketches with the mayor before she left town. Who knew? Someone might find some inspiration in her work in ten years and pick up the permanent market project. Or not. She wouldn't care.

Except she would.

Brittany drained her glass. "Let's go have a look at Arleigh's place."

"Now?" Paula looked up.

"Sure, why not? She'll probably be there, right? Let's drop by."

After a moment, Paula shrugged and stood. "I'll drive."

"Okay."

A few minutes later they'd climbed into the overheated SUV. It wouldn't cool before they got to the greenhouse.

As they drove, Brittany realized she didn't know Paula very well outside of the market and Green Acres connections. "Have you ever been married?"

The SUV swerved a little as Paula pivoted to stare at her. Thankfully, she recovered before hitting the stoplight at the corner. "A long time ago."

Interesting. "What happened, if you don't mind me asking?"

The other woman's mouth tightened.

"Never mind." An ugly divorce wasn't the sort of thing Brittany needed to know. Just look at Treyan's mess with Kayla. "It's none of my business."

"He was a pedestrian struck by a police car chasing a suspect in a bank robbery."

Wow. Brittany leaned back. "I had no idea."

"In New York."

She gulped. It could have happened anywhere, of course. Even in Galena Landing, not that Brittany suspected either of the local detachment's officers knew how to drive at high speed. Obviously, the NY cop hadn't been able to control his car, either.

"I'm sorry."

"That was the last straw for me with the city. I know you think it will be great there, but I can't figure out why more than eight million people want to live packed like stressed-out sardines." Paula gestured toward the lake as they crossed the bridge heading out of town. "Not when wide open places like this exist. Places where you can see some nature, see the sky, and see evidence of the existence of God."

Paula hit her signal light, slowed, and swerved into Arleigh's driveway, saving Brittany from having to reply.

She didn't really have an answer. She was an extrovert, and that meant she derived energy from being around other people. Right? That was what she'd always been told. Clearly, Paula was at the other end of the spectrum.

But the results of Britt's search for a shared apartment were sobering. Strangers jammed into those flats, practically on top of each other. It wouldn't be like sharing space with her cousin. It'd be crowded and probably co-ed. Could she really do this?

But what was the alternative? Not back to Spokane. And she couldn't stay in Galena Landing, either. Not since Treyan had frozen her out. She'd asked him point blank a couple of days ago if Kayla had left Tyrell. He'd said, "no," and walked away.

Brittany exited the car and looked around. A last-century trailer, a far cry from the manufactured homes she and Treyan had toured in Wynnton, sat tucked amid several tall cottonwoods. Two greenhouses with a small shed connecting them nestled near the riverbank. A small field of riotous bloom that nearly overwhelmed Britt's senses with a plethora of mixed fragrances lay beyond the mobile home.

She couldn't help stretching at the luxury of it all. Not the decrepit home, though it was cute in a vintage sort of way, but of all the glorious flowers turned toward the August sun.

Arleigh came out of the shed, stripping off a pair of gardening gloves. She wore overall shorts with a pink tank top beneath them, and her blond hair had been pulled into a ponytail... and come partially undone hours ago, by the looks of it.

She looked between them. "Hi. To what do I owe this honor?"

"I hadn't had a chance to see your operation yet." Brittany smiled. "Nice place you have here."

Arleigh shook her head but grinned. "Rental only, sadly. I mean, it's not much, but finding a few acres with greenhouses already on it was an amazing coup. I've had to sink some money into upgrades, and that's been hard since I don't own them."

"Sounds amazing, though. Paula says you're interested in hosting our fall market?"

"Maybe? I don't heat the greenhouses that time of year. Someday I'd like to overwinter some exotics, but I'm not there yet."

"Do you have a heating system, though? Can we cover the cost of running it through the fall, at least enough to keep the temperature above freezing?"

"I do have heat. I start seedlings in late winter, long before I can work the ground outside. In some ways, the timing is ideal in that you only need the space during my slowest time. But, I warn you, it's not cheap to heat."

"Do you have some numbers for us?" *Or a better idea?* But Brittany couldn't ask that.

"Sure." Arleigh pointed to a patio table on a pad of mulch beneath the cottonwoods. "We can have a seat over there. It's too hot inside this time of day with no AC."

Why had Brittany avoided making friends in Galena Landing? She could like Arleigh O'Neill, given half a chance. At first, it hadn't seemed worth the bother. Then she'd been too busy dreaming about Treyan to think about girlfriends. Now, when she was nearly ready to leave town, she knew she'd been shortsighted. Just because Arleigh's goals in life were clearly not similar to Brittany's didn't mean they didn't have a lot in common. For one thing, they both loved beauty.

Paula took the lead when they sat. Arleigh laid out her break-even numbers.

The manager winced. "We'd need at least ten more vendors than we have over the summer to meet that. I'm sorry."

Brittany leaned forward. "I think that's doable, but I also think our vendors would be willing to pay a higher stall fee for those twelve weeks."

Paula looked aghast, while Arleigh merely looked confused.

"First, don't let them pay by the week. They need to make a commitment to the whole season. If they miss a week, they don't get a refund."

"They won't like that," Paula warned.

"I think you're underestimating the potential for a fall market. I'd say we go for it. Ask all our current vendors for payment by September first. Meanwhile, we start advertising the expansion—"

"With what for money? We'll need every penny to heat the greenhouses." Paula turned to Arleigh. "Not that I think you're charging too much, but Galena Landing is a small town that—"

"That wants an extended market season," Brittany interrupted. "The *Galena Herald* will probably write it up as front-page news, so that's most of our advertising, right there. We'll make fliers. Downtown businesses will put them in their windows, and we can hand them out to shoppers every Saturday. Between all that, I'm sure we'll get more vendors *and* create some buzz from excited shoppers."

"And if we don't?"

"Then we give out refunds and call it a day." Brittany leaned into the chair and folded her arms over her chest.

Arleigh bit her lip. "Sounds foolproof. I won't be out a heating bill if we cancel before the market even moves in."

Paula opened her mouth and closed it again before finally nodding. "That could work."

Apparently, that was the highest praise Brittany was going to get for her genius. But Paula wasn't stingy with praise once it was proved.

Best of all, Brittany had a creative outlet designing those fliers, and she'd be in town long enough to see it pay off.

But not long enough to see the market in action.

TREYAN MADE sure to enter and exit the office along with other employees for the next week, but Leask and his crew didn't seem to be lurking. Maybe they felt they had their say already. Maybe they were scaling up in the background for the final public meetings that would be immediately followed by voting.

Then he'd know if he'd be presented as the town's hero or become the scapegoat Leask threatened to make him. Not that the entire project was his. Just that he'd somehow become the face of it.

Drat the fact that the only viable day for the open house at the old fire hall was a Saturday. Treyan hated that it encroached on his weekend with Scarlett. On the other hand, it meant he couldn't hang out at the Farm Fresh Market, and that was probably a good thing, though his kid was whining about missing her salted caramel cupcake. Mitch had offered to pick up half a dozen. Treyan wasn't sure he could eat one without choking on thoughts of Brittany.

He parked a few blocks away from the fire hall to leave room for the visiting public, even though half the town lived within easy walking distance.

"Good to see you, Ackerman." The fire chief, Simon Melnychuk, held out his hand at Trey's approach.

"Likewise." Treyan gave it a firm shake. "My daughter, Scarlett."

"Hey, little lady."

Scarlett half-hid behind Trey's leg. "I'm not a little lady. I'm a mermaid wolf."

"A...what?" Simon laughed. "Okay, then. Can't say I ever saw one before."

Treyan stroked Scarlett's hair. "She's one of a kind." He'd been watching carefully, but whatever was going on in the Burke household wasn't producing noticeable issues for her. He prayed every day that God would give him wisdom to know when or if he should intervene. It nearly killed him to send her back with Kayla on Sunday afternoons.

"Want to take the tour?" asked Simon. "Or, just a minute. I see a few people approaching. They might want to join us."

Treyan glanced toward downtown. No way. There was Leask's crew, waving their placards and making it difficult for pedestrians to pass. "Do I need to call the police?" he muttered.

"They're within their rights. Just barely." Simon fingered his phone. "I'll give Jared a heads-up just in case."

"Thanks. Better you than me."

"Better neither of us. Why can't they just back off and let the people have their say?"

"It shouldn't even have come to that." Treyan thumbed toward the aging clapboard building. "It should be painfully obvious to anyone with a pair of eyeballs that this project isn't a tax grab to make the town look good."

Simon shook his head. "You're preaching to the choir, man. I just can't figure out why this is such a huge hurdle to Leask and..." He glanced down at the top of Scarlett's head. "And you know who."

"Well, for TB, it's probably because it's my project." Treyan wasn't going to name Tyrell in front of Scarlett. Not in this context, anyway. "And you'll notice he keeps a low profile publicly. I think he's funding some of the actual costs, but they haven't accrued many of those that I can tell."

"And Leask?"

Treyan studied Nolan Leask as the farmer engaged with a middle-aged man on the sidewalk. "I wish I knew. He does own a couple of business properties in town, so he'll see a tax hike. On the other hand, so will everyone else in the tax base, and most of them are in favor, I think. I just can't figure out how he thinks you guys can work out of this indefinitely *and* protect his assets."

"I know, right?" Simon scratched his head as a man circumvented Leask's position blocking the sidewalk.

"Hey, mind if I have a look around?" asked the man.

"I was just about to give these two a tour, if you'd like to join us," Simon offered.

"Sure." The guy nodded at Treyan, obviously not realizing who he was.

That was totally fine by Treyan. He trailed behind Simon and the stranger and listened to the spiel. How they had no decontamination space. How they had no safe storage for chemicals. How the wooden building itself was a fire hazard.

Physician, heal thyself.

Treyan couldn't help but think of the biblical phrase in this context. This fire station wouldn't even be capable of rescuing itself.

The fellow asked questions about the structure and building codes then asked to see the mockups for the new building. Treyan took over on that part, freeing Simon to head back to the truck bay to chat with more curious townspeople.

One thing was clear, they needed to offer more opportunities for residents to tour the facilities so they felt invested. Treyan might have lived in the area for eight years, but he didn't know half the people who were hanging around today. He knew more of Leask's crew than the others.

He turned to the man he'd been chatting with. "I don't believe we've met. I'm Treyan Ackerman. How long have you been in Galena Landing?

The man shrugged and gave a deprecating smile. "I don't live here. I'm in construction and was just curious about what's happening here. That's all."

"Ah, I see." And to think Treyan had wasted half an hour on someone who couldn't even vote. "Well, thanks for stopping by."

The guy extended his hand and gave Treyan's a firm shake. "Name's Jeff Sutherland out of Spokane."

"Sutherland Commercial Construction?" That was one of the companies that had entered a bid.

"Yeah. I hope you don't think less of me for coming out in person. It seemed too good of an opportunity to get a real feel for the town and for the project."

"Fair enough. I hope we've answered your questions adequately."

"You have." Jeff thumbed out to where Leask and his placard had a few more people stopped. "How can anyone look at this building and think a new structure isn't necessary?"

"You've got me there."

"One more thing. Do you mind pointing me to the lot where the new build is going? Does the town already own the land?"

Treyan hesitated. It wasn't exactly confidential information. "Sure. It's just up the highway across from the Super One."

"Thanks." The man took a few steps then looked back. "Say, you work for the town, you said? You wouldn't happen to know a gal by the name of Brittany Santoro, would you? Word has it she moved up here a few months ago."

Why did this dude want to know? Trey narrowed his gaze at him but couldn't get a read. Bland face as though it didn't really matter. But if it didn't matter, why had he asked? And why was he still standing there expectantly?

Treyan wasn't into lying, but was the truth always necessary?

"Miss Brittany is one of my favorite people." Scarlett had been so quiet Treyan had nearly forgotten his little shadow was nestled against his side.

Sutherland's gaze sharpened at the little girl. "Is that so? Is she a good friend of yours?"

Scarlett nodded. "She has *so* many sparkly gel pens."

"Sounds like the same Brittany, all right." The guy laughed and raised his eyebrows at Trey. "And if your kid knows her, you must, as well. What does your *wife* think of her?"

Treyan fell back a step as he stared at Jeff. "My wife?" What did Kayla have to do with this? What was the guy insinuating?

"I shouldn't say this in front of a kid, but you should know. Britt's a home-wrecker."

Anger surged up, begging to come out in a punch to the guy's smooth-talking face. He couldn't know the same Brittany he did, even if the name and the gel pens matched.

Jeff chuckled and lifted a hand as he walked away. "I was thinking of looking her up while I'm in town. Maybe I still will. She can't be serious about a country bumpkin like you."

Trey's fists tightened at his sides. He should say something professional. Tell the guy to have a nice day. Thank him for coming to the open house. But there were no words for this moment.

"Ow, Daddy."

He released Scarlett's hand. He'd probably all but broken her little bones. "I'm sorry, pumpkin." Then he winced, because a nickname like pumpkin sounded too much like bumpkin.

Jeff crossed the street and slid into a sleek BMW. He waved as he drove away, a smirk on his pasty face.

There was no way a guy like him could know the things he'd insinuated about Brittany. She wasn't that kind of woman.

But what did Treyan really know? She'd never let him get close. Not for long enough to be sure.

Sounded like she'd been closer to Jeff Sutherland. *Much* closer.

Treyan's stomach roiled.

CHAPTER
TWENTY-SEVEN

Brittany growled in frustration. Should she have taken Jeff's call? He'd phoned twice, but she recognized his number and left both unanswered. He was persistent, though. The third time, he left a message.

Her hands trembling, she tapped to listen to it.

"Hey, Britt. I'm in town and hoped we could get together for coffee, though I've got a couple of hours, if you know what I mean." He chuckled and cleared his throat. "I met your boyfriend down at the fire hall — I'm bidding on his little project — and his kid says you're her best friend. What kind of game are you playing here, babe? Does he know about us? Give me a call back. We should reconnect and talk about it."

No, they absolutely should not, even though it sounded like a slightly veiled threat. What had he said to Treyan to figure out so much, so quickly? She didn't want to know. She wasn't going to ask. She and Treyan'd had the beginnings of a sweet little summer romance, but it was already over. Maybe he'd told Jeff that.

The worst thing was Scarlett overhearing nasty things. Letting Treyan walk away from her was one thing, but poor Scarlett didn't deserve being dumped along with the fledgling relationship.

Never mind that Brittany had fully planned to do the dumping herself in a few weeks. She'd known all along it was temporary. So had Treyan.

Did he even know she'd flirted with the idea of staying here just for him? Galena Landing had grown on her. As spring had morphed from mud season to daffodil season to full-blown summer, this little town had wormed its way into her heart.

She'd never admit it now.

Not knowing what Jeff had said to Treyan knotted her gut up so tight she thought she'd puke. She would never ask either of them for clarification or details.

Any idyllic dreams had been shot down as though by a chemical bomb. Jeff would love knowing that was what came to her mind. She could see his smirk in her mind's eye.

There was only one thing left to do. Apply for positions in New York City and, quite frankly, anywhere in the USA that wasn't Spokane or Galena Landing. A new job, a new location, was what she needed. A new start. She wouldn't make the same mistakes again.

Brittany flipped open her laptop and resumed her search, widening the parameters. If she needed another short-term position — maybe a couple of years to get to the magical five everyone wanted — that was okay. She'd get to her dream job eventually.

But was New York still her wish? The cost of living, the crime rate, the cut-throatedness of big business warned her away. It didn't matter anymore. All she desperately needed was to get away from here as soon as possible.

Surely Brittany could spin her story to Ms. Kozak to get an excellent reference early? She'd explain about how she and Treyan had started dating, but he'd called it off, and how hard it was to work together now. The mayor was female. She'd understand.

Ms. Kozak was also Ms. Durant's sister. And there was no reason at all to believe her former boss hadn't told her own sister why she was banishing Brittany. The mayor had never spoken to Britt about it, but she couldn't assume her current boss was in the dark.

History was repeating itself.

Not exactly, but too close. She could see the reference now: *Ms. Santoro is an excellent, creative designer, but she has a weakness for men that will, sooner or later, affect her ability to do her job.*

Aargh! Why hadn't she thought of this possible outcome before taking a second look at Treyan Ackerman? Why hadn't she clung to her first impression of a grumpy man with no endearing features, either in looks or in personality?

But his face had grown on her. Treyan might not be movie-star handsome, but he definitely wasn't homely. His love for his daughter, which he was finally figuring out how to prioritize and display, brought a glow to him that was most appealing. And when the man smiled and laughed?

Yeah. He looked amazing.

She'd gone and totally fallen for this guy. This *farmer*. The man who'd been shunning her for a couple of weeks now.

The only good thing about that was he could have denied any relationship with her to Jeff and been telling the total truth. But what poison had Jeff tried to infuse? Because he had. That was his nature. He didn't really want Brittany back, Jenna's leaving notwithstanding. At least not for more than a fling to convince himself he still had it. Whatever *it* was.

What was Brittany's nature? She couldn't help wanting a relationship. Someone to make her feel special. Apparently, she also couldn't help ruining everything as soon as she came near. Call it the anti-Midas touch.

But she also had eternal optimism that next time, things would be better. Next time she wouldn't make the same mistakes. Next time she'd fall for an appropriate guy. One who most definitely wasn't currently married or still entangled in a past relationship.

First, she needed a job.

Atlanta? Dallas? Chicago?

Any. It no longer mattered. She'd apply for dozens of them and take the first one that was offered.

Anything to leave her past behind. Galena Landing hadn't been far enough. Sisters for bosses. Living with her cousin's family. And Jeff following her all this way to keep interfering.

Did she need to warn Treyan about not awarding the contract to Sutherland Commercial Construction? That meant admitting Jeff had been in touch so, no, she couldn't advise him. Treyan was a smart man. He could figure it out himself if he cared to.

Brittany was done with it all.

It was time to move on.

Should he talk to Brittany about Jeff Sutherland's veiled accusations? The thoughts battled in Treyan's mind the rest of the weekend.

Driving the tractor in circles in the hay fields along Thompson Road gave him far too much time to think and too little time with Scarlett, who was playing by herself in the cleared lot where the new house would sit in just a couple of short weeks.

He could see her every time he circled the field. Scarlett had several dolls diving in and out of the kiddie pool he'd set up in the shade. No doubt, they were all mermaids today. He hated ignoring his little girl when he had so little time with her, but hay didn't cut itself, and Mitch had enough to do with all the picking that needed doing. The guy was working dawn until dusk — long hours in the north, this time of year — to harvest and sell all those vegetables.

Treyan's child wasn't the only one suffering from paternal neglect right now. Lincoln and Hudson were running wild over the entire farm in some kind of cops and robbers game. Thankfully, they seemed to have accepted Scarlett's *no* for an answer this time around.

He skipped church. Not because he made a habit of working the fields on the Lord's Day so much as he couldn't bear to see Brittany there with Gina's family. He didn't know what to make of Jeff's words, other than they'd settled into the depths of his gut like he'd eaten an entire bale of hay himself.

Jeff had insinuated that he'd had a relationship with Brittany that resulted in the destruction of his marriage.

Brittany had been in a relationship with a married man.

The married man had allowed it, mind you, possibly encouraged it. But still.

The Brittany Santoro Treyan knew was bright and vivacious and could, yes, catch the eye of about any man between the ages of sixteen and sixty. But she was also a hard worker, imaginative, giving, friends with her cousin, good with kids, in church most Sundays... the list of her good qualities went on and on.

Treyan had fallen for her. Not just a little, but a lot.

He might even love her.

The tractor swerved as he jammed down on the brake at the end of the row slightly harder than necessary. Scarlett was still there, splashing in the kiddie pool.

Did he love Brittany?

Treyan shoved the gear shift angrily. It didn't matter. She was leaving. She wasn't the right woman for him. She'd had an affair with a married man.

Because Jeff's wife wouldn't have left him over a lingering glance or two, would she? There had to have been more.

He really, really didn't want to think about it, but maybe it was a good thing he'd found this out before he'd made a fool of himself and begged her to stay.

His reason for holding back was still valid. Kayla.

Speaking of which, he glanced at his watch. It was about time to clean up a bit and take Scarlett to meet her mom.

Forty minutes later, he pulled into the parking lot by the lakeside playground. Kayla's car wasn't there. That was okay. It gave Treyan a few minutes of actual one-on-one time with his little girl.

Scarlett had shot down the slide half a dozen times before Kayla pulled up beside his truck. She leaned into the back of the truck and moved Scarlett's backpack over. Then she straightened and came toward them.

Even on what was arguably the hottest day of the entire summer, she wore jeans, and her long-sleeved sweater hung open over her bulging belly.

But when she came nearer, Treyan focused on a slight discoloration on her cheekbone. A bruise? A bruise mostly concealed behind more makeup than Kayla usually wore?

"What are you staring at?" She scowled at him.

He brushed his hand over the coordinating spot on his own face. "Everything okay?"

Her gaze shifted away. "Of course. Why wouldn't it be?"

"Watch me, Mommy!" Scarlett scrambled up the slide's ladder.

Treyan edged closer. "Kayla. Get help. Get out. Don't put up with this."

"You already told me you wouldn't help me."

He huffed an exasperated sigh. "There are places set up to help. A former spouse is not one of them."

"You don't care about me, anyway, Trey. You never did."

"I did so!" Possibly not as much as he should have, but then she'd also held back in their marriage. She'd been seeing another guy on the side most of the time.

Had Jeff's wife, too? Were they both complicit in their

failed marriage? And why did he have to think of that loser right now?

"Don't even bother." Kayla sliced her hand to cut off his protest. "Nice sliding, baby! Come on. It's time to go home."

Scarlett ran toward them, and Treyan scooped her up. "Love you, pumpkin. See you in a few days."

She squished his face between her palms. "See you, Daddy. Be nice to the mermaids."

"I promise." He gave her a tight squeeze then let her down.

Scarlett grabbed her mom's hand and swung it as they walked to the car.

How could he let his little girl keep going to Burke's house when he had such strong suspicions things weren't safe there? What was he supposed to do?

He'd talked to Jared a few times. Called his lawyer about his suspicions, but nothing had come of it. Mitch was right. At the very least, Treyan should get some counsel from Pastor Ron. Maybe the man would have some resources Trey didn't know about that he could pass on to Kayla.

Would it make a difference? Not when she seemed heavily into denial except for that one phone call a few weeks ago now. Should he have let her come to the farm? Encouraged her to?

It still didn't seem right. He'd felt used, manipulated... but wasn't Scarlett's safety worth everything? And Kayla's, too, of course. He might not want to start a relationship with his ex again, but didn't he owe her a champion who could still come to her rescue?

Kayla's car sped out of the parking lot.

He shaded his eyes with his hand as he watched her drive down the street and turn south on the highway.

Yeah. He'd drop by the pastor's house and see if Ron or Wanda had any advice for him. Having them knowledgeable and praying would be a good start.

Because Treyan absolutely didn't know what to do.

Brittany called in sick on Monday morning. "Sorry, ma'am, I seem to have caught a bug over the weekend. It might be better if I work from home today and not infect anyone with whatever it is I caught."

"Oh, I'm so sorry to hear that, Brittany. We do have that meeting at three thirty with the Parks commissioner. Do you think you can make that, or should I get Donna to reschedule?"

Gah, she'd forgotten. They'd been going to go over how the current location for the market was working out. Paula would be there and a couple of members of the council. "I'm sure I can make it. In the conference room upstairs, right?"

"Yes. I hope you can. Derek has a lot happening this week since he's taking vacation the rest of the summer, so it won't be that easy to move."

"I'll be there. I'll do what I can to be ready for it and try not pass on any germs."

This would be a Treyan-free meeting, right? He'd sat in on a few early meetings regarding the market, since he had a vested interest in the whole thing, but as the summer wore on, he'd separated from the process.

She could probably sneak in and out of the building without running into him. And if she did, well, she was there on town business with a meeting to attend, and she'd be too busy to stop and chat. As if stopping and chatting was an actual thing she'd do with him.

No, what she really wanted was to feel his arms around her, hear some whispered endearments, and then feel a kiss potent enough to peel the copper polish off her toenails.

That wasn't going to happen. Not today. Not ever.

Brittany put as much brightness as she could into her voice. "I'll see you this afternoon, ma'am."

She'd get all her notes together for the meeting and then spend a couple of hours searching for that elusive new job. A flexible position like she had here definitely had its perks, but she'd make sure she had forty full work hours by the weekend.

CHAPTER
TWENTY-EIGHT

The phone on Treyan's desk rang. He sighed as he reached for it. It had been such a frustrating day — Monday to its core — that he'd welcome a chance to get blasted by Nolan Leask. "Treyan Ackerman here."

"Where is she?"

He blinked and reoriented to his office in town hall. The office with Brittany's vacated desk in it. But the irate caller wasn't asking about Brittany Santoro. Not unless Tyrell Burke was even more twisted than Treyan had ever guessed.

"Who are we talking about?"

"Don't even pretend, Ackerman. Kayla left you a long time ago, but I know she still talks to you."

Of course, she did. They shared custody of their daughter. Treyan's hands shook and his head buzzed even as his gut clamped tight. "I haven't talked to her since she picked Scarlett up at the park yesterday. Why?"

"Where is she?"

"I don't know." Maybe she'd actually taken Treyan's advice and left this loser. "Apparently not with you?"

Tyrell snarled a few choice words.

Treyan took that as a negative. He shifted the phone to his other ear, nearly losing his grip. His trembling hands were clammy.

Tyrell Burke might care about Kayla's whereabouts, but Treyan's surge of panic was all for his five-year-old. Well, there was a bit for Kayla, too, but if she had really run away from her abusive live-in, all Treyan could do was cheer.

Except for Scarlett.

"If she shows up at your doorstep, let me know, okay?"

Treyan's eyebrows rose. As if. "She's her own woman, Burke. If she wants to leave you, what's it to me? She won't come to me if she has problems with you. We were over years ago." As Burke very well knew.

"Just don't even think of interfering."

"Wouldn't dream of it." Which wasn't the total truth, but not in the way the beekeeper meant. Trey might help Kayla escape and get counseling, but he wouldn't invite her back into his home, into his bed. That part of their story together was forever done.

If only they weren't permanently linked by their daughter... but there was no way Treyan would wish Scarlett away. She was the best part of his life.

She was due to start kindergarten today.

His heart pounded. There'd been no indication that Kayla wasn't planning on putting their daughter in school today. Scarlett was registered. Treyan had seen the paperwork himself. Had she spent the day at Galena Landing Elementary or not?

Not a chance was he going to ask Burke what time Kayla

had disappeared, but he'd hazard a guess they'd left this morning instead of dropping Scarlett off at the school.

Burke let loose another tirade then hung up.

Trey definitely wouldn't wish for Kayla's return. Burke's reaction proved their relationship wasn't based on any definition of love.

What had Pastor Ron said last night before they'd prayed together? That Treyan needed to be watchful and prayerful but agreed with the police chief that he couldn't intervene unless he had proof Scarlett was in danger.

No proof, but Treyan knew in his heart of hearts that Burke was unhinged. When he caught up to Kayla and Scarlett, no one would be safe.

He pulled his cell phone out and tapped Kayla's number. It rang until voice mail picked up.

Had he really expected her to simply answer the call? When had she ever? Her favorite thing seemed to be ignoring him over and over then eventually returning his call without so much as a hint of apology.

Treyan tapped her number again. "Hey, Kayla?" What if Scarlett was listening along with her mother? He needed to be careful what he said. "Just wondering where you're at. Ty called me looking for you, which makes me think you're not in Galena Landing." Although she could be at a friend's house, right? And Scarlett might have been in school, too. Was he making a mountain out of a molehill? Was Burke? "Give me a call, okay?"

He pulled to his feet and paced over to the window. Who were Kayla's local friends? She'd complained about not having anyone close while she was still married to Trey. If

Burke was as controlling as it seemed, it was unlikely she'd forged deep friendships in the past three years.

A bird flitted through the magnolia tree, letting loose a cheerful song.

There hadn't been a single thing cheery about today before this, and now there was even less. He drove a hand through his short hair. What was he supposed to do? Call Jared again?

But he had nothing to go on except Tyrell Burke's anger. Kayla could take Scarlett for a shopping day in Coeur d'Alene without telling Treyan. He had no recourse until she didn't show up Friday afternoon. Ninety-six hours from now. Although he could call the school tomorrow and see if Scarlett was in attendance.

He had to assume they were safe. Certainly safer away from Burke than with him. He couldn't do much of anything for four full days.

Not true. He could pray.

Like I haven't been?

Treyan shook his head as he slumped back into his office chair. He had been praying, but he definitely needed to kick it up a notch. He should call Mitch. Pastor Ron.

Brittany?

He parked both elbows on his desk and massaged his scalp. He couldn't call Brittany. He'd pushed her away and, by her response, she'd accepted that as a permanent reality. There wasn't any other reason she would've vacated the office completely, staying away from any place she might run into him.

But Brittany cared about Scarlett. She'd want to know

that Kayla had taken Trey's little girl and run away. Wouldn't she?

Because that was what had happened. She'd abducted Scarlett.

No, she hadn't. Not until Friday afternoon. Until then, she had every right in the world to spend time with Scarlett wherever she chose, so long as they didn't cross any international boundaries. So, they wouldn't have gone north to Canada.

East. West. South. Kayla's parents lived in Lewiston, a few hours' drive south. They had a fragile relationship, but wasn't that still the most likely place? He probably still had their contact information somewhere, even though he'd never been the most favored person in their life.

He'd give Kayla until late tonight to reply to his voice mail before he contacted her parents.

But what if she'd gone somewhere else? What if they didn't know where she was? What if, by waiting, Scarlett disappeared all the way from his life?

Kayla wouldn't do that to him. She wouldn't. She was eight months pregnant with Burke's child. It looked like she wouldn't give the loser the chance to be around the baby. She'd said Burke didn't want his child anyway.

What kind of man said that? The same kind who might hit the woman he'd claimed to love.

But Kayla knew Treyan wasn't that kind of loser. She knew he loved Scarlett and would do anything for her. If she'd decided she was tired of being Scarlett's mother — if having two children dependent on her alone was too much — wouldn't she know all she had to do was bring Scarlett to him?

They could have the court order rewritten and make a new agreement where she saw Scarlett however it worked out.

Kayla would be in touch in the next day or two.

The alternative was unfathomable. Unthinkable.

Prayer was still a really, really good idea.

BRITTANY STUFFED her laptop and folders into her giant messenger bag and left the conference room. Sandwiched between the mayor and the market manager, she managed not to glance down the hallway toward her office. The one that was, first and foremost, Treyan's and that she was abdicating to him. He'd be working for the Town of Galena Landing long-term. She, not so much.

The mayor turned toward her own office at the head of the stairs. Derek stopped at the Public Works office. That left just Brittany and Paula, but they were already halfway down the steps with Treyan nowhere to be seen.

"Good meeting, I hope!" Mrs. O'Neill said cheerfully from behind the counter. "Arleigh is so pleased to be hosting the fall market in her greenhouses. I'm glad that seems to be working out."

Brittany smiled at the woman. They needed a few more vendors to confirm attendance, but interest had been solid. But she couldn't really divulge information to Arleigh's mom, even if she worked for the town. Everything was a victim of due process, far more than had ever been the case in Janice Durant's company.

Ugh. Politics, even at the municipal level.

Everything in Brittany wanted to tell the mayor and Treyan not to let Sutherland Commercial Contractors win the bid. Not that Jeff didn't do good work — he probably did — but she didn't want him around, poisoning anyone's mind about her.

But what did it matter? She'd be gone in just a few short weeks. A couple of the openings she'd applied for had already closed to more applicants. In offices in far-flung corners of the country, recruiters were looking at her résumé, making impulsive decisions between deleting her application or actual consideration.

The waiting was killing her, and she was pretty sure she hadn't added anything useful to today's conversation about the future of the market, other than confirming that an April start was way too early. She could pretend it was because she was training Paula to take over more than daily operations, but it was mostly because Brittany was so distracted.

Treyan. Jeff. The market.

God.

She didn't want to think about any of it, least of all God. How could Mom say that God had been so near in her times of trial and mourning? It didn't even make sense. God had looked away from Brittany back when Dad died, and He hadn't tossed so much as a glance in her direction since.

Nor had she sought Him out. If He were really God, He knew where to find her and how to get her attention.

She descended the concrete steps outside, Paula beside her.

"Thanks for everything, Brittany. Have a good evening!"

"You're welcome, and you, too."

Paula walked to her SUV, parked beside... Treyan's truck. Not only his truck, but with the man himself standing beside it. Watching her.

Great. Ignore her for a few weeks and then stare at her like some kind of creep. She hugged her messenger bag to her chest and hurried down the length of the parking lot to the sidewalk beyond. It wasn't far to Gina and Chris's house.

"Brittany?"

No way. After all this? But her name sounded so sweet in his hesitant voice that her steps faltered. And, once she'd given away that she'd heard him, she couldn't very well keep going. Right?

She glanced over. "Hey."

"Can we talk?"

"Gina is expecting me." Or was her cousin working at the lodge this evening? Her schedule was hard to keep track of.

"It'll just take a minute."

Paula drove out of the lot with a wave. No one else seemed to be around. Fine. She could do this.

Brittany straightened her shoulders and lifted her chin. "What is it?" If Treyan was going to throw Jeff in her face, she'd just stand here and take it. Admit nothing. Deny nothing. Move on.

"Burke phoned a bit ago looking for Kayla."

Brittany blinked as her brain shifted gears. "She left him?"

"Sounds like it."

"That's good, right? Except..."

"Except she has Scarlett. I called her, but it went to voice mail."

Would Kayla really go into hiding with their daughter? Maybe Treyan had been right to break up with Brittany. He was embroiled in Kayla's mess up to his eyeballs.

"What are you going to do about it?"

He shook his head. "I talked to the police chief, and I can't do anything until she doesn't show up on Friday afternoon. The worry could all be for nothing."

"But you don't think so."

Treyan shrugged and huffed a breath. "I don't think so, but a hunch isn't something that will move the police to act before it's clearly a case of abduction."

Brittany's blood chilled. Abduction sounded so... real. So nasty. She didn't like Kayla — who could blame her? — but the woman wasn't going to hurt her own daughter. In fact, it was far more likely she was actually protecting her.

"I'm sorry. Is there anything I can do?" Like maybe cross the ten feet or so between them and wrap her arms around him and hold him close?

"No. I wish there was." He swallowed hard. "Even Jared said there's nothing to be done right now."

"Any chance she just went for a shopping day in the city and neglected to tell Tyrell? Or did tell him, and he forgot?"

"Anything is possible." Treyan's eyes looked haunted. "Pray for Scarlett, okay?"

"Sure." Not that God answered any of Brittany's prayers. The little girl would probably come home sooner if Brittany didn't bother. Her pleas to God for Dad's restoration and healing certainly had fallen on deaf ears.

But that was a lot to dump on Treyan. Let him gain whatever comfort he could from thinking she'd pray. That it would make a positive difference.

"Brittany, I—"

She put up a hand to stop him. "Don't."

"But I—"

"It doesn't matter. I'll be gone soon, and then you can get back to your own life. Your new home will arrive — it'll all be good. You'll see. You'll thank God I'm out of your life." At least if Scarlett was okay. She would be. Brittany would cling to that.

"Brittany."

"No, really. How well do you know Arleigh O'Neill? You should ask her out. She's really nice."

"I don't want—"

"Never say never, Treyan. And now I really need to get going." With major effort, she forced her feet to turn her body toward the sidewalk that would take her to Gina and Chris's.

Why didn't she hear Treyan's footsteps coming behind her? Why didn't she feel his arms catching her from behind and pulling her against his chest? Why didn't he look deeply into her eyes before kissing her?

Because not only was he tangled in Kayla's mess, he knew about Jeff.

He knew Brittany was totally, completely unworthy of being loved.

Even God couldn't love her, and wasn't that saying something? Dad — Brittany's breath caught in a hiccup as she hurried up the sidewalk — Dad would be horrified to hear her say that, but it was still true. Even when God loved someone, someone perfect like Dad, it still wasn't enough.

Wasn't that proof positive that He didn't care a speck for Brittany?

Mom had found Charlie. Great for her. Charlie was fine. He'd had a rough go back in his first marriage. Britt had heard him say he'd graduated from the school of hard knocks before he'd learned to give his life over to God.

But Brittany had tried to trust God. She'd tried to pray, to be the devout, good little girl, and where had that gotten her? Her life was a mess. She was a pariah, and God certainly hadn't shown up for her.

She swiped tears from her eyes, but more flooded in. It was a good thing she knew her way to her cousin's house. She stumbled up the driveway and in the front door.

"Britt? That you?" called Gina from the kitchen.

But she didn't answer. She scrambled down the half-flight of stairs and into her room, then locked the door behind herself. She dropped her messenger bag on the floor and threw herself across the bed.

"Oh, God, why don't You care about me? Don't take Your hatred of me out on Treyan and Scarlett. They don't deserve it. They're good. Scarlett's just a little girl..."

The tears came in a torrent like the river flowed through the rapids near Wynnton. Had that only been a month or so ago?

The sun had shone. The world was bright and happy, and Brittany had dared to kiss Treyan.

He'd waited until the next day to return the favor, but the kiss had been worth every second of the anticipation.

Why had she dared to dream for that brief moment? She knew she wasn't cut out for happiness. For blessings.

But... God? Why was that?

TWENTY-NINE

Never had four days seemed so incredibly long. Never had Treyan prayed so hard. He'd trusted only a few friends with details of the unsettling situation. Pastor Ron and Wanda had asked some of their colleagues in distant places to pray. Mitchell's pacing and growling was only surpassed by Treyan's.

The boys had started classes, Lincoln in second grade and Hudson in the preschool across the way. Neither had asked about Scarlett, but why should they? They didn't usually see her during the week, and never before at school.

Kayla's parents must have dropped their land line since Treyan had first known them, since the number was out of service. Short of driving to Lewiston, he had no way of reaching them.

Treyan had explained the situation to the mayor, and he was working from home this week with the final wrap-up for the referendum on Friday. That meant he didn't have to see Brittany again. Didn't have to see the hurt in her blue eyes. See her shoulders hunch as though to protect herself.

He might not have hit her like Tyrell had done to Kayla, but Treyan had hurt Brittany all the same. He hadn't meant to. But anyone who got close to him suffered in one way or another. He couldn't even protect his own child, let alone anyone else.

Treyan sat at a table to one side of the community center, Leask at a table a few feet away. Jared, with the police force, stood with the mayor nearby, watching the residents as they filed through to cast their ballots in the other half of the space.

Jared's presence kept Leask from getting in people's faces. A few people wandered over and talked to Leask. Even more asked questions of Treyan. That wasn't the competition. The real thing was taking place with every folded piece of paper dropping into the slots of the ballot boxes.

The hands on the wall clock had never moved so slowly. At five o'clock, Ms. Kozak would take his seat, and he'd be free to drive down to the park to meet Kayla and receive Scarlett from her. But would his ex be there?

He couldn't bear the thought that she might not be. Treyan squirmed in his seat.

"Nervous, Ackerman?" Nolan Leask jeered. "You should be. Your tax grab is going down in flames."

"In flames, huh?" Treyan raised his eyebrows. "Interesting choice of words. I'm wondering who's going to put the fire out."

Leask waved his hands dismissively. "Just a saying. Anything that catches fire, the volunteer fire department will put out. That's what they do."

And that was what they needed support for. But Treyan was done arguing with his nemesis. It wouldn't serve anything at this point in time. If they lost the referendum, Treyan's own job might be on the line, since he was the face of the project. He might be sacrificed for a fresh start. But if Kayla had taken Scarlett to her parents', there wasn't anything tying Treyan to Galena Landing, anyway.

His brother didn't need him. Mitchell should figure out how to take care of the boys on his own at some point, anyway.

And Brittany didn't need him. She wouldn't even be here.

There'd be no reason not to follow Kayla wherever she went, just so he could see Scarlett on weekends. How pathetic was it to trail his ex around the state? But he didn't know for sure she was gone. It wasn't like Kayla made a habit of returning his calls.

He might have thought Burke was just messing with him, except that Scarlett hadn't been in school.

He shifted in his chair and glanced at the clock. He'd know in an hour.

Ms. Kozak stepped closer. "Do you need to leave now? I can cover. There haven't been that many last-minute questions."

Treyan shook his head. "It's too early."

"Don't worry about it. Looks like you could use a mental health break beforehand."

Smirking, Leask leaned closer. "Am I too much for you, kid? Getting stressed out? It's almost over, and you'll see that the community doesn't back your gouging ways." He poked his chin toward the mayor, his eyes narrowing. "Or yours, neither."

Treyan forced a laugh. "You only wish you had that much power over the state of my life." Wouldn't it be great?

Then it really would all be over once the ballots had been counted.

As it was, who knew what Kayla was up to?

He glanced at the mayor. "I'll take you up on that."

She nodded and gestured for him to vacate the chair. He laughed and held it for her. Then he turned to Nolan Leask and held out his hand. "No hard feelings, Leask."

"Speak for yourself."

Well, Treyan had tried. He nodded at Jared then strode from the room.

Another blistering afternoon waited outside with not even a hint of a cool breeze off the lake. Sweat plastered his button-down to his skin in three seconds flat. Thankfully, the truck had air conditioning, not that he'd be riding in it long enough for the cooler air to make a difference.

A quick drive through the parking lot by the lake didn't reveal Kayla's car, but then he was forty-five minutes early. Plenty enough time to go home, get changed, and return. He managed that venture without alerting Mitchell, and soon he was back at the playground, slightly more comfortable, at least. If anyone could be comfortable while fearing his child might be in some sort of danger.

Treyan parked the truck with the windows down. He paced over to the picnic shelter, remembering the day that had started out so well and ended so badly. He shoved his hands into his shorts pockets and stared out at the lake.

A few minutes later, he realized he wasn't alone. Someone had taken a seat on a park bench overlooking the beach. Brittany! What was she doing here? Should he approach her and ask? But he already knew. She was looking out for Scarlett. Looking out for Treyan, too. She wanted to know his little girl was safe as soon as he did.

And if Scarlett wasn't okay, Brittany wanted to know that, too.

He'd pushed her away, and she was here, anyway. Sure, he'd done it for her own good. But maybe, just maybe, it had mostly been to protect his own heart. If so, it hadn't worked.

She looked up. Met his gaze across the expanse of sand cushioning the playground equipment.

The sound of an approaching vehicle broke through the buzz in Treyan's mind, and he pivoted toward the parking lot. Burke's truck! He'd never thought he'd see relief at the sight of it, but this wasn't the first time Kayla had borrowed Tyrell's vehicle to drop off or pick up Scarlett.

A grin crossed Treyan's face as he all but jogged toward the truck.

Tyrell Burke stepped out of the driver's side and slammed the door. He planted his boots, crossed his arms over his chest, and glared at Treyan.

The brief reprieve in Treyan's spirit faded and took his smile with it. Kayla hadn't come. She hadn't brought Scarlett. Not yet, anyway. And if Burke's presence meant anything, she wasn't likely to show up now. It was obvious Burke was just as determined to intercept Kayla as Treyan was anxious to see his daughter.

Ten after five.

He glanced back at Brittany, but she still sat in the shade where he'd first spotted her. Just as well. She could witness whatever happened next.

"Where is she?" Burke asked belligerently.

"I don't know. She hasn't been in touch."

"If you're lying to me..."

"Why would I? I'm here *because* I haven't heard from her. I was hoping you were wrong."

"I'm never wrong," the man growled.

"That makes one of us. I'm wrong far oftener than I'd like to admit." Maybe Treyan was babbling now, but talking was all he had to kill the time until he had to admit Kayla wasn't coming. *Then* he'd panic.

"Like that stupid referendum."

Treyan shrugged. "The referendum wasn't my idea. Leask pushed it."

"Right, you'd rather have just rammed it through without a dedicated vote."

"I've been wondering. What's it to you? You're outside town limits, but the fire hall serves the entire area. You'll benefit from better equipment, better training, all that."

"Simon doesn't deserve it."

"Simon? It's not about the fire chief. It's about safety for the community."

"My dad used to volunteer with the department."

News to Treyan, but he hadn't been in town his entire life. Apparently, the Burke family had. "Oh?"

"They told him he was too old to be chief. That they wanted a townie anyway."

Treyan narrowed his eyes. "So you're against the new fire hall because your dad once wanted to be chief and someone younger got the job?"

"They drove him out."

"I haven't heard anything about all that. Want me to look into it and see what happened?"

"It's none of your business."

"Okay." The phone in Treyan's pocket buzzed.

Tyrell took a few steps closer. "Gonna get that? It's probably Kayla."

"I don't usually take a call when I'm in conversation with someone." If Kayla wasn't here, at least she hadn't gone back to Burke. That had to count for something, and Treyan wasn't going to lead the guy right to her.

"I don't mind. In fact, I insist."

"You know what? I don't want to answer my phone right now. Whoever it is can leave a message. I'll listen to it later. I want to hear more about your dad." He racked his brain to remember if the senior Burke was still alive.

The phone stopped ringing.

Tyrell stood within arm's reach, flexing his hands. The guy was big and muscular. If he got aggressive, Treyan was not likely to come out on top.

"I don't want to talk about my old man."

The phone started ringing.

Burke lunged at him, and Treyan sidestepped, his heart pounding. Burke grabbed for his T-shirt again.

"Fascinating video I'm making here," Brittany said casually. "I'm sure the police will be interested in seeing it. There. Just sent a copy to my cousin, and I'm starting again. Smile for the camera!"

BRITTANY'S HEART pounded as she zoomed her phone camera in on Tyrell Burke's livid face. She zoomed it back out quickly to showcase his restless stance.

He looked between Treyan and her a couple of times, fists still clenching and unclenching.

Was he going to make a grab for her phone? She'd stayed far enough back that he'd have to take a couple of steps first. That would give her a split second to react. Give Treyan a chance, as well.

"Is this really how you want this to go down?" Brittany kept her tone casual and her phone trained on Tyrell.

"You can't do that. It's illegal to film people without permission."

"It's also illegal to threaten people. The police will be interested in that bit."

He growled and narrowed his eyes, but he didn't come for her.

Good, he believed she'd sent Gina the video. She hadn't. Yes, yes, she knew lying was bad, but she couldn't afford not to record every second of his confrontational posture and words. She couldn't afford the few seconds of distraction while she managed the send.

"Burke, probably a good idea to go on home and let Kayla take care of herself. I imagine she'll be in touch sooner or later."

Treyan had stepped out of easy range of Tyrell's swing. That definitely eased Brittany's breathing a little.

Tyrell looked between them again before his shoulders settled just a little.

Maybe this wouldn't end with a call for police or medical intervention, after all.

"I miss her, that's all. And she's carrying my baby."

"The one she keeps saying you don't want?"

Oh, Treyan. That might have been better left unsaid.

Tyrell tensed as he turned back to Treyan. "It's still my kid."

Brittany tried to imagine Treyan speaking that way about Scarlett. Failed, utterly.

Meanwhile, Treyan's phone had rung a few times again and silenced itself again. He was obviously itching to find out who was calling and why. It did seem most likely that it had been Kayla, but it might have been his brother or the mayor or nearly anyone else.

Brittany kept the recording going. "Trey's right. There's nothing you can do here. It's five thirty, so obviously Kayla isn't coming. I'm sure you've phoned her a time or two this week?" She was pretty sure Treyan had been calling, possibly on auto-redial.

"None of your business. You don't belong here. You don't even know Kayla or what she means to me."

Like a punching bag? "I don't need to know her." Though they'd met a few times. "All I know is you're not giving off the vibes of a man who truly cares."

Tyrell sneered. "What, like lover boy there? All mush and tender feelings? He might as well be made of flowers and rainbows. Real men don't have to stoop to emo stuff like that."

Well, wasn't that a fine opening? Brittany sidled closer to Treyan. "Real men actually love their women and want what's best for them. They don't try to control them or demand stuff."

In her periphery, she saw Treyan turn slightly toward

her. He should probably still be focusing on Tyrell like Brittany was. She didn't trust the guy as far as she could throw him. Despite having taken a few years of Brazilian jiu-jitsu as a teen, she didn't like her chances with a hulk like this one. She should've kept up her training.

Keep talking. Sooner or later, he'll get tired of your voice and depart.

"So, my guess is that Kayla will be in touch when she's ready. Putting on some bravado like this isn't going to make that happen sooner. Quite the opposite, I'm thinking."

He glared at her.

"Because real love isn't controlling." What was that whole bit in 1 Corinthians? She'd memorized the chapter as a teen at Dad's insistence. He'd wanted her to know how to measure God's love to her, as well as a hormonal guy's interest.

Oh, Dad. I miss you. If only he hadn't died, she would have been fine. She wouldn't have struck out and walked away from God. She'd have kept trusting. Wouldn't she?

"Love is patient, love is kind." Treyan cleared his throat and continued. "It does not envy, it does not boast, it is not proud. It does not dishonor others, it is not self-seeking, it is not easily angered, it keeps no record of wrongs. Love does not delight in evil but rejoices with the truth. It always protects, always trusts, always hopes, always perseveres."

Tyrell rolled his eyes. "Now you're some kind of preacher boy? No wonder Kayla dumped you."

"Hey, man. I saw you in church a lot way back when. I know you know better than what you're doing now."

"What I'm doing now?" The guy's chin came up. "Whatever. Tracy was into church. I went for her, and what good did that do? Nothing. She still left me."

Good for Tracy. If Tyrell had treated his ex like he'd treated Kayla, no wonder she'd cut ties.

"Going to church because someone else says we should isn't how to get a relationship with God." Treyan's voice was a little stronger now. "That only comes when each of us realizes we need God for ourselves, not because someone else thinks so."

Wasn't that what Dad used to say? He'd told her God didn't have any grandchildren. The only way to become part of God's family was by having a direct relationship, by becoming God's child based on her own repentance, not that of her parents. She'd done that. She'd been baptized on confession of her personal faith as a young teen.

She was God's child, but she sure hadn't been acting like it. When times got tough, she'd turned her back and decided God didn't love her or He wouldn't have let her go. Did she want a God who bullied her into sticking around like Tyrell bullied Kayla? That would be no kind of God she'd want any part of.

He *wasn't* that kind of God. He was the 1 Corinthians 13 type. Patient. Kind. Protective. Hopeful.

And Treyan Ackerman strove to be that kind of man. But he was still the guy who'd shunned her without explanation after he'd found out Kayla was possibly being abused. Brittany had wondered if he still loved Kayla and wanted her back. It would make sense, in a way. She was Scarlett's mom, after all. And wasn't there a prophet in the Old Testament who'd allowed his whore of a wife to return to him, over and over?

That didn't mean Treyan would. He loved his daughter, but he said it was totally over with Kayla. He'd never lied to Brittany. Shouldn't she trust his words? But there had been things he'd held back. Hadn't told her.

That was part of the reason she'd come to the playground today. Not only to see for herself if Kayla returned Scarlett as per their court agreement, but to see Treyan. Yeah, she could see him most any day at the office, but he'd put up professional walls there.

Tyrell glared at Treyan. Glared at Brittany. Glared back at Treyan. Then, with an explosive huff, he stalked over to his truck. A moment later, he peeled out of the parking lot, leaving a cloud of dust.

Brittany tapped to stop the video recording. Wow, that was a long one. She'd hang onto it for a while before deleting it, though. The situation wasn't resolved.

She felt a gentle touch on her arm and looked up.

"Thanks, Brittany. You defused him." Treyan's dark eyes searched hers.

Brittany couldn't seem to look away. "You were doing a fine job yourself."

"Pretty sure he'd have beat the tar out of me if you hadn't said you were recording it all. Were you?"

"I was. But I didn't dare take a break to send it to Gina or Chris. What if I missed the part with the most evidence?"

He let his hand drop away, causing a chill on her arm even on this warm evening. "You do know that won't be admissible in court, right?"

Brittany shrugged. "I figured. But it did deter him, and that was the first thing it needed to do."

"Thank you." Treyan swallowed hard, still searching her face.

She stepped back. It was either that or throw herself in his arms. "Was it Kayla who called?"

He blinked and reached for his phone.

THIRTY

Treyan pulled his phone out of his pocket. Five calls from Kayla then, finally, a voice mail. He tapped to listen on speaker.

"Trey, I'm in Lewiston with Mom and Dad. I'm sorry I'm not there. Scarlett's furious with me." She sighed heavily. "I just can't come back yet." Then she'd ended the call.

"At least now you know she's okay." Brittany folded her arms around her middle as though protecting herself.

Totally legit. Treyan had been half a breath from kissing her before she reminded him of the phone call. How could he have forgotten Scarlett even for two seconds? His daughter had to come first. And things hadn't changed. Not really. Yes, Kayla had left Tyrell, but that didn't necessarily free Treyan up to pursue Brittany. Kayla was still part of his life. Always would be.

Brittany deserved better than to be dragged into his mess.

"Guess I'm going to Lewiston this weekend." Then he growled in frustration. "Except I can't. I have to bale the hay.

It's been down for a few days, and it's perfectly dry. It's supposed to rain by Tuesday. I can't leave it."

"I'm sorry." Brittany looked about to say more, but thought better of it. "It's just one weekend?"

"Only one weekend *so far*. What if she decides to stay there? It's a four-hour drive from here." He shoved his hand through his hair. "She can't do this to me."

"You used to complain that you were tied to Galena Landing because of the custody agreement. Maybe you should move, too."

"Are you crazy? I've got a new house coming next week." He glared at her. "Which means I can't go to Lewiston next weekend, either."

Brittany shrugged as she poked her sandal into the grass. "Sell the house or cancel the agreement. It's nice. Someone will want it. Isn't it worth following your dreams?"

"Like you're doing with New York?" He couldn't keep the frustration out of his voice.

"It's not like I have any reason to stay here."

A tiny flare of hope bubbled. He could give her that. He wanted to. But... Kayla. The ex who'd taken his child and left town.

"I'm staying." His voice came out stronger than it had seemed inside his head. "God's been talking to me about contentment. About being thankful for what I have, not whining about what I don't have. And I share a farm with my brother. I could be an absentee owner. He could eventually buy me out, but you know what? I don't want to."

Brittany flicked a glance at him then looked down again.

"Kayla hated the farm, but I love it. She's gone, and I'm not living my life to meet her expectations anymore."

But wasn't he doing just that by declaring Kayla a barrier in a potential future with Brittany? Huh.

"But... Scarlett. She needs her dad."

"I'll figure it out." Deeper realization crept in. "God knows all this. He knows the answers, too. I'll figure it out with His guidance. I'm not smart enough on my own." Was he really going to trust God with Scarlett and Kayla? Then how about trusting God with Brittany?

It felt like that day he'd watched Scarlett jump a dozen times, trying to reach the rings on the monkey bars that were way beyond her reach. She'd finally admitted defeat and let him lift her. She'd be big enough to do it on her own in a few years, but not yet.

He'd been trying and trying to keep control of it all by himself, and he was just as unequipped as his little girl. Scarlett needed to depend on her daddy, yes, but her daddy needed to turn to God in the same way.

I'm sorry, Lord. This mess, it's all Yours.

How was it going to work out? He didn't know. Scarlett was registered for kindergarten here but hadn't attended. She was only five. Missing a few weeks of school wasn't that big a deal. Her safety — Kayla's safety — was far more important. But it was in God's hands, not his. That felt kind of freeing, actually.

"How did the referendum go?"

Treyan stared at Brittany. Way to crash back to reality. "I have no idea." He checked his watch. "Polls close at seven, so results should start trickling in soon after."

"Chris will probably have the local news channel on. They'll report, right?"

"Yeah. I'm sure." Or Treyan could ask Brittany to dinner and they could watch for the results together.

"Cool." She managed a semblance of a smile without meeting his eyes. "I should be going. Um... I wanted you to know I'll be in Chicago for a couple of days this coming week."

Wait, what? "Chicago?"

"Yeah. Job interview with a big marketing company."

She didn't sound all that excited about it. But still, she was pursuing her dreams. He had to let her do that.

"Great. I hadn't heard you mention Chicago before."

Brittany shrugged. "There are opportunities in big cities everywhere. This one sounds interesting."

She was leaving Galena Landing. He'd known she would, all along. For a few weeks, he'd wondered if he could be enough to make her want to stay. Hadn't that been egotistical of him? Then he'd shunned her... and now he'd never know if things might have been different.

"Well, that's great for you. When is your interview?"

"Wednesday at two. I'm driving to Spokane Tuesday after work and fly in and out Wednesday. My flight back is pretty late. The mayor said I could be back in the office Thursday afternoon."

"Nice." Treyan shifted from one foot to the other. So much for inviting her to The Sizzling Skillet tonight while they waited for referendum results. She was moving on. He needed to do the same, even though it felt like his heart was, once again, ripping in two. "Maybe I'll see you around the office. I'll pray you'll know if that job is the right one for you or not."

"Thanks." She hesitated then turned to walk away.

347

He watched her go in her knee-length linen shorts and the cute floral top she wore sometimes to the office. Not quite as formal as she'd been back in April, but summer heat demanded some concessions. She was gorgeous whether her hair was up in a bun, down around her shoulders, or in a low ponytail like today.

Brittany was walking away. If he were going to do something about it — make his case, tell her he loved her, plead with her to forget Chicago and New York and anywhere else on the planet besides Galena Landing — this was the moment.

He let her go.

And when she turned the corner of the sidewalk to hike up the hill to Chris and Gina's, he tapped Kayla's number. He had unfinished business with his ex.

"THANKS FOR MEETING MY FLIGHT." Brittany gave her mom a hug in the Spokane International Airport late Wednesday evening.

"I'm delighted to have a few extra minutes with you." Mom clung to her, rocking side to side for a long moment. "I miss you so much living in Galena Landing, and now maybe Chicago? It's closer than New York, but it's still way too far for this mama's heart."

Brittany extended the handle on her carry-on. Even she could pack light for a trip as short as this one. "About Chicago."

Mom linked her arm through Brittany's free one. "Was it amazing? Tell me everything."

"The job sounds cool." She could allow that much.

"Oh, honey, they'd be crazy not to make you an offer."

Mothers. You had to love their stalwart encouragement. "And the city is interesting, right on Lake Michigan like that. It's ten times the size of Spokane, you know. A real cultural hub."

"Ten times!" Mom sounded in awe as they left the coolness of the airport for the still-warm outside air. "I'm not sure I'd like that."

New York was something like three times bigger than Chicago, but Mom was right. Chi-Town was plenty busy enough.

Circling Spokane then landing had felt like coming home. She'd burned her bridges here, though. Also in Galena Landing. Where did that leave her? Was Chicago really the best option?

Or... Brittany could stop running. Face her mistakes. Okay, call that fling with Jeff what it was, a sin. She'd never be free of him if she didn't own up. Look at the way he'd intruded on her life in Galena Landing.

"Whatever happened with that wonderful young man from your office?" Mom pressed her key fob, and the taillights of her car flashed further down in the parking garage. "I'm sorry we haven't made it to one of your markets in the past few weeks."

"Treyan?" Brittany forced a laugh. "There was never a real possibility of anything there."

The trunk lid raised on its own, and Brittany slung her carry-on into it before coming around to the passenger door.

"He seemed very taken with you. Connie told me he's a respected man in the church and community."

Thanks, Aunt Connie. "He doesn't feel free of his ex-wife, and I don't actually blame him." Liar. She did blame him. "His relationship to his daughter comes first, and Kayla has primary custody. Right now, Kayla is in Lewiston with her parents, and Treyan's going crazy trying to figure out how to see Scarlett."

"We'll pray for God to give him wisdom. Do you think he's holding out hope for that marriage to be restored?" Mom slid in and started the car.

Brittany shook her head as she pulled the seatbelt across her body. "No. Kayla is expecting another man's baby. Treyan's only connection with her is Scarlett. I feel sorry for that adorable little girl. She's such a sweetie, and she doesn't deserve her mom using her as a bargaining chip."

"Divorces can be very hard for people to heal from. It takes a lot of God's grace."

Mom should know, since Charlie had been divorced. Yeah, it had been ages ago, a long time before Mom met him. But still.

"The thing is that God gives peace. Charlie's forgiven Julia and asked her to forgive him. He's also asked it of his daughters."

"Well, I know Katri is cool with him." It was through Charlie's daughter's engagement to Brittany's brother Dominic that Mom and Charlie had met in the first place.

"And Evie is coming around. Whether Julia ever forgives Charlie or not is no longer his problem." Mom glanced at Brittany as she drove from the parking area into the starlit night. "Charlie told me you and he had a talk back in June."

"Yeah. In my head, I kept blaming him for stuff that wasn't his fault." Brittany swallowed hard. "I miss Dad. He understood me like no one else ever has."

"I know, honey. I miss him, too."

"Isn't that disloyal of you to say? After all, you're married to Charlie."

"Your dad will always be part of me, Britt. Charlie knows that. He understands. And... in a way, the same is true for him. Julia is the mother of his daughters. They were married for many years. She will always be part of him, too. Our past experiences — our past loves — make us who we are today."

Kayla would always be part of Treyan, but a person could accept that and move forward from there. Could Brittany live with the ghost of Kayla? Could Treyan? Because if he was stuck in the past, it wouldn't matter what Brittany thought.

"Tell me everything about the job interview."

She didn't even want to think about Chicago. It hadn't been terrible. She'd told Mom the truth. The job sounded interesting. But what was the real appeal? Only that it wasn't Spokane or Galena Landing. It represented a completely fresh start.

Was that what Brittany really wanted?

Was that what God wanted for her?

Did she care about that part? More than she had a few weeks ago.

Brittany watched for the massive rocks that defined the airport exit as they merged onto I-90 heading toward the heart of Spokane. Even in the darkness, the beauty of eastern Washington seeped into her heart.

"Honey? Do you want to talk about it?"

She'd been Daddy's girl. She couldn't recall that many

heart-to-heart talks with her mother. But Dad was gone, and Mom loved her, too. "I'm not sure about Chicago. I'm not sure about anything these days."

Mom nodded. "Finding our places in the world as young adults can be very challenging."

"You married Dad right out of college. You had doubts?"

"About him? Never."

Brittany shrugged. "Then I'm not sure how you know." Ouch. That might have been too harsh.

"There's more to settling into adulthood than finding a partner."

"I love being a graphic designer."

"And there's more than choosing a career, too, though that's a legitimate part."

Then what else? Oh. Here it came.

"How are things between you and God?"

Bam. The other shoe had dropped. But hadn't Brittany decided it was time to take stock? And that meant actually analyzing every angle of her life. Which included her belief system.

But, ugh. Not with Mom. Except there was no one remaining on earth who loved her more, who cared more about every part of her than the woman who'd given birth to her.

Brittany took a deep breath. "It's been better."

"When was that?"

"Before Dad died. We prayed and prayed and prayed. We believed God would heal him, but He didn't. How could I trust a God like that?"

"How could you not?"

Mom spoke so quietly Brittany barely heard her. Barely

believed what she heard. "How can you say that? If God has all the power in the universe, how could He let Dad die so senselessly? We needed him! I needed him. Mikey needed him. *You* needed him."

"I don't think the things that happen are supposed to make sense to us. We can't see the big picture. We caught a few glimpses with your dad's friends, colleagues, and acquaintances who came to Jesus through his witness. Your dad loved the Lord more than anyone else I've ever known."

Brittany crossed her arms. "And an early death was his reward."

"His reward is living forever in the presence of his God and Savior, honey. Time is fleeting, and everyone will die sooner or later. Do I agree that I wish your father had come home that night as he had every other night, full of stories of the people he'd worked with that day, full of energy to take Landon and Michael on at the basketball court, full of kisses for me? Of course, I do. We had a very good life. So blessed of God."

"Until God yanked His blessing away."

"That's not what happened, Britt. I don't deny that it was a dark period. I felt like the sunny path I'd been walking had suddenly taken a left turn into a deep, dark forest. Birdsong was gone, replaced by an eerie, echoing silence. I couldn't see the path and felt like I was tripping over every rock and root."

When Mom paused, Brittany nodded. This confession she could understand. She'd been on this path, too. Still was, honestly.

"I cried out to God. So many of David's psalms gave voice to my agony. His circumstances were different, of course.

Saul was actively hunting David with intent to kill him. David could have looked at that as God ignoring his pleas for help, and that's where I identified. But when David spoke of clinging to his shield, his strength, his refuge, he was talking about God. And that made all the difference. God's blessings are new every morning. It took me a while to see that."

What, like a week? Her mom had been so strong right from the first minute. So strong that it hadn't seemed natural. Huh. It hadn't been natural. It had been God.

Mom angled the car off the interstate toward Bridgeview. "And when I threw myself on God's mercy, that gloomy, miserable forest went away. I felt like I'd emerged into a wide, pleasant place where God's sunlight shone again. Read Psalm 18 tonight, honey. Look for that picture of David's. There's solace there."

Brittany swallowed hard and tried to blink back the tears. "I had no idea."

"That's on me, my child. It felt like such a personal journey, but I can see it was something you and your siblings might have needed to witness. I was trying to protect you all, especially Michael."

"Mom... thanks."

"One more thing. Your nonna likes to quote that poem called 'My Life is But a Weaving.' It was written by Corrie ten Boom. In case you've forgotten who that was, Corrie and her sister were Jewish women in a Nazi concentration camp who let their Christian witness stand in the darkest times. She definitely had a much harder life than we can even imagine, but in the midst of all the misery? She knew God was there."

God was there.

Had God been there for her, too?

THIRTY-ONE

One o'clock on Thursday.

Treyan hadn't heard a peep from Brittany in almost a week. Sure, she'd been at the celebratory party on Monday morning, where town employees toasted each other with Redband Roasters coffee on the success of the fire-hall referendum. She'd disappeared before anyone else.

He'd prayed for her interview as promised, but that was nothing new. He'd been praying for her for months now. Praying for himself in regard to her. Asking God to make a way if it were His will.

1:05. Was she back from her trip? Would she come into the office at all?

He paced over to the window, then leaned across her desk to look out, but he couldn't see the parking lot through the magnolia tree. If the janitors didn't dust her workstation, it would have a thick layer by now. It had been weeks since she used this space.

He'd driven her to that.

Treyan took a deep breath and loosened his tie. He needed to see her. Talk to her. Tell her the upshot of his negotiations with Kayla.

Find out if Brittany was moving to Chicago or if he might get one more chance with her.

He should wonder more about Jeff, but the man's veiled accusations didn't line up with the woman Treyan knew.

He whirled at the sound of heeled footsteps in the corridor. He'd left the door open. Let the mayor catch him not working. He didn't care. Ms. Kozak was riding high on the referendum win. This week, at least, Treyan could do no wrong.

If only that were true in every area of his life.

Brittany paused in the doorway, looking as amazing as ever, her blue eyes catching on his. "Hey."

Treyan managed a smile. "Hey. How was your trip?"

"Okay."

That told him exactly nothing. "Good interview? Did they let you know how you stand?"

She shrugged, hugging her messenger bag to her chest. "It went okay, I think. I should hear something by Monday."

He swallowed hard. "Do you... do you want it?"

"Maybe?"

His heart surged. "And maybe not?"

"I... there's pros and cons."

"I'm sure." He glanced at the clock. He could do no wrong this week, remember? And Brittany's contract was nearly up, so maybe the same was true for her, too. "Want to clock out and go for coffee? I've got stuff I want to tell you."

Brittany shook her head. "I have a meeting with the mayor shortly."

"Oh. Can't bail on that, I guess."

"Not really."

"After that? I'm the golden boy this week. She won't mind if I leave early."

"I... I'll see."

That was more than Treyan had expected, honestly. He'd thought he'd get a flat no. But if she didn't care at all, she wouldn't have shown up on Friday afternoon to check on Scarlett.

She cared. He might have made all kinds of mistakes in life and love, but he'd stake everything on the fact that Brittany cared. Whether he'd hurt her too much for her to forgive was the bigger question.

He'd had way too much time to think this week. So many things had gone right. The referendum. The bales of hay stacked in the pole barn. Scarlett's safety and the discussions with Kayla and the family lawyer.

It seemed somewhat hollow without Brittany.

She offered him a fleeting smile as she turned away. Her heels tapped as she proceeded down the corridor. The mayor's voice greeted her. A door clicked shut.

Treyan closed his and sank into his chair. "Lord, help me to accept Your will. I don't want to want a future with Brittany if that's not what's best for both of us. But I'd be lying if I pretended it would be easy to accept. Please, Jesus. I need Your peace."

"Good afternoon, Brittany. How was your trip?"

She perched on the edge of the visitor chair in the mayor's office. "It went pretty well, ma'am. Of course, I don't know the results yet."

"I see." Ms. Kozak toyed with her pen. "I have to say, I'm really impressed with everything you've done for the Farm Fresh Market and its positioning within the town's marketing portfolio."

"Thank you." The mayor wasn't normally effusive with her praise, but she didn't usually withhold it, either. It was good to hear it flat out.

"In fact, I've been talking to the town's CFO about our budget for the next few months and on into the new year. I'd like to invite you to consider staying on as a regular employee."

Brittany clutched her messenger bag as her vision swam. "Ma'am?"

The mayor leaned back. "You heard me, I think. We'd like to keep you here. Now, I'm perfectly aware that Galena Landing wasn't your dream job. I heard enough a few months ago to know."

Heat crept up Brittany's neck. "About that. I'm not sure what your sister told you..."

Ms. Kozak met her gaze unflinchingly but didn't speak.

All right, then. Brittany was sinking or swimming on her own merits. Probably sinking. She clung to the vision her mom had presented. The one where the dark, foreboding forest gave way to a sunlit vista. It wasn't going to fall into her lap without effort. She had to take that step and make it happen.

"I was indiscreet. I had an affair with a client. One who

was married, though I didn't know it until later. But that wasn't really the important part. I should never have gotten involved in the first place."

The mayor nodded slowly. "Jeff Sutherland."

"Yes, ma'am."

"He's placed a bid on the fire hall."

"I suspected as much. It pains me to say it, but he's a good contractor. A sleazy human being, but a good contractor."

"We're not going with him."

Relief flowed over Brittany. "Okay. That's probably better." Because could she actually consider the mayor's offer if Jeff was going to be in town running his show for months on end?

"Brittany, normally what employees do after hours isn't any of a boss's business."

"I crossed a line, and I'm sorry. I can't tell you how much."

"You did. It's true. But if you're sorry — and I believe you are — then we don't need to speak of it again."

She blinked. "Ma'am?"

"We've all made mistakes. What matters is that we reserve the right to make *new* mistakes in the future, not get bogged down in repeat performances."

It almost sounded like the mayor was making a joke of it. Brittany was still much too close to the situation to find any humor there. "Your forgiveness means a lot to me."

"So... the employment offer stands. I don't know what Chicago is offering, though I do know what Marketing by Design was paying you. It helps to have a sister in high places. But I've had HR type up a formal offer. I'd like you to take a copy and read it. Are you willing to at least consider staying?"

What had happened to the woman who'd sneered at small towns? She'd faded away and been replaced by someone who saw value in communities. After growing up in Bridgeview, she should have known better than to spurn the concept.

"Is returning to Marketing by Design an option?"

The mayor flinched slightly. "I could ask Janice. But I really hoped you might have fallen in love with our small town."

"I just wanted to see all the cards face-up on the table." Brittany hesitated. "I may have changed my mind about Galena Landing, but I'm not sure."

"Treyan Ackerman."

The woman knew far too much, which also shouldn't surprise Brittany.

"He's one of the good ones."

There was no denying it, so Brittany nodded.

"I'm in no position to give relationship advice, but do give him a chance. Talk to him before you give up on him and our picturesque little town. Mr. Sutherland made some comments to him, according to my sources, but there's not a one of us fit to throw the first stone."

Was the mayor a believer? Maybe. Maybe not. A lot of biblical phrases had made their way into public vocabulary.

Ms. Kozak thumped a sheaf of papers together on her desk then held them toward Brittany. "Have a look over this, if you're willing. Feel free to ask any questions. Could we have a reply by Monday afternoon?"

The offer felt foreign in Britt's hands. Gina had teased

that she should ask for a permanent position, but she'd always thought it was rather a long shot. Brittany knew why she was here, and Gina didn't.

But now...

If the mayor was willing to offer her a job, she'd write a good reference, as well. If the firm in Chicago pursued her, Ms. Kozak would get that opportunity.

But did Brittany even want that anymore? Had she ever, really?

She realized she was still sitting in the office. That she'd been asked a question. "Yes, ma'am. Monday is fine. I have a lot to think about. Pray about."

The word sounded foreign even to her own ears. She used to pray about stuff. Her parents certainly always had. Sometimes, God said *no* as He had with Dad. Maybe Brittany could come to accept that in time.

"Hopefully we aren't a day late or a dollar short. Oh, and if you're concerned about sharing office space with Mr. Ackerman, please note the offer includes a separate work area."

Brittany rose to her feet and tucked the sheaf into her messenger bag. "That's good to know. Thank you for the consideration."

The offer for her own office was helpful, but it wouldn't make a significant difference. If she and Treyan couldn't move forward together, she'd be crazy to take this job.

She walked down the wooden corridor past Treyan's now-closed door, listening to her heels on the old floor as she took the steps down to the main lobby.

Mrs. O'Neill looked up as she passed by. "Heading out already?"

"I am. See you tomorrow." She pushed the doors open and breathed in summertime in the small town she'd grown strangely attracted to. The magnolia tree shaded the entire side of the building. Beneath it sat the bench where she and Scarlett had colored together. There'd been daffodils back then. Now the roses bloomed, filling the air with their sweet perfume.

A gentle breeze stirred up from the lake. She'd only been swimming a few times. Never begged someone to take her out in their boat. Never taken a weekend course at Green Acres Farm.

She hadn't seen the market through to the next phase, but maybe that wouldn't be her job. The paperwork burning a hole in her bag would clarify her new areas of oversight. Even if she wasn't in charge of the marketing anymore, Paula would be happy for a sounding board. They needed to create a board of directors, actually.

There was so much to do.

So much time to do it in, if she said *yes*.

What about Treyan? He'd asked to talk. That was a step forward right there.

Brittany glanced at her watch. Two thirty. She'd been in the mayor's office longer than she'd thought, but Treyan didn't clock out until five. He'd said he was the golden boy, though. Had he meant it?

She pulled out her phone and opened her texting app. Found his name. It had been a while since they'd exchanged messages.

Should she?

Yes. He'd already extended the olive branch. She needed to let him know she accepted it.

I'll be at the picnic shelter near the beach for a while, mulling over my conversation with the mayor. Come find me if you have time. If you want to.

Send.

A mental picture of bouncing the basketball toward him came to mind. Would he catch it? Sink a basket?

Time would tell.

It took Treyan an hour to wrap up the demands in his queue, since he had no intention of coming back to the office until Monday. He'd replied, but would Brittany be waiting still? He had to believe she would.

Even before he parked his truck by the playground, he could see a lone figure in the picnic shelter. He watched her a moment. *Lord? Help?*

That was about as coherent as his thoughts could be at the moment through the blood thrumming through his entire body.

He'd wasted two seconds worth of thought on going home first to change into shorts, but that meant an extra twenty minutes not spent with Brittany. Of course, she might send him packing. That was still a distinct possibility.

Treyan jumped out of the truck. At the sound of the door closing, she looked over and tugged on the end of her ponytail. He walked toward her, hoping no kid had left a toy, because he'd trip and fall flat for sure. He had no eyes for anything, anyone, but Brittany.

Everything in him screamed to round the table, lift her to her feet, and kiss her soundly, but they weren't at that place. Maybe soon. Maybe never.

He pressed his hands on the picnic table as he settled on the bench across from her. "Hey. You wanted to talk?" Oh, how dry his mouth felt.

How gorgeous she looked. But it wasn't her beauty that attracted him, not as it had at first. Now it was the essence of her.

"Treyan, I..." Brittany took a deep breath and met his gaze. She pointed at the papers on the table. "Maybe you know all about this."

He glanced down. It looked like a contract with the town's logo on it, and his heart leaped. "I don't, but is it what it looks like?"

"Only if it looks like a contract. Ms. Kozak — the town — wants me to stay. This is a permanent position. It isn't straight-up tourism marketing, but that's part of it."

"Are you going to take it?"

"Should I?"

Trey knew what she was asking. She wasn't seeking career advice. He had a whole list of things he needed to tell her, but maybe he should start with the most important one. He laid his hands on top of the papers, palms up.

She looked down at them, but he waited for her gaze to rise and meet his.

"I love you, Brittany."

Tears welled immediately, catching on the ends of her impossibly long lashes.

"Don't cry, sweetheart. Not unless you don't feel the same."

"Treyan, I don't deserve your love. Jeff—"

"You can tell me about him if you want. Or not if you don't. It's not going to change anything. I'm no perfect little choir boy myself. But I do love you more than I would ever have thought possible."

Slowly, moisture still trembling on her lashes, she placed her palms against his.

His blood sang. Their gazes held.

"I... I love you, Treyan."

The table was too wide, created too much distance. He hated to let go of her for even a second, but he needed to. He made it around the table in record time, straddled the bench beside her, and wrapped both arms around her as he buried his face in her hair. "Oh, Brittany. I love you, I love you, I love you."

There were probably things they needed to discuss. He'd thought of a few of them himself, but they all evaporated in the heat of the moment.

Because she turned on the bench and clung to him as their lips met. Melded. Made promises.

Promises Treyan was sure he could keep.

CHAPTER

THIRTY-TWO

T his is amazing." Brittany held Scarlett's hand as the little girl dragged her through the new house. "Which is your bedroom?"

"This one!" Scarlett exclaimed in triumph. "See? The same as last time, except there are different trees outside."

Behind them, Treyan chuckled.

Brittany thrilled at the sound. So much had happened in the past week, it was crazy. They'd had so little time together, one on one, but it was a busy season, and she knew Treyan hated that as much as she did.

He'd met Kayla and Scarlett in Coeur d'Alene on Friday, where they'd connected with a family lawyer and signed a new custody agreement. Now Scarlett would live with her dad during the school year and with her mom on holidays. Kayla had no intention of returning north. Her parents were going to help with the baby, and Scarlett would be the doting big sister when she visited.

And then the new house had arrived, and he'd used his vacation days to help the crew with all the hookups and final construction work, melding the parts into one weatherproof unit.

The office had seemed empty without him, but it was possible she'd accomplished more than if he'd been present, tempting her with a kiss here and there. Thankfully, he'd taken time Thursday evening to go through the official offer with her. He'd suggested a few minor tweaks the mayor had approved on Friday.

The longer it took Chicago to call, the more certain Brittany was of her answer. *No, thank you.*

Treyan slipped his arms around her from behind, and she leaned back against his strong chest, reveling in the feel of him.

Scarlett sat on the edge of her bed, bouncing a little. "Daddy, I want a mermaid room like Emma's. *Please?*"

Brittany choked back a chuckle at Treyan's low groan in her ear. "I think that's a great idea. Mermaids are so cool."

"Traitor," he murmured.

"I'll help you, Scarlett. We can make it so pretty."

"Can it be sparkly like a gel pen?"

"We'll make it happen. I'm not sure how, but we will."

"Yay! Thank you, Miss Brittany." The little girl darted across the room and crashed into Brittany, rocking her harder against Treyan.

His arms tightened. "I've got you."

Brittany stroked Scarlett's hair. She'd never have guessed how much she could love this kid. Kayla's loss was Brittany's gain. Well, and Treyan's. Not that they'd spoken of a permanent future together, but there was plenty of time for that. They hadn't even known each other half a year yet.

"I love you, Miss Brittany." Scarlett's words were muffled by the pressure of her face planted in Brittany's leg.

"I love you, too, little mermaid wolf."

"Wolves can't be mermaids. That would just be silly."

"Oh. I thought they could."

"Of course not."

Treyan chuckled against her neck. "See what I have to put up with? I'm not against decorating her room. Don't get me wrong. But I'm not redoing the theme every second week. I'm just not."

"But I love mermaids! And princesses." Scarlett looked up at them.

"We'll go shopping, you and me. Maybe Daddy will let you come to Spokane with me, and we can go shopping with my mom or my cousin. They know all the good places to buy stuff for little girls."

"Oh, can I?"

"Maybe I should come, too." Treyan's lips nuzzled the side of Brittany's neck.

"Maybe you'd be too distracting."

"Maybe distracting is good. Pumpkin, why don't you make a picture for Miss Brittany to take back to her house?"

"It's not *her* house, Daddy. It's Emma's house."

And that was another thing to think about. She might not be in any hurry for future plans with Treyan, but should she be looking for her own place? Gina said no. She was just thrilled to have Brittany there a while longer.

Christmas. That was when she'd decide. That was just three months longer than the original arrangement.

But Scarlett had dashed across the room to the kid-size

table and chair by the window, where coloring supplies were already laid out.

Treyan backed out of the room, pulling Brittany with him.

Not that she was protesting, exactly. She turned in his arms once they were out of Scarlett's sightline. "You are *so* distracting."

"Everyone has their talents." He set his hands on her hips and drew her flush against him. "Now, where were we?" He teased his lips across hers.

She arched back a little. "We were making plans for a girlie shopping trip."

"I don't think so." He kissed her nose. "I believe it was much more serious."

Her heart skipped a beat. "Mermaids are serious business, Mr. Ackerman."

"Is that so, Ms. Santoro?" He nuzzled her cheek.

"Absolutely certain. There's paint to be considered — sparkly paint — and fabric and—"

His mouth descended on hers, and all thoughts fled.

All she wanted was him.

"Well, excuse *me* if I'm interrupting something important."

His brother's dry voice broke through into Treyan's brain. He waved his hand in dismissal, not wanting to disengage his mouth from Brittany's long enough to use actual words on Mitchell.

"I'll just wait here. Better yet, I'll go back to the greenhouse and get Lincoln and Hudson to hang around here. They can call me when you come up for air."

Brittany's lips curved in a grin under Treyan's.

He supposed he needed to deal with whatever burr was under Mitch's saddle. "What?" He couldn't look away from Brittany, though. Those blue eyes of hers were like a summer sky. She—

"Dude."

Brittany turned, still in Treyan's arms. "Hi, Mitchell."

"Well, hello, Brittany. You've got more manners than my brother does."

"Your brother is busy," Treyan growled.

"The waterline over to the greenhouse sprung a leak where they spliced in the line for this place."

He closed his eyes, hunting for patience. "Does anyone care about that?"

"Yeah, I think we probably do. There's basically a geyser coming out of the ground, which the boys think is pretty cool, but I don't need to tell you the well doesn't have an infinite amount of water in it, so..."

Brittany eased out of Treyan's arms, which suddenly fell to his sides, cold and limp. "I'll just be over there planning for mermaids." She disappeared into Scarlett's room.

"Planning for *mermaids*?" Mitchell raised an eyebrow at Treyan.

"Maybe they're behind this. Trying to create a mermaid pond."

"You have so totally lost it."

"Maybe?"

"Meanwhile, there's a geyser. Can you give me a hand before the mermaid pond becomes a reality?"

"Yeah. Sure." There'd be no separating his life from Mitchell's, even now that they didn't live in the same space. He followed his brother to the door. "Where's the lea — whoa."

The plywood lid covering the hookups had shifted to one side from the pressure, and water shot into the air. "That's at the new junction then. At least it's accessible."

"Good thing." Mitch pushed aside the plywood and jumped into the deep concrete ring. "The break is on the other side of the valve. How do I get it turned off?"

This was going through a lot of water. He might still have pressure in the new house, as it was closer to the well, but the animal pens and main house would already be reduced to a trickle.

"Over by the well house."

"Of course." Mitchell started to hoist himself out of the hole.

Treyan was already halfway to the shack that covered the well and housed the pumps. He turned off the pump then the valve before glancing back across the yard. The waterspout was gone.

That only solved the problem of hemorrhaging water. They still had to fix the line, and Treyan was no pipe-fitter.

A van painted over with gaudy flowers pulled into the yard. "Hey, saw your water fountain. Is everything okay?"

"Arleigh!" Treyan gripped their neighbor's hand after she'd erupted out of the driver's seat. "We've got a broken waterline. I was just going to give Ed's Plumbing Shop a call."

He had no idea why it was called that. The forty-something man who owned it was named Bob, not Ed. And Bob probably wasn't eager for a call-out on a Wednesday evening.

"Let me have a look."

Treyan exchanged a glance with Mitchell. What could this wisp of a woman with overall shorts and Bogs that matched her van do about their problem? Probably nothing but commiserate.

But he stepped back and gestured at the location. "Sure, have at it."

Arleigh dropped into the hole. She was so short she'd need a ladder to get back out. "Oh, I see what happened. Do you have any plumbing tape and solder? Just need to get this spot dried out and rewrapped. I think the guy was just in too much of a hurry."

Mitchell looked at Treyan with wide eyes. "Um, I'm sure we've got some tape in the mudroom."

"I'll go look. Blue roll, white tape, right?"

"Yeah, that's the one." Arleigh's voice was muffled. "If you don't, I can run home and get some."

"You do your own plumbing repairs?" Mitchell crouched beside the pit.

Treyan cringed at the disbelief in his brother's tone as he jogged toward the house.

"What's happening, Unca Trey?" Hudson wanted to know.

"Yeah, why's there a girl out there?"

"Miss Arleigh is our neighbor, and she stopped to help." Treyan pushed the door open and began searching for the needed supplies.

"But girls can't do stuff like that," whined Lincoln.

"Why not?" Treyan moved a box of mouse traps. Ah, there it was.

"Because..."

"Hold that thought, buddy." Treyan jogged back over to Arleigh. "Here you go. What else can I do?"

Mitchell's eyebrows hadn't come back to earth yet. No wonder his boys thought a girl couldn't fix pipes. Mitch didn't think so, either.

"Drop me a block?"

"Sure. Or a five-gallon bucket, anyway."

"Perfect." She dusted her hands together. "I've got some goop in the van. I'll go grab it."

Treyan handed her a bucket, which she upended and climbed on, then hoisted herself out.

She strode over to the van and opened the back doors, revealing the hippie floral wrapped all the way around.

"What does she think she's doing?" Mitchell hissed at Treyan.

Trey pivoted and shoved his chest against his brother's. "Being a good neighbor, which you are *not* doing. How about you give her a little credit and respect?"

"What could she possibly know?"

"Obviously, she knows more than you or me, and if she saves us a call-out, we're way ahead. Plus we'll have water. If she doesn't fix it? We're no worse off than we were ten minutes ago."

"But..."

"Your chauvinism is spewing as much as the water line was." Treyan turned back to Arleigh as she approached with a bag of supplies.

She looked between them, saving a glare for Mitchell, and hopped back down.

"Miss Arleigh! Your van is so pretty." Scarlett towed Brittany across the yard.

"I'm glad you like it. Hey, Brittany."

"Hi there."

"Miss Brittany, could my room look like Miss Arleigh's flowers instead?"

"It could, but you have to be really sure." Brittany turned laughing eyes on Treyan. "I think Daddy is happy with the mermaid theme, though."

Compared to eighties-vibe flowers? Definitely. But he could barely keep from laughing out loud. Until he looked back at Mitch, who stood with his feet braced and arms crossed as he stared down at the top of Arleigh's head.

Was it possible...?

Nah. Mitchell wasn't going to fall in love again. And if he did, it would be with a woman who had designs on taking care of his house, not a plumber-wannabe like Arleigh O'Neill. But wouldn't it be fun to watch?

Treyan's gaze caught on Brittany. How had he gotten so lucky? She definitely wasn't what he'd been looking for. Which, to be fair, was exactly who Mitch was looking for — no one.

But God had given him a second chance at a real home, a real family, something that, unlike his brother, he'd never had.

He tucked Brittany against his side and reveled in the sensation as she tucked her thumb through his shorts belt loop and rested her head against his shoulder.

This. This was what he'd been missing, and he hadn't even known it.

IT WAS THANKSGIVING, and not the first time Brittany had brought Treyan home to her family in Bridgeview. They'd met Kayla in Coeur d'Alene so Scarlett could spend the weekend with her mom, grandparents, and baby sister. It was kind of too bad. Brittany knew Scarlett would enjoy the Santoro cousins, but she wasn't about to poke a stick into the delicate balance Treyan and his ex had formed. It was working. Kayla'd set a restraining order against Tyrell Burke and wasn't sniping at Treyan anymore, even from a distance. Peace reigned. It was bliss.

Well, bliss amid chaos. The Bridgeview community center was full to the brim with Santoros. Nonna held court not far from the main doors, her oldest son nearby. Uncle Ray's eyes warmed when he spotted Brittany and Treyan coming in. He hurried over and shook Treyan's hand before kissing her on both cheeks. "It is so good to see you, mi tesoro."

His treasure. Just like Dad used to call her. This time, the pain was only a little twinge. Bittersweet. Life went on. Charlie and Mom ran the kitchen today along with Gina's brother Tony, who was a chef. Not Tony's wife — Kenna could burn pure water, but she was a good nurse and kept an eye on Nonna.

"I like your family." Trey's hand warmed the small of Brittany's back.

"I kind of like them myself." How long she'd fought against them, though. Felt stifled. Felt invisible in a crowd instead of special. But being an only would have been so lonely. This family might be crazy, but it was hers. "Come, let's say hello to Nonna. Then we can mingle or help out."

He guided her toward Nonna then crouched in front of her, taking both Nonna's hands. "You look well today, Marietta."

Nonna's shrewd eyes assessed him then focused on Brittany. "You should keep this one."

"I think I will. He's pretty special."

"My Salvador was so strong and straight, too. Something about his eyes." She stared at Treyan until Brittany squirmed. What must he think of her grandmother?

He squeezed Nonna's hands. "I'm honored that I remind you of your husband. I never knew my own grandmother, so I'm doubly happy to have met you. You mean a lot to Brittany, you know."

"I do?" Nonna's voice turned coy. "She keeps that to herself."

"Oh, Nonna. You know I love you. And..." Brittany lowered her voice as she leaned closer. "Thank you for all your prayers for me. God hears."

"He does, child. But I'm not done praying for you. When is your wedding day?"

Oh, no! Brittany gasped, half choking on the intake as heat flushed up her face. "Nonna, I—"

"We haven't really talked about that yet." Treyan leaned closer to Nonna. "But how does spring sound to you?"

Brittany clapped her hands over her mouth, suddenly aware of Mom and Charlie and Gabby nearby.

"Spring is good." Nonna nodded. "It always reminds me of redemption and new life. God redeems our mistakes, you know."

"I'm so thankful He does, and I'll take your preference under advisement." Treyan was still low to the floor in front of Nonna, but now he swiveled a little to face Brittany. And was that an open ring box in his hand? How had that happened? When?

She gave a little stomp of excitement, her hands still pressed over her mouth as she stared down at his beautiful dark eyes, soft with emotion.

"Brittany Lina Santoro, I love you with all my heart. Would you do me the honor of becoming my wife?"

"Yes?" Her voice squeaked. "Yes!"

Then he rose to his feet. His fingers trembled as he tugged the ring from its nest and slipped it on her finger.

It was gorgeous, a diamond fit for a princess. Or maybe a mermaid. She slid her hands up around his neck and felt his arms wrap her close. His lips touched hers, tentatively, reverently, then with more passion.

Brittany could hear laughing and clapping and whistling — one of her brothers or cousins, no doubt. She didn't care. She was surrounded by her family, and she was home in her beloved's arms.

THERE'S MORE!

She needs a job and a greenhouse. He has a greenhouse and needs a nanny. What they don't need is each other.

Just after giving notice at her day job, Arleigh O'Neill's fledgling flower-growing business takes a lethal blow when the river overflows its banks, demolishing her rented greenhouse and drowning her fields. Finding a replacement location on zero budget is impossible, unless she can sweet-talk the vegetable grower down the road into some sort of deal.

Widowed farmer Mitchell Ackerman is at wit's end with his two rambunctious boys, especially since his brother is getting married and moving out. When the frivolous flower farmer asks to rent greenhouse space, Mitch turns her down. He needs every inch for vegetables, but when his son destroys flats of seedlings, Mitch realizes he needs help more than he needs space. But... a deal with *her*, of all people?

Arleigh thinks he's arrogant. Mitchell thinks she's flaky. What will it take to get them to see into each other's hearts and grasp a green and vibrant hope?

Look for *A Green and Vibrant Hope,* the second Farm Fresh Market Romance, today!

valeriecomer.com/hope

Are you subscribed to my email list? This bi-weekly newsletter is the best way to be kept up-to-date on what I'm working on, what's for pre-order, and what sales or promotions might be happening. Plus, you get a free e-copy of *Promise of Peppermint*, the prequel to the Urban Farm Fresh Romance series, as my thank-you gift.

valeriecomer.com/subscribe

If that's a fuller inbox than you prefer — but you're still interested in occasional news — follow me on Bookbub and/or Amazon to keep up with new releases.

See you again soon in Galena Landing!

FARM FRESH MARKET
ROMANCE
BOOK 2

A
Green
and
Vibrant
Hope

USA TODAY BESTSELLING AUTHOR
VALERIE COMER

DEAR READER...

Thanks for reading *A Wide and Pleasant Place*! I'm so honored that you chose to spend the last few hours with Treyan, Brittany, and me. You are appreciated.

I'm an independent author who relies on my readers to help spread the word about stories you enjoy. Would you take a few minutes to let your friends know? Facebook, Instagram, Goodreads... wherever you hang out online.

Also, each honest review at online retailers means a lot to me and helps other readers know if this is a book they might enjoy. I'd sure appreciate your help getting word out!

I welcome contact from readers. At my website, you can contact me via email, read my blog, and find me on social media. You can also sign up for my newsletter to be notified of new releases, contests, special deals, and more! You'll receive *Promise of Peppermint*, the novella that introduces the Urban Farm Fresh Romance series, absolutely free as my thank you gift!

~ Valerie Comer
www.valeriecomer.com
https://valeriecomer.com/subscribe

ACKNOWLEDGMENTS

Thank you for loving the Farm Fresh Romance stories and bemoaning the end of the Urban Farm Fresh Romance series. I hope you've enjoyed this trip back to Galena Landing, where it all began in *Raspberries and Vinegar* back in 2013!

Thanks to my fellow author and friend, Elizabeth Maddrey. She prods, cheers, and commiserates as needed, then offers helpful brainstorming and critiques. If you haven't read her Christian contemporary romances, go find them and get started!

Thank you to Lynnette Bonner. Not only did she master-mind this multi-image cover, but she's been a great motivational buddy as we spur one another on to meet our daily word counts! Check out her fun contemporary romances under her pen name, Brynn Stewart.

Thanks, too, to Paula Dye, whose namesake graces this story and the remainder of the series. She ably moderates my Facebook Reader Group and has proved a true friend.

Also thanks to Gretchen Atcheson, friend and professional farmer/ farmers market vendor, for taking time to check for accuracy. It's entirely possible I still missed a correction or two. (Sorry if so!)

Here's where I always thank my amazing editor. This time, Nicole's schedule and mine crashed and burned. Huge thanks to Lesley Ann McDaniel Editing for stepping in at the last minute. I appreciate the stellar and timely copyedits so much!

I'm also grateful for the Christian Indie Authors Facebook group and my sister bloggers at Inspy Romance. These folks make a difference in my life every single day. I'm thrilled to walk beside them as we tell stories for Jesus!

Thank you to my Facebook friends, followers, street team, and reader group members for prayers, encouragement, and great fellowship. If you'd like to join other readers who love my stories, please find us at Valerie Comer: Readers Group.

Thanks to my husband, Jim, whose love for me never fails and who encourages me in every endeavor. Thanks to my kids, their spouses, and my wonderful grandkids for cheering me on. To them, having an author for a mom/grandma is "normal." Imagine that!

All my love and gratitude goes to Jesus, the One who is my vision, the High King of Heaven, the lord of my heart. Thank You. A thousand times, thank You.

Valerie Comer Bibliography

Farm Fresh Market Romance

1. A Wide and Pleasant Place

Urban Farm Fresh Romance

0. Promise of Peppermint (ebook only)
1. Secrets of Sunbeams
2. Butterflies on Breezes
3. Memories of Mist
4. Wishes on Wildflowers
5. Flavors of Forever
6. Raindrops on Radishes
7. Dancing at Daybreak
8. Glimpses of Gossamer
9. Lavished with Lavender
10. Cadence of Cranberries
11. Joys of Juniper
12. Together in Thyme

Pot of Gold Geocaching Romance

1. Topaz Treasure
2. Ruby Radiance
3. Sapphire Sentiments
4. Amethyst Attraction

Farm Fresh Romance

1. Raspberries and Vinegar
2. Wild Mint Tea
3. Sweetened with Honey
4. Dandelions for Dinner
5. Plum Upside Down
6. Berry on Top

Cavanagh Cowboys Romance
(Montana Ranches Christian Romance)

1. Marry Me for Real, Cowboy
2. Give Me Another Chance, Cowboy
3. Let Me Off Easy, Cowboy
4. Kiss Me Like You Mean It, Cowboy
5. Choose Me for Always, Cowboy
6. Trust Me With Your Heart, Cowboy

Saddle Springs Romance
(Montana Ranches Christian Romance)

1. The Cowboy's Christmas Reunion
2. The Cowboy's Mixed-Up Matchmaker
3. The Cowboy's Romantic Dreamer
4. The Cowboy's Convenient Marriage
5. The Cowboy's Belated Discovery
6. The Cowboy's Reluctant Bride

Garden Grown Romance
(Arcadia Valley Romance)

1. Sown in Love (ebook only)
2. Sprouts of Love
3. Rooted in Love
4. Harvest of Love

Miss Snowflake Pageant

1. More Than a Tiara
2. Other Than a Halo
3. Better Than a Crown

Riverbend Romance Novellas

1. Secretly Yours
2. Pinky Promise
3. Sweet Serenade
4. Team Bride
5. Merry Kisses

valeriecomer.com/books

About Valerie Comer

Valerie Comer's life on a small farm in western Canada provides the seed for stories of contemporary Christian romance. Like many of her characters, Valerie grows much of her own food and is active in the local foods movement as well as her church. She only hopes her imaginary friends enjoy their happily-ever-afters as much as she does hers, shared with her husband, adult kids, and adorable grandchildren.

Valerie is a two-time *USA Today* bestselling author and a two-time Word Award winner. She writes engaging characters, strong communities, and deep faith into her green clean romances.

To find out more, visit her website at www.valeriecomer.com, where you can read her blog, explore her many links, and sign up for her email newsletter, where you will find news, giveaways, deals, book recommendations and more. You can also find Valerie blogging with other authors of Christian contemporary romance at Inspy Romance.